GUERRILLA GIRL

Helen D. Gamanya

A Girl's echoing voice in the
Zimbabwe Chimurenga

Published by Helen D. Gamanya
Publishing partner: Paragon Publishing, Rothersthorpe
First published 2009
© Helen D. Gamanya 2009
The rights of Helen D. Gamanya to be identified as the author of this work have been asserted by her in accordance with the Copyright, Designs and Patents Act of 1988.
All rights reserved; no part of this publication may be reproduced, stored in a retrieval system, or transmitted in any form or by any means, electronic, mechanical, photocopying, recording or otherwise without the prior written consent of the publisher or a licence permitting copying in the UK issued by the Copyright Licensing Agency Ltd, 90 Tottenham Court Road, London W1P 9HE.

Condition of Sale

This book is sold subject to the condition that it shall not, by way of trade or otherwise, be lent, resold, hired out or otherwise circulated in any form of binding or cover other than that in which it is published and without a similar condition including this condition being imposed on the subsequent purchaser.
No part of this book may be reproduced or transmitted in any form or by any means electronic, chemical or mechanical, including photocopying, any information storage or retrieval system without a licence or other permission in writing from the copyright owners. Reviewers are welcome to quote brief passages should they wish.
ISBN 978-1-899820-71-9
Book design, layout and production management by Into Print
www.intoprint.net
Printed and bound in UK and USA by Lightning Source

TO MY FAMILY:
    My late husband Zebbediah
    My son Tafirenyika
    My two daughters – Rufaro and Wadzanai

    By foreigners we were enslaved
    And like oxen bled
    Until no more than the living dead;
    Now thy work is to guide the misled,
    Direct the astray
    Your work remains incomplete,
    Until aspirations are fulfilled
    Will you, say, each one of you?
    "I've done my bit".
              (Alexander Galloway)

Chapter 1

The guerrillas took turns at the observation post, up a tall Musasa tree. The tree was a few kilometres off the main road from Salisbury to Sinoia (Chinhoyi) and Karoi, some small country-towns. The road passed Sinoia through jungle, to the border between Zimbabwe and Zambia.

At sunset, Shupai, the guerrilla girl, was already up the tree. It was her turn on the observation post. She could see every movement, far along the road in all directions. The western sky, she observed, was clear and bright with the amber light of sunset. But the eastern sky was dark. There were dark clouds which moved furiously, forming all kinds of ugly gigantic shapes and images. Occasionally, sharp strokes of lightning warned of heavy rain. 'Threatening thunderstorm! You and your meddling features!' Shupai accused as she watched the eastern horizon. 'You stay where you are. We've got work to do here!'

The guerrilla unit to which Shupai belonged operated in that area. Earlier in the day Hupei had visited nearby villages, as part of her other duties, to detect and collect any information about the movement of the colonial forces. She had learnt that the colonial troops were, that night, going to move along that main road on their way to the border. One of her reliable information sources had replied to one of her cunning questions saying:

"You see, my dear girl, these terrorists are launching their attacks on us from the border."

"Really? How far true is that?" Shupai had encouraged the man, an African Policeman on patrol around the villages.

"It's true. They usually attack and retreat into the other country," the man went on, "now, the strategy is the concentration of troops along the border. The barbarians will be halted while they cross the Zambezi and this will reduce their infiltration into the country drastically."

"So the objective is to kill them before they even enter the country?" Shupai asked, urging the man to continue.

"It's a brilliant idea, don't you think? It really is!" he emphasised and rode off on his bicycle before Shupai could say anything more. She just shook her head looking after him:

'What these settlers don't know yet,' she said to herself, 'is that more and more guerrilla militants, for example, I myself are now being trained inside the country.' With this war that the colonialist settlers had forced upon the African people of Zimbabwe, the underground movement had managed satisfactorily to organise a network of counter-informers. 'Following the Maoist tactics of involving the people in the liberation struggle,' she went on thinking, 'it is getting more and more certain the settlers can never win this war. Particularly if girls like me,' she laughed silently, 'could readily get first hand information about their strategies like this.....' she giggled to herself. 'It's very interesting.' She thought, 'if only that policeman had known the real person he has been talking to....' She felt elated.

She had hurried deep into the jungle and reported her findings to Munongwa, the unit commander, who started issuing orders excitedly. Preparations got under way, feverishly, for an ambush. The commander and two combatants went to the road on reconnaissance, to locate a suitable place to mount an ambush. A tall Musasa tree not far from the road was chosen as an observation tower. "Comrade Munda, you start your guard duty up this observation post straight away" commanded Munongwa. "You know what to do and you know the sound to make when you see anything of importance."

Back at the base, Munongwa told the rest of the combatants, "We'll have to move fast and take our positions just after dark. The enemy troops should be taken as they move along the road."

"So it means we have to spread ourselves along both sides of the road?" asked Shonhiwa, the guerrilla who was second in command to Munongwa.

"That's the idea, though, there may be last minute alterations after assessing the condition of the enemy," answered Munongwa, and he went on, "Comrade Shonhiwa, I think you should be the last on the observation post until you spot the enemy convoy. Make a proper assessment of the enemy's strength and formation before we make the final decisions on how to attack."

An hour or so after Shupai had been on duty up the Musasa tree, the storm which had been threatening from the east seemed to be subsiding. Shonhiwa came to relieve her. He said "Wait for the others here. By the way, what did you do to the storm?" he asked laughingly pointing to the east.

"I rebuked it and accused it of meddling in our affairs" she answered jokingly.

The spot for the ambush was well chosen. At dusk guerrillas moved and took their appointed positions. They waited quietly and tensely for the enemy. Every one knew what to do. Get-away routes for the combatants had been carefully mapped out and surveyed earlier on so that everyone knew exactly where to go when the commander gave the order. The night was still and only occasionally was there a breeze under the heavy cover of the jungle thickets. The chirping of the crickets added tension and anxiety to the still night. Blood was running hot in the veins of the fighters. 'The enemy must be dealt with decisively,' Shupai thought. 'He must not be allowed to escape now, that he is about to pass where we lie waiting.' The guerrillas had taken position along both sides of the road. Shupai was the only woman in this unit, but like everyone else in her unit at that moment she waited for the enemy's arrival with reasonable impatience and anxiety.

Minutes passed. Finally, the familiar bird-like whistle was heard. This was the signal from the observation post, warning the comrades that the enemy had been spotted and was moving nearer. Everyone made sure, for the last time now, that everything was well set and ready. Every guerrilla waited eagerly for the action, the action to rid Zimbabwe of settlerism and oppression. 'We must succeed!' Shupai repeated to herself. She was excited as she, like her comrades, held firmly on to her AK/47 rifle and hand grenades. The guerrillas were certain that this battle would be won and bring honour and raise the morale of their unit and people of Zimbabwe even higher.

After assessing the condition of the enemy convoy formation, Shonhiwa came down to report. His report to the commander was that there were about five heavy-duty vehicles coming, probably full of soldiers, weapons and other materials that their unit needed. "The first two are certainly carrying men as I could observe lights from cigarettes," Shonhiwa reported. "The third and fourth seem to be all darkness except for the headlights; the fifth one," he went on, "I'm not quite sure but that, too, could be carrying people."

"Good," said the commander. He then relayed the news, "Five vehicles coming. We will let the leading ones hit our land-mines ahead and then we attack the ones following. Remember we need some supplies! Everyone be ready!"

'We are ready,' Shupai thought nervously as she waited for the target to arrive. Through the foliage, Shupai and the other guerrillas could see the approaching head-lights. The vehicles drew nearer and nearer, and then the first two lorries packed with troops, weapons in their hands, passed and hit the mines just a kilometre ahead. The explosion was deafening and with it came chaos, cries of pain and death of the enemy troops. Those who were not killed by the mines were thrown into the air, but that only brought them into the guerrillas' view. They were shot at and many fell dead. Those who crawled to hide among the trees and bushes along the road side were quickly eliminated. There was no way out for them. They were completely wiped out. Shupai saw that all the five vehicles were now on fire and there were some explosions, probably of the ammunition. The signal was given. The combatants went cautiously to the vehicles to try to rescue some ammunition and weapons and supplies of food.

As Shupai came close to one of the lorries which was burning a little but badly damaged, she heard a slight movement behind her, she turned quickly, "Look out!" she shouted, at the same time pulling at the trigger of her gun. Bang! She fired at an enemy soldier, who was still alive but seriously wounded. Shupai had turned just in time to see him lying on his tummy with his head up, holding his gun aiming at Munongwa, the unit commander, a few paces away. Munongwa responded to Shupai's warning by throwing himself to the ground behind a nearby bush and at once letting loose several bursts of automatic fire, making several bullet holes into the already dying body. Everyone had thrown themselves to the ground, to take cover in response to Shupai's warning and the shot she fired. No movement was detected then. After a brief silence the unit commander ordered everyone to move quickly and take whatever was useful and move away from the scene swiftly. Within moments, the unit had vanished from the area. The unit had replenished itself with British hand grenades, Belgian rifles, West German machine guns, pistols and other NATO automatic weapons without suffering any casualties. 'This is what we call an ambush,' Shupai said to herself. The guerrillas moved toward the rendezvous.

After inspection of the 'loot', Munongwa ordered the unit to a resting place for the rest of the night. At about six in the morning the following day, Shupai was the first to awaken to the sweet tunes of the Zimbabwe birds. The sky was cloudless. With the previous night's action out of her mind and while lying on her back with eyes shut she heard a sudden shuffling of leaves right above her. She jumped up in fright, grabbed her gun, ready to shoot, only to discover that it was a little monkey jumping from one branch to another. She sat down and stared at the little monkey, thinking, 'What freedom these animals have in their world!'

She wished she were as free in her own world as those animals were in their own. 'People are born to be free. Free to live and reside where they want to. I want to be free to choose and pursue a career. Job Reservation curtails my freedom. Buying from special kaffir shops, travelling in 'Native train coaches' from city to city; being administered by a special 'Native Affairs Department', living in specially designated 'Native Locations', and 'Native Reserves', all these things dehumanise me. They dehumanise Zimbabwe. Segregation is designed to make us inferior. It is designed to deprive us of the pride which people of all nations have sought to have. Labouring under such laws as the 'Law and Order (Maintenance) Act', 'Industrial Conciliation Act', deprives us of our genuine human-rights, the rights of workers to strike for better pay and better conditions of service. I'll be free one of these fine days, just like that small monkey,' she felt suddenly angry and hungry.

Shupai stood up and started to open a tin of baked beans taken from the enemy the previous night. She heard from behind her the commander's voice saying:

"Thanks a lot comrade Shupai."

"What for, for this?" Shupai asked, giving him a tin of baked beans.

"You saved my life last night."

"It's not necessary to thank me comrade Munongwa. But tell me," said Shupai, "Why did you have to waste all that valuable ammunition?"

"Which ammunition?" Munongwa was surprised.

"Four precious bullets you poured into that dead man's body?" Shupai answered. Every member of the unit burst into laughter at the joke. The tension which had built up since the previous day's operation loosened.

"Actually, in such a situation, one does not really stop to think of what one is to do. You just act instinctively," said one of the combatants as if replying on the commander's behalf.

"That was a great performance you staged last night comrade Shupai," commended Shonhiwa Gidi, and they all joined in a hearty laughter and congratulations. A jovial mood had set in. They were all having their "breakfast" of tinned beans, in high spirits, recalling their victory over the enemy forces the previous night.

Shupai looked round at her male comrades with great satisfaction. She raised her right arm high, and with her two fore-fingers, made a 'V' sign to the comrades. They all responded by showing the 'V' sign with their fore-fingers also. For Shupai, the victory was more than just one victory after an engagement against the enemy. It meant victory not only for the Zimbabwe Liberation Forces but also for the Zimbabwe women-folk. As one of the few women, in this liberation army at that time, Shupai was proving that if women took their rightful place in the nation, they could do everything that men did. She was quite satisfied with her contribution to the armed struggle.

Many women were involved in the struggle for the liberation of Zimbabwe. Shupai had been one of the first women to be fully engaged in guerrilla warfare in Zimbabwe against colonialism, imperialism and the exploitative system of capitalism. She was an attractive 24-year-old with brisk movement. She was too quick to be described as pretty. She stood at five feet four inches, with black and bright smiling eyes. Even at first sight it was impossible not to notice that she was an intelligent and mature woman. Men looked at Shupai twice and would wish to talk to her, talk to her about some things other than the struggle for the liberation of Zimbabwe. She had a great sense of humour and was always trying to keep her comrades cheerful, especially when they faced a difficult situation.

"The struggle is difficult, but it is of no use brooding over difficulties without searching for solutions," she would always say. She was an extraordinarily inventive person. In really awkward situations she could think of unusually cunning ways of getting out. Often it would mean her going into the danger zone herself. This won admiration for her courage from some of her male counterparts. She had strong nerves, ingenuity, and perhaps, somehow, lucky too. This won her a special place in the hearts of her comrades especially those with whom she worked closely, for example, Munongwa, Shonhiwa and several others.

Munongwa was a bearded young man. His beard seemed to be trying unsuccessfully to conceal a prominent scar which ran across his right cheek from ear to chin. Munongwa had incurred this scar from a barbed wire fence when he had escaped from Bindura remand prison. He was quite tall and thin, but without any suggestions of frailness, with an athletic stature. He walked easily, as if his feet were automatically lifted up from the ground and pulled forward. He could jog for a long time without tiring easily. He was one of the several guerrilla trainers, who had been well trained in guerrilla warfare outside the country. He was among those who infiltrated back into the country through the Centenary area, and was assigned to the Sinoia (Chinhoi) area to open a guerrilla training base. He trained several combatants as well as receiving already trained ones who were arriving from across the Zambezi. Munongwa was the commander of the guerrilla unit which staged the famous Sinoia battle against the colonial forces a few months before. It was this particular battle which heralded many other different operations by the liberation forces throughout the country which led the colonial army to concentrate their troop activities along the borders with neighbouring countries to the north and East. Among the combatants whom Munongwa trained was a young man whom they called Shonhiwa Gidi.

Munongwa later chose Shonhiwa Gidi to be his second in command. He became a tough, seasoned guerrilla, a little bit heavier than Munongwa but they were of the same height. He tried to keep his beard closely shaven but, guerrilla life made it hard to shave regularly. He had been observed to have his right hand on his itchy chin all the time, particularly when decision making. Most guerrillas did not even bother to shave.

Looking at Shupai now, Munongwa recalled the first time the girl was brought to his base for training. "What is this?" He had protested bitterly. He even left the camp that day to travel all way to the headquarters of the local underground movement to register his complaints: "Sending that girl to me! What are you trying to do to me, may I ask?" Munongwa spoke, quivering with rage, pointing at Jakwara, a mall bearded man, who was the attendant at the secret office in Sinoia.

"Don't you worry, comrade Munongwa," Jakwara answered calmly and said, "Comrade Shupai is quite alright."

"Comrade, indeed!" Munongwa's face registered his disgust.

"Yes," said Jakwara. "Everyone here and elsewhere, is convinced she can be a capable fighter. You see...." His sentence trailed away. Munongwa had interrupted him:

"But comrade, are you aware of the implications, politically, militarily and....otherwise?"

"There is no problem, comrade Munongwa. She's been thoroughly screened. After all, she's worked with the underground movement in several areas, for a long time now." Jakwara went on to explain how Shupai worked as a secret agent and that she could still be utilised as such as well as being a fighter.

"Yes? Then why don't you keep her here with you?" asked Munongwa and went on, "You know how women behave. I'm afraid discipline among the men is not going to be easy to maintain anymore, once they have a woman among them. Every one of them would strive to have her and this may lead to fights and hatred. No comrade Jakwara. I'm not going to have it, period!" He left the office, banging the door loudly behind him. Jakwara tried to follow him, but could only shrug resignedly.

When he came back to the camp, Munongwa found Shonhiwa talking quietly to Shupai. He ignored them and just threw himself on the makeshift bunk bed, away from them, and closed his eyes. Shupai remained calm and unaffected. Shonhiwa was saying: "You see, sister, the work here is quite taxing and quite involved. You see ...."

"I beg your pardon, comrade," She interrupted him. "In the Underground Movement and even at Headquarters I'm also addressed as C-O-M-R-A-D-E," she slowed down on the word "comrade" as if to spell it out for him. "I've seen the commander's reaction. But I'm determined, and I mean business about this training. Why don't you try me? People always pass or fail...."

"Comrade Shonhiwa!" Munongwa called loudly. He sounded somewhat irritated. Shonhiwa went to him. "What's going on, are you already courting comrade?" Sarcasm sounded. Shupai did not hear what Munongwa had said to Shonhiwa.

"Don't be irritating, comrade commander," said Shonhiwa quietly.

"Then what's going on? How long have you been talking to her, and what have you been talking about? Who, who gave you the permission to talk to her anyway?" Munongwa's questions ranted on.

"Too many questions comrade commander," said Shonhiwa, still calmly and added, "She is a human being, first of all, sitting there quietly. The commander of the camp just stormed away without any word to her. What is she supposed to do? Someone had to, at least, talk to her, perhaps, about what is involved here."

"You hadn't even consulted me," Munongwa said, suddenly sitting up. "Then what did you tell her? You know we can't have women around here. They are too much of a nuisance you know." He sat there glaring at Shonhiwa who just looked at him calmly. After a while Shonhiwa said:

"You, comrade Munongwa, you surprise me now. You are the one who thoroughly trained me. You are also the political commissar around here. Are you contradicting your own teachings? Have you forgotten the Maoist tactics you are always talking about?" Shonhiwa went on, "You have always talked about how the Chinese, the Cuban, the Algerian and the Palestinian women had carried arms against the colonialist oppressors. Are our Zimbabwean women any different?" Munongwa did not answer. "Can you, please, answer me comrade commander," pleaded Shonhiwa, insistently.

"Our women are not yet ready, you know," he answered.

"When do you think they are going to be ready if they are never given any chance?"

"I don't know. Don't ask me!" he cut Shonhiwa harshly, not looking directly at him. This was uncharacteristic of Munongwa.

"Well, this one seems ready and has made up her mind."

Munongwa laughed cynically. "No woman's mind is ever made up," he said. "They are constructed for the purpose of having their minds made up for them. How else do you think the human race survives?"

"Congratulations! Congratulations, comrade commander!"

"What do you mean by that?" Munongwa snapped at Shonhiwa.

"Why don't you give her a chance commander?"

"You go ahead and do that. I'm not going to have it. Dismissed, comrade!"

"I'm sorry if I've gone too far comrade commander. It's a matter of opinion, you know." Shonhiwa withdrew to where the others were, who also seemed to have questions to be answered by the commander.

Pregnant silence ensued. All the men were waiting for the commander's decision or what ever. Conversation became strained. No one dared come near Shupai. She kept sitting where she was, waiting, watching the sun setting, watching the commander sitting there rigidly looking straight ahead of him, brooding. It was going to get dark. She thought, perhaps the commander was waiting for the darkness to take her back to where she had come from. She had not heard the talk between Shonhiwa and the commander. But she had sensed some opposition atmosphere from the commander. Then Munongwa stood up and called all the men to him and said: "Now, comrades what do you think of this?" he asked, pointing at Shupai who just watched them from where she was. Most of the men just shrugged their shoulders looking at each other.

"Comrade commander," said Munda, "there are about four of us here who know her. She is the teacher who received and looked after us and others at Charara School, when we first came from Zambia, and also during the Jeaney Junction Operation, and others. And now that she's decided for armed struggle, I think she's quite a capable freedom fighter."

"No one has asked for your personal opinion, comrade Munda," said Munongwa. 'Sarcasm still,' thought Shonhiwa who kept looking down at his feet. "Okay, I'll give her a trial training," he said looking straight at Shonhiwa, then round at the others. "Now, don't start having any funny ideas. No courtship around here. She must just be treated as one of us, okay? She must be watched very carefully," he emphasised, "I mean, very carefully. Understand?"

"Hi, comrade commander!" the men agreed in unison.

'Watched carefully for what?' Munda and a few others asked themselves silently. The commander didn't elaborate. What do we watch her for?

Shupai had heard the "Understand?" and the man's unison answer, "Hi, comrade commander!" 'What ever they are conspiring about me....' She stood up. 'I'm losing my patience,' she thought, 'I've got to do something.' She moved gracefully towards where the men were gathered, and said "Comrades," addressing the commander, specifically. "I thought I was supposed to be one of the group?" gesturing around with her stretched arms. "Now can you tell me what's going on?" she asked. "It seems I'm going to be an outcast, or am I already one?" she pretended to be calm.

Silence...All eyes on the commander. Munongwa was taken by surprise. He had not expected this encounter with the girl, he thought. He had wanted to take his time. First of all he had planned on actions which would show her that she was completely unwelcome. Preach to her, roughen her up so she could lose her temper, perhaps, and finally lose her discipline. Then he would have had a pretext to send her back to where she had come from.

"Don't you think I know the problem, comrades?" Shupai asked, her eyes still trained at Munongwa, interrupting his thoughts. "Oh, yes I do know what's going on, indeed," nodding her head slowly. "In this liberation war, the Zimbabwean woman is caught between two very aggressive enemies.

Can anyone of you mention these two enemies to us?" She looked around at the men. Her eyes resting again at Munongwa, waited a little, no one spoke. "Number one," she continued, "is the oppressive minority regime; the regime that has created hell for every Zimbabwean black man and woman. This enemy, I clearly associated with the international imperialist movement which is tenaciously linked to the global capitalist system," she sounded as if she was in one of her history classes, but she went on steadily and they seemed to be listening attentively. "The second, very, very sickening and aggressive force is the so-called strong sex, you, all of you," she pointed around to them. "You think women can't fight a war. You all say wars are for men alone. And so, the war of liberation and all that has to do with the running of the state is a prerogative of men and men alone. I'm telling you, comrades here and now that, this is sheer male chauvinism." The last clause she uttered slowly and emphatically. She was trying to drive deeper into their minds the nail of what she thought and believed could help her be accepted as an equal among equals, especially in the struggle for the liberation of Zimbabwe. The silence that followed....then:

"No, no one has said anything of that sort," Munongwa seemed to have recovered from Shupai's spell and did not know exactly what to say. He sounded apologetic. "You see sister, life in these jungles is not easy and I feel you are better off at home where you belong."

"Umm...I've heard that one before. I know what your kind thinks, comrade. You think women are soft-hearted and soft bodied and so wars are for the tough and hard-bodied men. You think women are meant for the kitchen, the bearing of children and the badza (hoe)? Then you are mistaken comrades," she went on, "Women are oppressed also, you know and don't want anymore to be used as objects for men's admiration. Now, I'm here to stay and train as a combatant just like everyone else here," she had now become a bit emotional. She checked herself, and kept quiet. A minute of silence, then she said more persuasively, "Please, give me a chance to show my ability. I'm eager to learn and to do more for the struggle than I have been doing so far. In fact, I feel as if I was paying lip-service to the struggle." Shupai was polite and respectful but when necessary she could be tough and aggressive. She discovered that she had to be like that against those that attempted to divert her efforts from doing what she thought was right for the struggle.

The training turned out to be really hard. She chose the name Shupai as her guerrilla name. Munongwa had kept to his word for a trial training. Most of the difficulties that Shupai encountered were pre-arranged, just to make conditions tough for her, so that she could give up in despair, at least this was how Munongwa had viewed the whole thing. She seemed to have detected this scheme of Munongwa's and she became even more and more determined to fight this enemy. She secretly condemned Munongwa and all those of her comrades who exhibited chauvinistic tendencies which indicated that as men they felt that women could not be fully involved in the armed struggle.

Shupai, however, noticed that there were a few men including Shonhiwa, the second in command to Munongwa, who acted differently towards her, Shonhiwa was one of the first men to recognise her as an equal in the struggle. He admired her courage and determination. He also admired her as a person, Shupai noticed, and not as a woman but just as an oppressed Zimbabwean eager to rid the country of all forms of oppression and exploitation. Shonhiwa approached Munongwa one day and asked, "How long is the trial training going to last?"

"What do you think?" Munongwa snapped.

"Well, I personally, don't think it's necessary anymore, what do you say comrade commander?"

"To tell you the living fact, I don't think it was really necessary in the first place. But as you can see, she's become one of the toughest combatants I have trained so far, let alone her, being a woman."

"I was hoping, comrade commander, you'd never mention the sex issue. Well, I guess some of these things are ingrained in some of us, so that it's hard to believe otherwise."

"Comrade Shonhiwa, we've got work to do. Don't start....But you know what?"

"What?"

"You, a few others here and this woman have taught me something. Don't ask. It's my own secret."

Munongwa's unit had decided to move to the 'Mikute', further into the jungle, to the west, away from the previous ambush point. The guerrillas particularly knew the area well. They knew most of the corners to hide themselves from the enemy. Green foliage of all kinds in that jungle provided them with excellent traditional guerrilla camouflage, all the time. The Mikute trees at this place were nice and green and Munongwa always told his guerrillas: "the care free, comfort craving colonial soldiers don't usually venture into these corners for fear of snakes and....The settler soldiers after all, were still convinced that the guerrillas still hit and run back into the neighbouring countries except South Africa," he told the combatants.

Munongwa had ordered his unit to spend the whole day lying low under the Mikute trees, with combatant watchmen taking turns at the guard duty. They had three of them on top of tall trees, apart, for viewing farther distances. The enemy was usually spotted from afar and was usually ambushed or just assessed and let to pass.

"Several copters from Sinoia are flying to and from our spot of operation of last night," one of the combatants from one the observation posts came to report to the commander.

"The enemy must frantically be removing their dead, assessing their losses and trying to clear the road of the debris before the civilians noticed the damage," commented Munongwa with satisfaction and continued, "The civilians are made to understand and believe false reports as the radio announced this, 'A gang of terrorists last night attached a security force, abducted and killed innocent peasants in Sinoia area'. True or false?" he laughed.

"What a farce!" Shupai had said, switching off the radio, "Added lies to sow seeds of hatred among the peasants against the freedom fighters."

"After all, they merely talk of an attack," said Shonhiwa, "and not the fact that their entire convoy had been wiped out."

"It's a cheap common propaganda line by the settlers to demoralise us, and discourage the peasants from supporting the guerrillas," said Katema, a Rhodesian trained soldier, who had decided to join the liberation army. "They have to seal the area and work over-time to clear the spot before the villagers noted the real damage." He went on, "I remember the time I was still in the settler army when they used to use some of us to broadcast some false interviews over the radio pretending to be captured "terrorists" or deserting ones, to denounce the leader, the armed struggle and so on. This activity used to bore me to death. The day I was forced to appear on T.V. was the limit. I just disappeared. And in the tracking down of the "terrorists" we, the African soldiers are sent in the front while the white soldiers follow in the rear. Most of us used to die a lot from the mines than anyone else. So you see, blacks against blacks; it's okay by them."

Spotter planes zoomed high and low. They sometimes flew so close to the guerrillas that they were forced to remain carefully under cover for the whole day. The biggest man-hunt operation had been declared. The enemy infantry division, the radio report said, had poured men into the Sinoia area and the area along the border to track down a gang of terrorists that had attacked a security force unit and killed innocent peasants.

Munongwa realised that the settler soldiers may venture into the jungle and flash them out. He conferred with his second in command;

"Comrade Shonhiwa, there is definitely going to be a bigger contact with the enemy. We are so few. No doubt we'll be wiped out like flies."

"We'll need some reinforcements," suggested Shonhiwa. "Perhaps comrade Shupai can go and call for some more men to come and help us."

"That's a good idea," Munongwa said, "Somehow she knows how to go about it." He crawled to where Shupai was and said, "Comrade Shupai, we need reinforcements. You'll have to try and leave for Masowe School, to contact Mjiba Doro, for more combatants as soon as possible, right now we do have enough supplies, what we need is numbers."

"Right way comrade commander," she whispered. She did not hesitate.

"Be careful how you move, comrade. Watch out for those spotter birds. They do mean business," he warned and added, "We don't want to lose you, you know." She just nodded as if to say, don't – worry – you – know – I'll – do – it.

Behind a bush, she changed into civilian clothes and was on her way. When necessary she would run very fast, jog or start to gather some firewood. She then tied the firewood into a bundle and carried it on her head. With the bundle on her head, she thought, she was safe from any suspicion. At around eleven o'clock that morning before she reached Chiromo Village near Masowe School, she met five soldiers on foot, three Africans and two whites.

"You, where do you come from?" one of the soldiers asked, pulling her hand roughly. She screamed, letting the firewood bundle drop onto his arms, chest and onto the ground. "You foolish bitch, I'll...." his hand rose to strike, but one of the other soldiers, the biggest of them all caught the hand in mid-air and said:

"Why don't you leave her with her firewood?" Turning to her he asked, "Are you from that village?" pointing to Chiromo.

"No, the school, sir," she answered and added, "Thank you very much, sir, for your kindness," politeness a bit exaggerated.

"Where do you gather your firewood?"

"The forest just behind me sir."

"You didn't see, see any people there, men?"

"No, sir," she replied, bending down to lift her firewood bundle. The big soldier helped her. "Thank you, again, sir. You are very kind." They let her pass. That was close, she sighed. She walked for a few metres and looked back. The soldiers were heading towards the wrong direction, she thought. When she left the base, she had circled, crossed the main road and joined the path to Chiromo village as if she was coming from the opposite direction.

When she reached Chiromo, she gave the firewood to an old couple, friends of hers, Mr and Mrs Taita. They welcomed her sadly, thanking her for the firewood, and the old man asked, "Are you going to the funeral, my grand child?"

"To the funeral, who has died?" she was surprised.

"Oh! You haven't heard? The soldiers have shot and killed two Chifamba village youths. Not so long ago. The boys were just herding their cattle near the river down there," the old man jerkingly explained, pointing to the direction the five soldiers were coming from.

"Gosh! Where are these soldiers now?" She thought of the ones she had just met. "Did they pass through here? How many were they?"

"You can't ask how many. They are many. They are moving in groups of four, five, six, even more. They must be everywhere, all over," answered the old man emphatically stretching his arms pointing around.

"But killing children...." The old lady, Mrs Taita sighed sadly, looking at Shupai, shaking her head slowly.

"That's terrible! Let me go back and inform teacher Doro and the others. I had just come to see how you are, my grand parents."

"Be careful child," the couple said simultaneously waving to her.

She delivered the messages from the front to teacher Doro. She estimated the number of combatants needed to reinforce Munongwa's unit. "They are needed immediately." She gave the directions to where Munongwa was and where he expects to meet the other combatants. "Mr Doro you know the place and you will have to guide them there if they don't already know." Most of the guerrillas who operated in the Sinoia, Karoi, Hurungwe areas were quite familiar with the surrounding jungles. Most of them either had been trained there by Munongwa or had been sent to him as they come in from training outside the country.

"This particular group, the nearest from here, knows the place you are talking about. There won't be any need for me to guide them." said Doro already preparing for the trip to the local underground headquarters. "Alright, I must run along now," she said, finishing to eat the food Doro had given her.

"Now, comrade Shupai, I don't think you should go back, today," protested Doro. "The way you explained everything, I think it's not safe anymore, for you to travel back alone. You stay here. I'll go...."

"You've missed the point Mr Doro. You and I have to do our work. You go ahead and do yours and I'll do mine. Good bye." She went out of the house, leaving Doro standing there with a pair of boots in his hands, mouth open, as if he wanted to say something but was not given the time.

On her way back, she did not retrace her previous route. She met a few peasants, here and there and spoke with them pleasantly. One of them may be an informer, she shivered. It's true, the going back is more difficult and dangerous, she thought, she could not use the firewood camouflage anymore.

They could suspect her the moment they see her. She had to move cautiously and went deeper into the jungle. She met no one then.

She moved a few more metres further then she heard a whistle. That warned her that she's been spotted by one of the comrades at the observation posts, as well as informing the others of her approach.

"Congratulations comrade Shupai," Munongwa hugged her warmly when she arrived.

My heart kept on jumping into my mouth each time I thought of you meeting with trouble," said Shonhiwa, also hugging her heartily.

"I almost did; on my way there; just before I reached Chiromo village." She went on to tell them what had happened and what she heard about the soldiers' movements and activities.

"So you see, comrade Munongwa," Shonhiwa said, "your suspicions are fulfilled. The enemy will eventually advance this side. Hope the comrades manage to reach here before it's too late." Thank God she's back, Shonhiwa prayed secretly. He had developed a special liking for Shupai. She had also realised it and had admired him for his ready understanding and his acceptance of her as a person and guerrilla, as a comrade in arms and ....well, Shupai had gone on thinking about Shonhiwa and admiring him. He was a liberated man, Shupai praised Shonhiwa, quietly. He could make a suitable husband in a liberated Zimbabwe, she thought, she wouldn't mind him as a future life partner.

Shupai's capacity to gather information, vital information which helped the liberation struggle and her performance in real combat had drawn men in her unit, and those who had worked with her elsewhere to accept her as an equal. Men like Munongwa, chauvinistic as they were, had no choice but to accept her and give her, her rightful position in the armed struggle. She, however, still had to fight her way into the minds of some die-hard who she thought, still refused to accept the facts that women could fight side by side with men with equal zeal, courage and determination and win. This part of Shupai's struggle was very difficult, she thought. Although she always won in the end, she realised it was difficult as she, could be transferred from one unit to another, or her unit could work in conjunction with another unit whose combatants did not know her. During such circumstances she always met fresh opposition and fresh resentments from male chauvinistic comrades. The worst difficulty, Shupai thought and realised, was that in each case she had to deal with individuals rather than a group. Where she had to deal with a group, she thought, the task was relatively easier.

Chapter 2

Munongwa's unit, after Shupai's arrival, waited until it was dark. Then they were safe to gather and plan for the next strategy. "We will now move from here to the rendezvous with the others." Munongwa said. "The 'Grey Stone', we all know where. Comrade Shonhiwa and his advance party have already left." He went on, "We must, as always, not leave any tracks behind us. We'll march in small scattered groups of two or three. The enemy must never know which direction we took from here. Any encounters with the enemy, you all know the signal to give and warn the others. Avoid using the fire arms as much as possible. Our knives are still effective as usual. Let's destroy all tracks," he added.

They left the 'Mikute', heading towards all directions. Some had to circle the place to head towards the stated Grey Stone. Sporadic gun fire was heard from the direction of their previous operation area. Shupai was marching with Nhamo and Chamu. She said, after the sound of the gun fire.

"They must be killing the innocent civilians."

"I wonder what they are shooting at," said Nhamo.

"Ask me. I know them, those cowards," said Chamu, one of the former Rhodesian soldiers who had deserted the colonial army, and ran out of the country through Botswana to join the liberation army. The army vehicle they had travelled in, with four of his colleagues, Museve, Katema, Sango and Rukwa, was found abandoned inside Botswana, just near the border. Chamu went on, "They probably must just be shooting at random into the bushes to frighten us away, or just to give each other morale. You must remember, they get paid and they have been given the mandate to shoot the "terrorists," he went on, "the sound of the guns is a message to their bosses that they are doing their work, an honourable job indeed, don't you think?"

"It's honourable, indeed," commented Shupai. "It serves us an honourable service by informing us of their whereabouts." They reached the rendezvous, a one hour's march from the Mikute. The Grey Stone place was well camouflaged with some very tall trees and thick undergrowth of shrubs and creeping plants. Looking at the so-called Grey Stone one would be surprised how it had become so famous. They were actually two ordinary looking, fixed stones in the middle of which was one of the tallest trees in the area. The guerrillas had adopted a system of giving names to certain particular land marks for easy reference in their several operations.

One combatant on top of that tree had observed that enemy activity was still concentrated on the other side of the main road around their last ambush spot. It must have taken the settler soldiers a longer and harder time to clear the place, thought the guerrillas. The road seemed to be out of use for some time.

At dawn, a whistle was heard from one of the observation posts announcing the arrival of the other combatants who were to join Munongwa. The commander of this unit was called Tichaona, Ticha in short. He was one of Munongwa's very first locally trained cadres. Most of his men were also trained by Munongwa and they knew the area around the Grey Stone in and out. Tichaona , himself, particularly knew this area because there was a time when he was serving a prison sentence with hard labour for contravening the Law and Order Maintenance Act. Tichaona and the other inmates were the ones who constructed that military road from Darwendale to Sinioa up to Chirundu. When he had completed the prison sentence, he joined the underground movement at the time Munongwa and the other foreign trained cadres had just come back into the country. Tichaona was the one who had suggested and recommended to the underground movement the Chirundu/Sinioa/Karoi area as one of the best training bases. He never wanted to go and train outside the country: "What a waste of time and money," he had argued, "If there are a few who have thoroughly been trained, they can also train the others. I wouldn't want to waste time going out of Zimbabwe or else I may lose track of Sergeant Fielding." He went on, "Sergeant Fielding is the well known colonial terror at the central police station in Salisbury. I'll never forget him. I'll have to deal with him and wipe his image out of my face." Tichaona commanded one of the crack guerrilla units in the country, good at commando operations and good at walking long distances.

Tichaona and Munongwa exchanged comradely greetings. The combatants stood in small scattered groups among the trees. Tichaona looked around and when he saw Shupai he got so shocked, at the sight of the girl, that Munongwa noticed it clearly. He looked closely, and immediately recognised her. 'I thought I had warned that girl to keep away from this,' he muttered to himself angrily. He turned quickly to Munongwa.

"What's that girl doing here?" he asked angrily and went on, "Where did you get her? I thought I had warned her to stay out of this job long ago. It's about time someone took some action about her." He glared at Munongwa as if Munongwa were responsible for her presence there among the combatants.

Then he switched his gaze to the fringe of trees where Shupai was, then more visible and talking confidently with her comrades, most of whom had long ago accepted her as a good fighter.

"How do you mean?" Munongwa asked, and added, "Do you mean comrade Shupai?"

"Comrade Shu, what? That's not her name. She's called Lucia. That's the girl I told you about, remember? The girl I said was arrested together with me in a bus on our way from Gomba to Salisbury?" He went on breathlessly fast "Remember, the one, the teacher who was in charge of transportation during the time we staged the Wiltshire Estates thing. You must remember man. I told you about the lady teacher who met us, transported and kept us at her school on that day we burned up the pigs at the Wiltshire Estates piggery. That's her," he said pointing at Shupai. "I told you I loved that girl."

Tichaona kept gazing towards where Shupai was. His face was tense, his eyes fixed unblinkingly ahead. He decided he'd talk to her again, more sternly, this time. Then his body seemed to relax a bit. He glanced at Munongwa and grinned, seemingly happily concerned. All tension had smoothed out of his face. "From now on, comrade, we can forget what I've just said. We have this that we have set out to do." He glanced back at the girl, smiled, and then turned back to Munongwa. "What did you say her name was, Shushu?" he asked, mockingly.

"Comrade Shupai," Munongwa answered, tone sounding very confident in the girl, there was no doubt about it, Tichaona noticed.

"Hmm.... Shupai" What a waste, he thought. I'd like her for a wife not a comrade. I've been in love with her ever since I saw her at Chakarara School, and been wondering about her and yet all along she's roaming the jungles with a group of cut-throats. How ungodly! He decided he had to try and discourage her. She can't be left to go on like this. She needs a good adviser, me, he thought. He said, "Excuse me," to Munongwa, and walked to where she was. He stood for a while watching her. She looked soft and pleasant there, among the male combatants in combat gear. He hated the idea badly. But he found himself tingling with desire to touch her, to feel the warm roundness of her body under his hands. At last he moved nearer her.

Shupai smiled invitingly when she saw him. Tichaona was tall, just a few centimetres shorter than Munongwa and Shonhiwa, she noted. But he had become wider at the shoulders, had developed thick, tight muscles, due to walking long distances carrying heavy loads, she thought. Except for the muscular, over trained body, she thought, he looked surprisingly the same. His face was unmarked and the expression was still somewhat boyish. "At last we meet again, comrade Tichaona," she said extending her hand to greet him. Actually, she felt, she was happy to see him again.

"Hello, so we meet again," he said, shaking her hand. "I'm very happy to see you Lu...." He almost called her by her real name, Lucia. Most of the guerrillas use code names except a few, such as Tichaona himself. "Would you like to come for a walk with me, it's a warm morning," he said quietly, smiling.

"A walk, but we have serious work to do." She looked up at him quickly. "Well, yes, why not? But remember the enemy could be anywhere near." They went round behind a bush and moved on a little farther from the others. Shonhiwa watched them go and just wondered, what the hell does he think he's doing parading her like that?

Tichaona sat onto a dry log and called softly, "Come and sit down. What did they say your name was?" He asked, obviously sarcastically, she made a mental note of that tone. She looked at him with slight frown, but made no comment.

"Shupai," she answered, kept standing.

"Is there a last name that goes with this one?" His tone sickening, she felt.

"Shupai Zvenyu," she answered the slight frown still on her face.

"I totally disapprove of this. I would like to call you by the sweetest name I know, Lucia." She did not answer. She kept looking at him. In her mind the bell was already ringing, warning her to sharpen her defences. The good old Tichaona, she reminded herself of a bitter confrontation she had with him, a few years ago, when he had discovered that she was the one who had been appointed to look after him and his colleagues after the Wiltshire Estates operation, and to transport them to their other operations. Tichaona could not believe that a woman could be of any use in the struggle, let alone the armed struggle. The argument was a bitter one, she remembered, now there he was again. Still backward as usual, she thought.

"Tell me," he went on, "who finally encouraged you to leave your befitting teaching job to do this?" He gestured towards where the other combatants were. His face, a mask of sarcasm, she felt she was going to vomit.

"I beg your pardon!" she said. Her face became serious, almost turned to leave him.

"You see, I can't stand the idea that you really have decided to put yourself into the danger zone like this. I love you Lucia, remember?" He continued. The sarcastic tone was getting replaced by a more persuasive one. "Leave this job to the men. It is a man's job. I promise I'll do your part. I do...."

Shupai shrugged her shoulders and suddenly kicked at the ground with her right foot, sending a shower of sandy dust up. Then she flung up her head and looked straight at him almost defiantly. "You surprise me," she said, her hands clenching and unclenching. "Because you are a man, like every one of them, you do not think otherwise because of your male chauvinistic attitude."

She was like an animal that is cornered and has turned at bay. "You'd better go now. We are not on the same side and, it seems, we'll never be."

He got up slowly to his feet and went towards her and said, "You are very bitter, aren't you?"

"Bitter?" her eyes stared at him angrily. "Of course, I'm bitter, more than bitterness itself. I had thought, after the argument we had last time, you had become one of the very few Zimbabwean men who had seen the light, the light of liberation. You really astonish me!" The fire in her eyes suddenly died out of her and she turned away from him. "We are on the opposite sides of the wall. We are like two people who've caught sight of each other through a crack in the wall that separates us." She added "I'll live for the day when every Zimbabwean, man and woman will be liberated. What else have I to live for?" Her voice sounded unhappy.

He reached out and put his hand on her shoulder, but she shook him off, "Leave me alone! Don't touch me!" Her voice was sharp, almost hysterical. And in a moment her mood changed and she turned towards him, "I'm sorry. You can't help. I should not have talked like this to a commander. I will go now?"

"But listen," he pleaded.

"Please, let me go," she insisted. "Others are waiting for you, for us."

He hesitated. "Alright," he said. Then held out his hand: "Good-bye then Lu....Shupai."

"Good-bye?" Her fingers touched his. He felt they were very cold despite the warmth of the air. "Yes. I suppose it is good-bye, comrade Tichaona."

"Friends?" He asked, still holding her hand.

"Friends yes. Yes friends and comrades in arms, for the liberation of everyone in Zimbabwe." She lifted her eyes to him. Her fingers tightened on his hand. He saw her eyes were suddenly alive, almost excited. "I'll watch you." She took her hand out of his grip and walked with him to the others. "It'll be good and interesting to watch you....fight, comrade Tichaona," she said. The words were a little more than a whisper but decisive enough to worry him.

It took some time before Tichaona could concentrate onto the task at hand. 'It's such a pity,' he thought. 'Yet I can't blame her. Every black man and woman in Zimbabwe is oppressed. Every effort is needed to rid everyone of this oppression. But she's a woman man,' he went on thinking stubbornly. 'She can do other things and leave the gun to the men.' He watched her. She had resumed her position among the men, with an AK47 in her hand, she seemed contented. 'The wall between us is high indeed,' he said to himself. 'A man has to be superior and feel more superior than the woman,' he thought.

"Comrade Tichaona," he was aroused by Munongwa's voice, "What happened back there? You look as if you had a fight with her?"

"It was tantamount to a fight, indeed."

"What happened?"

"That girl is too stubborn, that's all," he replied and went on, "But I've just been thinking. One never feels superior with her, even if being in-love with her, you know. She's just…." He terminated his sentence and looked at Munongwa defiantly.

"You need to know her better. Let me tell you something comrade," said Munongwa. Tichaona kept looking at him. "The first time they brought her to me for training, I almost jumped into the lake. It took me almost just an hour to reach Sinoia to protest bitterly, giving all sorts of reasons why I could not take her. She x-rayed my thoughts immediately and she started preaching to me. Then I decided to give her the hardest trial training that I could think of, hoping she'd be discouraged and eventually give up. I failed comrade." Munongwa stopped talking, looked at Shupai and shook his head a little. "What a gallant fight she put up. She's tough, comrade, physically and mentally. Since she came, she has even helped to maintain discipline and high standard of performance among the combatants here. Do you know what she told me one day?"

"What?" Speeches and speeches, Tichaona told himself, but he listened, this time with more interest.

"She said, 'You know comrade Munongwa, for me, a man who likes to feel superior over a woman, is one who thinks that a woman is a chattel. He's a non-progressive man and a reactionary.' She went on. She said, 'You see, comrade Munongwa, I feel terribly dispirited whenever I think that many men in Zimbabwe are still so un-liberated in their thinking towards their female partners that they sometimes act foolishly.' She ended her speech. I'm telling you, it started me thinking."

"She's a speech maker alright." Tichaona just commented. He sounded disappointed and bitter, Munongwa thought.

"And a good fighter too," commented Munongwa looking at Tichaona's face. "Well, comrade Tichaona, you are entitled to your own opinion, you know. But I'd say, the more courageously such women fight, in the armed battles, the more victories they win for Zimbabwe against white minority rule, and for women against some of our attitudes towards them, the women, our mothers and sisters. Anyway," he looked around, "It's getting lighter. Let's get on to the task at hand. Let's all assemble under the tree between the Grey Stones. Introductions have to be made. I'm afraid, comrade Tichaona, your negative reaction towards comrade Shupai has, somewhat, disrupted the normal trend of events. I hope you'll act normally and work with her as an equal in the battle coming."

Tichaona just grimaced at him and walked over to the combatants and delivered the commander's message for the assembly at the Grey Stones. The combatants had to take up the positions Munongwa had told them. "We'll wait for the enemy, scattered around here. The wait may be long but, I've a feeling that, today, at any time, they'll turn their search to this side of the road. We must be ready for them."

"The special commandos must be ready to position themselves in a certain formation" suggested Tichaona. "We must try as much as possible to use as little fire as possible and yet try to capture more weapons."

The special commandos were those who were trained in the hand to hand combat with the enemy using fists, kicks, knives, gun-butts, arrows, even axes and so on. They were good at knife throwing. In this group, they included Munongwa' himself, the trainer, Shonhiwa, Tichaona, Chamu, Nhamo, Museve, Sango, Katema and five others.

"Alright," agreed Munongwa. "Now comrades Tichaona, Shonhiwa and two more, you must set out on a reconnaissance to locate the best spots to position the commandos," he went on turning to the others. "The rest of you position yourselves behind fallen dry logs, large stones, tree trunks, ant-hills and so on, avoid too bushy bushes. They are the most suspected enemy targets."

They had been maintaining three observation posts. It had been quiet. The guerrillas watched the sunrise in the Eastern horizon. Suddenly, they heard automatic gun fire. Munongwa, who had been talking to some of the combatants said, "Good, the enemy always announces his position."

"Who's being machine gunned like that anyway?" asked one of the combatants, worried. "Comrade commander, do you think comrades Tichaona and...."

"Morale comrade, morale," cut in Munongwa, "The soldiers are very generous with their automatic fire. Most of the time they are giving each other some morale, or just shooting at the bushy bushes because they think the 'terrorists' hide in them. That's why I warned you to avoid thick bushes, shrubs and tall grass as much as possible."

Tichaona and Shonhiwa returned and reported, "The enemy is not far from here and is surely going to approach from there," pointing to where they had gone.

"We'll try to make up a formation where the enemy can move past us, then we attack from the rear," Tichaona suggested and asked, "What do you say comrade Munongwa?"

"It's alright with me," answered Munongwa. "But the special formation may be dictated by the enemy condition. Let's, however, place ourselves ready. Comrade Tichaona will try and make proper assessments of the enemy and sound the necessary whistles. You all know our retreating routes. We'll rendezvous at the 'Three Trees.'"

They waited. The sun was going higher and getting hot. The humidity was promising to be unbearable. Waiting was the worst in this trade, Shupai thought, while stretched out on her tummy, behind a large dry tree which had fallen. She admired the lovely dry branches. Good firewood, she thought, I guess the villagers have no need yet to come deeper here to fetch the firewood. They still have plenty near their villages. Her thoughts drifted to the scene with Tichaona that morning. He's got a warped mind that guy, she said to herself. Don't think he can tell anything right from anything wrong. She went on ruminating. He could make a well built, handsome husband but his superiority complex is an incurable disease. It is in fact, a creation of his own warped mind. I don't think I can stand him. Then her mind switched on to what they were waiting for, alerting herself at once. The waiting may be long and boring, she thought but once the enemy appears, the excitement starts and all the fantasies about the Tichaonas of Zimbabwe would be brushed aside. She observed Munongwa moving and occasionally stopping to whisper something to his fighters. Some may probably be dozing off, she thought. We hadn't had any sleep or anything to eat. It's easy to lazy off and fall asleep when hungry, she thought.

A plane hovered above them, and a sudden burst of automatic fire sounded. It was repeated several times. The fire seems not to be very far from here, Shupai thought. After the plane had passed one of the sentries came down to Munongwa and said, "Two helicopters have just dropped some more soldiers from Sinioa. It seems they've pitched camp not far from here," the sentry went on fast, "We don't even know how many they are now commander."

"Afraid comrade?" asked Munongwa. "We never knew how many they were, and we don't need to know how many they are now," he assured the combatant. "Now take your position and wait for the signal. I don't think we'll wait long now."

At about two o'clock a whistle sounded, announcing that the enemy has been spotted. Shonhiwa, who had whistled from the observation post saw the first soldiers appear. He tried to assess their strength. They are many, he thought, and more seemed to be coming, heavily armed. He also noticed that they were moving in small scattered groups not too far apart. He thought of his strategies and smiled to himself when he saw that they would surely fall into the guerrilla trap like blind foxes. He came down and reported to Tichaona. "With the commandos dispersed like this, and with this formation, we are sure to deal with them, no matter how many they are," Tichaona commented in answer to Shonhiwa's report. "They'll be surrounded and be attacked from all sides." They waited. Every guerrilla waited for the signal from Tichaona which tells them that the commandos have started their silent attack.

The front groups approached. They were the ones who were shooting at random, at intervals. The following ones, some warily ready to shoot, some carelessly carrying their weapons on their shoulders talking to each other; and some looked wearily as if they had been on the march for days.

"We've been moving all night and all morning without any contact. I've a feeling this manoeuvre is useless," one of the young soldiers, passing near where Shonhiwa was, was saying to his companions.

"Why?" asked the other.

"The terrs have since gone back to Zambia, don't you think? That's what they do".

"Yeah," agreed the third one. "We'll comb the area, anyway, then we'll rest after a while."

The first groups and the following ones had passed the commando formation into the ambush zone. Tichaona, after receiving the sign from the observation post that there were no more enemy soldiers coming, he gave the signal for the commandos to attack the rearguard. First a volley of knives and arrows from the guerrillas followed by another and rifle butts to finish the fallen soldiers off. Munongwa then gave the signal to open fire on the vanguard.

Volleys of gun fire from the surrounding guerrillas rained, taking the enemy soldiers by surprise. In confusion some returned the fire, some somersaulted to take cover only to fall into the hands of more guerrilla fire. Many did not have time to do anything except to throw their weapons down and either clutch onto their deadly wounds or just falling to their death. The forest sounded like the Guy Fauks Night with deafening, crackles of fire from the automatic pistols and rifles. Moans, shouts of pain and shouts of commands; all were lost in the crackles and booms of bazooka and hand grenades. A plane flew by and hovered above a little and immediately circled back.

More soldiers soon, Munongwa thought. There were still many of them there. He sounded the whistle for the retreat. Many enemy soldiers were dead or wounded. Some were shooting wildly, aiming at the trees around. The guerrillas began to crawl out and break engagement. Rounds of fire whistled overhead, slashing the branches and leaves or burying themselves in the tree trunks. There was a thick bush from which heavy enemy fire was coming. Munongwa, including Tichaona and other guerrillas saw Shupai dangerously, exposed herself in a split second and threw a hand grenade at the bush. Bodies and guns went up in an explosion. That Shupai is a good fighter, and she is courageous, said Munongwa to himself. So what? Chuckled Tichaona to himself. Showing off, that's all. How can she expose herself dangerously like that? She'd die very soon if she's so careless....

Shupai's quick action gave the guerrillas a better chance to crawl out of the opponent's range, because the fire had been slowed down a bit. They crouched down and ran. They had been scattered but all had to run towards the Three Trees. As Shupai ran, two of Tichaona's men were running parallel to each other in front of her. Suddenly, about five or six metres away in from of the two guerrillas, an enemy soldier, a frightened young man was struggling feverishly with his gun, trying to aim at them. Instead of them firing at him, Shupai, coming from behind saw them halt, threw their guns down and quickly raising their hands up. She fired, instantly killing the soldier. Apparently his gun had jammed or he was shocked to be so face to face with the terr's, she thought, or else he'd have killed the two as well as herself. He definitely had an upper hand, she realised. She ran past them a little and looked back. They had kept standing there looking down at the dying man, their guns still on the ground, as if they had not realised what had happened.

"Run, comrades, run!" she shouted at them. It's probably their first engagement with the enemy, she thought, or else why did they get so scared stiff?

Some of the guerrillas including Tichaona had witnessed this incident from a short distance. Tichaona had felt the urge to run and push the boys forward. Thanks to the woman. She's saved the men's lives, he thought. She sure is a good fighter, quick and courageous. But who does she think she is, shouting orders at my men? I still want to tell her to stop this business of wanting to be boss, he thought stubbornly. He thought jealously, she must go home where she belongs, in the kitchen where women should be.

The sound of Shupai's gun had enabled the enemy soldiers, who had been firing randomly to turn and concentrate their fire towards that direction. The first motor shells began to fall. Munongwa whistled, signalling for a detour to avoid the fire as well as a diversionary measure against the enemy pursuers. The detour made the distance to the rendezvous longer, but this was a clever move, the guerrillas realised. The enemy proceeded to fire and passed the guerrillas who had diverted fast away from the enemy range of fire. They could tell where the soldiers were heading to. One of the guerrillas came to Munongwa and said:

"Comrade Commander, they are going toward our rendezvous."

"Yes," agreed Munongwa. "We'll have to hide here, wait until they go past the place, then we can follow their tracks. Comrade Chamu, find a good observation post and see how and where they are actually heading to." He signalled to the rest to halt and take cover. Munongwa and Tichaona conferred. Tichaona went scouting. After walking for a short distance, he climbed a tree. He could clearly observe the colonial soldiers moving fast on their search and destroy mission, spreading their motor fire generously, tearing the trees. Tichaona remained up the tree until the soldiers neared the Three Trees and passed, then he descended and retraced his footsteps back to the others. The whistles from the sentry announced his return. Munongwa went to meet him and said:

"Some of our comrades have been wounded, not seriously, thank God," he prayed. "Comrades Shonhiwa, Museve and some others are not with us."

"Let me go back there and see what's happened." Tichaona offered. At the same time they heard several bursts of automatic fire toward the direction of the point of encounter. "Now, what's that?" Tichaona asked.

"Mmm...." answered Munongwa. "Those enemy soldiers were many, you know; that's why I called for retreat."

"I agree with you, comrade Munongwa. Perhaps some of the soldiers remained behind and are probably shooting at our missing comrades back there." Tichaona said, deeply concerned. "Now let me...."

"No, you let me go back. You and these proceed slowly towards the meeting place. Any sign of the enemy, whistle and take cover."

"Isn't it advisable to take some of us to go with you, comrade commander?" Shupai suggested. Tichaona eyed her angrily. She doesn't want to be in my company, he suspected.

"A group'l easily be noticed," argued Munongwa. "Now go, comrades. Comrade Munda must lead the scouting team. Comrade Shupai and .... must look after the wounded.

Munongwa circled the point of ambush cautiously, and came nearer. He did not encounter any of his comrades except dead or fatally wounded enemy soldiers and many abandoned weapons. He wished he had come with at least two more combatants to help carry some of the necessary weapons.

He gave a calling whistle. No reply. What happened to Shonhiwa and the others? He thought desperately. The latest fire sounded from this side.

Somebody fired the guns alright. The comrades or some of the enemy soldiers could be alive somewhere around here, he thought with conviction. He hid himself behind a bush for a while, listening. He wondered around a little further, climbed a tree for better view, could not see nor hear anything except for the distant sound from the enemy artillery fire. Then from the direction of Sinoia, three choppers were heading directly towards him at very high speed.

Operation evacuation! He chuckled, descending the tree like a frightened monkey. Abandon the search and run, Munongwa told himself. His arrival at the Three Trees was announced. His comrades converged around him relieving him of the load of guns and ammunition he had managed to collect and to carry. It was now five o'clock pm. Munongwa reported: "No sign of them. But knowing Shonhiwa and Museve," he tried to assure his worried comrades, "I'm convinced they must be alive, somewhere." He looked around. No one said anything. "For the war communiqué," he tried again, "the enemy suffered heavy losses."

"The evacuation of the dead and wounded must have started now," Chamu commented. "I spotted three copters which were heading there a while ago."

"Yes, I had to run away from the area when...." They spotted three more heading for the ambush point. After a short while they heard a deafening explosion.

"A bomb dropped on our comrades, may be!" Shupai exclaimed. One combatant from the observation post came down and reported:

"One of the copters has just fallen down. Seemed to have separated itself from the others and headed west."

"Pilot may have lost control or...." said Katema, one of the several men, who had deserted the settler army to join the liberation forces. "Such disasters are very common. They usually panic a lot, those young pilots of theirs."

It was getting darker. All were more worried and Katema was offering to go back and look around again. After an hour they heard a calling whistle from a distance, followed by another, a reply from one of the sentries.

"That must be the comrades!" Shupai announced excitedly.

Shortly, they arrived. Everyone was jubilant to see the five of them. Museve had a wound on the left shoulder. Shonhiwa had sprained his ankle. The other three comrades, Rukwa, Murimo and Sango, the last two, who were from Tichaona's Unit, were alright except for a slight wound in Murimo's lower thigh. Shupai and the other comrades straight away examined the wounded. Museve reassuringly said:

"I'm alright comrades. There's no bullet inside. I've lost a bit of blood though."

"What were you hanging around for back there?" asked Shupai, then to Munongwa, "I'm sorry commander, I guess it's your question." The commander just nodded looking at Shonhiwa.

"We were cut off behind enemy lines from the rest of you," Shonhiwa explained. "We couldn't escape through the previously stated route. We had to run westwards a bit then skirt round this place."

"What about the shooting we heard?" asked Tichaona. "Man, were we worried!"

"Three enemy soldiers, I think they were on the run," Museve replied. "They were very close. Both of them and us were all taken by surprise. Comrade Sango here," Museve said touching Sango's shoulder, "who was behind them opened fire killing two of them. The other started to run shooting wildly before we dropped him. Guess we all shot at him, no one couldn't."

"What about the chopper, comrade Museve, which broke away from the others and headed directly towards us?" asked Sang excitedly.

"Oh yes," replied Museve, "seems it had lost control or something."

"I thought they had seen us, but they were not shooting," commented Shonhiwa.

"Usually, they want to capture us alive so that they could parade us," informed Katema, one of the former colonial soldiers.

"Well, whether the chopper had lost control or not, it was almost upon us." Museve went on, excited. "Reflexes were in chaos, I'm telling you. Comrade Shonhiwa threw a hand grenade. It landed clean inside the chopper hitting the pilot. We had to jump away from its falling target." Museve turned to Shonhiwa, "By the way, comrade Shonhiwa, at what point did you sprain your ankle?"

"I think, I should say the time he threw the grenade," answered Rukwa. "I had to drag him from the falling chopper's target just before it hit the ground."

"I saw you, comrade Museve. You finished the chopper with your grenade, just before the explosion. I stood up, tried to run but fell. A little black out I guess, coz I can't remember being dragged." He looked at Murimo who had sat on a stone. "How bad is comrade Marimo's injury?" Shonhiwa asked.

"Not bad at all," Marimo replied. "Actually we never stopped to examine anything."

"Can someone take a look at comrade Shonhiwa's leg? We couldn't walk faster because of him limping like a wounded crab." Museve said jokingly, slapping Shonhiwa on the shoulder with his good arm. Then he turned to Shupai. "Comrades, we have grand fighters in the Zimbabwe Liberation Army. Comrade Shupai, that quick grenade of yours saved us a lot. We only managed to move out after the heavy fire from that thicket had ceased." He was shaking Shupai's hand amicably. Then the two comrades, whom she had saved from the frightened young Rhodesian soldier, also came and shook her hand quietly....while the others cheered happily, except for Tichaona who intervened:

"Any guerrilla could have done the same. And, by the way," he said looking directly at Shupai, "that didn't mean you should've taken the command ship, did it?" Tichaona warned harshly, moving away from the group, briskly.

"What's wrong with him?" Shupai asked, puzzled, a deep frown on her forehead, looking at Munongwa. The others were also puzzled....

"Don't worry," said Munongwa consolingly, taking her by the hand, moved a bit away from the rest. "There is nothing wrong with comrade Tichaona. You see, comrade, a man does not like to see that the woman he is relating to does not feel inferior." He went on, "some men do feel bad to know that a woman can be brave. Can even be braver and cleverer, perhaps, than themselves. They feel even worse to see that a woman can do better than them in a real combat situation when some of them drop arms and run for their lives." Munongwa led her and joined the others, when Shonhiwa was saying to his comrades:

"The problem with these colonial guys is that they think they are frightening the terrorists away by shooting at random making all that noise."

"They don't know that the noise serves us a lot," commented Rukwa, one of the former Rhodesian soldiers, "In these jungles their sophistication doesn't help them either."

"Today they fell beautifully into our trap. They were taken nicely, like sitting ducks, if it wasn't for their numbers," said Katema, also a former soldier in the Rhodesian army.

"Another problem for them is, that their friends can't distinguish the random shooting from the real engagement with the enemy," spoke Shupai laughingly and continued, "by the time reinforcement and rescue come, the guerrilla would have hit and run." Shupai was still talking when Tichaona returned.

'Speech maker, speech maker,' Tichaona said to himself. 'The star of the jungle, go home,' he thought and then said aloud, "How about something to eat, comrades. We have to move while the going is still good. The enemy is going to comb this area like short hair. What do you say, comrade Munongwa?"

"Sure," Munongwa answered. "Your unit will move further to the East of the road. The enemy was quite active there for the last three days." As you say, they'll be this side for the next, I don't know days." He went on: "We're meeting another group further to the south, who needs to replenish itself."

He turned to Shonhiwa, Museve, Murimo and the other two, Shaya and Pasi who had been wounded, "You need to go for treatment!" he commanded. They all refused politely. They thought they were not that serious. He turned to Tichaona, "Comrade Shupai'll go into the villages tomorrow," he informed. "One of your men should travel with her to Masowe School now. Then he'll communicate to you, any vital information she finds out."

They all had something to eat, baked beans and corned beef and destroyed their tracks. The Three Trees was one of the guerrillas' land marks. These actually, were three large Muhacha trees, not very close to each other, but seemed very near each other when viewed from a distance. Thick undergrowth surrounded the Three Trees that the guerrillas were provided with unquestionable traditional camouflage. It was not hard for the guerrillas to conceal their tracks at the Three Trees. They shook hands good bye. "Good luck, comrade Tichaona," said Shupai, shaking his hand. "Hope we'll meet again." He just nodded his head saying to himself sarcastically, she thinks she's so dependable, stupid woman....

'His male chauvinism is an addiction to him,' Shupai thought. Struggling against men's chauvinism, and general social and cultural backwardness was more difficult, she thought, than firing an HMG (Heavy Machine Gun). But, she felt, this played a big part in shaping her patience and physical energies. Her bravery always showed itself in the field of battle, when some of the most, egotistic and most chauvinistic of the comrades, she realised, were usually the first ones to throw down their AK47s, surrender, or run for their dear lives. She remembered the events since the second encounter with Tichaona. He had demonstrated such hostility against her that most of his men never spoke to her until after the battle. Only after the battle, she sighted, after demonstrating her fighting abilities. Well, she vowed, the firm fight continues.

Tichaona turned to Munongwa and said: "Okay comrade Sango'll go with her to Masowe. Hope you know what you are doing?" He looked at Shupai and then turned to leave.

"Go well, comrade Tichaona," Munongwa said and to Shupai, "You'll meet us at the cave, comrade. We won't move from there until you return." Munongwa announced this to Shupai to show Tichaona that there was real confidence in her participation as she did.

At eight o'clock that evening Sango and Shupai marched to Masowe and arrived at the school, at about half past one in the morning. Doro recognised the knock on his door and quickly opened it.

Chapter 3

Shupai, then Lucia, was a trained Primary School teacher, therefore, a civil servant in the Rhodesian Government. Civil servants must not have anything to do with politics; this was what the colonial government in Rhodesia believed in. Teachers, however, were some of the best people the Party and the underground movement could use as intelligence workers. Many teachers, male and female were engaged in this activity and yet were the least suspected, especially females. Shupai's work in the movement took her to teach in the most remote schools, areas of active guerrilla operations. She was in charge of looking after the 'boys', the name given to the guerrillas by the local people, transporting them to and from their respective operational parts of the area, hiding them and feeding them and so on.

In this work, she also pretended to be working for the colonial police. The settler police in turn regarded her as a very reliable informer and maintained her accordingly. Each time she got a transfer from one remote school to another, she would have suggested it herself to her "police superiors" following instructions from the underground movement. Some officials in the colonial Ministry of Education knew her as a "police informer", so that her requests for the transfers were never questioned. For easy and quicker communication with her "police superiors" from those remote areas she had requested for transport. She was given a mini-station wagon. Bravo for the Liberation movement, thought Shupai. She used this car to travel around, running errands for the movement. As an "informer," the settler police never suspected her of harbouring "terrorists" in her school accommodation. She could even divert the police attention to the wrong directions in order to pave way for the guerrillas to escape.

Masowe was the last school she had worked. Before she joined the actual combat, she had mobilised a lot of people of different calibre, in that area into the underground movement. They included fellow teachers. So, Mr James Doro was one of the teachers at Masowe Primary School whom Shupai had closely worked with in the movement. He was one of the main Mjibas in the Sinioa/Karoi/Chirundu area who was very active and also respected by the colonial police as their well trusted informer.

"Mjiba" in the Liberation war, were the link people between the guerrilla field forces (the boys or the comrades) and the underground movement activists and the local people including the peasants and workers. The movement maintained Local or District offices, Regional offices, up to National headquarters.

The Mjiba were in charge of the feeding, treatment and clothing of the "boys" and so on. James Doro, as a teacher did exactly what Shupai used to do. He had only come to this school to replace her after she had left to join the armed combat.

Shupai would come to Masowe School to visit James Doro as his "cousin". She was known at Masowe School, to have been transferred to another Primary school in Sinioa town. So, her constant presence at Masowe was not a surprise to anybody who might be suspicious of her movements. And some members of the police force in the district still recognised her as their reliable informer.

On intelligence gathering missions, Shupai dressed accordingly. She wore an ordinary civilian dress and looked just like any of the smartly dressed local girls. She was very shrewd at this work. She would pose as an agent of the settler police when the situation calls for that. But she would identify herself appropriately to the right people and at the right time and place.

That day she discovered very vital information. The settler enemy, she found out, worried by the effectiveness of the guerrillas, had decided that he would eliminate the guerrillas, now, without firing a shot. She had gone in the morning, to Chiromo Village, as if to visit her elderly friends, Mr and Mrs Taita. She had brought them some bread and sugar. The old lady was happy to see her: "You've just missed your grandfather," greeted the old lady.

"Where has he gone, to the field?" Shupai asked cheerfully and said, "Let me make you a cup of tea Ambuya (Grandmother), the bread is nice and fresh."

"He's gone together with the others to the council offices. They were called for an emergency meeting yesterday. All the villagers were called."

"I wonder what the meeting is all about, have you any idea?"

"I don't know my child," the old lady went out of the room, looked around, satisfied there was no one near, picked up a few chips of firewood and came back. "Do you remember that day you brought us the firewood?" She whispered as if there were others near by.

"Yes," answered Shupai. "The soldiers had killed some youths of Chifamba village."

"Hm, there's a rumour that the boys killed many soldiers and destroyed some army lorries."

"Where, when did this happen?" She asked enthusiastically, seemingly surprised.

"That day you brought us the firewood."

"This war...." Shupai just sighed, shaking her head and then asked, "Do you think that has anything to do with the meeting at the council?"

"I don't know. It's my suspicion."

Shupai said goodbye to Mrs Taita after she had brewed some tea for her. She went out and headed for Chifamba Village. She was now anxious to know what the meeting was all about. She had a feeling that the meeting must have been very important. If only she could see Headman Chifamba himself, she wished. Headman Chifamba was one of the several villagers in that area, who had begun to give full support to the freedom fighters. He was one of the most reliable persons Shupai had known in the area. By the time she reached the village, the meeting was over and Mr Chifamba had already arrived.

"Oh, you have come, my child," Chifamba greeted Shupai, shaking hands warmly. "You have just come in good time. Get into the house, your mother," meaning his wife, "is in there." He went round the house and shouted, "Nora! Come back!" He called, then entered the room, "I had just sent Nora, my grandchild, to call teacher Doro here. It's an emergency, my child." Without waiting for Shupai to say anything, he went on, urgency in his tone, "There is going to be danger all around us now, my child. I don't know how the 'boys' are going to survive now, and even ourselves."

"What is it, please tell me quickly!"

"We all have been to the Police Camp this morning. The Mujonhi (the white sergeant major), himself addressed us. That sergeant Marova (the black sergeant), was interpreting for him, he said....and he was angry today, he said, 'Everyone here listen very carefully. Anyone found harbouring terrorists in his house, will be dealt with very severely. I repeat, severely dealt with.' He started reading from a piece of paper. 'Listen very carefully. You are all forbidden, until further notice, to fetch drinking water from the following sources: Chiromo, Madenyika, Chifamba wells; Radoka, Kwaedza ponds,' and other water sources he mentioned which I don't know, have never heard of. Perhaps the other villagers know them. The Mujonhi repeated the names sternly three times."

"All those wells! Foul play," Shupai suspected, and she continued, "Where are you expected to get your drinking water then? What about washing and all, domestic animals and others?" Shupai asked anxiously, almost stood up to go.

"All the villages will get their water from very few sources. As for us here, the Mashumba pond, though quite a distance away, is the nearest. It's worse for people from Chiromo because they are the farthest from any of the wells not mentioned. We will have to...." The sentence trailed off because Mrs Chifamba had interrupted.

"E-e-e, old man Chifamba! These walls have ears, you know," his wife warned. "You don't want to put us into trouble, do you?"

"Now did the Mujonhi say why you are all forbidden to use those water sources?" asked Shupai.

"Come to think of it," Mrs Chifamba said quietly. "That policeman did not tell us why, or perhaps I was not listening?" she said questioningly looking at her husband.

"No. He didn't tell us. No one dared to ask. The threat was just that anyone seen nearing those forbidden water sources will severely be punished."

"Mmm, so no one knows why the restrictions?" Shupai said, as if to herself. "Well, I better run to teacher Doro, then. This information is very disturbing. Mrs Chifamba," she said, "Thank you so much for the food. It's been a long, long time since I ate sadza with sour milk."

As soon as she left Chifamba village, she decided to visit the police sergeant Marova first. The news about the water restriction was scanty, she thought. The best person to give her full information was Marova himself. She jogged towards the police camp. When she arrived, Sergeant Marova was in his office talking to some young police recruits. He saw her coming and called to her jovially:

"Come in, come in my sister, long time no see," he said gesturing her to have a seat.

"Hello sir," she answered confidently. "I've been too busy lately, you know, with all the business about the terrorists," she said, going straight into the subject of her visit. "I hear the villagers are complaining bitterly about our latest strategies against the terrorists," she said, thinking to herself, 'if he was to ask what she meant, she would say....'

"The idiots!" the police sergeant scolded and went on, "They still think we don't mean business about getting rid of terrorism."

"Do they know? They think they are clever," Shupai said seemingly sarcastic.

"Aha-a, let them wait and see. The poison is going to eradicate the terrs just like flies after a Killem spray."

"Poison in the drinking water!" Shupai almost gasped with shock. She bent down, pretending to pick on her shoe in order to conceal her shocked face. This is the worst shock she has ever had in her life in the struggle for the liberation of this country, she thought, ever.

"Yes. And if any one of those foolish idiots in the villages is stupid enough to go against the directives from the law, it's their own bloody funeral." He was really boasting about this, she felt sick, but she had to get as much information as possible. She went on:

"That's great, sir, really great," she said pretending to be happy about the whole idea about the poison but craving to get out of there and run. "But, sir, did you tell the villagers the names of the water sources that haven't been poisoned? Remember," she went on, "we have very good informers in some of the villages whom we rely upon very much."

"They've been told. No, we haven't done so yet. But, by the end of the day they should have collected enough water for the day. Here is the list." He gave her the list of the names of the wells to be poisoned and those to be left for the people. The list, she noticed covered the whole of the Sinioa/Karoi/Chirundu area.

"Do you think, sir that poisoning the water in this area alone," she said, pointing onto the list on the paper, "would be effective enough to eradicate the terrorists who are all over the country?" She probed, wanting to find out whether this move was country wide or just specific areas.

"It has to be all over the country where the bloody terrorist menace is. What do you think?"

"It's the best, so far," she answered, her heart aching madly.

"Of course, it's the best. The bustards will drink the water and die instantly. The rest will be forced to move out," he reasoned, "back where they came from in the first place."

"That is if they get a chance to move out before drinking the water," Shupai said, pretending to be cheerfully sarcastic, but saying to herself: The SOB! Can't he see he's breaking my heart? "Well sir, it was nice seeing you again." She extended her hand to him and shook his.

"Come back soon," he called "It's nice talking to one civilised person around these parts."

She returned quickly to Masowe. So, she thought, to the settler forces, poisoning water would help bring the war quickly to an end. This is serious! How can the comrades all over the country know this conspiracy by the enemy to have a quick-kill of all the people's forces, before it is too late? I wish I were ten people in one, she thought. She found Doro and Sango waiting for her anxiously. Sango could see that there was something very wrong, shown by Shupai's breathlessness. She sat down to calm herself down a little. Then she explained to them what she had found out about the enemy's new strategy.

"Mai we-e!" Doro exclaimed. "How fast can this news reach the comrades scattered all over the country?" He was already getting ready to travel. "Comrade Sango, you'll have to remain here until dark. I'll drop comrade Shupai a little further down the road on my way to Sinioa. Hope comrade Jakwara is there so that he could relay the news to the other underground movement branches as soon as possible."

Keeping watch, checking in all directions to make certain she was not being followed, Shupai reached her unit. With obvious excitement she made her report, in detail to her commander, Munongwa, ending with, "the enemy is resorting to real devilish tactics as deadly weapons against the Liberation forces, in fact, against everyone in the countryside."

All the combatants were shocked, stunned to deathly silence. Only the sound of the distant guns interrupted their silence. Each one was obviously cracking their heads for a possible solution.

"Why don't we do this," Shonhiwa started, arousing everyone from the deep thoughts. "Why don't we try to identify these poisoned wells?"

"How can we do that, if I may ask?" Munongwa spoke, with obvious hopelessness.

"We can get a few cats and dogs and let them drink the water. Then we can observe the results," suggested Shonhiwa and went on, "That'll also serve to test the effectiveness of the poison."

"Yes, man," Munda said. "By the way, comrade Shonhiwa used to work as a lab technician with the CAPS Pharmaceutical Laboratory. We may even be able to identify the type of poison used."

"That's possible!" exclaimed Shupai.

"Possible, what?" asked Munongwa.

"I mean possible to test the water. The best person to approach is headman Chifamba. He knows the others he works with." Shupai said with enthusiasm, ignoring Munongwa, who kept looking at her as if she was talking nonsense.

"But why should we do this?" he asked. He was still adamant that they do this. "You have been told the names of the water sources to be poisoned, haven't you? He went on, "And you said the villagers have also been warned at this meeting, so....?"

"Comrade Munongwa, you see," Chamu, one of the former Rhodesian soldiers, spoke. "When these people are instructed to do a duty, they do it. My experience is that they are rough and negligent. Ask comrade Museve or Katema there."

"No! We can't afford to trust them with the people's lives," Katema supported Chamu and continued, "There was this time, in the Wedza area, a group of soldiers, led by the police, were sent to a certain house suspected to harbour 'terrorists'. They burned the whole village and killed everyone including children."

That's why the liberation army is full of former colonial soldiers, Shupai thought. They deserted because they could not afford to carry on being used to kill their own people like that.

Munongwa was also thinking. Then he started, and immediately ordered an "Operation Identification". With the help of headman Chifamba and some of the other peasants from the surrounding villages, the poisoned water sources were easily identified that night. The animals, mostly cats and sheep or goats were generously offered by the peasants. The villagers who were involved in that operation witnessed all this. They were completely baffled. The poison was deadly. One of them, called Nyanga whispered to Chifamba:

"Can you believe it? We were going to drink this water alright! What do these people want from us? He was absolutely taken aback. "Some of these wells were not mentioned this morning, remember?"

"For sure, they don't care if we all die," Chifamba whispered back, and said, "Thanks to the boys who thought of this plan. Imagine what would have happened." Chifamba suggested that the message to test the water be sent to all the villages and to all guerrilla operational areas throughout the country.

The act of poisoning the sources of water for the peasants was not without it's own adverse effects. The peasants were now forced to walk long distances to fetch water. They had to wake up at four o'clock in the morning to start their journey. Three women from Chiromo village on their way to Mashumba pond were complaining bitterly about how cruel the colonial regime was treating them. One of the three women called Raina said: "I'm really incensed against this government of the white people," she whispered loudly, "I feel like dropping this tin and go into the forest to join the comrades." She was a retired nurse aid. Her husband, Sairos, the eldest son of headman Chiromo, was working in Salisbury as a tailor.

"I-we (you), you'll be heard," warned Jesika, the sister to Raina's husband.

"What? Do you think this is right?" Raina asked harshly, walking even faster. "Now we women folk have to traverse the whole district in search of unpoisoned water."

"Ah! Let her talk," encouraged the third woman, Sekai. Her husband worked in Sinoia town as a cook. "What's not death now? It's all the same now, whether you drink poisoned water or you walk long distances in search of unpoisoned water. From there can you go the field? You'll be so tired you can't even cook a meal."

"Imagine the old woman, Mrs Taita," said Raina. "Can she walk all this way? She's old. The husband is worse and sickly." She went on, "yesterday my mother-in-law had to give them some water to drink and cooked their evening meal."

"We have to take turns to supply them with water. We must also store some for the comrades, you know," Sekai suggested.

"At Chifamba that's what they are doing." Jesika informed.

The peasant women, through out the country stored fresh water for the freedom fighters. The water was cleverly and secretly delivered to them.

"Not a single patriotic soldier died of the racist minority's poison." This was the report from the district headquarters of the underground movement to Mjiba Doro. He had been sent by Shupai and her Unit to find out the results of the poisoned water in other areas. "Thanks, to the ingenuity of comrade Munongwa and his unit and to comrade Shupai Zvenyu's resourcefulness." The report continued. "The evil scheme by the enemy of the people of Zimbabwe, was shattered. Praise and thanks be to the patriotic men and women peasants in the various villages who gave their unflinching support to the Liberation forces. Forward with the struggle! Down with the settlers and their evil tactics to end the liberation war! Down with the lackeys of the racist regime!"

As animals, both wild and tame wandered through the affected districts, they drank the water from the poisoned sources. They began to die like flies, sprayed by deadly insecticide. The liberation forces could not do anything about it. The villagers were infuriated. Secret meetings began to be held in the villages to work out strategies to combat the situation.

The headmen of Chifamba, Chiromo, Mashumba, Madenyika, Kwaedza and Radoka villages invited their counsellors and advisors to a secret meeting. Chifamba himself chaired the meeting:"

"Hama (relatives)," Chifamba opened the meeting. "As you can all see what's happening around us. The government is seizing the slightest opportunity to make life harder for us." He went on cautiously. He was aware that some of his colleagues in there were police agents. "Look at how our women have to work in order to fetch unpoisoned water. Look at how our animals are dying of the poison. Hama," he continued, "On that meeting with Mujonhi, we were told the sources not to fetch water. But it was found that even those which were not mentioned that day had been poisoned. What do you think of the poison? Do you think it was aimed at the magandanga (terrorists) alone? Every one of us needs water including the animals." Chifamba spoke calmly but provocatively. He was trying to incite his audience to reason the way he himself did.

"Then why poison the water?" Asked a pipe-smoking counsellor from Mashumba village, called Chenjerai. He was a notorious settler police informer. Shupai had warned Chifamba about him long back. Chifamba looked at him and thought, 'you and your back-biting and selling of our resolutions. This time the game is up. You'll be dealt with very severely. You just wait and see.' Chenjerai went on, "This government is planning real hell for us black people. Now they are killing our cattle, sheep, goats, dogs and all. The next thing is that they will kill all of us." The others looked at each other in surprise.

"You? Don't you know?" asked Nyanga, one of the villagers who had witnessed some animals dying instantly on the night of the "Operation Identification" by the "boys". "They nearly did, if it wasn't for the clever boys, the ones you call magandanga. You,Chenjerai...." He sat down letting his sentence trail off. It was not time, yet, to deal with the police informer, Nyanga had noticed Chifamba shaking his head in a negative gesture. One of the advisors angrily interrupted:

"Let me tell you, Chifamba. When I went to visit my sister in Rusape last month, I saw the police beating people and confiscating their cattle. The people were told that they had to pay collective fines for helping magandanga." He went on. "Everyone in Rusape is suspected of helping and harbouring the magandanga. Everyone is made to suffer while the white farmers are merry-making in their farm clubs around the country. They experience no such problems. Only black people have to suffer in their own country."

"If only we ruled ourselves, life would be different, I'm sure," said another old man quietly as if addressing himself.

"It's true," said headman Chiromo who usually just sits, looking down on the floor up to the end of the meetings, "Things are bound to change," Chiromo continued, "These aliens brought war to this land. They'll keep fighting us by all means." They all started talking together to each other. Others were pointing at Chenjerai as if accusing him ...

"Alright! Alright!" Chifamba interrupted them for order. "What do you think has to be done then?" asked Chifamba, the chairman. He had let them talk. He asked this question, his gaze directed towards Chenjerai, the police informer. His eyes demanded an answer from the settler agent.They need to be fought," declared Chenjerai.

"How? By putting poison their drinking water?" asked Nyanga. Some laughed a bit but the atmosphere was getting serious, Chenjerai realised this for the first time since he came to the meeting. He said:

"First of all, all those who sell information to the police must be stopped...."

"Must stop it right away!" Interjected Nyanga, "and help the boys in every way possible."

"Do we all agree with that?" asked Chifamba, again canvassing for support, gazing at Chenjerai.

"Yes, we do!" the answer was unison."It's alright then. We all know that to liberate ourselves from this evil we need collective effort in supporting the boys, fully," Chifamba announced. "All police informers must stop going against their people. They must all realise that if it hadn't been for the clever plans by the "boys", even they, the informers and their families would have died together with ordinary people like me," he said, pointing at his chest with his right thumb. "Now Chenjerai, you will be in charge of flashing out all the enemy informers and stop their counter-revolutionary activities forth-with. Do we agree? The rest, we know what to do."

Tension between the settler forces and the peasants increased. Some of the villagers who were police agents were uncovered and were severely dealt with. Anyone who, to the peasants, symbolised the regime, a pretext was used to prey on him. The settler police were forced not to move about in small numbers, but in large foot or mechanical mobile patrols. The settler forces tried to send some informers, especially the mercenaries, the Selous Scouts, into the villages dressed like freedom fighters. The villagers were able to identify the true and genuine fighters of the Zimbabwe Liberation Army from the traitors. Slowly, a solid identity of objectives between those of the peasants and those of the freedom fighters became clear.

Chapter 4

In an adjacent area was another guerrilla group led by comrade Tafirenyika (Tafi in short). His unit had run out of ammunition. It had to carry out a special requisition operation to replenish itself. To do this it had to work in collaboration with Munongwa's group, which had just had a replenishment operation itself recently. The target this time was an army ammunition dump out-post. It was manned by the military police and well guarded by armed soldiers. Tafi's unit commandos had been carrying out close surveillance on the out-post and managed to study the characteristics of the place. The commandos had realised there was much activity during the day and seemed quiet after dark. They had also noticed that the majority of the soldiers and the military police did not spend the nights there. They were brought in by trucks in the morning and were returned to the major barracks in Sinoia just before six o'clock in the evening. Those who remained there, all except those on guard duty, had supper at seven, in the mess. The armoury had been identified without difficulty since Tafi himself had an idea of the whole set-up during the time he had worked with the Army Supply Transport Division.

When the two units met to plan the logistics for the forthcoming operation, scepticism ran through the ranks of Tafirenyika's unit at the sight of Shupai. The men were wondering whether the girl they were seeing among the freedom fighters understood the meaning of guerrilla war-fare. They wondered whether Munongwa or the people who allowed that woman to be present in the forest, at that particular moment knew what they were doing. Did Munongwa properly understand the importance of the operation they were about to undertake? Didn't he realise that an operation such as this was a task for not even the ordinary men, but for the tough seasoned guerrilla fighters.

"Can you see what I'm seeing?" One of the men in this unit exclaimed to the commander, Tafirenyika.

"Sure. No one is blind around here, is there?" answered the burly commander, lifting his AK47 to his shoulder as if to get ready for an attack. Tafi was a heavily built man, wide at the shoulders, with hard thick muscles as if a weight lifter. He was somewhat loud in speech. He was a man exhibiting immense physical strength and drive and authority.

"Can we know what that woman is doing around here?" a stout thickly set fighter called Shingirai (Shingi in short), whispered to Tafi, pointing to the other group. Shingi was the second in command to Tafirenyika.

"This is terrible!" exclaimed another one called Monday.

"We can't work like this," said Shingi. "After all what can a woman do in this work?" He went on, "People must be joking when they talk about waging an armed struggle, 'haikona'?" Shingi was already beckoning the others to retreat saying, "This is a set up, commander." For a split moment Tafi's unit members thought they had been smartly delivered into the hands of the enemy. They started to back away. Tafi kept rooted to the ground, breathing heavily with rage, clenching and unclenching his fists. Tafi's experience in the struggle was that many beautiful girls were in the service of the minority government's security services to detect and sniff-out the freedom fighters.

"Come commander. What do you think of this?" Monday asked and went on, "Have you forgotten the account you told us about the women, the women who...." he let the sentence trail off. Monday had noticed that Tafi's gaze was beyond. He was thinking deeply.

Tafirenyika will never forget how he had suffered in the hands of some women. He reflected back to the time just before he joined the armed struggle. He grew up and went to school in Harere's Highfield African Township – the heart of African politics. He had obtained a driver's licence, class two, but could not get employment. In 1971 the Rhodesian army advertised for drivers for the Army Supply Transport Division. Answering the advert at the African Employment Exchange, Tafi, together with the others, seventy five in all, twenty five Africans and fifty colours, were taken to Inkomo Barracks for training as soldiers. The training, he recalled, was tough. Really tough, he thought. He worked with the Army Service Corps (ASC) delivering food, clothes, spare parts, weapons and transporting South African and Rhodesian soldiers and arms to areas of guerrilla activities. For example, when the Centenary was declared an operational area, the Rhodesian army launched the 'Operation Hurricane'. This was to try and wipe out the guerrillas as they came in from Zambia or Mozambique, before they spread throughout the country. A futile action, Tafi thought.

It was that former girl friend of his, Seria, he reminded himself, who enabled the army authorities to get wind of his activities in the Camp, with the underground movement and the Party. His friend, a soldier instructor had told him that he was going to be arrested and be detained by the military police the following day. This was going to be done at seven thirty in the morning, the time he used to leave with the truck for the trip to deliver the food and spare parts to Mr. Darwin. His adrenalin level increased now at the thought of that incident. His heart started to pound madly as he stood there looking at the girl standing among Munongwa's combatants. He remembered how he decided to take a chance and leave the military camp earlier in the morning hoping that the guard at the gate would not know about his impending ordeal. Perhaps only the one who would come on duty at seven thirty would be informed, he had reasoned.

The following day he succeeded in leaving the camp. He drove the Land Rover truck with the spare parts and the other supplies towards Umtali (now Mutare), up to Macheke. He left the truck parked at the shopping centre and hitch hiked back to Salisbury. In Highfield he took off his military clothes, stayed with an aunt for about a few weeks, while the search for him was concentrated around the Mutare area up to Mozambiqu. He managed to escape into Malawi while the search for him was still concentreated around Mutare/Mozambique border area. In Malawi he was discovered by the Malawi Special Branch who harassed him and wanted him to return to Rohodesia. Friends, including a Reverend, Pastor James, managed to hide him in the Hotel Continental in Blantyre.

While at the Continental, a girl he knew from home as a Party activist, Eliza, met him. Boy, was he happy to see her! He remembered the way he opened up straight away, told her about his escape from Rhodesia and the problems he was facing. Eliza was an African air hostess with Air Rhodesia. She had been with this airline since the days of the Federation of Rhodesia and Nyasaland. Tafi knew her as quite an active Party supporter and was used to carrying vital communications between the politicians at home and abroad. It was, however, discovered later, that she was working with the Rhodesian Special Branch. Most of the information she pretended to transport usually ended in the hands of the enemy. Eliza seemed thrilled to see him and promised help as soon as possible. The next thing, early in the morning, two plain clothed men came into his room and forced him out at gun-point.In their car they hand-cuffed and blind-folded him. They drove for some time, stopped and dragged him out of the car into a room. He stayed blind-folded for about two days, he thought. The period had been endless. He was almost blind when they untied the blind-fold. For the next few days his eyes could not focus properly and he had terrible headaches aggravated by the beatings and torture they gave him. They had decided to bundle him and send him back to Rhodesia. Fortunately, for him, the men who were to drive him back to Rhodesia decided to drive him to the border with Tanzania and Mozambique and left him there. He could not forget the hardships he encountered on his journey to Dar-Es-Salaam.

In Dar-Es-Salaam the Party officials, many of whom knew him very well as a Rhodesian soldier but a Party supporter, welcomed him. There were many

Zimbabwean girls in Dar-es-Salaam, all party members. He became friendly with one of them called Memory. And as usual, he told her about how he escaped from the Rhodesian army. Memory fell pregnant and Tafirenyika swore he was not responsible for the pregnancy. The girl was so angry and confused that she told the party officials that he was still a Rhodesian army soldier working for the Rhodesian Special Branch. He had been sent to Tanzania to join some of the informers among the exiled Zimbabweans. The Party used to deal with these informers very severely if they were found out. So the Party acted accordingly towards Tafirenyika. Did he suffer! Tafirenyika recalled. For almost four weeks he was detained until one Party official who had come from Zambia released him. Tafi remembered how he staggered around for weeks to try and regain his strength.

Now that it was known who he was, the real informers were actually happy. They had hoped that he would be killed or something. But when he was released they tried something else. There was this woman called Rosa from Rhodesia. She had been in Tanzania since it was Tanganyika. She had a good job with the government, in charge of the Parliament House activities, and she had a good house right there, and was well known by the Tanzania government officials. The Zimbabwe Party Officials used to trust her very much as a staunch Party supporter but did not know that she was a very well trusted informer, in charge of the operations in Tanzania, Malawi and Mozambique. The Party officials used her place for entertainment and other party activities, even serious meetings.

This woman, Rosa, almost died of poison which she had aimed at Tafirenyika. He had suspected something fishy when he was invited to the woman's house together with a few Party officials. Why only him, he had asked himself, and not the other boys? The glasses with beer were brought from the kitchen, and Rosa herself, as cheerful as ever, was handing them to the guests, one by one. "I'll have that one, Rosa, the one you are holding," requested one of the guests happily. Rosa refused.

"No. This is for Tafirenyika," she said jokingly.

"Why? Is it different from the others?" asked one of the guests, and they all laughed. It was a happy atmosphere really, Tafi thought. But a warning bell had rung in his mind. He had accepted the glass of beer, pretended to drink and put it on the table. She kept on watching him, he noticed. Then she finally urged him to drink:

"Tafi, you are not drinking your beer. I know you drink beer." Then one of the guests, grabbing the glass, said laughingly:

"Why is he so special to you? Let me drink it for him." That was it! Rosa moved so fast and snatched the glass from him that the beer spilled onto the table, saying:

"No, don't! Please, it's for him." Giving it back to Tafi, "It's for you! You better drink it now before they do it for you, these drunkards," the last two words were added in to cool off the command. Now, Tafi remembered when he off-handedly took the glass from her, grabbed her and forced her to drink the beer:

"You drink it yourself. It's your beer!" Tafi said harshly, holding the glass and pouring the beer into her mouth. She spat it the first time. By the time the other guests apprehended Tafi, Rosa had swallowed down a few gulps. Before the scuffle ended she had already begun to complain of terrible heat in her throat and tummy:

"Please, take me to the hospital now! I'm going to die," she gasped the words out. "Please!" she was bending, clutching, with both hands, over her throat and abdomen. "I wanted to kill him. I've put poison into his beer. He's a traitor. He's an enemy of the people. He must die." She was sent to the hospital. By the time she reached the hospital she had lost consciousness. But she had just confessed everything about her activities with the Rhodesian Special Branch connections, to the three Party officials, who had taken her to the hospital. Tafi had escaped again, through the eye of a needle. He had vowed never to trust any woman. Women can be very deceitful, he thought. The Rhodesian Special Branch uses most of these so-called nice, well placed, and polite women to get information about the strategies and plans of 'the underground movement'.

Now, this woman, among Munongwa's boys, he thought, can she be different? Thus, Tafirenyika's men, especially Tafi himself, were sceptical about the presence of a woman in their ranks. Why should the woman particularly emerge just before the launching of an important attack on an enemy post? These women are never to be trusted, never. Tafi turned round and joined his group. The men had moved a short distance away and had waited for him.

Shupai was quick to notice the anger, scepticism and curiosity that ran down the faces of the comrades her unit had just joined. She stood upright, straightened the load on her back, leaned her AK47 rifle against her, hands akimbo, and stared straight at them as if weighing their abilities on the battlefield.

But to Tafirenyika and his men, at least the majority of them, the feeling that Shupai might be a plant, and that she may be in the pay of the enemy, remained quite strong. She had already detected the hostility.

Munongwa also quickly detected this feeling that seemed to dominate among the ranks of Tafi's men. He advanced to them. He greeted them and said, "What's going on, comrade Tafi? We haven't seen each other for quite some time."

"You tell me, us, what's going on," replied Tafirenyika, gesturing towards Shupai. Everybody else waited anxiously, others with anger and yet others with curiosity on their faces.

"We have an important mission, comrade Tafi, that's what is going on," Munongwa said, pretending to evade the subject.

"An important mission? With women around? How do you know we have not been sold out already? We'll run straight into the hands of the enemy, I'm telling you." Tafi was a bit emotional about this. Munongwa knew about Tafi's ordeal involving those few women, especially the incident in Tanzania. He began to reassure Tafi and his men that Shupai was a genuine comrade-in-arms. Munongwa went on:

"It's true, comrade, that some Zimbabwean women are used by the enemy against their own people. But it is also true that there are equally some, beautiful Zimbabwean girls, such as comrade Shupai, there," he pointed at his unit, "who are genuinely and bravely committed to the struggle for the liberation of this mother-land. Infact, many men, including myself," Munongwa tapped at his chest, "used to think that women preferred feathers and flowers and not the rigours of an uncertain forest life, the life of fighting the ruthless settler forces."

"Comrade Munongwa, I know you like making poetic speeches," said Tafi, "But this is serious business. We'll have to call off the operation. I mean it!" Anxious note in his voice, he went on, "Let's move comrades," he said to his men already moving away.

"Truly, comrade Tafi," Munongwa pleaded, "Shupai is a woman, but she's a tough and courageous freedom fighter, and in-charge of intelligence." He continued. "She's the one who discovered about the poisoned wells as well as the concentration of the enemy forces and mercenaries in the villages in this area." As soon as he mentioned this, great surprise showed clearly on all the comrades' faces.

"She....?" The men said, almost together. Apparently they had heard something about the comrade who had been mentioned to them to have discovered the information concerning the poison. They had never dreamt that comrade to be a woman. This served to dispel distrust. But Tafi was not convinced. He thought he would have to watch the girl very closely. If she tried any monkey trick, he vowed to himself, she would be the first to get his first burst of fire. He excused himself from Munongwa and took his men aside and reassured them:

"I do hope everything is alright. We must try to forget our doubts and remember why we are here in the forest." He glanced towards the other group. "But we must be aware of the enemies within...." He let the sentence trail away. For a few of his men, however, Shupai's presence was a pleasant surprise. They were happy to see that, at last some women had actually stopped lip servicing the struggle to join the ranks of those who carried arms. Great indeed!

The two groups then finally met. After the introductions, greetings and glances from Tafirenyika's men to Shupai, Tafirenyika, who was in-charge of the operation, carefully briefed the combatants about the topography of the place of operation and the logistics to follow. "Any questions?" Tafirenyika asked, throwing his glances around and then settled directly at Shupai.

"If the particular question is for me," said Shupai, "I don't think I'm such a slow learner...., comrade commander," The 'comrade commander' phrase was an after thought for politeness' sake, thought Shupai. The two commanders, after answering a few technical questions from the combatants, stood up to leave to be by themselves. One of Tafirenyika's men burst into a revolutionary song:

"Iyi ndiyo nyaya yatinotaura yokuti uyai tirwire Zimbawe."

Chorus: "Zimbabwe, Zimbabwe, Zimbabwe," (baritone)

"Ngatirwire nyika tose. Ngatirwire nyika tose, Ngatirwire nyika, nyika yedu ye Zimbabwe."

(This is the issue we always talk about. You should all come so we can fight for our country. Let's fight for our beloved country Zimbabwe).

Revolutionary songs in a revolution, the guerrillas knew, were used to rally the morale of the fighters. They served to help the combatants maintain in their minds the purpose of the revolutionary struggle. The commanders, Munongwa and Tafirenyika, who had left the group for a private consultation, were caught in their tracks. They rushed back to join the fighters in the singing.

In the meantime it had become dark. The time for the operation was drawing nearer. The guerrillas were then told to march towards the scene of the operation. They moved on to their respective positions. Each combatant knew exactly what to do when the signal was sounded. Escape routes had been identified and well defined. Members of the two units had to withdraw from the battle spot, they had been instructed, not to run back to where they had come from but towards the opposite direction.

"The commandos would create a mine-field behind us," instructed Tafirenyika, and went on, "The enemy as you know usually observes the direction where the fire started. He usually starts his search from there thinking we always withdraw back where we started."

"But don't forget, comrade commander, that some battle circumstances may alter our programmes," reminded Shonhiwa, and continued "Then we must all remember the mine-field or else the whole set-up may back-fire on us."

"Sure, comrade," Tafirenyika agreed and commended, "That's a necessary reminder and warning. So," he looked around, this time avoiding the temptation to stop his gaze at Shupai, "We must always remember or else.... we fall blindly into our own trap. That would be great!" he said emphatically.

The evening was a little bit chilly but quiet. The chirping of the crickets and an occasional hoot of an owl acted as harbinger. These added an anxious note among the combatants, a few of whom had to fight a relentless battle to push their hearts away from their mouths back to their chests. Tafirenyika looked at Shupai. He was anxious to see her in combat. He had earlier vowed to himself to watch her very carefully. He thought he would remain as close to her as possible. Shupai was unaware of this. She was calm and composed, and ready for action as usual. She had thought of the negative attitude towards her from some of the combatants in the other unit. That was not a new story for her, these male chauvinists....She told herself, there is going to be a battle. In battles contenders either die or live; and those who live would be lucky and not necessarily brave. Her morale had also been heightened by the revolutionary singing.

When one of the scouts arrived from the observation post and reported the movements of the enemy, the time for absolute alertness and readiness had come. Nerves had to be still and be cool for this could be the time for life or death. After an order, the combatants moved forward to their positions. At the appropriate moment the signal to attack was given. The guerrillas burst into action. First of all, the guards had to be silenced as quietly as possible. The selected commandos had to rush to the armoury quickly, break in and grab as many necessary weapons as they could carry, and must run immediately. The others had to burst into the soldiers' mess where the soldiers were having supper merrily unawares.

Most of the soldiers had no time to return the fire. The settler force was nearly destroyed when the sound of helicopter gun-ships was heard. Apparently one of the settler soldiers had managed to send an SOS signal to Sinoia. The guerrillas had, by their initial success, got carried away.

They thought they had acquired an upper hand to over-run the enemy out-post. They noticed the gun ships so close that, for a split moment slight confusion reigned before focussing their attention on to the approaching copters.

Munongwa gave orders to break engagement and beat a quick retreat. During the retreat, two gun ships which were dangerously strafing the retreating guerrillas were shot down. This served to pave way for the safer exit of the guerrillas from the battlefield. The enemy's attention was drawn towards the fallen helicopters. The soldiers were now frantically trying to rescue their colleagues before the copters burst into flames.

Every member of the two units made for the rendezvous. There, Munongwa, in his usual sharp way, realised that Shupai and a few other combatants, including Tafirenyika were missing. He quickly gave orders:

"Comrades Shonhiwa and Shingi, march on ahead with the rest to, the River," another of the guerrillas' land marked hiding spots in the jungle. "I'll go back to try and investigate what's happened to our comrades."

"Why don't I go with you, comrade commander?" Shingi suggested emotionally. His beloved commander Tafi was missing, he thought, he should be the one to return there.

"Two is a crowd," answered Munongwa. "Very dangerous," he said breathlessly, already on his way. There he goes again, thought Shonhiwa. Always volunteering for the danger zone, all by himself. It was such brave acts, at such desperate moments, which had earned Munongwa the rank of commander of commanders among his comrades. Shonhiwa thought he should have gone back there himself to look for Shupai. He could not stand the reality that she could be dead. No, please, he pleaded silently. That one shouldn't die. Zimbabwe is not yet free. No sir, he thought, looking up to the sky as if searching for an invisible person who held the answer.

Munongwa carefully made his way back towards the scene of action. He advanced towards the enemy forces and the heavy sound of gun-fire. Crouching behind a bush at a vantage spot, Munongwa could see that the major enemy force was busy at the scene of battle. He guessed they were trying to salvage whatever they could from the ravaged unit. He could still hear the sound of exploding land-mines and the crackling machine-guns. He carefully climbed a bushy tree to have a clear view. He was happy about what he saw towards the direction of their initial attack. He said to himself, the enemy is now learning a very good lesson. You don't just randomly pursue a guerrilla unit. You sink into the mines. The machine gun bursts, he concluded, the enemy was firing at random as usual, a sign of fear and desperation.

He got down the tree and proceeded cautiously, pushng forward from bush to bush and from tree to tree. Presently he saw two figures advancing towards him. He quickly took cover, cocked on the hammer of his FN rifle (one of the guns the guerrillas acquired from the enemy force the other day). The two figures were moving very slowly. As they moved closer to him, Munongwa recognised Shupai, moving slowly, supporting a man he could not readily recognise.

"Comrade Shupai!" Munongwa called in a whisper from behind a bush. The two figures halted and Shupai went for her gun and aimed.

"Weyu, don't fire!" Munongwa had to be quick to announce himself using the unit code name. At this point he could recognise the other figure besides Shupai. It was Tafirenyika. He had been badly wounded. He had three deep wounds bleeding profusely. He had sustained one wound on the left leg, another on the shoulder and yet another above his right eye. He was unable to walk unsupported. "Comrade Tafi!" Munongwa whispered, touching him by the shoulder and Tafirenyika flinched, violenetly with pain, muffling a loud cry. "My goodness! You are wounded badly!" exclaimed Munongwa leading them to under a tree.

"I pleaded with her to leave me and run for her life," Tafi choked. "But she could not listen. She insisted, risking her own life like this." The wounded commander sounded thankful as he told Shupai's superior with great difficulty since pain was having the better of him.

"How could I leave a comrade to die or be captured by those settler dogs?" Shupai asked, handing Tafirenyika over to Munongwa. "We must bandage his wounds and try to stop this bleeding. He's losing a lot of blood." This was the point Munongwa noticed Shupai also limping badly.

"Comrade Shupai, you are hurt. I can see you're limping badly."

"It's nothing. I think I sprained my ankle that's all," replied Shupai, dismissing her own injury as nothing.

"I'm very sorry, comrade Shupai," pleaded Tafirenyika, twisting his face, lying on his back while she and Munongwa bandaged his wounds.

"What for, comrade commander?" asked Shupai rather softly.

"For bothering you now and....for ....for doubting you when I .... I first saw you this afternoon."

Oh! You did that?" she pretended surprise. "Well, don't worry about that now," she smiled soothingly. As they finished bandaging Tafirenyika, Shupai announced soberly, "We have left some of our comrades back there. I touched two as we inched our way out with comrade commander here." Her voice was quivering, "I think they have fallen." She blew her nose and went on, "Wish they could be removed from there before the enemy uses their bodies for propaganda."

"It's true," conceded Munongwa. "The enemy propaganda instruments always report of 'a large number of "terrorists" killed and captured,' whenever one or two bodies of freedom fighters are in their hands, just to frighten the people away from joining us and supporting us." Munongwa asked, "But why didn't you break engagement and run when the order was given?" The question was directed at Shupai.

"I joined comrade Tafirenyika and two others to stage a diversionary stunt to woo away the major body of the enemy from the main guerrilla force towards our mine-fields," Shupai explained quickly.

"Whose orders were those? Was that the strategy comrade Tafi?" Munongwa sounded his disapproval.

"Circumstantial action, comrade....very dangerous I know," Tafirenyika was having problems. He could not explain further. Shupai took over:

"No one ordered me to follow him. I just thought that would work. The stunt was very effective," she sounded excited and proud, Munongwa thought. "But the gun fire was heavy that I had to fall down and lie prostrate on the ground as if dead. I could feel my heart alive in my mouth, was afraid the pursuers could hear the pounding heart. They all, quite a large number, jumped over and rushed towards the mine-field." Shupai was definitely thrilled about this lucky adventure. Munongwa decided he was not to damp the excitement. He urged her to go on as they stood up to support Tafirenyika.

"They fell into the mines. I could hear the deafening explosions. Comrade Tafirenyika, shake my hand," she shook Tafirenyika's left hand saying, "Mission accomplished. Dangerous move, but effective, very effective," she emphasised excitedly.

"Very effective," Munongwa repeated and asked , "Then?"

"Then I decided to run. On my way I came across comrade Tafirenyika here lying on the ground....in a pool of blood...."

"Alright, comrade Shupai,a medal for you. One of these days when...." Munongwa discontinued his sentence and said instead "You and comrade Tafi try to move slowly ahead. I'll go back and see if there's any chance of removing our dead."

"Comrade Munongwa, you can't do that," protested Tafirenyika. "Unsafe. Very slim chance. We declare ourselves lucky, thanks again-to-comrade-Shupai- here."

"I'll go there anyway," Munongwa insisted. Shupai just shrugged her shoulders desperately all the excitement she had sounded a few minutes ago drained out of her.

Munongwa only managed to reach a spot where he could see the settler soldiers frantically loading their dead or wounded into the choppers and ambulances. He also noticed a lot of activity around the area where the guerrillas had planted the land mines. The mines were still exploding, accompanied by a lot of machine-gun firing. 'Hope they shoot at each other,' thought Munongwa, 'there are no guerrillas that side anyway.' He decided it was hopeless for him to do anything or move any further. He retraced his footsteps to follow Shupai and Tafirenyika. On the return, Munongwa found Shupai and Tafrenyika sitting under a tree. They could not move anymore. Her ankle was swelling rapidly and the pain had increased. She was no longer able to support Tafirenyika. Then the three started to walk slowly, Munongwa in the middle supporting the two. Tafirenyika was in greater pain and was getting weakier. Munongwa half carried and half dragged him. When they reached the River, Munongwa announced to the anxious combatants: "Comrades, our operation was very successful. But," he went on in a low voice. "We lost two of our beloved comrades, Batanai and Rongai. They and comrades Tafirentyika and Shupai had decided to create a stunt to divert the enemy towards the mine-filed and pave way for most of us to escape. A heroic move indeed comrades. Heroic," he whispered.

A second's silence. Shupai detected deep emotion in Munongwa. A rare occurrence, she thought. Munongwa continued, "They have fallen. They'll be remembered in the history of the struggle for the liberation of Zimbabwe, for ever." The two fallen combatants belonged to Tafirenyika's unit. Munongwa looked at Tafirenyika lying on the make-shift bed on the ground and Shupai sat on a log. "Two others, as you can see, were badly wounded. They need immediate treatment.Everybody, attention!" The combatants followed the command. "With our right fists raised high, we shall have a moment of silence in honour of those fallen gallant fighters of Zimbabwe."

The order was carried out. Most of the combatants were in tears induced by emotion at the thought of their dead comrades. Shonhiwa was, however, relieved to see Shupai and was busy bandaging her ankle with a crepe bandage. Shingirai and others were preparing make-shift stretchers for carrying Tafirenyika and Shupai. Shupai broke into a revolutionary song. She sang quietly, and the other guerrillas joined in softly and emotionally:

                 Zimbabwe shall never forget this....
                 Brutal murder of her sons,
                 By the hands of vile oppressors,
                 Zimbabwe-e- shall be free.
Chorus: Zimbabwe, Zimbawe, Zimbabwe....
                 Zimbabwe-e
                 May their souls go marching on.

After the emotion rendering of the song, Munongwa gave orders, "Comrades Shonhiwa, Museve, Monday and Chamu take comrades Shupai and Tafirenyika quickly to Mjiba Doro for treatment. Comrade Shingi you command the unit. Remain here with your men until Monday returns. Some of us will march over back to the Cave."

With great reluctance, Shupai agreed to leave her unit for treatment under the care of Mjiba Doro, the teacher, and doctor Mutero in Sinioa Town. She was secretly happy however, to be accompanied by Shonhiwa whom she got very fond of. And Shonhiwa, on his part wished to stay for ever with Shupai, right through her treatment. On arrival at Masowe Primay School, Doro wasted no time. He drove the two injured, including Shonhiwa, straight to Sinioa.

South of Sinioa Town was an African Township called Chinhoi (now the name of the town and the whole Sinioa area). It was one of the segregated African Townships where Doctor Simon Mutero ran a private surgery. He was also employed as a consultant Residential Orthopaedician at the Local General Hospital for Africans. Doctor Mutero was one of the several African doctors who belonged to the liberation underground movement. He had worked very closely with Shupai before she joined the armed struggle. She was in fact doing the job that is now performed by James Doro in that area. Mutero's role was to look after the health of the combatants operating within this area. He was one of the very few Africans who had done their medical training at the Sir Godfrey Huggins School of Medicine of the University of Rhodesia. He had gone out of the country to specialise in Orthopaedics and had returned home. He could not be permitted to open a private practice in the town centre. The segregatory law formulated and enacted by the settler authorities reserved the city centre for whites only.

For purposes of the struggle, however, it was a blessing in disguise, thought Dr. Mutero. Now Shupai and Tafirenyika and many other combatants could be treated and looked after without fear of being captured by the enemy. It was not particularly easy for the maze of the enemy's extensive informer network to suspect or detect anything against Dr. Mutero.

Sinoia was a small but rich and busy town. It was surrounded by all the fertile settler commercial farms and thriving mines such as Mutorashanga, Rhaffingora, Trelewney, etc. The famous Mhanyame (Hunyani) River runs through that area on its way to the Zambezi, up North. Sinioa Town was a typical colonized Zimbabwean set-up.Exclusive African Townships on one hand and white suburbs on the other. Chinhoi Township itself was a slum, without any street lighting nor tarred roads. Dirt, filth and the stench of uring mixed with the smells of cooking were the common companions of the inhabitants of Chinhoi African Township. The township was controlled by a council headed by a white man known as a superintendent. He never bothered to furnish the Africans with enough garbage removal trucks. People were using tin-toilets and communal bathrooms. Dysentery, Bilharzia, Typhoid fever, Diarrhoea, Diphtheria, Tetanus, sore eyes, Poliomyelitis, etc, Wooping cough and other chest problems were the commonest ailments of the residents of Chinhoi.

Dr Mutero tried hard to keep his surgery and its surroundings under clean and hygienic conditions. He was helped by his wife, Ruth, who was a trained nurse. He could admit some of his "special" patients for serious treatment in his "spare-rooms" behind his private surgery. Shupai, Shonhiwa and Doro, with Tafirenyika, who had lost consciousness, arrived at Dr. Mutero's surgery before dawn. The dark township was still asleep, it seemed. Doro and Shonhiwa had to return to Masowe while it was still dark.

Dr Mutero quickly examined Shupai and ordered her to be put to bed after a good pethidine injection.

A glance at Tafirenyika, finger tips on his wrist pulse, Dr Mutero diagnosed severe haemorrhage straight away. "Blood transfusion stat," he called on to his wife and went on, "Let's put up a glucose/saline drip right away and sample his blood." Mutero remembered a coloured friend of his, an orderly, who looked after the blood-bank at the African General Hospital. The friend worked under a white man, supervisor. But he also carried the keys to the blood-bank. These whites like to live as comfortably as possible, thought Dr Mutero. They can't afford to be waking up at night for any emergencies. Mutero was sampling Tafirenyika's blood and found that it belonged to the universal blood group 'O'. The task was going be easier and he was happy. With fifty dollars in his pocket, he left his wife in-charge and sped to the house of his coloured friend on the other side of the town. He knocked and waited for a short while. The door opened slightly;

"Who's it?" the anxious coloured man in a bath robe asked, but recognised Dr Mutero right away. "Doc. Mutero! Why?"

"Please, don't get worried. May I come in? I want to talk to you. There is an emergency." Mutero whispered loudly emphasising the urgency of his presence. "Oh! Please, do come in. What's the matter? asked the orderly, a bit apprehensively.

"I need your help urgently." Mutero said handing the orderly the fifty dollars. "Can you get us two or three pints of group 'O' blood, now." The man looked down at the money in his hand and said:

"No problem doc. Let me put on something."

Doctor Mutero worked very hard for the greater part of the time removing bullets from Tafirenyika. A bullet had lodged itself in his right shoulder, and another one had found its way and hid itself into the upper part of his left thigh. The lost blood was now being replaced and prognosis could be classified as satisfactory. Fortunately, Dr. Mutero thought, there were no broken bones. The situation had been contained.

It was at about eight o'clock in the morning when Tafirenyika gained consciousness. He opened his eyes slowly. He noticed he was in a strange place, and with an intravenous blood drip running. A confused smile appeared on his face. He however felt he was in good hands. He closed his eyes again. He did not notice that Shupai was sitting in a chair at the other corner of the room waiting. When Dr. Mutero opened the room, Tafirenyika turned towards the door, saw him and gave a questioning smile. He had an orange stain of antiseptic above the eyebrow that gave him a clownish, lopsided air. Dr. Mutero cocked his head aside admiring his work. He had put a few stitches on the slash wound above Tafirenyika's eye, put a pad of gauze and strip of elasto-plast (adhesive tape) over the wound. When he saw Shupai, Tafirenyika smiled crookedly and closed his eyes. Shupai thought Tafirenyika was not fully awake. He did not seem to recognise where he was. He lifted his left hand and touched his scarred, puffed face with a diagonal white strap of elasto-plast above his eye and with a start he opened his eyes:

"Shupai! Comrade, what in heaven are you doing here?" He almost sat up, but winced back, and his left hand went up to his right shoulder. The pain there reminded him. He made another critical look at Shupai, who was now standing beside his bed talking to him soothingly. He looked around the room he was in, touched his hair and mumbled:

"If I had known you were coming, I'd have...." He trailed back to sleep peacefully.

"Dr. Mutero decided to admit Shupai into the women's surgical wing of the Sinoia African General Hospital where he was the resident consultant. Shupai's ankle had swollen tremendously and she actually could not stand on it, let alone walk with it. After weighing the pros and cons he admitted her under a false name, Sarah Mutamba. The x-rays showed a crack on one of the tarsal bones in her ankle coupled with a severe dislocation. This meant complete bed rest. Shupai thought she would be bored stiff lying in bed for many days. What idleness! She found that the hospital bed was not as exciting as jungle life or battlefields. She lay there, ruminating....

She remembered her comrades back in the jungle including those who had died in combat. Ayiwa!(No}. Besides she had to struggle to remember her assumed name, Sarah Mutamba. Mutamba was Mrs. Dr. Mutero's maiden name. So she was said to be Mrs. Mutero's cousin.

Shupai's ankle was painful, she could not even walk, yes, she thought. But for a person of action like her, it was boring, she anticipated, lying in bed day and night doing nothing but staring into space and listening to sick women's talk. She was lying in bed on her back with a Plaster of Paris around her ankle and on a mild traction. What a position in which to lie in bed! She thought, worse still the idea of having to have her toilet in bed tormented her. She hated the smell of antiseptic and methilated spirit that was the order of the day in hospitals. She had unsuccessfully protested to Dr. Mutero against the complete bed-rest. Well, Shupai sighed, looking around the ward. She saw another patient, also on traction. Shupai thought the other patient looked more miserable and in more pain than herself. Perhaps that patient needed the traction and the complete bed-rest more than herself. She thought Dr Mutero had no need to pamper her like he did, though she realised he was the expert.

While lying there in bed, Shupai remembered Munongwa, Shonhiwa and the others. She wondered how they were faring after last night's operation. Perhaps they must be lying low until dark because the hunt by the enemy must be really hot. But how in Heaven did she sustain the injury? She asked herself. She tried to retrace in her mind, the beginning of last night's activities up to the time she discovered she had been injured. She could not place how and when she got injured. She went deeper in her thoughts, back to the past. How did she come to become what she was, a militant freedom fighter against colonialism and settlerism in Zimbabwe? She asked herself. Guerrilla life is no tea-party. It is hazardous, why then did she choose this life? Shupai recalled that during guerrilla training and active combat, she had been too pre-occupied and too busy to think of her past. In fact, she thought, what past? Life had never been easy for her. She had to fight her way through many varied difficulties ever since she was a child. She knew she had grown to regard life as a battle-field rather than a play-ground. And what a gallant fight she put up, Shupai commended herself. Through this life-long battling against various hardships, she had learnt that to succeed in what ever, one had to "fight". And for the people of Zimbabwe to be free, from colonial bondage they had to be prepared to sacrifice, suffer and serve. They had to fight, she had declared to herself, and continued to flashback to the past, now that she had nothing else to do.

Chapter 5

Salisbury! The meeting! The N. D. P. meeting! That Sunday morning! Shupai recalled, and everything started to flow back into her memory. It's been a long time, she thought. How many years now? Strange that one could be so involved as to have no time to idle and reflect back to one's past. By the way, my real name! That name, Lucia, I had even forgotten that name of mine, now that my names have become so numerous. She thought if someone had to call her by that name now she would hesitate to answer. The name however, reminded her of what she termed the dark ages in her life, she thought.

Before Shupai assumed her guerrilla name, Shupai, she was known by her Christian Catholic name, Lucia. Her father Mr Jonas Kashungu, a staunch Roman Catholic, had been able to maintain contact with her indirectly. Ever since she had gone underground he had constantly been informed about her well-being. He never knew where his daughter was at any given moment. He repeatedly demanded, from the people who constantly informed him about her, to see her, talk to her. It was impossible, he was told. It was against guerrilla rules. He had finally concluded that his daughter had perhaps, gone out of the country, or....He had bitterly complained, "So my daughter has completely forgotten about me. I wish she hadn't joined those town hooligans like her uncle Gumbo." When he had mentioned Gumbo he became very emotional. He had gone on, "It was that Garikai Gumbo, who was responsible for making my daughter forget all about me, about God. He plunged her into the so-called politics," he accused, "You people," pointing accusingly at the two men from the underground movement who had come to see him. "You are all the same as that stupid Garikai Gumbo, who happens to be my deceased wife's brother, and that town wife of his. You led my beloved and obedient daughter astray," he had repeated angrily, shaking his head, "Astray! Now she has become a lost sheep." Jonas Kashungu had stopped talking, looked down on the floor. Then he had said quietly, "God will, however, bless her, my poor daughter. I pray that, one day she will realise she is doing wrong." Those were the daily prayers of Shupai's father.

It has been a number of years now, Shupai reflected. As Lucia, she was visiting her Uncle Mr Garikai Gumbo in the Harare African Township of Salisbury. To her memory, this was the first time that her father had ever allowed her to stay with her Uncle. Her father had never at any time, allowed her to go to town. But that time she had been given permission to visit her

Uncle and had to return within a week and never to stay in town any longer than that one week. He had warned her:

"I don't want you to be influenced badly by that man, who unfortunately, happens to be your late mother's brother." He advised, "Town life is horrible! It is corrupt. It is Godless, therefore, evil," he stressed. "Your Uncle, Gumbo used to be a very good person, now he has turned out to be a notorious hooligan ever since he left home. He never comes to visit us, the common country folk." Shupai's father continued talking, as if preaching, while she listened quietly. "And now, all he does is getting drunk and never goes to church. That wife of his is not of any help to him, either. To make matters worse, they now think that fighting the white people is a useful profession. Little do they realise the power the white people have. They can fly through the air, make cars, trains, sewing machines, electricity. They can even talk to each other while they are in their own houses or even in separate countries through a simple wire. I tell you, my daughter, these people," he maintained, "can do other things which we can never be able to do if they decided to leave us alone here, of course, the white man is an earthly god," he looked at a portrait hanged on the wall, of the Holy family, Jesus, Mary and Joseph, surrounded by angels and other people and he went on, "Don't you see, the angels are white, the disciples of Jesus are white." He looked at his daughter. "You are young my daughter," he said, "Do we then wonder why and how white men can perform miracles on this earth?" Kashangu asked with conviction and went on advising his daughter. "Fighting the white men's power is sheer madness. These people are too powerful for anyone of us to cheat ourselves. We must never pretend that we can fight them. These are God's people sent to us. The white man is the saviour of the black man. He brought to us education, hospitals and above all the very true word of eternal salvation-the Holy Bible," he concluded. There was silence. Shupai's father kept on gazing at the portrait of Mother Mary on the wall, as if praying silently.

"Father," Shupai called, and said after he had turned to look at her enquiringly, "My Uncle Gumbo and his wife are so nice to me that I can't imagine them being a bad influence on me, and...." She was interrupted.

"Anyone who despises God and is faithless, is not worth emulating in any form," he argued on, "No, no reasonable and faithful parent would allow his daughter to mix up with such characters."

"But they seem to be respectable enough and I think they deserve a better description and credit than you give them, father." She sounded persuasive. She had made up her mind. I'm old enough to look after myself and I must go and visit my Uncle, she thought and said aloud, "I thought I'd go and stay with them for just a week or so father," she pleaded. He stared at her for a whole minute:

"Alright," he conceded with a sigh, "Just a week and you come back here as soon as the week ends."

Mr and Mrs Gumbo's house was in the, so-called, New Location of Harare (now called Mbare), one of the largest and densely populated African Townships in Salisbury. The house was semi-detached with two small bedrooms, a small dining room and a small kitchen in which there was a narrow fire wood iron stove with just two plates. The difference between the New Location and the Old Location was that there were only two or three large communal bathrooms and latrines in the Old Location for the whole population. In the so-called New Location only two families shared one latrine with a shower. The toilet was a big bucket which had to be emptied every evening by Council employees (Katsekera). A family could be made up of five, six, eight, ten or even twelve members. The two townships had certain similarities and characteristics, however. They were both located long distances away from the inhabitants' places of work and quite a distance from white suburbs. Both townships had narrow streets and passages starded with buildings. The streets were rarely tarred and lit.

Mr and Mrs Gumbo did not have any children and therefore they had a lot of room in their house. When Lucia visited them, she occupied the room at the back facing Ngano Road, one of the few tarmacked roads in this township.

One Sunday morning, three days after Lucia had been in her uncle's home, she was busy preparing to go to church. She had finished putting on her best Sunday dress and looked very smart and beautiful in it. She had also put on one shoe and was ready to wear the other one when from a distance she heard a deep man's voice: "N.D.P.!" the voice was saying. "ONE MAN ONE VOTE. COME TO THE NDP MEETING TODAY!" The voice went on. It was drawing closer, getting louder, and louder. "COME ALL TO THE CHAMINUKA SQUARE!" the loud voice urged. "THE OPPRESSED PEOPLE OF ZIMBABWE, LET US COME TOGETHER AND GET RID OF EXPLOITATION AND OPPRESSION ONCE AND FOR ALL!" Now the voice had become quite loud, almost deafening.

With one shoe in her hand Lucia stood behind the curtain and peeped out through the window. She discovered that the voice was just a few meters away from where she was standing.

It was coming from a yellow van parked near a house on Ngano Road. It had three loud speakers – two in front and the other at the back and there were a few people in it. Lucia noticed two or three women; she was not sure, among them. On both sides of the van were written in bold red lettering. "NDP! ONE MAN ONE VOTE!" The man's loud voice had stopped, and then women's voices immediately took over – they sang a tradtiotional war song, "Tora huta hwako toda kuenda kunorwa hondo! Chave Chimurenga, kunorwa hondo. (Take your bows and arrows – we want to go and fight a war, the war of liberation). The mood of those who sang was inciting as it filled one with emotion and anger. Lucia was somewhat stuck and rooted where she stood, with one shoe on and the other in her hand. She could understand the meaning of the words very well. That was a war song, urging people to collect all their weapons and go to war.

But war against whom? She mused. The song did not specify clearly who the enemy was, she thought. The words from the man's voice and those written on the yellow van were not so familiar to Lucia. She was surprised, even a little afraid. As she watched, another man and a woman join those in the van. Life in Salisbury is very strange indeed, as my father tells me, she concluded. What is going on? She asked herself wishing for someone to answer her and explain all this.

The van had started to move away slowly and the man's voice began again, roaring after the singing by the spirited women had stopped. "YOU OPPRESSED PEOPLE OF ZIMBABWE, WE HAVE A RIGHT TO OUR COUNTRY, HAVEN'T WE? The voice continued. "WE HAVE A RIGHT TO LIFE; A RIGHT TO TILL THE LAND; A RIGHT TO OWN AS MANY CATTLE AS WE CAN. THIS IS OUR COUNTRY, ISN'T IT? WHAT WE ARE SAYING, BELOVED CHILDREN OF ZIMBABWE, IS THAT WE NO LONGER PLEAD TO BE TREATED WITH FAVOUR! WE NOW DEMAND THAT WE RULE OURSELVES. WE WANT POLITICAL POWER TO BE FIRMLY IN OUR HANDS. ONLY IMPERIALISM AND COLONIALISM STAND BETWEEN US AND OUR FREEDOM, COMPLETE FREEDOM! WE MUST, THEREFORE, UNITE AND GET RID OF THESE EVILS NOW, AND WE SAY NOW!"

These brief, tough speeches were repeated at intervals in between war songs by the women. Each time the man's voice spoke; new and stronger words were used, urging the people to go to a meeting where issues were to be discussed. Issues of land, Lucia realised. Land, where Man's life begins and ends. Land, the very life of man.

Lucia watched the van disappearing behind the houses. The voice faded away but the words continued to ring in her ears. She continued to visualise in her mind the yellow van with its big red letters. She kept hearing the voices urging people to a meeting. The words rang so loudly in her mind that she could not hear Mrs Gumbo, her Aunt knock at her door. A strange mixture of feelings and emotions had gripped her. She felt anger inside her chest. At the same time her mind was busy posing many questions and demanding answers. True this is our country, she thought, we are not permitted, by this government, to rear as many animals as we want. People can't plough the land or graze their livestock where-ever they want. We, African teachers, are paid less than European teachers of the same qualifications or even less. The questions ran through Lucia's mind and repeated themselves over and over.

After knocking for a little while, Mrs Gumbo was surprised by getting no response from inside. So she had decided to open the door and entered. She found Lucia there, fixed to the spot near the window, still holding one shoe, and looking out through the window, with the other shoe on one foot. Mrs Gumbo stood besides her and looked out to find out what had taken Lucia's attention so much. She could not see anything of importance except children shouting to each other: N. D. Fee, ONE NEM ONE DEF and playing on the road behind the house. Lucia looked sad, Mrs Gumbo noticed but she decided not to ask why. Instead she said, "Lucia! You look nice. Where are you going? Are you coming to the meeting with us?"

With a start, Lucia turned away from the window and looked at her aunt as if dazed. She looked as though she had received a terrible blow on her face. Mrs Gumbo became worried but did not want to show it...

Now lying in her hospital bed, Shupai smiled to herself. It had been a long time since that Sunday morning. The yellow van belonging to the Party had passed near her uncle's house in Harare Township, to give her the first contact with the struggle. She continued to recall and to imagine herself standing behind a window curtain peeping through to view the yellow van as if looking at the revolution itself through that window.

A few children, Shupai, remembered, had rushed out to the van not at all surprised, as she, had been. They had come out to cheer the Nationalist leaders in the van. She remembered two of the children running after the van shouting "ONE MAN ONE BOAT!" and "NDFII, ONE NEM ONE DEF!" It was also fun for the children, perhaps deliberately mispronouncing the slogans. For her it was strange. What was being released right before her very eyes and which was also touching the core of her being, she realised, was an awakening of the deepest consciousness of a life of contradictions she had lived as all Zimbabweans had done.

Why had it taken so song for this awakening to come? She was visibly upset as she tossed and tried to turn in her hospital bed and continued to recall what had happened that Sunday morning.

She had turned to look at her aunt, Mrs Gumbo who had just said something about the 'meeting'. She was still quiet and sad. Her aunt called out to her husband, "VaGumbo, come and see our muzukuru (niece)." Gumbo came into the room at the call by his wife and stopped there by the door whistling joyously admiring his niece, he said:

"Good morning Lucia. Wow! You look beautiful, very smart, where are you going to so early in the morning? You haven't had your breakfast yet? You must be careful. A beautiful girl like you is likely to meet ugly, hungry wolves here in this town." Gumbo was teasing her happily. He had not noticed how sad she was.

"But why does she look so sad?" asked Mrs Gumbo worriedly. But Lucia continued to stand with one shoe on and the other still in her hands. She did not seem to have heard what they were saying. She was still reciting 'N.D.P. ONE MAN ONE VOTE!' in her mind, looking blankly ahead.

"Are you going anywhere Lucia?" her uncle asked, coming closer to her, not as jovial as he was when he first came into the room. Lucia turned slowly and looked at him with sad eyes. She, whose eyes always carried a permanent smile, had changed drastically, Gumbo noticed and thought she was ill. But then why was she getting so well dressed up for? "Are you going anywhere, my dear?" He asked again, putting his right arm around her shoulders.

"Good morning sekuru (uncle)." Lucia greeted him and answered quietly, "I am going to church."

"But you do not look well, why do you force yourself to go to church if you are not feeling well!"

"I am alright," she replied quietly sitting on the bed, looking up at her uncle, still with one shoe in her hand.

"Ah! So that's it? You people from the 'reserves', you still like to go to church!" Mrs Gumbo exclaimed. "I would rather go to the N. D. P. meeting than waste my time going to the white man's church to pray to his 'Mudzimu' (ancestors). The N. D. P. meeting is more important to me than the church," she continued, turning to her husband, "We must get ready or we will be late."

"Yes indeed," said Gumbo in support of his wife, "Archibishop Pascal at the Catholic Church says nothing these days except urging the Africans to register as voters for the white man's government system. Who does he think we should vote for, while our leaders are all locked up in the white man's jails, detentions and restriction camps?"

"The Archbishop himself is a British settler colonialist, remember?"

remarked Mrs Gumbo. "What can we expect from him? He is just as bad as the others. They are his kith and kin."

In her whole life Lucia had never heard anyone utter such words against the church and let alone the Catholic Archbishop. She was surprised by Mr and Mrs Gumbo's bold utterances. This is sacrilege, she thought, and was beginning to be afraid for them. My father did warn me against these people.Now....

She had grown up at a Roman Catholic Mission. She had learnt to believe in nothing else but the Catholic Church, Mother Mary and Heaven or Hell after death. Her task on earth was to pray hard through Mother Mary so as to enter without difficulty, the Kingdom of God – that precious Heaven, she thought.

But what are these people talking about? Lucia wondered. It must be that N. D. P. thing which is responsible for the things my uncle and aunt are saying and the way they are thinking. She was now almost convincing herself that there was something very wrong with her uncle. Her father, after all used, time and again, to warn her against her uncle Garikayi Gumbo, who, he said had become a ruffian and a gangster, and a godless man. Her father didn't want her to be mixed up with Garikayi and his lot, she recalled. It seems as if my father was right. How surprising! They talk of MUDZIMU instead of God, the Creator. They talk ill of the holy fathers and the white people generally, instead of thanking them and being grateful to them for bringing to us the very Holy Word of God and civilisation.

And yet on the other hand, Lucia could vouch before God himself, that the N. D. P. thing was telling the truth. The Africans in their own land of birth are oppressed by strangers. There was complete silence in the room. Lucia went on thinking. But what is this

NDP anyway? I don't even know what those letters on the van mean. There is going to be a meeting, though, and I must go and find out more about it. After a little while Gumbo came back asking his wife to hurry up so that they would be in time for the

N. D. P. MEETING. Lucia decided to ask, "Uncle, what is the N. D. P.?"

"The National Democratic Party," he answered with a surprised voice, "Are you telling me you don't know the N. D. P, you Lucia, a trained teacher? You surprise me!"

Lucia shook her head sadly.

"Not even the ANC?" the uncle asked.

"No," answered Lucia with a very low voice. "What is the ANC?"

"The ANC, the African National Congress, was the first real effective nationalist political movement in Rhodesia (Zimbabwe)."

Gumbo sat on the bed beside Lucia and continued to explain, "The ANC demanded that the people of Zimbabwe be given the right to vote. Thus they demanded for African adult suffrage. It was banned. Two more parties were formed after the ANC. They advocated for the same rights for us. Both these political parties were banned by the settler colonial government and the leaders were arrested and are still languishing in jails and detention camps." Gumbo stopped. After a short pause he said: "But my niece you surprise me. A primary school teacher, twenty years old and you have never heard of all these things? But the National Democratic Party is well known even in the reserves, and even by small children," he paused.

Lucia, after her mother died, grew up and was educated on a Catholic Mission school, St. Pauls. She was trained as a primary school teacher at another Catholic Mission farm school, Monte Carlos, and on completing her training, worked there. She had been very much involved in religious work with the nuns. The literature she was encouraged to read was only about angels, saints, prayers and the Catechism – for a better and happier life hereafter. No politics was discussed among the mission population which consisted of priests, a few brothers and many nuns, most of them being German nationals. In fact, political discussions were discouraged by the Mission authorities. Political discussions, she was taught, were vain earthly distractions, unimportant to a true Christian.

"I know your problem my niece," Gumbo thought he sympathised with Lucia. "I too nearly fell under the influence of those priests and nuns. I know what they can do to innocent black people, to make them serve this government without questioning. Those Priests and nuns can do nothing else except to brainwash and mentally oppress young people like you in their early stages of life. They do not want the black youngsters to aim for anything else in life besides working for the so-called happy life after death. The white man, priest or non-priest, enjoys his heaven right here on this earth, a heaven created by black people's sweat and blood." Gumbo sounded and looked quite emotional. Lucia looked at him and said:

"All that we hear from the fathers and nuns at the Monte Carlos Mission is that, 'the ungrateful Africans in towns are forming groups for aggression against the good, civilised and God-fearing government of this country.'

We are told this nearly everyday, especially during the mass sermons," Lucia said, seemingly regretful. She seemed as if she had come to realise something she had never thought of in all her youthful life. "But what does ONE MAN ONE VOTE mean anyway?" She asked her uncle, becoming a bit lively.

"Africans as you know are disenfranchised. No African is allowed to vote for members of Parliament. That so-called Parliament is full of whites only, voted for by whites only, making the government a white-only government. Those people – the white government – make the laws that put you and I in detentions, restriction; laws that demand that we carry a pass on us every day of our lives. The Parliamentarians make the stupid laws that refuse us compensation when we get maimed at work and die three thousand feet underground, in their mines, digging the gold, copper or asbestos that enrich the white man." He continued, "What we are saying is that we must choose our own people to go to Parliament to make laws that are for us and not laws that are against us. We are demanding that every adult must vote regardless of colour, creed, sex or property owned." Gumbo went on, "You see, if we can all vote we will be able to create our won black government. We should get rid of the colonialists and their oppressive forces and govern ourselves. Above all," he went on, "this country is ours. It is we, Zimbabweans who must rule any other nationality that chooses to live in our country." Mrs Gumbo, who had been dressing herself in the other room, now came to join them. She was dressed in a long black skirt, with many small pleats at the waist-line, which made her rather too big two inches below the waist, Lucia noticed. An inch or so above the hemline, small, white and red beads were sewn around the skirt, making very beautiful embroidery about four inches wide. The blouse was a simple and sleeveless, leaf-green cotton with four rows of the same white and red beads embroidery along the neckline. She looked at Lucia and:

"When are you going to church, Lucia?" asked Mrs Gumbo cheerfully. Lucia did not answer the question. Instead she asked about the N. D. P. meeting:

"This meeting, is....er....is it the same as those meetings that the priests and nuns at Monte Carlos describe as gatherings of Africans for aggressive and subversive purposes against the Christian, civilised government?"

"There is nothing like that," answered Mrs Gumbo. "After all, some of those so-called fathers and sisters are some of the cruel oppressors and the worst exploiters of Africans that I have ever known in all my Christian life," she continued. "And Catholicism is the most conservative and the most oppressive religion of all religions ever introduced into Africa by white settlers.

They use it as an effective weapon for subjugating and humbling the African people for easy enslaving and exploitation! They use it as a very effective instrument for the pacification of the primitive people of Africa, remember?"

"Let me tell you muzukuru," her uncle took over. "I grew up in the Catholic Church. I know what those fathers and nuns have been doing to you. I almost fell victim to their persuasive lies." He went on, "They are the most cruel religious people, I have noticed, who are up to destroying our culture and traditions. Their aim is to replace these with their naked culture which is marked by cruelty, hatred and discrimination." He looked at his watch. "I could tell you more about your so-called fathers and sisters, but we don't have time now. We must rush to this meeting."

"See you when we come back Lucia, wish you good praying," said Mrs Gumbo, picking up her black hand bag.

"I am coming with you to the meeting," Lucia declared with a low but lively and excited voice. "What about my dress? Is it suitable for this meeting?" She asked, looking enquiringly at Mrs Gumbo's dress. Lucia had thought perhaps there was a special dress for this meeting. She was assured that her dress was, in fact, perfect. With this assurance from her aunt, Lucia added strength to her will and desire to attend the N. D. P. meeting instead of going to mass. In the back of her mind, however, lingered the important question: Is it not a sin, an offence against the Creator, to deliberately avoid going for mass? Is it not a sin to go to a gathering composed perhaps, of people like Mr and Mrs Gumbo with their sacrilegious talk? Well....

Shupai, lying in her hospital bed, was suddenly roused from her ruminations by a crashing noise. One of the ward maids had knocked down a water glass from the locker next to her bed. The glass had broken into small pieces and the ward maid had rushed out of the ward to fetch a broom and a dust pan. "Watch out for the broken glass!" Shupai warned the patient, owner of the glass, who had gone out to the toilet and had almost stepped onto the dangerous broken glasses bare footed.

"Oh dear!" exclaimed the patient. "Who did that, you?" she asked irritably pointing at Shupai accusingly.

"No, it's me," replied the ward maid who had just entered and asked, "How could she? Ah! You Nelia, and your madness! Go round and get into bed, now!" The ward maid commanded the patient, called Nelia and went on to remove the broken glasses.

Shupai, who was still on traction just looked at the other patient in surprise and returned to her thoughts, and going back to that Sunday morning in Harare Township. She imagined herself hurriedly putting on the other shoe, heart pounding madly, and followed her aunt, Mrs Gumbo, who had already gone out of the house for the bus stop without waiting for her husband.

Chaminuka Square ground was in the heart of Highfield Township. The ground was surrounded by a six-foot high wall with barbed wire fence on top.

Four gates led into the Square from four different directions. Inside, all round it, were benches made of concrete arranged in rows step by step with those at the back higher than those in the front. In the middle of the Square, stood a permanent four-cornered platform made of hard wood.

Lucia (Shupai), Mr and Mrs Gumbo entered through the eastern gate together with many other Zimbabweans who were flocking into the Square. They sat on the concrete benches in front of the platform, but not nearest to it because they had arrived a little late and the nearest benches had already been occupied. Thousands of people, males and females, young and old, gathered in the Square on that Sunday morning. The crowd anxiously waited for the speakers to begin speaking. The thing that struck Lucia most at first was the large number of uniformed black and white policemen. Some were outside Chaminuka Square, surrounding it completely, and others were inside. Some of those who were outside stood in their open trucks, with others walking about, and some just sitting quietly, loaded in big lorries. All the policemen were fully armed. Several were handling huge, blood-red eyed bull dogs, which looked as if they had had no food for the last few days. The dogs seemed terribly hungry or angry over something, she thought. They kept on barking, grumbling and howling for a chance to have a bite on something or someone. Shupai, now remembered how she shuddered at the sight of those vicious hounds. Little did Lucia know that among the people filling the Square were hordes of plain-clothes policemen from the Special Branch of settler regime.

Lucia curiously looked around the Square and noticed a number of women, most of them dressed exactly like her aunt, Mrs Gumbo. Most men had short sleeved green shirts, the same colour as the women's blouses, and black long trousers.

Her uncle did not have a green shirt on. But he wore a pair of black trousers.

"Is it a uniform?" Lucia had become curious enough to enquire from her aunt.

"Yes," replied Mrs Gumbo, "It is our traditional or our national dress."

Lucia listened to a conversation between two youths sitting behind her. They sure do despise the white people, she thought. I wonder why they are not even afraid of all these policemen around. A sudden uproar from all the corners of the Square startled Lucia from her wondering mind. Everyone was on their feet waving their clenched fists looking towards the main entrance. A single voice shouted, shouted through a loud speaker:

"RUSUNUNGUKO (Freedom)!" The crowd answered:

"ONE MAN ONE VOTE!" These words were uttered simultaneously and repeatedly by everyone except Lucia. It is not that she did not want to join in the cry for "One Man One Vote," Lucia was a stranger in this environment, she thought. The same words that the loud voice was shouting just an hour ago, from the van, she realised, are being uttered by all these people, all in one voice. Lucia was taken aback. She noticed that the younger ones in the crowd, those of her own age, were most outspoken and the most emotional and seemingly the most violent in their actions.

Five men and two women had entered and were heading straight for the platform. They were also waving their right fists in fraternal response to the crowd. Mrs Gumbo, who was sitting next to Lucia, in a whisper, introduced the leaders to her, one by one as they took their respective positions on the platform:

"The bearded man is Mr Tapera, our national chairman; the second one is Mr Marufu, the vice chairman; the third is Mr Murambiwa, the General and Publicity Secretary," Mrs Gumbo went on, "Mrs Chake, the Secretary for Women's Affairs; Miss Regayi the Treasurer; Mr Tichafa and Mr Musekiwa, the two committee members." Lucia observed that Mr Tapera seemed a very simple man, simply dressed in khaki shirt and khaki long trousers, not like the rest of his colleagues who had the same uniform as some members of the audience had-the green shirt and the black trousers....

I wonder if Mr Tapera is the owner of that deep voice from the loud-speaker, this morning, Lucia wondered. He is not likely to possess the voice I heard an hour ago, she thought she would like to hear his voice again and what he had to say this time.

Without any delay, Tapera took the microphone: "RUSUNUNGUKO! (Freedom)", he shouted amidst loud cheers of "RUSUNUNGUKO! ONE MAN ONE VOTE! from the audience. "Vana vevhu (Children of the soil) greetings! Greetings to you all sons and daughters of the motherland," he began. "Let me say, I am, for one, very glad to see such a large number of us gathered here this morning. This shows that we are ready to free ourselves from the colonial bondage. We must be free to govern ourselves in our own country. How many times, brothers and sisters," he asked, "have we begged these colonialists to give us back our land which they seized from us by the use of violence?

"MANY TIMES!" the crowd replied.

"Vana vevhu! We have talked for too long. The oppressor does not listen. He does not understand our language of non-violence. He understands his own language, the language of violence. He answers our plea by beating us, by arresting us and our leaders; and above all he selects a few of us, whom he bribes into registering as voters for the settler general elections." Tapera went on, "In the first place, children of the soil, what do we vote for if the settler law forbids us to run our own country, Zimbabwe?"

"NOTHING!" shouted the crowd.

"Secondly, why should we vote and whom should we vote for when the same settlers have locked up our leaders in their jails?"

"NO LEADERS, NO VOTE!" replied the people loudly, in unison.

"This reminds us brothers and sisters," Tapera continued, "that today is Sunday. Our people are crowded in different churches helping these same settlers to pray to their ancestors for their continued rule over us." Lucia had been attentive since Tapera began his speech, but at the mention of 'Sunday' and 'Church', her heart started beating heavily as if some hot fluid had been poured into her chest. She became anxious, listening more carefully.

"We should know by now, brothers and sisters, that the church is the shepherd of the settler regime, evidenced by the speech of the Roman Catholic Archbishop, Pascal last week. He urged his African Catholics to register as voters. We still remember that only yesterday, the same Archbishop threatened the poor African believers with excommunication from the church if they were caught by the settler police throwing stones at the settler police and army. How can we be thrown out of the church if we are waging a struggle to liberate the oppressed souls of millions of God's own children never mind how black? This Archbishop, I know for certain, that he himself, though doing the preaching business here in Zimbabwe has his right to vote in his own country – Britain. I wonder whom these African Catholics are urged to be voting for. We must remember of course, that the Archbishop himself is one of the pioneer British colonialists into our country. What can we expect from him?"

"NOTHING!!!" answered the crowd angrily.

"When our country was being colonised," Tapera continued, "It was the missionary and his religion who also came here with the so-called Holy Bible in his right hand, while concealing a gun in his pocket and a bottle of whisky in his left hand.

The British colonialist soldiers and settles were just behind the missionary, fully armed, watching every move of our ancestors and waiting for any resistance by them." At this point, Tapera took the opportunity to remind his listeners of what Mzee Jomo Kenyatta of Kenya once said of the colonialist missionary, when he said that the white man taught the African to pray looking up to the skies closing his eyes. As the African prayed, and begged, with his eyes closed, the white colonialists stole the land from under the feet of the praying African. "The missionary was the first foreigner to destroy our traditions and our culture. He even wanted to destroy our language. He replaced our names with his own, intimidating us into believing in his religion by saying: 'You must believe in God. You must be baptised and be given a Christian name or else God will not accept you into the Kingdom of Heaven.' Actually the missionary meant that we must have English, Hebrew, Italian or French or German names in order to be accepted by God! What is wrong with our own names?"

"NOTHING!!" shouted the audience.

"Vana vevhu, our names have very clear meanings which we understand. What does Antonio, or Wilson or Bridgette or Lucia or Benedictus mean to us?"

"RUBBISH!" roared the crowd. Lucia was shocked to hear her name from the speaker. Her adrenaline level had become too high and was actually shaking inside, causing her heart to palpitate violently. She listened.

"What is wrong with our names like Murambiwa, Tapera, Tichafa or Marweyi?" Asking these questions, the speaker was encouraging the audience to participate fully in the debate and really aroused their thinking and their anger.

"THERE IS NOTHING WORING WITH OUR NAMES!" They answered rather disjointedly, and had become a bit restless.

They began to shout all kinds of political slogans, and some people, especially women, were so emotional that they broke into sobs. Shupai, now, remembered how she, as Lucia had joined them, although at this point she did not understand or know why she was crying. She chose to cry quietly. Tapera had mentioned her name, Lucia, among the colonialist names. I was given that name when I was only a baby, she thought. I don't have any other name besides this Lucia and I don't even know what it means. All I was told was that it belongs to a Saint, St Lucia. Lucia went into deep thought.

Taperal had said that the church was the shepherd of the settler regime. So, all those so-called Ten Commandments and especially the Ten Roman Catholic Church commandments are actually meant to corner the African Christian into obeying the cruel rules of the colonial regime, not God as such? She questioned herself.

While Lucia was deeply involved in some revelations, another speaker, Miss Regayi, the Treasurer had taken the stand. She started to speak. She was rather persuasive, but firm. She was dark in complection and beautiful, about twenty three or twenty four years old and of medium height. Lucia fixed her eyes on Miss Regayi. She admired Regayi's courage to address such a big crowd.

"Sons and daughters of the soil," Miss Regayi shouted into the microphone. "Those people there," she said, pointing to the white policemen, "should be in the churches now, not us." The church seems to be their target, these people, Lucia thought, they are not afraid of the Creator, either.

"Those whites are the ones who should be in the churches thanking their gods and ancestors for what they have today." Miss Regayi went on. "We should be here at this meeting, all of us, talking to our ancestors to help us take our country back from these foreign usurpers. We have nothing. The whites have everything. They have cheap labour from us. They live in luxury, in mansions. Each and every one of them owns a car. Their banking accounts are more than fat. They have more clothes than they need. More land, all of it usurped from us. Each one of them has at least an African cook, a garden 'boy', a nanny and a 'house boy'. I can go on. But let me ask you; do you know why they did not go to church today?" She asked, and without waiting for an answer from the audience, continued, "Because they know that we, the African people, people of this beautiful Zimbabwe, the colonised ones of Zimbabwe, do the praying for them. They have come here instead to arrest us for not going to pray for their perpetual reign over us. A slight move on our part, I'm telling you children of the soil, they will fire." Miss Regayi was herself becoming hot and agitated. She was a forthright, powerful and a penetrating speaker. The audience moved with her accordingly, Lucia noticed.

"Sons and daughters of Zimbabwe, Zimbabwe is a rich country. The British colonialists want to entrench their imperialist, capitalist oppression and exploitation by using us. I can see the sons of Zimbabwe over there," pointing at the African policemen, "handling hungry dogs, ready to let them loose upon us, to let them feed upon us, their own brothers and sisters. To top it all, there are many among us, not uniformed, but enemies of our struggle all the same."

"SHAME! SHAME!" cried the crowd. Lucia looked at a group of policemen. One black policeman adjusted the position of his sten-gun, and moved his feet uneasily. Another, shakily fixed his cap; yet another looked to the ground. The rest of them were as still and silent as the dead ones in their graves.

"Children of Zimbabwe," Miss Regayi went on. "It is high time we knew our enemy and his tactics. He uses us. He uses a few people against the rest of the nation. Let us refuse to be used as tools of oppression against each other. This is an appeal to you," pointing to the African constables, "brothers over there, as well as those secret informers, sitting among us here," waving her hand around the crowd. "Let us fight for our nationhood. A nation that is oppressed by another is not nation at all. We can only win this nationhood, and be a people among people of the world, only through a concerted and prolonged struggle. We can win this war only when we are united and working together against the enemy; united we win, and divided we fall. Sons and daughters of Zimbabwe, who is our enemy?" she asked.

"THE WHITE SETTLERS!" shouted the crowd.

"Yes," she said, "and their running dogs, our own brothers over there!" Miss Regayi said pointing at the black policemen again and concluding her speech, amid angry shouts from the crowd. The crowd was agitated; they were shouting all sorts of insults pointing at the policemen.

"WHITE PIGS!" a group of youths behind Lucia were shouting together, "RUNNING DOGS OF THE WHITEMAN!" And they asked, pointing at the caps of the policemen, "MUDENGU MUNEI?" (What is in the basket?) – a derogatory expression in reference to the type of khaki basket-shaped hats or caps that the African policemen wore.

Some women were sobbing without restraint with helpless anger. The men were shouting angrily at the police. The atmosphere had become tense. Mr and Mrs Gumbo noticed that Lucia had also joined in the sobbing. Her shoulders shook violently. She had covered her face with a handkerchief and blowing and sneezing endlessly trying to suppress her violent shaking. Mrs Gumbo was very much disturbed by Lucia's crying. What could she be crying for? Mrs Gumbo thought, a little confused.

To the masses at the rally and the sprawling segregated African townships, Mrs Gumbo knew the police were the visible symbols of the power of oppression. They were in fact, the Government. An attack on or against the visible police force was an attack on the oppressive white minority government.

Lucia was completely moved by Tapera's and Miss Regayi's speeches. She was moved into the realities of the actual life which her mother, father, brothers and sisters and other relatives who did not live in mission stations as she did, lived through. This was a revelation, of some kind of life which she had never thought of; a life which had been hidden away from her. She felt angry with the people who were responsible for her upbringing – the priests and nuns at both Monte Carlos and St Pauls; the church – the shepherd of oppression and exploitation of the black people in their own country. She thought, it was as if a very dark cloud had been covering her eyes and mind. Now those speeches had unveiled the dark cloud and there was a bright light shining and showing new happenings which had been hidden behind the dark veil. Lucia had been born an oppressed black woman, yet, because of the teachings of the church, she thought, she was unable to realise that she and her people were an oppressed nation. She stopped crying decidedl and was looking around her.

A third speaker had taken the floor. "Is that Murambiwa, the General and Publicity Secretary?" Lucia asked Mrs Gumbo. Her voice sounded quite composed and calm, to the surprise and pleasure of her aunt. The crowd was shouting, "THAT'S OUR MAN – GO ON COMRADE!" That was the first time Lucia heard of the word 'Comrade', she noticed. "Yes," answered Mrs Gumbo. "That one is more dynamic and aggressive than Mr Tapera. Just listen to him," so she listened, attentatively, thinking:

I think I like Mr Murambiwa. He seems more active and more charismatic than the chairman. Could he be the one who had been shouting through the loud speaker this morning inviting people to the meeting? He could be, she told herself.He was a handsome man of about five feet ten inches. He was dark in complexion with a very deep voice that sounded rather harsh and provocative as he shouted into the microphone:

"FREEDOM! ONE MAN ONE VOTE!" The crowd loved him, and they responded to his slogans vigorously. He was popular. It seemed as if people were waiting for him rather than any other nationalist speaker, Lucia noticed. He had to plead for silence from the audience. He had a way of tantalising his audience. He, obviously, had made himself the darling of the masses. Almost everyone around Lucia and her aunt kept on saying "That is our man!" This heightened Lucia's interest in the speaker, even more. She was anxious to hear what Murambiwa was going to say which had not already been said by the previous speakers. Murambiwa had nothing to say on the church.

Shupai, in her flash back, started thinking of Murambiwa. She had never heard of him ever since she went underground. Hoping he is not in detention until now, she prayed. That man, Murambiwa was my inspiration, she thought. His speech, that Sunday morning, was the one which opened this road that I'm walking on today. She thought back to Murambiwa on the platform, one hand holding the microphone, the other clenched and raised high in the 'Black Power' type salute. Just that salute alone, made his audience more anxious and more restless.

Whereas Tapera and Miss Regayi were persuasive in their speeches, Murambiwa, it seemed, was not persuading the oppressor, but he was challenging him. He was urging the Africans to be ready to attack the enemy. He was certainly provoking the enemy into fighting on that very day.

"Comrades,borthers and sisters!" Murambiwa started. "We have gathered here today to inform each other, once and for all, that the oppressor is an imperious being. He is crazed by his absolute power drunkenness, and the fear of losing it."

"TELL THEM BROTHER!" shouted the group of youths behind Lucia and Mrs Gumbo.

"Yes, we have been oppressed for too long. These settlers want to keep on holding on to their privileges. Their racism and animalism are a reign of terror to the blackman in his own country. Courts that dispense no justice! An administration that creates concentration camps! More and more dogs are being trained daily, to tear our flesh to shreds. There are, pro rata, more secret police in this country than there were in Hitler's Nazi regime. So many, comrades, that they constitute a whole new stratum that is firmly attached to the oppressive state power, the bourgeois establishment. Repression! Repression!" He repeated, "Repression, brothers and sisters! Repression of the worst and the highest order!" His voice was shaking. He was agitated. Sweat was streaming down his face and he did not even bother to look for a handkerchief to wipe it. He just did it with his forefinger. The crowd was roaring. Murambiwa had roused their temper even higher. He was increasingly charging the crowd. The crowd was restless. Lucia, among the crowd, was restless too. She found herself leaning forward; tense, on her patch of the hard concrete bench. When she looked around, the others seemed to be in the same condition – condition of apparent spiritual release. It seemed that the voice of the speaker was a sharp knife cutting the past from her, and drawing closer the bright future. The ugly past, she thought, and then described it as a record of ignorance, misery, brutality and stupidity. She found herself joining everyone in shouting: "FREEDOM! FREEDOM!" And other political slogans of the N. D. P. which she had heard for the first time only that morning.

Murambiwa gave the crowd the time to scream and shout. Lucia noticed that there were no more tears from the women but cries of anger instead. Everyone including the policemen, it seemed was ready for any eventuality.

"Children of the motherland," Murambiwa continued and the crowd fell silent. "We have talked for too long. We have persuaded and begged for too long. We have suffered for too long. We have sacrificed and served for too long. The time to end talking should be now! The time to serve our country through action should be now! It is time to move with determination to build a revolutionary movement for a revolutionary change. We must strike at the oppressor's nerve – centre and keep him in fear, fear of the attack which he does not know where, how and when it cometh. The oppressor seized our country by plundering and killing our forefathers and grandmothers. He used a gun against innocent and defenceless peace loving people. The oppressor is the owner of violence. He is the teacher of violence. We have to learn from him. Violence can bring freedom to a people. Violence is the key to our liberation. Comrades, let us unite against the oppressor in speaking in his language, the language of violence, but against his injustices, exploitation and oppression. Look over there, in their arms," he pointed to the police. "They are hugging the violence itself – the gun, the tear-gas canisters, the hound dogs. The oppressor oppresses us with the gun. He rules us by the gun and those other instruments of oppression and violence. He believes in the night of the gun. What can we do with our bare hands, without the gun? Only the gun understands the gun. He, the oppressor, will certainly understand his own language, brothers and sisters. His own language spoken by a determined, united people. United! United comrades, we will organise a violence of our own, hard and more aggressive. As for those running dogs of the white pigs, and the plain clothed ones," he said, pointing to a group of black policemen, "let them wait. The day of reckoning, the day of black judgement will come. We will ask them, 'where were you when the others were struggling for freedom! Where were you when we were fighting the oppressors?' Our judges will be on the throne, waiting for them. Black judges comrades. Thank you, comrades!" Murambiwa stepped down. He was breathless, sweaty and shaking with anger.

The people were up on their feet in an outburst of political slogans. Murambiwa had done it. He had pressed the red button. Anger and excitement were running wild among the people and they were ready for action against the nearest symbol of enemy oppression – the settler police surrounding the square.

Lucia glanced at the six-foot battle dressed policemen. She could see some, feverishly clutching on to the sub-machine guns, sten-guns, tear-gas launchers, and some, struggling with the ugly and hungry man-eating dogs. Many horror scenes raced through her mind as she imagined what could happen if all those instruments of oppression were let loose upon the defenceless but angry crowd of freedom-demanding Africans. Actually the dogs seemed more ready for action than the police men handling them. This is it, Lucia told herself. Can they surely kill all these people in cold blood? She looked at the crowd of angry, defenceless people, armed only with the love for their usurped country. Somehow she was not afraid anymore, although this was her first time to come into direct confrontation with the white man's instruments of oppression – the police force and the hungry dogs. Murambiwa's speech had strengthened Lucia. He had managed to dispel all the fear that she had when she first came to the meeting that morning. She felt like shouting at the top of her voice like the rest of the people, especially as the youngest ones were doing. She felt like crying. She checked herself because she thought that was no time for tears. She had felt like crying a while ago. And she cried, she thought, to express her anger against her ignorance of the truth about her own country's history. She thought she had been too preoccupied with religious work and had viewed the white priests and all that they stood for as the symbol of godliness and freedom. Now, the fathers, brothers, and nuns and all they stood for and preached, was now to her, a symbol of evil and repression. Slowly she was feeling, within her, the strong urge to do something about the life of her people in Rhodesia. Obviously, she thought, her people in their country, were modern slaves of the white minority regime.

While these thoughts engulfed Lucia's mind, she noticed that Mrs Chake, the Secretary for Women's Affairs had taken the stand when, 'B-O-O-M!' was heard. A tear-gas gun had been fired by the settler police. Within seconds a loud 'B-A-N-G!' was heard, then another 'BANG', and yet another....

The settler agents and police were now determined to put an end to the rally. They had had enough of the castigation of their master regime by the African politicians. The crowd started and rose to its feet. There was chaos! People began to run in all directions, pushing this way and that way. People stumbled, falling on top of each other and pushing and shoving each other in the struggle for the exits. The panicking developed into utter confusion and pandemonium. Are they killing people? Lucia thought. But the people have not done anything except talking. Why are the police shooting? Lucia was really stunned, but surprisingly not afraid.

While people struggled for the exits, she kept her eyes on the platform. She saw Mrs Chake, the Secretary for Women's Affairs, grab the microphone and spoke with a very high, cool and firm voice. She attempted to calm the people by asking them not to panic:

"Do not panic," she shouted and repeated, "Don't panic. Let's go to our homes quietly. Let's not do anything to those cowards now. They are only rats armed to the teeth. Our time will come, comrades," she went on, "Our time, when we can strike at them effectively. That will be the time the people's long arm will strike at the nerve centre of the enemy and his dogs. We are er...." Her voice tailed away and stopped suddenly. A white policeman had wrestled the microphone from Mrs Chake. At that point Lucia had looked back over her shoulder only to see Mrs Chake being grabbed by a burly and tall settler policeman in full riot-dress. Mrs Chake and the other leaders were being pushed violently down the platform and led towards the southern gate at gun-point. Lucia suddenly became furious. She stopped walking and felt the urge to go back and join Mrs Chake, Miss Regayi and the other leaders. She checked herself. What am I going to do even if I go back there, a wretched, helpless fool like myself? Lucia checked her urge to go back. She was not going to rescue them or help in anyway, she thought. She stood there for a moment as if rooted to the ground, looking at the leaders being pushed around by the police. Her uncle shouted:

"Let's go, Lucy!" He tugged her towards the eastern gate. Within a few minutes they had struggled out of the enclosed Square. Before leaving, she turned to look back once more and managed to see the six leaders being pushed and hustled into a police truck outside the opposite gate.

The truck was surrounded by four black and white policemen handling the hungry dogs and several plain-clothes men. Lucia shuddered at the sight of the ugly dogs which were barking and growling, jumping and leaping furiously. They jumped as high as the height of the tall handlers who had to struggle hard to control them.

What have they done to deserve such treatment? Lucia questioned herself, as the truck disappeared. There goes the people, Miss Regayi and the others. I had wished to see them after the meeting, but....Lucia was lost in her thoughts. These people had brought light to her. Those who had removed a dark blanket of ignorance off her mind had diasappeared with the police truck, may be, never to be seen again, she thought. They had now been arrested. Lucia had become interested in politics and wanted to know more. She had thought she would know more only from them.

The image of Murambiwa, the General and Publicity Secretary of the N. D. P. was the most dominating in her mind. Murambiwa had inspired her more than the other speakers. His speech was the one that had strengthened her desire to join the struggle. It had dispelled all the doubts she had about politics and the fear she had suffered the first time she had a glimpse of so many armed policemen and their bull-dogs, who had surrounded the ground. She had come to the conclusion that only people of Murambiwa's calibre could give her the very much needed political footing without fear. She had made up her mind, during the meeting, to meet the leaders as soon as the meeting was over, but the police....! She was very disappointed. She was trying very hard to fight back burning tears of anger that were pricking her eye-lids as her uncle took her hand and led her to the bus stop. Well, perhaps there is going to be another chance, she concluded her private debate. She was trying to cool her anger even though tears were blinding her eyes. She could not see properly where she was going. She was just being led away. At that particular time in her flash back, Shupai, in the hospital, was aroused by a nurse, offering her a cup of tea. The tea, Shupai noticed was very thick and dark brown.

Some patients were saying, "Nurse Raina, we don't want your tea. It's not nice and it's also cold and too strong." Shupai also noticed that the patients were just joking with nurse Raina, who, it seems, was kind of popular among the patients in that ward.

"You keep quiet now," commanded nurse Raina and went on, "You are disturbing the others who are feeling worse than you." Turning to Shupai, nurse Raina asked, "How are you feeling now, Sarah?" Shupai hesitated. She had forgotten that in the hospital she was to be called by the name Sarah. She almost had forgotten the name Sarah after having been thinking of herself as Lucia. Too many names! She sighed, and politely she told nurse Raina that she was quite alright and not hungry yet.

Shupai imagined herself drinking tea at half past ten in the morning! What a farce! She remembered her comrades she had left in the forest. The combatants do not care what time or what day they eat, let alone drinking tea at ten in the morning, she thought. Sometimes they go for hours without having eaten a thing. At this particular moment, she imagined her comrades must be on a very fast march or run. Or may be they are just lying low, heavily camouflaged in order not to be spotted by enemy spotter planes. Shupai was thinking that, after the operation in which she sustained her injury the previous night, the settler forces must be combing the area, hunting them down like the devils themselves.

But knowing the tactics the guerrillas use in escaping from the enemy, she thought, she had all the faith and confidence in her comrades. She knew that the enemy would have a very hard time trying to find Munongwa and his unit.

Munongwa's men, after Shupai and Tafirenyika were taken for treatment, had marched in silence, further away from the point of their previous encounter with the enemy forces. It was not until the following day that Munongwa and his other comrades realised how much Shupai had meant to them. She had done more than just fighting side by side with them. By her brightness and her cheerfulness even at tight moments, her mere presence, they thought, she had cushioned the tense exhaustion of their efforts. She had provided a background for them in which they could momentarily relax and gather strength for another day's sustained effort. The whole atmosphere, the guerrillas, especially Munongwa, realised, seemed flat without Shupai.

The results of the previous operation must have stretched Munongwa's nerves to the utmost. But he never showed it, his comrades observed. He set out to instil confidence in his men and renew their interest and enthusiasm. He did this by the force of his personality, by implanting in them his own encouraging feelings. They reacted accordingly. Tafirenyika's men, who had felt more heavily the absence of their commander and the death of their two comrades, were relieved. They felt as thought Munongwa had stretched out his hand to lift them up to his own pitch of mood which sprang from deep within him. The mood was natural and real. They went ahead scheming and planning for their next move. Munongwa was now in-charge of the two units and proper camouflage was their immediate target. They decided to lie low under cover until dark. Munongwa, however, kept on wishing for Shupai's presence. He could send her now to spy and gather more information about the reaction and the movements of the enemy forces after the operation yesterday....

The radio had earlier reported that there had been an attack on the "terrorist" base by the security forces. Now the ten o'clock news report went on: "Last evening's attack on a terrorist base was carried out by the air and ground units from the joint military commands of both Karoi and Sinioa. About more than thirty terrorists are known to have died in the attack," the report went on, "The surviving terrorists fled towards the border, carrying some of their wounded with them," the announcer went on, "According to the security officers who participated in the operation, troops pursued the terrorists up to the border. Heavy fighting took place, near the border, between the fleeing terrorists and the units of the Rhodesian security forces. At the terrorist base, the armed forces freed some villagers who had been abducted previously by the terrorists who...." Munongwa switched off the radio abruptly:

"Empty settler propaganda stunt!" he remarked, "Aimed at creating hatred and mistrust between the peasantry and us. What empty lies!"

"The peasants, however, are now aware of this," said one of the combatants from Tafirenyika's group. "The enemy can't reverse the trend any longer. They are fighting a losing battled, that's for sure."

Chapter 6

After tea, the ward became quiet again. Shupai went on thinking of her comrades and the previous operation. She thought of the two fallen comrades they had left behind. Pity they could not remove their bodies before the enemy saw them. She felt dispirited lying flat, sick in that hospital bed, with one of her legs lifted on traction, helpless, she thought. She was, however, not in too much pain then. Her mind lingered back to the scene in her uncle Gumbo's house in Salisbury's Harare Township after the meeting in Chaminuka Square. She was very green then about the struggle, she chuckled to herself. She remembered herself listening attentively to her uncle's narration about how the struggle began. He was trying to cheer her up, she thought, by telling her a short history of Highfield African Township. He was telling her about some of the interesting events that took place in Chaminuka Square and the Ceiril Jameson Hall, as far back as before the African National Congress days.

Highfield Township, Gumbo started, was built some few years after Harare's New Location. Because of an African influx into Salisbury in search of employment, Highfield had become a sprawling large township. It was capable of taking in most of the African job-seekers. The most interesting spot in Highfield was the community centre, not far from the Chaminuka Square. Most pleasure loving people used to say, "If you really want to enjoy yourself, go to 'Highvillage' – Highfield! Marriages, be aware!" Africans from other small townships like Mabvuku, Mufakose, etc, in Salisbury would go entertainment seeking to Highfield. Everyday, and especially during the week-ends, they would remain there up to past midnight, drinking mostly, in this famous beer-hall garden. The "Kaffir" beer (Ngoto), Chibuku and women! The "natives" were not allowed to drink any other type of "European" beer or alcoholic drinks such as Gin, Brandy, Whisky etc. So these were not found in these African beer-halls.

After some time, "European" beer such as Castle, Lion Lager etc were allowed, by legislation, to the "natives". Then a cocktail bar was built near the beer-hall in the same grounds. The cocktail bar was upstairs, a semi-open roof-garden, and it served only "European beer". People would either drink inside or outside in the open. Only 'gentlemen' dressed in suits and ties, and their ladies "dressed to kill" in evening gowns, were allowed into the cocktail bar, the "kokotero", as people used to vernacularise 'cocktail'.

The beer was expensive, and it was somewhat costly to be allowed to enter the bar. But one found the poor Africans struggling to get suits and ties in order to make it into the "kokotero". In fact, it seemed, the tie was the only important item of clothing that enabled one to pass as a 'gentleman' at the entrance. What happened inside was one of the guards' business. So, some three or four naughty men would sometimes use only one tie to enter the kokotero. One of them would put on the tie, went up into the bar while others wait downstairs in the garden. He would remove the tie and clandestinely threw it down to the others. Another would put it on, entered the bar, removed it and follow what the first one did, and so on until all three or four of them managed to go in.

The music from the "kokotero" was nice, commended one of the housewives from the Lusaka section of Highfield. The music was beamed throughout the township through loudspeakers, especially around four in the afternoon. Housewives would be seen dancing, rock and rolling and jiving excitedly to the sweet tunes of groups like the Dark City Sisters, and De Black Evening Folleys, the City Quards, Elvis Presley, Cliff Richard and the Young Ones, Dorothy Masuka and her Pata Pata tunes, Miriam Makeba and many others. Many men would not reach home in good time after work, after having stopped first at the "kokotero". On Fridays and month ends, most pay packets remained at the "kokotero" before reaching home. Marriages were in real trouble.

Highfield Township was also the hub and the heart of African politics, and trade unionism. It was the birth place of many workers' organisations such as, the Commercial and Allied Workers' Union, the Tailors and Garment Workers' Union, the Artisans Union, African Railway Workers' Union, Transport Workers' Union, the Textiles Workers' Union and so on. All these were affiliated to the African Trade Union Congress (ATUC).

The African National Congress (ANC) and now the National Democratic Party (NDP) were all born in Highfield. Most political and trade union rallies were held in the Chaminuka Square or the Ceiril Jameson Hall on the Northern side of the Square. Not only the African politicians and trade unionists used the Chaminuka Square and the Jameson Hall for meetings; the government officials also did when they felt like addressing the "natives" on anything.

Government Primary Schools in the Salisbury area used, also to gather in the Chaminuka Square to participate in the singing competitions. These were organised by the Mayor of Salisbury in conjunction with the Native Education officer and the Superintendent of Highfield, a white man. In these contests, each school was allowed to sing one optional song, and one which would be the only competition song: "God Bless our Gracious Queen. Long live our noble Queen..."

To many parents, it was marvellous to watch and hear their children sing the "National Anthem", conducted by "educated" African teachers. The African politicians, the nationalists, bitterly and angrily watched and listened to the African children entertaining the settler mayor and his group of white dignitaries with singing the British National Anthem instead of "Mwari Komborera Africa/Zimbabwe – God Bless Africa/Zimbabwe". The settler mayor, his wife, other Town Councillors, the Highfield Township Superintendent, his wife and other interested settlers attended these annual competitions. It was an evening of entertainment for them alright. Some Africans had a soft spot for the mayor. They said, "The mayor is a very nice white man. He is quite different from some of the white administrators. He is not a racist," they asserted, "Otherwise he would not attend native singing contests." These people, Gumbo said, did not know that the mayor came to these events merely as a matter of obligation, and ofcourse, to "civilise" the "natives". They also did not know that the settler mayor had to encourage the "natives" to sing praises to the British government and to colonialism.

The settler government, Gumbo went on, fearing the impact of the African National Congress among the Africans, decided to unilaterally declare it a prohibited organisation. It was banned without explanation. The regime arrested and detained the ANC leaders. The Africans were disappointed. After a few days, Mr Redhead, the settler government Prime Minister promised, in an announcement over the radio, that, he would address and explain to the Africans why the ANC was banned and why their leaders were arrested. The meeting was going to be held in the Ceiril Jameson Hall in Highfield on a Saturday afternoon.

The Jameson Hall became famous throughout the country, Gumbo declared. It was in that hall, that same Saturday afternoon, when the settler Prime Minister, was prevented by the masses from addressing them. Gumbo went on excitedly. This Prime Minister had tried to explain and justify his banning of their political party, and the arrest and detention of their leaders. The Prime Minister's security men had to save him by throwing him out through the window. The people had started to throw whatever they had, umbrellas, handbags, etc, at him. Some were already advancing towards the stage.

Lucia, who had been listening quietly but attentatively, had become quite interested in her uncle's narration. She asked, "Why uncle? Why were the people doing that?"

"The Prime Minister could not be allowed to go on talking. Because, as soon as he had begun his talk, he attacked the people's leaders and the ANC, which had just been banned. He had called it 'a party of terrorism organised by hooligans and terrorists'. That did it! The people began throwing things at him. They advanced towards the stage, shouting, 'You white settler pig. Who do you think you want to fool?' Some asked angrily, 'Get him down here! Kill him!' His settler security men were taken by surprise. They delayed a little, while the mob was doing its 'talking' and 'throwing' against the regime's leader. It was only after a brief spell that the bodyguards realised that the Prime Minister was in danger. They had been taken by surprise. Then, they moved quickly to whisk him down the stage and out of the Hall through the window because the doors had been blocked by the mob. Then wielding their revolvers, they were ready to shoot. That was an incident and a half! They shot a few shots into the air."

"Then what happened?" Lucia asked, urging him to continue. Excited? Her uncle thought he detected a note of excitement in that question. He went on:

"After this, the Hall was all tear-gas. The tear-gas bombs were being generously lobbied into Hall, landing on the packed crowd of Zimbabweans. People started to scramble for the exits, trampling on each other, coughing and choking, with streaming of eyes, sneezing and vomiting. But some daring youths of the ANC were having fun by managing to quickly pick up some unburst tear-gas canisters and throwing them back to the settler police. One of the canisters landed in a truck full of settler police, who had no masks. To the settler police, this was no fun at all. They were so much used to tear-gassing the people generously, but this time....They scrambled out of the truck, a bit too late. So they also participated in the game of coughing, sneezing and streaming of eyes. Chaos and confusion reigned. Some of the policemen, covering their noses, tried to apprehend and arrest those who tried to escape. The settler police ran riot that Saturday afternoon. Reinforcements had to be called in. They started to arrest every African they laid their hands on, some passers by too. Hundreds of people were arrested that day. No one escaped. Can you guess where they were taken to?" Gumbo asked but did not wait for an answer from Lucia. "They were all pushed into the Chaminuka Square like cattle into a dip-tank. The people spent two nights and two days in that Square, in the open, heavily guarded like run-away murderers. Talk of the cold! Talk of the hunger! Many people had not eaten on that Saturday. Most had just proceeded to the Hall straight after work on that Saturday afternoon".

"Were you there in the hall, uncle?" asked Lucia.

"Eye witness," answered Gumbo boastfully. "In fact, participant. You should ask your aunt how I appeared when I was released the following

Monday evening. An un-ironed shirt squashed in a box for many days looked better." He went on humorously:

"A rumour swept round, not only in the Salisbury area, but the whole country, that the settler Prime Minister was hospitalised as a result of the shock he received at the Jameson Hall that day. During the attempts to save him from the angry crowd, the settler bodyguards roughened and manhandled the Prime Minister and threw him out through the nearest window. This caused him some bruises and some injuries. You see, Lucy," Gumbo pointed to his niece, "Both the Prime Minister and the security personnel had not expected the type of reaction they received from the African people on that day. They had never before experienced such a harsh reaction from a crowd of black people. Usually, they addressed the docile people, on anything at all, in the Hall or in the Square without any trouble. They expected a smooth scolding and despising in a smooth meeting as usual. They did not know that the Natives had become really angry about the banning of the ANC and were ready for any eventuality. That was the last day that the settler Prime Minister or any other white personnel had ventured to address the Africans, on anything, in any of the segregated townships. Now, only violence is the means of communication the government uses."

"Very interesting!" Lucia said and she sighed. She was quiet for a long moment. Then she said, "So this....this struggle started a long time back and you, uncle had been part of it all along? And Auntie?" she asked ruminatively, as if ending her uncle's narration.

"Yes", joined in Mrs Gumbo. I was in the Tailors and Garment Workers Union when this happened. By the way," she went on. "Your uncle was a member of the Commercial and Allied Workers Union and the Transport Workers' Union – all affiliated members of the Southern Rhodesia African Trade Union Congress (ATUC). That's where we met – me and your uncle, you know. He is quite a loud mouth as you see him," she laughed jovially, trying to lighten the atmosphere that had accompanied the narrative about the history of Highfield African Township and the beginning of the struggle.

Lucia was so moved by the events of that day at the N. D. P. meeting that she spend the whole of that Sunday afternoon quietly in her room. She thought she would join the forces of liberation, and hoped it was not too late. But Mrs Gumbo was a bit worried about what she termed, "Lucia's unusually quiet behaviour," that whole day after the meeting.

Lucia had refused to eat anything, even to talk. "What do you think is the matter with her?" Mrs Gumbo asked her husband and continued. "Do you think she is regretting going to that meeting after all, instead of going to church?" Mr and Mrs Gumbo started blaming themselves for taking Lucia to the N. D. P. meeting. "She is usually not such a ruminative, and quiet character," commented Mrs Gumbo, and asked her husband "What do you say Garikayi?"

"I wonder," replied Gumbo. "May be she feels it was a great sin to have gone to a gathering where the church was so much castigated and criticised," Gumbo suggested, "She must be thinking of how to present this grievous sin to the priest in the confession box." They laughed quietly, but they could not get an answer to this puzzle. In the evening, Lucia had eaten very little supper, and was sitting quietly, as if ill, in a corner of a couch. Her uncle said, "Now this is too much for us, Lucy. Your sulking the whole day long after this morning's meeting in Highfield...." He trailed off his sentence, then went on more persuasively, "Tell us, Lucia. Are you afraid the police might come here and arrest all of us?" Her uncle asked, deliberately, avoiding to mention the church issue.

"No! Not that at all," Lucia replied with a sigh, and then asked, "Tell me uncle, what will happen to those people? I mean those – those leaders?" She looked worriedly at her uncle.

"Oh! Those!" Her uncle was surprised. He looked at his wife, shrugged his shoulders, as if to say, so-we-were-wrong-after-all. His wife also replied with a shrug of her shoulders. Looking back at Lucia he said, "They might be charged for threatening settler interests and for contravening the notorious Law and Order (Maintenance) Act."

"What ever that is, it's terrible!" Lucia exclaimed. "But they didn't do anything wrong at the meeting," and emphasised, "They only spoke to the audience."

"Well," said her uncle, "The speeches were seditious as far as the settlers are concerned. You see, they are now very afraid of the African people. They know they are oppressing us and that we are up in arms against this oppression, against them. So they employ all sorts of tactics in order to keep us helplessly quiet and...." At that moment there was a knock at the door. Lucia tensed. Could it be the police, she thought, probably looking for everyone who had been at the N. D. P. meeting? Gumbo went to the door and opened it. A close friend of Gumbo, call Rungano (story), entered. Rungano was a teacher at one of the first and oldest government primary schools in Harare Township, Chitsere. He was a staunch supporter of the N.D.P. After an exchange of traditional, cordial greetings, Lucia was introduced to Rungano. He was tall and on the stout side, almost the same structure as her uncle.

These two people must be of the same age, she thought, I'm sure they think the same and act the same. After a few exchanges between Rungano and Mrs Gumbo, Rungano and Lucia, Gumbo said,

"Rungano, listen. I was just trying to tell my niece here about how the settler regime oppresses us using such laws as 'The Law and Order (Maintenance) Act' and others," he went on, "You see Rungano, my niece grew up with the Missionaries, the Roman Catholics. You and I know how those Catholics can brain wash some of these kids. Imagine, she seems not be aware of the political struggle that is going on between the government of the settlers and the black indigenous people of this country." Gumbo looked at Lucia and went on addressing her, "You see my dear, with the Law and order (Maintenance) Act, any one of these settlers, can say or do anything against us. We are not to complain. The police can arrest us even for a mild remark about the way we are treated in our own country. In short, Lucy," Gumbo said, "It is because we want to end this brutal and unjust treatment of the African people of this country, that the N D P and the ANC before it were launched. We intend to struggle on until we can rule ourselves."

"Can you explain to me more about these laws, uncle?" Lucia requested. With a smile, Mr Gumbo passed the request to Rungano whom he credited with being more knowledgeable on the oppressive instruments of the white minority system, than he was.

"But, first of all Lucy," said her uncle. "Do you believe that we are an oppressed and enslaved people in our own country?" he asked.

"Now I can say I am beginning to see the light uncle," she answered and said, "All along I thought the way things were was how God willed them, and we, as human-beings could subject ourselves to our fate in submission to God's will." She asked, "How could we challenge God's will?" Sarcastic, Lucy? Gumbo wondered.

"Well, in order to oppress and exploit us with minimum resistance from us the settlers use a set of laws. An inhuman set of laws for this task." Rungano started to explain to Lucia some of the laws that formed the corner-stone of oppression and exploitation of the black people by the white minority in Zimbabwe. Rungano, who talked in terms of imperialist, capitalist interests in Zimbabwe, was using, according to Lucia, a jargon she had never heard of before. Anyway, it sounded interesting, she thought, and was definitely impressive.

"There is the Land Tenure Act and the Land Apportionment Act, for example. The settlers," Rungano went on, "have divided our country into what they call 'black areas, the "Reserves", and white areas'. This means that there are certain areas in this country where you and I may never settle or buy land even if we have the money.

They are reserved for the whites. The reason is that by law, a black person may not settle or do business in those white areas. We live under the laws of private property ownership! This is capitalism of the worst order," Rungano emphasised.

"Do you remember the Ruware people?" Gumbo asked her, and added, "All those people were forcibly moved from their traditional homes to somewhere down, I don't know where. Their place was declared white area. What gave power to the single 'Native District Commissioner' – a white man – to move those people? These are the laws we are talking about. The peasants of Ruware could not argue without violating one of these laws."

"Even if they had argued the white commissioner would have simply pointed to the relevant law," said Rungano and continued, "On the basis of that law, he demands immediate and positive response to his orders. The peasants must move out or their eviction is carried out with characteristic force under armed guard. It is supervised as if it were a military operation to occupy the area."

"The peasants of Ruware were moved because their area was fertile and the new white settlers had to be settled there." Gumbo explained. "The land is fertile and there is plenty of water. Where the people of Ruware were moved to did not and does not matter. It may be a dry, hot, infertile and unhealthy area, the white regime does not care."

"The Land Husbandry Act," Rungano said, "has operated against our owning enough cattle for our needs. You know, to us, wealth is counted in the number of cattle one owns and the size of land one owns and cultivates. By these laws of daylight highway robbery, it is stipulated that a black family shall own only six herds of cattle and a small piece of land. Those black people caught exceeding the number stipulated by law will have their cattle confiscated by force and the cattle are auctioned. I do not have to tell you Lucia how big a herd of cattle or how much land a white farmer may own here in Rhodesia. You have seen the large estates they own. You have seen their cattle. They use counting machines to know just how many they have. Can you believe it?" asked Rungano looking at Gumbo. "Van Buren, that white farmer next to my village owns cattle, I'm telling you! But none of the villagers around have ever been able to know just how many herds of cattle this white man owns. They are too many, many times more than the total number owned by the Africans in that village.

"In the towns the white man has made sure that the black workers do not even earn enough." Rungano continued and Lucia listened attentively. "He has done this by enacting the Industrial Reconciliation Act. This sinister law makes it illegal for black people to strike for more money or for better working conditions.

A strike reduces profits for the capitalist and hurts the whites. That is why black people are prohibited from striking for more pay, better conditions of service or removal of an oppressive foreman. Disparity in pay between the black workers and the white workers is by law. That is to say, the law has stipulated that a white person will always earn much more than an African for doing the same job. There is no pension system for the black worker, and no workman's compensation of any kind in case of accidents at work.

"Every black person in Rhodesia is a 'servant' by law," continued Rungano as if addressing a class of students. "This is clear in the 'Masters and Servants Act'. Every white person is a 'master' by law. This law clearly makes a black person a permanent servant and a white person a permanent master. What could be more devilish than this? Don't you think, Lucia that such a thing simply means that slavery does exist in modern times? It exists right here in our country, not in Arabia, USA or anywhere else, but right here?" Rungano asked emotionally.

"I must remind you too," Gumbo took over, "that you and I, your uncle here, cannot choose any type of work we want to do, or learn freely. We cannot do so because the whites have against us in this country what they call 'Job Reservation'. There are jobs reserved for white people. Equally, there are jobs reserved only for black people. I mean you have seen this yourself, in those missions between the white and black nuns and priests. By order of things in our country today, whites reserve the best jobs for themselves and their kith and kin. They encourage many whites to immigrate from the ghettos of England and Europe." Gumbo talked harshly on this subject, as if he could strangle someone. "Those jobs regarded as 'superior' are for whites and those regarded as 'inferior' are for us. The dirty, manual jobs are usually ours, and pay us very little. Exploitation Lucia! Exploitation of the highest order, I'm telling you," Gumbo talked emphatically and went on, "If a white man wanted to do a job reserved for black people, he would do it without any legal or political constraint. In fact, they do it quite often. Once a white man decides to do that type of job, normally relegated to us, they are paid not a 'black wage' but a 'white salary'. And this is four or even more times our wage. His conditions of service are automatically and immediately altered to suit his skin."

"You see," said Rungano, "There is, in fact, no inferior or superior job. The white man creates inferior and superior jobs and conditions. He makes us believe that the jobs we do are inferior simply by paying less for them. He talks low of them and makes the conditions of service bad, as well as demeaning the jobs in every way he can. He calls them 'kaffir' jobs. Who does 'kaffir' jobs in Europe, Britain, Japan and so on?" asked Rungano looking directly at Lucia. "It is a war against our human dignity as a people," he declared.

"By degrading the jobs we do the white man at the same time, degrades those who perform or do those jobs. Equally, those who do 'superior' jobs, are expected to be 'superior'. You must have noticed this thing even at your mission there, as Gumbo pointed out a minute ago. The white fathers and sisters expect to do 'superior' work than the black fathers and black sisters. By doing so, they expect you to regard them as 'superior'. Can you imagine Lucia, 'job reservation' even in the House and Service of God?"

"But you all seem to think that all white people think alike," Lucia reluctantly broke her silence, and went on, "I have seen some very good missionaries at our place. To me, they didn't seem to have anything evil, racist or anything of the like in their heads. They were out and out to serve God," she asserted. "I also believe that even outside the mission stations there are some white people who are here to stay like us and work like us?" Hers became more of a question than an affirmation, Rungano noticed. But she seemed to be learning fast, thought her uncle.

"True, Lucia. Very true," agreed her uncle.

"You see Lucia, we are not fighting, in this country, against the white people per se," Rungano replied, and continued, "Our struggle may appear to you to be a racial struggle, that is, a struggle by black people against white people. The truth is that is appears that way because it is the white people who have decided to monopolise political power, power to make laws that run the lives of the people of this country. I talked a moment ago about laws that have permanently made a white person a 'master' and a black person a 'servant'. This law is evil. It is a law that makes a 'master' out of every white person including those 'good' missionaries you are mentioning right now. This law has made you a permanent servant of that 'good' missionary you are talking about. This is so whether the good missionary likes it or not. It makes you a servant whether you like it or not, whether you are aware of it or not. The 'good' missionary is white. He does not refuse or reject the social status bestowed on him by his white ruling society." Rungano continued: "The white man has made it difficult for us, the ordinary black workers and peasants, to see a difference between the small white ruling class and the rest of the white people living in this country including the missionaries you know. The white ruler, by his laws, has destroyed what in fact should be a class struggle. He has built into the minds of the black peasants and workers the idea that every white person is happy to see a black man or woman toil in serfdom forever. This has given a racial colouring to our struggle. Remember, Lucia, white people are strangers in this land," Rungano reminded her. "This is our land. No ideological or racial bias can change this position, the position that this country belongs to Zimbabweans.

In this land, the white workers, the white missionaries and the white farmers are collaborating whole heartedly with the white ruling clique to oppress the black people. You can say what you like. But we cannot tolerate torture in our own land forever. There has to be a day when we have to say, 'enough is enough'." Rungano sounded emotional this time.

"Well, the missionaries, that is, the nuns and the priests I grew up with never mentioned to us about any political struggle," Lucia said. "All I know is the struggle we have to endure all, so that we can enter the Kingdom of Heaven. No matter what hardships...." she let the sentence trail away.

"The white people in this country have not only bestowed upon themselves all politico-economic power and social superiority, as well as racial superiority, they are a pitiful minority for that matter," Rungano went on, "Nowhere in this world has a foreign minority ruling over the majority been democratic.

"Look at them," Rungano said, "They can legislate against the majority with such ease and impunity, to protect their minority interests. In the N. D. P's view, only a confident and progressive majority government can justly protect the interests of the majority. The notorious Law and Order (maintenance) Act, is such an example of racial segregation. This was a law resulting from the minority's realisation that we, the majority are now up on our feet. We are on our feet to fight, not to laugh and turn the other cheek anymore. So, they too decided that they will subdue us further by legislating against our liberation activities. This notorious law hardly applies to a white person in Rhodesia. It was never meant for him. In fact, it protects the white ruling clique and its kith and kin, missionary or not. By his law, we must not hold meetings in circumstances not approved by the white minority power structure. We cannot discuss certain things regarded by the white man as injurious and detrimental to his existence. Under the Law and Order (Maintenance) Act, you and I can be detained without trial, restricted, house-arrested or banished from entering certain areas of the country. All these things can be done to us and their law says we shall have no recourse to any court of law." Rungano, Lucia observed, must be a very good teacher and a confident politician.

Lucia was an educated girl by Rhodesian standards, a trained Primary School teacher. Strange enough, she found herself looking foolishly and unbelievably ignorant before her uncle and his friend. They were able to tell her all about the laws in force in Rhodesia. She had never thought about these things before, she realised. What her uncle and his friend were saying to her made her appear like she was entering a whole new country – a country she had never thought existed before. But they were revealing to her the true country, in which she was born, grew and was to die. She was being told of a mother country which the white oppressor and his religion did not wish her to know. Her uncle's friend drew her attention to another point:

"You see, Lucia, our oppressor wishes, by some of these laws, especially the Law and Order (Maintenance) Act, to hit hard and destroy the will, determination and bravery of our youth fighters, so that we are deterred from waging a relentless struggle against their oppressive rule. This, the enemy hopes to achieve by continuous imprisonment, and cold bloodied murders perpetrated in those prisons and interrogation rooms. But, I say to you, where there is oppression there must be resistance. We have the will, determination and bravery to resist and fight to the end. Our will and determination cannot be destroyed by detentions or imprisonments. For that reason, I am confident that we shall, one day, be masters in our own country, Zimbabwe." "Now," interrupted Lucia, "How can you be confident that we shall win, if the laws that you are talking about can send our leaders to prison, detentions or restrictions and even banishment, as you told me?" She asked. Interested? Gumbo thought.

"You see, Lucia, there is nothing this white minority regime can do about our liberation struggle," replied Rungano. "We are going to be free whether the regime likes it or not. In prison or out of prison, our leaders remain leaders of the Zimbabwean revolution. That does not stop our struggle. More leaders emerge and are chosen from the people, by the people and for the people," he emphasised. "Those of us who are now politically conscious do realise that our whole country of Zimbabwe has been turned into a giant prison," gesturing with his arms, "whose inmates are kept down by brutal force of arms." Rungano asked for some water and went on after emptying the whole glass. "To undo this situation, in my opinion, only an armed struggle is the remedy," Rungano declared breathlessly.

"Now, what's an armed struggle?" asked Lucia with interest.

"Your uncle will explain this to you later. For now you should know that our leadership will continue to be more revolutionary and more resolute than ever before. The enemy is bound to be weaker and be demoralised. There is no doubt that we will win." Concluded Rungano. There was silence for a long moment. Then: "Do you think I will be able to see those leaders, uncle? I mean, meet them and talk to them?" Lucia asked looking at her uncle who immediately showed very open signs of surprise. The conversation had become more of a political discussion than a mere talk between a consoling uncle and a seemingly frightened niece. Gumbo realised he had misjudged his niece. He had seen her as a frightened girl, who was regretting not going to church but going to a political meeting, where the church was so castigated.

He realised that the niece was, instead getting interested in the political issues and wished to know more. She wanted to shape a new future and shed her old past. But what was Lucia's experience of life so far? Her uncle asked himself, beginning to retrace his niece's background, from when she was born up to the present.

Lucia was born at a small village in Chikwawa Reserve. Baby Lucia grew up under difficult conditions, Gumbo remembered. That step-mother of hers, he thought, was not kind to her at all. Lucia's mother had died while the baby was only seven moths old. Garikai Gumbo recalled going to Lucia's father and requesting to take the baby into town and look after her. Lucia's father, Jonas Kashangu, had adamantly refused, saying, "How can I let my child be brought up under those crude, rude town conditions?" He had asked and went on, "She will learn to be a hooligan and will despise me." He added "No! God will punish me for being that irresponsible. I would rather suffer in poverty with my baby than have her become mannerless, without respect for me." He had asked, "How can I leave my child to a society that is Godless, faithless, cultureless, without tradition or custom to build her character?" Gumbo had left the child reluctantly saying:

"The people in the 'reserves' have dormant minds. They don't and will never understand life." From that time until Lucia's present visit to Harare, Gumbo had never had any real contact with her nor her father. He knew, though, that she was taken to a Catholic Mission School and was never allowed to see.

That was the time, at the age of seven, when Lucia's father had negotiated with Father Gilbert, the head of the St Paul's Mission Primary School. Lucia's father had requested Father Gilbert to keep her at the Mission until after at least a few years Primary Education. "Why can't you let your child attend school here in Chikwawa near you, her parents?" Father Gilbert had asked, and added, "You want to bring this child up as an orphan, why?"

"I wish for my daughter to have a bit of education, father."

"We do have places here but only for orphans," Father Gilbert explained. "Those with living parents have to pay for their schooling plus boarding and lodging." But Lucia's father had heard of this programme where some children stayed and worked at the Mission after classes and during the school holidays.

They stayed on at the mission and worked in the garden, at the laundry, in the convent and so forth, doing various jobs without pay. Father Gilbert was finally persuaded to admit Lucia into this programme. The work that these children did during holidays was to meet their tuition fees plus boarding and lodging.

Young Lucia was pretty, slender, very quick in movement and sensitive but polite. She was a quiet but cheerful type and was very good at most of her school subjects except for religious studies. She found it a little difficult to memorise the prayers, some of which were supposed to be said in Latin during mass and en masse. She also had to memorise the questions and the answers in the Catechism. Somehow she found this subject a bit hard. "You are only lazy, that is all!" Sister Hildegard, her religious lessons teacher, would shout at her. "Why are you so poor only in catechism? I know you are always top in class in all the other subjects." Sister Hildegard would make the whole class kneel down and make a direct payer in order to "get out the devil in Lucia." Lucia would suffer punishment after punishment because of having said a certain prayer wrongly. After some time, she solved the problem by being able to recite the prayers correctly. She then became one of the best girls in leading prayers, for example, using the Rosary, even teaching others. Sister Hildegard was then very happy about Lucia's progress. She (Sister Hildegard) thought, she had worked really hard on a difficult case of demon possession; this girl was surely demonic! That was the sister's conclusion, but now she was happy to have worked so hard.

Sister Hildegard, a German national, then wanted Lucia to join and start the nunnery or the convent life straight away. "Lucia must be a nun," Sister Hildegard had told Father Gilbert and she had prayed all the time for this. "Lucia can be a good nun Father, don't you think?" Sister Hildegard had urged and had even asked permission to visit Lucia's father in the reserves. Lucia was saved from forced entry into the nunnery by her father's very strong refusal. Though he was a staunch Catholic himself, he thought he was not in favour of his daughter becoming a nun.

"That is not the only way one can serve God." Lucia's father told the sisters who were sent to him to seek his permission for Lucia to be enrolled into the convent to be a nun. "I think my daughter would live a very frustrated life as a nun in the convent. Please, I plead with you, sisters, just leave her alone to decide her own future." Lucia's father had travelled to St. Paul's Mission to plead further with Mother superior and Father Gilbert to allow Lucia to stay on and to learn but not as a nun. Kashangu went on to remind those priests and nuns about what had happened to Lucia's uncle, Gregory Gumbo (now

Garikayi Gumbo) who had decided to run away from the mission and from his father, because he was being forced against his will to join the priesthood. "Besides, he was too young to make a valid and proper decision." Kashangu went on, "As a result he ran away from the mission and then he had become completely lost in the town and leading such a difficult life that he finally turned against the church," Lucia's father concluded his plea. Lucia, herself, had never thought of that career under any circumstances.

But she had fallen into the clutches of the Fathers and Sisters. If it had not been for her father, she would have had no choice and no power to refuse. She was a good girl yes. She had never done any mischief. "Wasn't that good enough in front of God?" her father had asked Sister Hildegard, who had pleaded, prayed and appealed. She had even made a special journey to Chikwaka, to see Kashangu, personally, about the issues of getting Lucia into the convent:

"She would make a very good nun. She would even rise very quickly and easily to the rank of Sister Superior for the African nuns," Sister Hildegard had tried very hard to persuade Lucia's father. She even knelt down on the mud floor of Kashangu's hut and started to pray:

"In the name of the Father and of the Son and the Holy Ghost. Holy Mary Mother of God, pray for us sinners...." But her prayers were in vain. Mr Kashangu had refused. Lucia however, was allowed to continue with her primary education at St Paul's Mission.

Conditions for Lucia's admission at St Paul's were that after standard six she would stay at the mission and work as a laundry girl for three years without pay. That would complete the balance for her school fees. She completed her standard six, that is, grade eight, and started her three year contract (even if nothing was signed) as a laundry girl right away. Everyday, for six days a week, Lucia had to do the washing and ironing of the clothes for the white nuns, a few brothers and priests, and those of the African nuns. These clothes for the different groups had to be washed separately on different days of the week. Lucia was a hard working girl. She and other girls were working with a white sister, Aquilina, the sister in-charge of the laundry. Sister Aquilina was very quick tempered with a high pitched voice which would get lost when she was very angry and shouting at someone, usually at the laundry girls. She was an avowed racist, the girls thought. She only wanted the girls' labour that was all. Sister Aquilina believed that her mission to Africa was to tame the wild, the unbelieving pagans and crude Africans into believers of God and into lucrative beasts of burden. Lucia was made in-charge of all the washing and the ironing and even the storage of the detergents.

Lucia, as head of the laundry girls was always in serious trouble with

Sister Aquilina. If the Sister spotted a tiny spot of dirt on any of those white habits and head scarves and so forth, Lucia would get all the blame. She would be forced to re-wash all the clothes as punishment by Sister Aquilina. The rewashing sessions were often carried out after normal washing hours, between four and five thirty, in the afternoon. Sister Aquilina would go there to watch Lucia wash what were in fact very clean clothes.

"Watch out Lucia, don't waste the soap, and water. The Mission has no money you know," Sister Aquilina would remark, and immediately start a different topic altogether. "Why did you refuse to become a nun? You know you wouldn't be doing what you are doing now." Lucia would carry on with the job without saying anything in reply. But Sister Aquilina would shout on, "Stop what you are doing and listen to me, you!" Lucia would stop immediately and look directly at Sister Aquilina in utter confusion. "Why did you refuse to serve God?" Sister Aquilina would ask in an insistent manner.

"I think I can serve God adequately and well without becoming a nun, sister." Lucia would reply politely, still looking directly at Sister Aquilina. The sister would remark, shivering with rage:

"Look at her, the way she looks at sister. One would think she is a witch." Lucia would often quietly resume her washing of those clean clothes. These incidents were repeated every time Lucia did a punishment of re-washing some clean clothes. One day, as she was in the process of re-washing a heap of white gowns, sister Aquilina came in and started her usual scene of shouting at Lucia:

"Look here, you witch! This is not a place for witches." Lucia straightened her aching back. She looked up, and said quietly:

"I didn't think you believed in witches, sister?" She asked.

"Shut up you fool! When sister is talking to you, you don't answer back, do you hear?" Sister Aquilina shouted, and continued, "It is you, primitive and demonic people, after all, who talk so much about witches." Then she added: "You listen! When sister is talking to you, you must stoop. You should not look directly at sister like that as if you want to bewitch her, you...." Sister Aquilina stopped shouting as she felt as if she was being ignored since Lucia had started to continued with her task.

Some of these nuns really, Lucia said to herself, bending down to carry on washing. They use such vulgar language! Does God really allow them to do so? I have to look down and appear as if I am guilty of a sinister crime. Do I have to face all this simply because I refused to become a nun? Please God, help me! Lucia prayed silently. I hope I have not done anything really wrong by not joining the convent to serve you as a nun, my God. I hope I can make my own strong vows without entering a convent. So many girls get married and live a happy religious life raising families. God what grave mistakes have I done to deserve all this?

"What do you think you are doing, you foolish devil?" Sister Aquilina shouted, her voice so pitched up that it got lost in the process. Lucia looked at the sister, surprised. Sister Aquilina's face changed from her light pink colour to something like purple as if she was choking: "Why are you using so much soap on such clean things after I told you to be careful? I told you the Mission has no money, didn't I?" asked the sister. "The mission could be having a lot of money if it were not for evil people like you. People who just want to be educated and eat like pigs without paying anything. God have Mercy! Mercy!" Sister Aquilina prayed and quickly ordered Lucia to stop what she was doing because: "I want Sister Superior to know how you are behaving. After all, the Mission had worked so hard to give you free education and civilisation."

"No, I believe I was and am still working for that education and for the food I am eating here," Lucia replied as if talking to herself, and beginning to rinse the things she was washing.

"What have you just said you ungrateful brat?" the nun demanded angrily.

"Sisters should not be answered back, sister," she replied politely, sounded sarcastic?

"Jee-su-s Mary and Joseph! This child!" sister Aquilina shouted, trembling with rage, taking Lucia by the arm, pulling and leading her to the Sister Superior's office. In this office Sister Aquilina dropped an empty packet of Blue Surf powdered-soap and said: "Mother Superior, this Lucia, this stubborn and unreasonable child! She is so ungrateful and so wasteful that she can really throw around this very expensive soap, washing already washed clothes," Sister Aquilina finished her report breathlessly, and added something in German, and then said, "I don't know what else to say about this child, Mother!" Sister Superior looked at Lucia with a stern eye. The way this woman was looking at her, one would have thought that Lucia had turned out to be something a dog had just vomitted, Lucia thought.

Sister Superior was a tall German woman (all white nuns at St Paul's Mission were mostly German), wide at the shoulders, with a big bust of about forty-eight or more inches. The waist line measured almost the same as the bust and the hips, with big fat legs. Her voice was big too, like a man's voice. She even had some strands of beard on her double-chin. Her eyes....

Everybody at the mission, especially in the convent, was afraid of Sister Superior. Very few people knew her name – Sister Praxcedes – she was commonly known by her titles, "Mother", "Mother Superior", or "Sister Superior". And if one were reported to Mother Superior, the crime was regarded as very grave indeed. And mother Superior herself would straight away regard the reported person as a dangerous criminal who needed to be dealt with very severely. After surveying Lucia for a moment she said: "Lucia! Do you have any reason for doing what Sister Aquilina says you were doing with soap?" She asked with that deep man's voice of hers. Lucia shivered inside. She looked down. She was afraid to answer just in case....

"Lucia!" Sister Superior barked. She was impatient already.

"Sisters should not be answered back, Mother Superior," Lucia said politely now looking straight at Mother Superior's fish-like grey eyes. "That's what I was taught by Sister Aquilina here."

"Just look at her!" Sister Aquilina remarked; "She is not even ashamed of herself, looking at Mother Superior like that, as if...."

"Answer my question Lucia!" demanded Mother Superior angrily.

"I don't think I was wasting any soap Mother," Lucia started, shivering visibly. "I had to wash the clothes again that had already been washed because Sister Aquilina had instructed me to do so. She had said that it was my fault that the clothes were not clean."

"Just listen to her lies!" Sister Aquilina interrupted Lucia. "You blinking devil! You, you will...."

"Sister Aquilina!" Mother Superior hushed down the enraged Sister Aquilina.

"Mother Superior, my goodness, are you going to listen to this evil brat and not to me? If so," sister Aquilina threatened, "I will ask for a transfer to Monte Carlos or St Mary's. I cannot be humiliated like this." Sister Aquilina had suspected that Mother Superior had rather believed what Lucia had said. Actually, Sister Superior used to like Lucia right from the beginning despite Lucia's refusal to be a nun. Lucia was an honest girl. Mother Superior had observed and had trusted her, and believed her account about the rewashing of the clothes.

"Please Mother, would you like to come to the laundry and see the clothes that I was washing? Honestly, I am not lying, please," Lucia pleaded with Mother Superior. She was now afraid of the consequences, now that sister Aquilina was raving like a mad dog. Sister Aquilina rushed out and was heading for Father Gilbert's office, shouting and cursing. Mother Superior seemed to ignore Sister Aquilina and immediately sent the pleading Lucia back to the laundry:

"You go and finish that washing and come back here." Lucia wanted to say something.... "Get out! I said." She went out quickly, tripped at the door and almost fell. Her eyes blinded by burning tears, she felt sorry for herself and wished she could leave that place, that mission immediately. She started to pray silently.

After all it was God's people who were doing their work, she thought. But the vulgar language that some of these people of God used? She wondered. She was taught that when in difficulties, pray, pray and pray. She returned to Sister Superior's office later and was sent away without a word said, causing her to even be more afraid of the unknown. The next morning she did not see Sister Aquilina at the laundry. Sister Superior herself came into the laundry room, looked around then she joined Lucia and the other girls. So Lucia worked with Mother Superior herself instead, for the next five days.

Though the atmosphere was tense and so thick you could not cut it with a blunt knife, no serious incident occurred between Sister Superior and Lucia or the other girls. Then another sister, Theresia, came to replace Sister Aquilina. She watched Lucia very closely, Lucia observed, but her only weapon was silence, and performance of her task conscientiously till the end of her three year bondage. She had hoped very eagerly to quit the place after three years. After all, she had passed her standard six very well and perhaps, she could get a job somewhere....

After the three years, Lucia was surprised when she was left to continue working at the Mission laundry for weeks without pay. Without anything mentioned about the end of the so-called contract, she went on working without complaint. It was God's will, she had prayed and had accepted the situation.

One morning Lucia was called, to Father Gilbert's office. He never apologised for not letting her off after she had completed her 'contract'. "Sit down Lucia," Father Gilbert greeted her and stood, towering over her. He was tall and burly with big hairy arms. He was good looking with handsome eyebrows. "Tell me, what do you want to do with yourself?" Father Gilbert said vaguely. Lucia appeared puzzled. "Now that you have finished your primary education?" he clarified. Before Lucia had said anything, he went on. "You know, you can stay here and continue here with your work and receive pay every week. Do you like to do that?" Father Gilbert asked. Lucia thought for a few minutes. Then:

"Father, are there any possibilities for a girl with my standard of education to teach?" She had no hope of getting any help on this from Father Gilbert. But she was surprised to see that he was very pleased to learn about her wishes.

"So you are interested in teaching? I didn't know." He sounded astonished alright. "I didn't think of it either." He continued, "well, we have a teacher-training and Domestic Science School for girls at Monte Carlos," he informed and added, "Are you still interested in going back to school?" he asked. Lucia answered very quickly and eagerly:

"There is nothing I would like to do more than going back to school, Father." She started to smile warmly, had not expected this, she thought, this would be great indeed and she prayed silently, 'Please, God, help me.'

"Then go back to your work. When I get a reply from Father Leo, the Principal of Monte Carlos, I will let you know." Lucia hesitated a little bit. She wanted to ask about how she could train as a teacher since her father was a poor peasant, who could never have enough money to even pay for her primary education, let alone teacher training? As though Father Gilbert had read her thoughts, he immediately informed her that the conditions for taking the course would be exactly the same as she did at St Paul's Mission. This is, work at the Mission as she attends school. She would also spend a period of three years teaching at one of the Monte Carlos' Primary schools without pay, but getting only food and lodging. "That would go towards payment for your training." Father Gilbert said, however, that for the moment they had to wait for the reply from Monte Carlos. Lucia was very grateful to Father Gilbert, who had offered to try and make all the arrangements for her admission into Monte Carlos Girls Teacher-Training School. She was jubilant, and thankful to God.

A week after her visit to Father Gilbert, Lucia was told to pack her few belongings for Monte Carlos Girls Teacher-Training School. Monte Carlos Mission was another Roman Catholic Mission Station, about forty-five miles east of Salisbury. It was made up of a teacher training and a Domestic Science School for girls and a co-education primary school.

Most of the teachers were white nuns, of German origin, a few African nuns, and a few African male and female teachers. This Mission was in another district quite a distance from Lucia's own district, and Chikwaka Reserve. The course was of two years duration and Lucia worked very hard on her studies. She wrote her final examinations and passed very well. The conditions of work here were different. She could at least go away from the mission during school holidays for some days, which she could not do at St Paul's. So teaching at Monte Carlos was more interesting, because she felt she developed a sense of responsibility, as a person. And the very interaction with other independent teachers and not nuns all the time, gave her the confidence she so much needed after her experience at St Paul's Mission. The Monte Carlos conditions permitted her to visit her father at home during the holidays, as well as visiting her uncle and aunt, Mr and Mrs Gumbo in Salisbury's Harare African Township.

Garikayi Gumbo was a brother to Lucia's mother, Prisca. He had run away from a Roman Catholic Mission school where he was doing his sixth year of primary school. His Christian name was Gregory. His father, Luke Gumbo, was a herdman at the Mission and was a staunch Catholic. His work was to look after the Mission farm cattle and was staying at the Mission. Gregory's father had conspired with the priests at that Mission to have him Gregory, become a priest. His father had imagined: 'The son of a poor herdman becoming a priest and conducting mass! He must be called Father Pio! (the name of the Pope of those days).' Gregory rejected this idea. They persuaded him. They prayed for him. They used every persuasive trick, until they started to use all kinds of coercive measures and threats; threats about God descending from Heaven to punish him severely because he was refusing to serve God. Life became more than difficult for Gregory. They actually used to punish him, saying it was God's will. He escaped from the Mission one Monday night. Then he started to live from one small town to another, form one European farm to another, doing all sorts of manual jobs. And most of the time he stayed or went without a job, so he went hungry, without shelter, and with very little to cover his body.

He had given himself the name, Garikayi, which means, 'Live well', instead of Gregory. He had changed his name first because, he thought, he wanted to break his links with the Mission as much as possible. Secondly, because he did not want anyone from the Mission to trace him while using the name Gregory. He also did not want to be recognised by any one of his father's distant relatives through this name. Garikayi moved on continuously until he settled in Salisbury where he eventually got a job as a 'house-boy'. Later he was employed as a bus conductor with the Salisbury United Bus Company. He worked for this company until he was promoted to bus driver position. And because of his level of education, he sometimes worked as a clerk for the same company.

Garikayi Gumbo became one of the black people in Rhodesia who were termed 'town-fellows'. He actually had no home to go to. He had developed crude and rough mannerisms in his daily dealings with hard life and his fellow Zimbabweans. He developed a very negative attitude towards religion and its propagators, and to him, they were the Catholic priests and nuns. He cultivated a special hate for Catholicism. He used to say: "Catholics, those priests, nuns and the so-called brothers and their chosen life of celibacy, are hypocrites in front of the Heavens. How can a man or woman stay without a wife or husband? God wants people to multiply. How can they?" Garikayi married Emma. Emma's father was also a 'town-fellow', and Emma was what people termed a 'born-location', meaning a child born and bred in the segregated African locations of the vast Rhodesian urban centre.

Such children were generally regarded by people from the rural areas, as bad mannered, lacking in traditional and customary behaviour that was a mark of the well behaved rural born and bred child. Emma had no experience of life in the rural areas. So, the two, Emma and Garikayi somehow looked down upon and actually despised people from the rural areas as 'uncivilised, uncouth and generally backward'. Gumbo and his wife were a great contrast to Lucia's father and his wife, her step mother, who were the typical 'reserve-fellows', simple and seemingly satisfied by their lot. That was Lucia's background too, simple and seemingly....

Chapter 7

The following day after the meeting, Mrs Gumbo requested Lucia to accompany her to town to buy some things. "We will go through the heavy industrial sites of Salisbury," said Mrs Gumbo. "You must see the hub of the white man's oppression in Zimbabwe." They boarded a bus labelled 'City via Industrial Sites'.

During their trip through the industrial sites, Lucia saw large notices almost at every gate they passed. The notices read; 'HAPANA BASA' (there is not work). At the same gates multitudes of men, Africans thronged the gates in the blazing sun. Lucia wondered what those people were doing around the gates. She whispered to her aunt, "I'm sure some of those men can read the 'hapana basa' signs?"

"Yes, of course, they can," answered Mrs Gumbo.

"Then what are they waiting for?" In her reply Mrs Gumbo said:

"Well, Lucia, you see, it's a long story," she did not want to discuss this in the bus as she was aware of the presence of police informers everywhere. So she said, "Can you raise the issue with your uncle when we come back home in the evening?" They reached the town. "Let's look for a pair of shoes for you Lucy. What size do you wear?" asked Mrs Gumbo.

They went from store to store looking for a pair of shoes. They entered an Asian shop. The Asian who stood behind the counter had seemed bored to death. But as soon as he saw them enter, he started to shout, his mouth red hot with whatever stuff he was chewing. Lucia could not tell what kind of stuff that makes one's mouth and teeth so ugly. The stout Asian with a bald head went on shouting, "Tenga lo, lokabudula. Lomatako kayena enayazi shakala, lokabudula enashala (buy this good pair of shorts for your son, his buttocks will wear out and the shorts will stay good)". As usual, the Asian shop-keeper has assumed that the two women were from the rural areas and were in the city shopping for their boys' short khaki pants for school. Lucia and her aunt ignored the Asian salesman and went on to look at a row of ladies shoes, displayed in the centre of the shop. Mrs Gumbo did not like any of those shoes displayed. Outside the shop, Mrs Gumbo turned to Lucia and said, "Did you notice the language that the Asian shopkeeper used in talking us into buying the boys' shorts?"

"Yes," answered Lucia, "And I thought it was a joke. 'All his buttocks will wear out, and the pants will remain? It was my first time to hear that one," said Lucia rather lightly.

"But it wasn't a joke. That's how we are talked to, you know." Mr Gumbo was serious. She went on explaining, "The Asian shopkeeper saw two nannies, whether from the bush or not, and he decided to advertise for boys shorts, using such derogatory language. We are disregarded so." They reached the city centre, and they walked into another shop in First Street. The situation was different there. As soon as they entered the main door, there was notice, "AFRICANS THIS WAY" with an arrow pointing to the side for Africans only. They went to this side. No one came to serve them. No one seemed to even recognise their presence. Lucia noticed that the shoes this side and those where the Coloureds, Indians and Europeans were shopping were almost the same. The price was the same also. Then why the discrimination? She wondered. They however, were eventually served by a coloured girl who seemed as if she would vomit if she touched African money. "This shop has the best shoes, though I hate shopping in here," Mrs Gumbo said as they left the shop.

"But the shoes were just as good as those displayed on the other side? Some of the people there were even as black as I am," declared Lucia.

"You see, in occupied Zimbabwe, Asian and Coloured communities benefit from the white man's system of divide and rule," explained Mrs Gumbo. "The way to pay the system for most of them is to act accordingly. They also must show that the blacks are inferior to them," she went on, "They accept, willingly, the segregation on which the system is based. And the Africans suffer left and right, forwards backwards. Some light skinned African men and women in Rhodesia are going out of their way to play coloured in order to enjoy the few privileges given by the settler system." That evening, after supper, Lucia had another discussion with her uncle:

"Uncle, when we went to town this morning we took a bus which took us through the heavy industrial sites." Lucia informed. "We saw an unbelievable number of unemployed African men crowding around factory gates. We did not see any white men or Indians or Coloureds standing around those huge gates. Why is this so, yet there were notices warning them that there was no work?" Lucia curiously asked her uncle.

Mr Gumbo smiled. He was enthusiastic to impart some political and socio economic facts to Lucia as his role in politicising her. "You see, my dear, the reason is simple. The Africans already working in these factories are exploited. They work hard but receive very low pay.

When they complain they are thrown out of the jobs and new employees are taken on immediately. The white employers know that there is always a large number of unemployed Africans who, because of financial hardships, are ready to work for any exploitative wage." Gumbo continued, "A certain friend of mine with a family of six children has been out of work for almost a year and half now. He had protested and refused the job he was doing because of very low pay, but now he is among those waiting at those gates, to accept any wage as long as he can get something for his family." Lucia was learning fast, Gumbo noticed.

In the second week of Lucia's stay in Harare Township, Gumbo took her one Sunday afternoon to visit a family in Mabvuku Township, on the eastern side of the city of Salisbury. The father of the family, Mr Masara, was a close friend. He worked as an interpreter at the "Native Commissioner's" (Kwamudvviti). They had talked for so long, about the political and economic system in the country, that they had not realised it was so late. Lucia and Gumbo had to rush back to Harare Township. They had to catch a bus to the centre of the city. By then there would be no bus service to their part of the town.

They had just got off the Mabvuku bus, at the Central bus station and were walking towards Harare Township, when a tall black constable emerged as if from nowhere: "Chitupa! Chitupa!" he shouted, extending his open hand toward Gumbo but his eyes towards Lucia. 'Chitupa' was the registration certificate bearing all the details pertaining to the individual adult African male. He must carry it on him all the time. He must always remember his number until he died. Gumbo had forgotten his at the house. "What's your number?" the constable asked.

"I don't remember it," answered Gumbo.

"You know you are not supposed to be in the city centre at this hour?" shouted the policeman. "What were you two doing anyway, where were you?" he asked sarcastically, looking at Lucia threateningly. Gumbo had started to explain about the problem of buses. The policeman interrupted him. "You are under arrest you bastard!" he shouted, already hand-cuffing Gumbo. Lucia was shocked! She could not believe her eyes and ears.

"What shall I do?" she asked. "Please. Help me," she pleaded, almost crying, "I'm new here in town. I don't know the way to Harare Township".

"You shut up and go to hell, you bitch!" shouted the constable. Gumbo tried to say something protesting. He was shut up with a smack across his mouth. "You shut up!" shouted the constable and led him to the police station in Railway Avenue. Lucia was left alone. Filled with fright and helpless anger, she had to find her way to Harare Township.

Mrs Gumbo was already in bed. But she was so worried and restless that she could not sleep, when Lucia knocked at the door. After Lucia had explained what had happened, Mrs Gumbo became sad. But rather angrily, she said, "Garikayi knows very well that no black person is allowed to be loitering in the city centre so late at night. He is too much of a big mouth. He should have....Oh well...." She sighed heavily and urged, "Let's go to bed. We'll see what we can do tomorrow morning."

Early, the following Monday morning, Mrs Gumbo and Lucia were already waiting at the office of the General Manager of the United Bus Company which employed Gumbo as one of the senior bus drivers and clerk. After sometime waiting for him to arrive at his office, and the necessary red tape having been cleared, they were finally let in. They met a stocky and harsh looking white man of about forty-five who was the boss. Mrs Gumbo explained to him what had happened the previous night. Without saying anything to her, he picked up his phone and dialled. In a second he spoke, "Mr Pickford, the Member-in-charge, please". After a minute: "Hello, Peter, Rod here. Very well ideed. They're okay. Listen, Peter, one of my boys was picked up last night by one of your boys. He didn't have his papers, I guess. I suppose he couldn't prove to the satisfaction of your boys that he was working for us as a driver," he said. "Gumbo is his name, Garikai," he said again, certainly in response to a question from Pickford. "He can come straight down here. Thank you, Peter. Okay, thank you. Say hello to Ellen and the kids." He replaced the receiver, told Mrs Gumbo, "You can go home."

Lucia could not understand how the seemingly complicated case of last night could come to an abrupt end as its beginning. The process appeared so simple. Her uncle was released without any charge? She was surprised indeed, how the two white men collaborated to bend the law.

"You see my niece, in our country; the white man makes and unmakes the laws as he wishes, as long as it is to his advantage." Gumbo told Lucia in the evening when he came home. "The law works for his benefit and where it is in conflict with his interests he bends it. That is what happened." He went on, "My boss can't afford to lose drivers. Buses would stop running. If it means bending the law so that all drivers are at their wheels, the law will bend." She understood. She thought she was learning very fast.

Another day Lucia went into town accompanied by a friend of Mrs Gumbo, Mrs Ruth Chari. After walking around the city for a long time, they were tired and decided to pass through the Cecil Square garden to sit down and rest for a while. "Come, let's sit on this bench here." Mrs Chari invited Lucia to a particular bench under a leafy Jacaranda tree. "This place reminds me of a terrible incident I will never forget in my life." Mrs Chari told Lucia as she sat on the bench. "I was still green in Salisbury, you know. I had come to look for a job as a nanny or house girl, and was staying with my aunt in Magaba, a crowded section of Harare Township. This was before the Federation of Rhodesia and Nyasaland. Segregation by colour was at its highest peek then. I had just blindly walked into the beautiful park without too much care and sat on this bench, this very bench. As I was settling down relaxingly to read the newspaper I had just bought...."

'Hey you there, can't you read?' the voice enquired sharply. I turned round and saw a tall black policeman standing at a short distance from me, staring down at me intimidatingly..

"Who? Me?" I had asked politely.

'Yes, you of course, who the devil do you think I am talking to? You can't sit there. Can't you see, there is a notice on that bench which tells you clearly that you have no right to set on it?' asked the policeman. I looked at him surprisingly and then at the bench. Sure enough, there was the notice, 'WHITES ONLY'.

"Alright, alright, I'll be going in a minute." I said politely, adjusting myself to a better sitting position.

'What? Aren't you getting off that bench just now? Are you out of your mind? Go and sit on those over there for 'Blacks only' if you want to sit in this park. Do you understand me?' he asked. 'Get going unless you want me to lift you up and throw you into the cell just now!' The policeman said threateningly. I stood up and looked at the policeman:

"Hey, you don't have to chase me like a dog. I did not see that I had sat on a 'Whites only' bench, I said, still very polite." 'Can't you read? Where did you go to school?' asked the policeman sarcastically. 'Open your eyes girl and learn manners.'

"What do you think? I retorted and continued, "My brother, this bench wont change colour and become black just because a black person sat on it. You just want to harass me for nothing. I wonder for what and for whom?" I said gathering my things. I was now angry and was almost crying.

"Before I could stand up the policeman had come closer and said harshly, 'Woman, I don't need your talk! Do you hear? You are wasting my time! I've been quite patient with you. Come now!' he commanded.'You can give your talk at the police station!' The policeman was already dragging me by the arm and pushing me roughly in front of him.

'Move! I have no time to waste arguing with a stupid woman like you,' he said. I could not say anymore. I was pushed and shoved and was taken to a cell, where I spent the night, shivering and very angry.

"The following morning I was brought before a white magistrate. My aunt and her friends had got worried when I did not return home the previous day. They had gone to the police station, the previous night, to report their niece's disappearance, only to be told that I was locked up. They had wondered what exactly I had done. Now they were already seated in the front row of the court room, anxious....

"I was charged with being a public nuisance and obstructing a police constable in the execution of his lawful duties. I was surprised! I had thought I would be charged with sitting on a 'Whites only' bench in the park, but not this one. I was fined ten pound." Mrs Chari went on, "However, this shocking segregation of benches in the parks was outlawed at Federation." Lucia was learning quickly, she thought of that day her uncle had spent a night in police custody for the so-called loitering in the city centre late at night, with a girl. Now this Mrs Chari too had had that sort of experience, but had to pay a fine; very interesting indeed. In both cases the settler regime's system had shown them its power to do or not to do.

The following day Lucia requested her uncle who was off duty that day to accompany her to visit the Party headquarters in Highfield Township. She wanted to see whether the Party was also a power capable of asserting itself so that the hateful system that ruled their country could be brought down. Lucia and her uncle were welcomed and were shown around the offices. She was introduced to some party full-time functionaries. They seemed to be men and women who were not afraid and were ready for any situation, she thought. The publicity office was a large room with two long tables. On each table was a typewriter and typists busy with their work. Two men were working on the duplicating machine. Others were sorting out the papers and stapling them.

This office had more people, both men and women, than any other office in the building, Lucia observed. The three women who were working in the publicity office inspired Lucia even more.

She wished she could be like them, to serve the Party and the oppressed people of her country. There was honour and spiritual satisfaction, she thought, in working for and serving the people and one's country. Lucia noticed a closed door at the far end of the large room. The door was marked, 'General and publicity Secretary'. That must be Mr Murambiwa's office, she thought and wished he was there to see her and talk to her. She went round the publicity room looking at the papers. She picked up one. On the cover were printed 'THE VOICE OF THE PEOPLE'. She was told that it was the Party's monthly publication, and she was given a copy as well as some back issues. Then someone went to a hidden corner of the shelf and fished out another copy and gave it to Lucia, saying: "This was the first issue of the party which was published when the N. D. P. was launched. The editors of this particular issue were arrested," the man whispered, "because of the editorial comment. They were fined heavily and were warned not to publish any more of such subversive articles." He added, "Go and read it; but be careful," he continued "It's a prohibited paper."

Lucia found herself, to her uncle's surprise too, encouraging and telling those men in the publicity office, "Don't you worry. Just continue steadfastly and don't be afraid, or be intimidated by that white power. We are behind you whole heartedly," she said. "The people will win, they are bound to win, no matter what." Her uncle decided they should leave the premises for Lucia was getting carried away. She was given more party literature to read at home. She also requested for the party membership card. Her uncle paid for it and they left the office. Outside the office, Gumbo tried to warn Lucia not to be in such a hurry. She should take things slowly and easy otherwise she would put herself in danger with the settler police informers who were all over watching every card-carrying member of the N. D. P.

From Highfield they went via some of the settlers' residential suburbs. She was really surprised by the contrast between these houses and those in Harare and Highfield Townships. This part of the town, her uncle told her, had been the most fashionable before the new suburbs began to sprout and spread. There were several avenues of big sprawling houses in big gardens.

They had been built for both physical and mental comfort, by people with money. They were an impression, in fact, of the type of colonialists whose families have been in the traditional habit of administering this part or that part of the fizzling colonial Empire. The colonialists were accustomed to making themselves comfortable in different climatic conditions provided by the empire. Lucia could see that comfort was their key-note at the expense of the black man. She saw and observed the so-called boys' Kaias, the 'servants' quarters. These small four cornered holes were built in a row along the end of the back gardens. She could see that it was not because these white people intended to make their servants comfortable, but because they meant to have as many servants as they could, and to have them as near as possible for easy use. "These people have such large houses. The rooms of these houses must be very large and cool," Lucia remarked. "Look at those enormous veranders, and the big the gardens!" Lucia said, "Ah! Uncle, I have had enough of looking at the oppressors' posh houses and comfort. It's been an eye opener anyway," she commented.

On their way back to the Harare's New Location, they passed through a small shanty African township called 'Magaba' – which means 'tins', Lucia remembered. This was where Mrs Chari was staying with her aunt before the Federation? Lucia could not help smiling sourly as the poverty deepened around her. Some of the 'houses' were made of nothing but sheets of plastic paper and a collection of tins spread out into sheets of zinc. These were patched together to form the walls and roof of a one roomed house; just a one-roomed 'house'. Some of those shacks held more than one family, her uncle explained. She could see miserable, ragged children everywhere, washed clothes hanging across door-ways, open gutters running filthy water. They were such concentrated slums; the kind of which she never thought existed in her own country. "Actually among these were the first houses built for African urban workers in those early days of colonialism," Gumbo explained. "The planning and development of all Rhodesian towns during this period was based on the assumption that African workers in the towns were sojourners. They could be housed in peri-urban shanty settlements," Gumbo continued to explain. "The Africans were only 'supplying the needed labour' to the white man's cities, and were therefore, not expected to be permanent residents of the towns and cities. Their place was in the reserved areas. And they could only come to the towns to solve a labour problem for the white man."

Lucia and her uncle moved on through the Old Bricks, another shanty settlement. They passed heaps of rubbish tins thickly covered, with the sluice of every imaginable kind of waste matter – filth! Filth, nothing else but filth! They passed the communal bathrooms. Holes in the back walls of the bathrooms, filled with strands from communal sponges. The walls and floors were covered with green moss and old soapy suds mixed with dirt, the scum of long ago. Water was trickling out of the baths and a strange nasty stench coming from there permeated all the air around the place. It was saddening, Lucia remarked. They moved in such surroundings until they reached the so-called New Location and Gumbo's house.

Lucia was tired, but she was pleased with herself for the work she had done that morning. She set out to read the Party papers that she had brought from the Party office. The first publication of the N. D. P, the one that prompted the arrest of the editors was more attractive to her. She had been told that it was a banned copy, she might get arrested if found reading it. So, she locked herself in her room and began to read:

"The struggle for the liberation of Zimbabwe started as long back as 1890 and 1896 when some strangers of a pinkish colour invaded our country from the south, and took our land. They used inexhaustive means of repressions to dehumanise, domesticate and to condition us both physically and psychologically. Violence was used to enslave us in our own country...."

"Only violence can uproot the colonialist settler. People, who are ruled by violence, must use violence to recover their lost land and rights. These were unconditionally usurped by force. The settler understood his own language – the language of force and violence. The people had to understand and adapt that language. The colonialist settler understands nothing but force! The people must answer settler violence with their own violence for national liberation," the editorial ended. There was also another article which reminded the people about how the Africans were enticed by false promises to join the colonial army to go and fight the Hitler Germans. For those who managed to come back, the promises were never fulfilled but their white-counterparts were fruitfully remunerated. No wonder the call for violence, Lucia thought.

She read the articles repeatedly. They inspire her to make a decision to join the struggle, just like the speeches she had heard at the meeting. Lucia had never actually known the true history of how the white people came to be masters of the people of Zimbabwe and elsewhere on the giant continent of Africa. She had known only that the white people had brought the Holy word of God to save the black people from eternal hell fire. In her history lessons nothing had been mentioned about how the people of Zimbabwe stood against guns during the period of colonisation. She realised that the colonialist oppressor needed 'violence' to oppress our ancestors, she thought, so we now also need 'violence' to free ourselves and our posterity. The people are sure that violence will stop this oppression just as they are sure that violence will perpetuate this oppression. Lucia felt the urge to fight theses oppressors? All men and women, including myself, must join this army, she thought. After all we will be far too many compared to the whites. I don't see why we can't wipe them out within a few weeks of the fighting. Little did Lucia realise the growing militancy in her.

It was a fact, she was spiritually and gradually developing militant nationalism, Gumbo and his wife observed when she suggested this to them.

From Rungano, the teacher, her uncle had brought her books on political philosophy. Some of the books which interested her most were: "Towards Colonial Freedom" and "Africa Must Unite", by Osagyefo Kwame Nkruma; "The wretched of the Earth," by Franz Fanon; "Freedom and Unity", by Julius Kambarage Nyererem and a few more.

After two weeks, before the end of her vacation, the leaders of the N. D. P. were released on bail pending trial. Lucia as well as many people was extremely happy. She thought there was now a chance to meet the people she had admired since that Sunday morning at the N. D. P. meeting. These people had changed her life completely. In the evening, Mr and Mrs Gumbo took Lucia to Mrs Chake's house in Highfield Township where all the leaders and other prominent Party members were grouped for the evening. Lucia was introduced to the leaders and other members of the Party. Her uncle told them that she had just joined the Party and how eager she was to meet the leaders. He also told them how ready, above all, she was to work for the Party in any capacity. She was welcomed with cheer and admiration. "She is a rare case," Mrs Chake told the others, "because many women and girls took a long time to join the struggle. They usually think that politics and the struggle are for men only. Did you say she is a teacher at Monte Carlos?" Mrs Chake asked and without waiting for an answer she went on, "That was my school. The brain washing that goes on there!" she added. "This child is one of the many Zimbabweans who have been kept in the dark for too long by one of the white minority regime's apparatus of oppression," she continued, "We must rejoice in the fact that she has now realised the truth that she had been cheated all her life. She is now embracing the idea of fighting for her country to shake off that blanket of darkness and oppression," ended Mrs Chake. She was quite an orator, Lucia thought. But she was telling the truth about her, Lucia told herself.

Lucia became the centre of attention that evening. She, in her quiet manner, was able to tell them more about herself. About how the priests and nuns in collaboration with the 'Native Commissioner' were telling people in the 'reserves' that they must not listen to the voice of the towns' people. The blacks in the towns were thugs and hooligans who were after committing grave crimes against the civilised Christian Government.

Murambiwa, the Publicity Secretary was much more interested in Lucia as a new member who could recruit more members for the Party in her area. She herself had admired Murambiwa right from the start. He was the one who had inspired her and encouraged her with his inciting speeches at the N. D. P. meeting, that Sunday morning.

Lucia had believed that Murambiwa would be the right person to teach her more about politics and the struggle. Murambiwa appeared a courageous person who was no talker but an actor and a fighter, she thought. And that was what Lucia wanted: to be a fighter, and not a talker.

"You are telling us that you would like to leave teaching, at Monte Carlos and come here," Muranbiwa said to Lucia. "Are you afraid to continue there while working for the Party?" he asked and added, "We would have liked you to stay there and recruit more members and open new branches in that area. Do you think you can do that?"

"I think it will be difficult because we are never allowed to move about in the surrounding villages alone without the sisters," Lucia replied. "Party officials would visit the area occasionally to help you and to address the villagers," Murambiwa suggested.

Mrs Chake said, "Lucia, don't be afraid of those white people, the so called Missionaries. All we need to do is show them that we mean business then they won't do anything to you."

"You seem to have all the courage needed in a political Party worker," Miss Regayi remarked. "There are very few women working for the Party. Most of the girls and women are afraid to involve themselves. They think we are hooligans and lawless."

"I still think more is happening here in the towns than in the reserves," Lucia insisted. "I'd complete my contract at Monte Carlos and transfer to teach here." "You are mistaken Lucia," interjected Tapera, the national chairman. "The people who need more politicisation are more in the reserves than in the towns. So, we need you to remain at Monte Carlos as long as possible," Tapera encouraged.

Lucia replied that if the leaders strongly felt that she should remain at Monte Carlos and that by so doing she would be of greater use to the Party, then she would gladly remain there. She, however, did tell the Party leaders that the priests and nuns kept a very sharp and close eye on every black teacher and every grown up student at the Mission.

"You have to be used to that Lucia," said Miss Regayi. Tough Miss Regai, thought Lucia. Miss Regayi added, "If you didn't know, as we are sitting here in this room, we are being watched like the devils themselves. All of us are watched whether we are in buses or walking down the streets or inside our own little shanty houses, day and night, by the enemy," concluded the touch Miss Regayi.

Back at Monte Carlos after the holidays, Lucia had become a different person. She had vowed to work for the N. D. P. no matter what the difficulties. In her History classes Lucia clandestinely started to discuss politics to Standard sixes i.e. grade eight. She even discussed this subject with other selected pupils whenever she had a chance. The other teachers were afraid at first. But she was able to influence some of the lady teachers. Her influence steadily spread to the Teacher Training-Centre. Every weekend on Sunday afternoons, the Sisters, with some lady teachers including Lucia, took off to go around the villages teaching Catechism as usual. Lucia and a few others took that opportunity to pursue their political education among the villagers. Lucia and her friends would, after selecting their groups, go on to tell the villagers, briefly and quickly about the N. D. P, what it stood for and what type of government it hoped to establish after defeating the white minority regime. Lucia became popular among some of the teachers and especially among the student teachers, some of whom came from the towns.

From the Party Headquarters, Lucia was sent a big pack of Party membership cards. Equipped with these, Lucia slowly and carefully proceeded to recruit some members in the villages around the Mission Station of Monte Carlos and a branch was formed with headquarters in one of the villages. Top Party officials often visited the branch to boost the villagers' morale and to explain current issues to the new Party members. The frequent visits by Party officials from Salisbury were important, Lucia thought. It assured the villagers that Lucia had the full backing of the Party. It also showed that the party was well organised and was powerful and was concerned about the plight of the villagers.

One weekend, a public meeting was organised for Sunday afternoon. The meeting was to be addressed by Murambiwa, the Publicity Secretary and other Party officials from Salisbury. Lucia had carfully prepared the villagers for the meeting at the local branch office in one of the villages. On that day many peasants attended the rally. Nuns, both black and white showed up at the meeting as curious observers, Lucia thought. She and her teacher friends coolly placed themselves among the audience. The three officials addressed the meeting. Murambiwa the General and Publicity Secretary, was the main speak. He was a good and powerful speaker as usual, Lucia observed. He urged people to unite so as to fight oppression. As usual, his speeches were inciting and provocative. At the end of his speech the people rose to their feet, gave him an overwhelming ovation. They were filled with anger, though the cheering appeared a happy one.

It was not until one of the peasants, an elderly man burst into traditional war song that the anger that had remained burning within the chests of the peasants burst out. The elderly man had started and others had followed:

Nyika yedu yeZimbabwe ndimo matakazvarirwa
(Our land of Zimbabwe that is where we were born)
Vana mai nababa ndimo mavanobva
(Our mothers and fathers that is where they come from)
Tinoda Zimbabwe nehuphumi hwayo hwese
(We want Zimbabwe with all her wealth)
Simuka Zimbabwe
(Rise up Zimbabwe)
Zvaireva vakuru zvoitika – Hondo!
(What the elders predicted is about to happen – war!)

Zvaireva neHanda zvauyawo – Hondo!
(What neHanda predicted has come – war!)
Nyika yedu yakatorwa nevayeni!
(Our country which was taken by strangers/visitors)
Zuva rayo guru rasvika!
(Its big day had come)
Chorus:
Zimbabwe!! (Barritone)
Tinoda Zimbabwe !!
(We want Zimbabwe)
Dzimba dzemabgwe! (Barritone)
(Houses of stone)
Torwira Rusununguko-o!
(We fight for freedom)
Zimbabwe! (Barritone)
Tinodawo Nyika!
(We want the land)
Zuva rayo guru rasvika!
(Its big day has come)

The villagers began to point at the nuns, some were shouting angrily: "You there! What are you doing here?" A group of young men started to advance towards the nuns shouting, "These are the informers, the traitors! What are they doing here?" They went on, "Let's get rid of them!" And the crowd was giving them way. The nuns were frightened to death. They huddled together not knowing what to do. They could not believe that that was happening to them. Those were the same villagers who came to church and made confessions. Those were the same people whom the nuns always visited and taught Catechism and the way of Christianity and Catholicism. What had come over them, these Christians?

Lucia, realising the danger the nuns were in, she moved forward quickly. She dodged the people left and right until she was right in front of the audience, and on top of the table which had served as the speakers' platform:

"My brethren, may I have your attention!" Lucia shouted on the top of her voice, at the same time clapping her hands: "Please listen to me," she repeated, "Listen please." The singing stopped, and she said, "Listen, relatives (hama). What are these sisters here? They are nothing! They are not the wielders of the power that oppresses the people. They are simple souls who happen to have a white skin. Those of our kith among them," she pointed to the black nuns, "Are just as deceived as all of us. Look, they have to come to your meeting. They perhaps may not be traitors but sympathisers and supporters of your cause. Or they may just be curious observers?" She went on pleading, "Do not harm them. They may be on your side. Aim your arrows where it matters, not to these poor creatures." Lucia concluded by urging the crowd to disperse peacefully, "The revolution mentioned today has to be organised properly so that it is effective, and must be directed to the right people, the colonial regime and its system."

The villagers had become calm during Lucia's brief and impromptu appeal. That was a clever move by Lucia, thought Murambiwa. The sisters were very thankful to her too. She had saved their skins. To the settler security agents present, the maker of that brief speech did not warrant positive 'marking'. It was a short speech that saved the day, however.

The crowd had absorbed every syllable that had come from her mouth. The nuns on the other hand were unable to disguise their fear as well as their joy and appreciation to Lucia. She had saved them. Their eyes glittered with the thought of what might have happened to them if all those villagers had descended upon them.

After the meeting those who wanted to enrol as members of the N. D. P. came forward to the speakers' table and were quickly enrolled. The Party officials from Salisbury were impressed by Lucia's efforts. There was no doubt in their minds that Lucia was a capable organiser. She had good qualities of leadership, thought Murambiwa. Lucia, on her part, complained to the party officials about her limited field of action, because of the ever watchful and suspicious eyes of the priests and nuns. She informed the officials that she wanted to be involved, full-time, into the struggle. Above all, she said, she had begun to loathe mission life. "Today, I may have come out into the open by that brief speech I made. I don't know what to expect from those nuns tomorrow." She talked nervously, "I don't want to be sacked," se said and suggested, "I think I would like to resign despite the contract I have not yet completed."

At the mission, Lucia was treated with calculated coolness and indifference. No one in authority asked her about the incident at the meeting or about the Party. But she sensed an uneasy atmosphere. She was a changed person, one of the sisters, who was at the meeting, observed. In church services she would be there as if to observe how the crowd responded to it all. She would sit there and listen to the priest conducting the mass. That foreign ritualistic formula used by Catholics in their church services, she thought. She would listen to the priest's voice raised in toning the sonorous Latin sermon. African believers did not even understand what the priest said, she thought. Catholicism! She had begun not to like it, especially its propagators, who were well protected by the segregatory regime.

All those prohibitions! Don't do that, don't do this, God forbids this, and that, were all repression and oppression of the worst kind. Oppression in the name of God, thought Lucia, 'Kusiri kufa ndekupi apa (what's not death here)?'

Father Leo, the principal of Monte Carlos Mission did not try to refuse Lucia's resignation when she applied for it. He thought Monte Carlos could be better off without 'ungrateful' girls like Lucia, so ungrateful she wants to start trouble here with the government. But Lucia had already sowed the seeds of revolution. The fathers and nuns were quick to notice that more and more villagers were no longer turning up for the usual Saturday confessions. The Sunday church attendance had dwindled too. The Fathers or nuns could not stop the fast blowing wind of nationalism merely by accepting Lucia's resignation from Monte Carlos, they realised.

Chapter 8

Lucia found a job as a teacher in one of the Government Primary Schools in Salisbury's Highfield African Township, the nerve centre of the African political activities. She became very active in the political struggle despite the settler regime's order that African teachers or nurses, as civil servants, should not participate in politics. She was very happy, to work with Tapera and his colleagues for a few days before they were sentenced to prison terms ranging from five to ten months. But usually, after they have served the stated sentences, some would be detained indefinitely, Mr Gumbo had informed her.

After a few months, the workers – the African Trade Union Congress (ATUC) working in conjunction with the N. D. P. declared a country-wide strike for higher wages and better working conditions. African cheap labour was vital for ensuring the comfort of the white settlers; the TUC leaders had weighed the situation. One or two days without the vital labour force, the entire settler industrial complex and comfort, would be reduced to rubble of chaos.

That was the biggest industrial action by African workers in the history of Southern Rhodesia (Zimbabwe). The settler industries were paralysed for three days, not to mention the accumulation of garbage in the white suburbs like Highlands, Newlands, Alexandra Park, Hillside, Mount Pleasant, Kumalo in Bulawayo and other white settler residential areas in the other towns. All the ATUC affiliated unions were involved.

When the police decided to move in to force the Africans to go to work, real trouble started. In Highfield Township alone, some policemen were killed and several others were wounded. Soldiers had to be called in to help the police. The riots were so serious that some African policemen and soldiers were disarmed and arrested bt the settler regime for refusing to carry out orders to beat people and force them to go to work. The United Omnibus Company lost four or six passanger buses in Harare and Highfiled Townships alone, not to mention what happened in other towns like Bulawayo, etc.

A state of emergency was declared. The N. D. P. and the Trade Union Congress were banned and all leaders plus many people, man and women were arrested. Party vehicles and property were confiscated. Schools were closed. Additional Police stations and police posts were set up in most Government school grounds in most of the African Townships, large and small. Large areas were surrounded by barbed wire and set up to accommodate all the people – women, men, boys and girls who were rounded up. Classrooms were used as temporary cells.

Lucia was not taken in, however. In fact, most teachers, nurses and other hospital workers were never touched. They were not supposed to be politicians but civil servants in support of the government.

Highfield was closed by surrounding it with rolls of barbed wire. All Africans who wanted to go in and out of Highfield Township had to be stamped with indelible ink on their left hand palms. They had to show these marks each time they passed through the checking points. Lucia's mark lasted for over four months. Lucia noticed that armed soldiers, riot police with their Alsatian dogs, were prowling the back streets of the locations and in beer halls day and night. They were arresting all those whose 'looks' they happened to dislike. That was the harshest and the longest state of emergency in the history of the country.

Eventually the schools were reopened and the numerous police stations and police posts were dismantled, leaving only a few. And the settler soldiers eventually returned to their barracks.

The situation became helplessly quiet, because thousands of people were now in jails, restricted areas or detention camps. Those who still walked the streets of the segregated townships were scared to death for their lives and those of their families. For a time, it seemed to Lucia, the settler regime had succeeded in breaking the spirit of resistance among the Zimbabweans. But under this silence was the continued deep seething hatred for foreign rule and oppression and repression, which was getting even harsher.

For Lucia and many others the situation was frustrating. However, as days went by, more and more people were returning from detentions and restrictions. The minority regime was carrying out what it called 'screening operation'. The hard core was left inside.

Teachers such as Rungano and Lucia were among a group of men and women who organised a secret study group. A new Party had to be formed. The people could not be left alone without any directive voice to follow. Things could not be left like that without anyone saying anything while the political situation deteriorated. One Saturday morning the group came up with the launching of a new Nationalist Party. It named all the detained leaders as it's office bearers. The new party, however, was destined for a short life. It was banned under the settlers' notorious Law and Order (Maintenance) Act, the law aimed at maintaining the so-called law and order, that is, detention without trial. The leaders of this short lived party got detained. Everyone who was connected with the new Party was taken in for questioning, and eventual arrest and detention without trial.

Lucia, like all other teachers remained free. She thought that was the end of the struggle for the liberation of the oppressed people of Zimbabwe. Couldn't she do something? She asked herself. But what could she do? Weeks and weeks of frustrating silence passed. Harsh, vicious and more repressive laws were passed by the colonial settler racist Parliament. These laws were to strengthen the Emergency Powers. Africans were manhandled at every turn in the street or at work. The secret informers, both men and women increased in numbers. The same oppressed sons and daughters of Zimbabwe, turned to the police as informants for a sickening fee. 'This is terrible!' Lucia told herself. The emergency regulations forbade any groupings. A group of more than three adult Africans was considered a mob, dangerous to the settler regime.

In these conditions, Lucia decided, it was not wise any more to remain in the city. She decided to leave Salisbury. Perhaps she could do more in the rural areas, giving political education to some primary school children most of whom did not know much of what was happening in the towns. She thought, maintaining contacts with the peasants could be better than brooding over the emergency powers of the settler regime. Resistance could still be organised somewhere, she thought.

She asked for a transfer and was posted to teach at Muzhanje Primary School in Chiweshe Reserve, to the North of Salisbury. During her History periods she privately gave political education, of course without any planned notes. She gave different notes to her pupils to write in their exercise books, just for the settler inspectors' notice. But most of the oral work was about the scramble for Africa and the political struggle for the liberation of Zimbabwe. Lucia began her clandestine and well calculated visits to the surrounding villages and other neighbouring schools to talk to other teachers and some of the peasants.

Peasants in Chiweshe Reserve had long been exposed to political activities by the N D P workers before the Party was banned. So it was not difficult for Lucia to start a political conversation whenever she visited any one of the villages. In Chakanyuka village, one day, she had been discussing with old man Munyoro and other village elders. Munyoro was quite militant. He was once arrested and was fined for burning his 'chitupa' and refusing to pay poll-tax. He was very bitter about how the peasants were being forced to follow what he called useless orders. He said, "Teacher Kashangu what you are saying is true," old man Munyoro was in agreement with what Lucia had just said. He went on, "Since the white man began to rule us we have never been allowed to till the land and plant whatever we want and as much as we are able to.

That is what our fathers did. Tell me," old Munyoro continued in a low voice, "What do I do with cotton or tobacco which they force us to plant?" He went on, "How can I feed my children on cotton and tobacco?" Old man Munyoro concluded, his face was tense and shaking his head. He was showing those who were looking at him, that, he was an angry old man. He was a man who had grown up and aged, tortured by the white minority regime system, Lucia noticed.

"VaMunyoro, don't forget that the 'Native Commissioner' also never forgets to demand poll-tax from each one of us," said a short, stout old man who had so far remained quiet and attentively listening to the conversation. "Although we don't have enough to feed ourselves, poll-tax must be paid in cash, without failure. Where we get money for this taxation, the 'Native Commissioner' is never interested," the stout old man continued, shaking his head sadly. "We are never allowed to own as many herds of cattle as our forefathers used to do."

As she listened to the discussion, Mrs Taneta one of the women who were present, suddenly felt she had a question, and without waiting for the men to finish their points she asked: "I wonder how these white people get to know just how many herds of cattle we have besides those they wrote in our cattle-books?"

"Have you forgotten that you take your cattle for dipping every other week?" Lucia sked, reminding her.

"Ho-o-o-o," old man Munyoro cut in, "I now see why the dip supervisor Jakopo is always in attendance on the dip days. He stands at the mouth of the dip tank, with pencil and notebook in hand and never winking for a second."

"Yes, man, I have observed him myself," said Mrs Taneta, "After calling the name of a villager and ordering the person to have his cattle splash in, he stands there counting continuously and closely examining each herd of cattle that jumps into the dip-tank and noting something in his notebook.

"Of course, that way he is able to compare the results of his count and what was recorded in your 'Dipping-book,'" said Lucia.

"Okay, from now on I will not take my calves for dipping. That way the devils will never know just how many more I have," Mrs Taneta declared.

"That won't help," warned Lucia, "because the other duty of the dip supervisor is to detect any pregnant or nursing cows and that's why he examines them closely before they dip."

"Ah! It is better then not to dip our cattle at all," resolved old man Munyoro.

"Yes, but imagine if we had our own government like the people in Nigeria, Kenya, Ghana, Tanganyika and so on, dipping facilities for our cattle would be provided for the health of our livestock, only and not for de-stocking" Lucia informed, "we would pay tax most probably, but that would be to enable our government to buy the medicine for the dip tanks, to build more schools for our children, better roads and more hospitals in the countryside,as well as providing better facilities for our cattle's health." She went on, "We would probably plant cotton and tobacco as cash crops, first, because our government would buy them from us at fair prices. Secondly, our government may ask us to plant these crops only after making certain that we already have adequate land from which to produce food crops. I am saying this because this is what our brethren in free African countries are doing." Lucia said this, fixing her eyes at old man Munyoro, who kept on nodding his head at his colleagues.

Such discussions would be repeated in several other villages where Lucia visited, and the participants always ended up with certain resolutions to counter the oppressive measures of the colonial regime. The effect of Lucia's political discussions with the villagers was seen when the peasants in Chiweshe Reserve refused to pay poll-tax and refrained from taking their cattle to the dipping tanks because, if any peasant was found to own more than the stipulated number of cattle, the extras were slaughtered or sold at an open market. The peasants thought it was wise not to dip their cattle and other livestock at all to avoid this.

One dipping day, early in the morning, the dip Supervisor, Jakopo, discovered two dip tanks filled with stones, sticks and sand. No peasant had brough their cattle for dipping that day. He notified the Native Commissioner. And within a few hours whole villages were swarmed with armed police. All the villagers in that area, including women and children were taken in open lorries to the nearest police station in Mazoe. Women and children were whipped and sent home. And none of the men escaped without a heavy fine or heavy prison sentences or detention.

On the wall map in the Police Commissioner's office in Salisbury, this area was marked with a red drawing pin identifying it as a trouble spot.

Although schools were not touched by the police during their raid on the villages, the District Native Education Inspectors who were always whites were on the alert. They started to visite the schools at any time without the usual notification. One day, on a Monday, a Mr Bloomfield came to Muzhanje Primary School very early in the morning, before the school started. The teachers and pupils found him roaming around the buildings as if trying to detect something suspicious.

Bloomfield's behaviour surprised and even annoyed the Headmaster, Mr Sanganayi, the teachers and even some of the pupils. "What is the white man doing here?" the pupils were asking each other surprisingly. They were even afraid that he could have brought the police and soldiers with him; but for what?

"We did not receive any word that an inspector would come would come to this school on this day?" The headmaster, Mr Sanganayi greeted the white inspector with the question and went on, "May I know whether this is an official visit or a private visit?"

"What do you think?" Bloomfield asked, and added, "And you have no right to talk to me like that! I am an education officer of the Government, don't you know?" Bloomfield shouted, throwing his hands recklessly in the air.

"Of course I know you, but, I have all the rights and reasons, and plenty of them," Mr Sanganyi replied with the same relevant force in his tone. The two men exchanged harsh words right there in front of the pupils and the teachers who were arriving at the school. Eventually the inspector, after the morning assembly, was accompanied in to every classroom by the head teacher. When they entered Lucia's classroom, the pupils did not stand up as was the custom. The teacher went on talking as if nothing had happened. The inspector was infuriated.

"What are you teaching here?" The question was thrown to the teacher with such a deafeningly loud voice that some pupils were startled. Lucia did not move she simply turned and looked at Mr Bloomfield for a second and turned back to her pupils, "Children...."

"Answer my question!" the inspector demanded furiously. Lucia did not answer the question. Instead she said:

"Mr Bloomfield, you are disturbing the progress of the lesson, please. This is very unprofessional, and is against the principles and practice of education, don't you think?" Lucia wanted to continue with her lesson disregarding Mr Bloomfield who was by now walking towards the front of the class, hitting the floor with his boots so loudly that the pupils sat very tensely in their seats. The settler inspector ordered the class to stand up. The class remained seated looking at their teacher.

"Stand up, I said!" he repeated the order. The pupils became afraid of the white man and were about to stand up when Lucia shouted:

"Sit right where you are children and don't move an inch!" The pupils obeyed their teacher and not the white inspector, whose face's pigmentation had turned to different shades of red, purple and pink many times over. The muscles around his eyes, nose and mouth were twitching madly with anger.

No one could predict his next action. Sanganayi, the Head teacher, had to intervene. The pupils were ordered to go outside. Then Sanganayi spoke, supporting Lucia's actions, at the same time blaming the behaviour of the settler inspector of education: "You disturbed the progress of the class Mr Bloomfield. Your question was irrelevant because you had not given yourself time to listen to the theme of the lesson. You just barked: 'What are you teaching here?' right at the door of the classroom and most pupils were startled." Sanganayi continued, "I think, Mr Bloomfield, you should admit your actions were unprincipled and unethical." As Sanganayi was making his remarks, the humiliated inspector was busy making notes in his notebook. His face never stopped twitching and his hand trembled with rage.

"What's your name, your full name?" the inspector asked Lucia. She spelt her surname out. Bloomfield wrote it down with great difficulty because of the shaking of his hands. He repeated the name to Lucia, and after getting the assurance that it was correctly spelt, he stormed out of the classroom without any other word. To the headteacher's surprise, Mr Bloomfield just walked away as briskly as he could. He had hidden his car away from the school yard because he thought he wanted to enter the school unnoticed. After Bloomfield's departure everything appeared tense. Lucia and the headteacher expected the settler police to appear at the school at any moment to arrest them or something, but nothing happened. After a month, however, Sanganayi was transferred to a remote school in another district, many kilometres away from any nearest town.

Lucia continued with her work as usual at Mujhanje School. The new Head Teacher was an elderly man, short, with an increasing obesity. He did not seem to be interested in what was going on at the school. He was just busy asserting to the teachers, especially, the ladies, how experienced he was and how the girls got a kick out of him. Lucia had a good chance to carry out her clandestine political activities in the villages until the end of the school term.

Shupai (Lucia) in her hospital bed, recalled all these activities in her life. She imagined herself in front of that class at Muzhanje Primary School. The shouting that took place in that classroom between the Inspector and herself in front of those pupils! She thought it was very interesting! She sighed, moving herself a little. She winced violently; the pain in her ankle throbbed, pulsating up and down her spine. The pain drug she had been given was wearing off. She stayed like that, in terrible pain for another hour. She looked around the ward. There was no nurse in view. Her eyes became heavy. She bit her lower lip and closed her eyes. She thought, this pain....she felt a cool hand touch her wrist.

"Sarah," a voice called softly. Shupai opened her eyes and saw nurse Raina. "Have you been sleeping all this time?" nurse Raina asked, feeling Shupai's pulse.

"The pain is killing me, nurse," Shupai hissed out the words through clenched teeth. "I thought you had been resting peacefully all this time? I came round several times and observed you sleeping, peacefully, and I never thought you were in such pain." "U-ugh!" Shupai uttered shivering. The nurse glanced at her watch. She went into the duty room and opened the dangerous drugs cupboard and took out a vial of pethidine. She came back with a hypodermic syringe:

"It's time for your medicine," she told Shupai, quickly, inserting the needle into Shupai's upper arm. Shipai felt only an itchy prick on her skin. Nurse Raina is good, Shupai told herself. The first injections she got on admission had been very painful, she compared. But this one is not. "Hope you'll feel much better shortly," informed nurse Raina, straightening the bed sheets and patting the pillows.

In the women's surgical ward of Sinioa Hospital, Dr Mutero conducted his normal rounds twice a day. The white ward sister always accompanied the doctors during their rounds to see their patients. One morning, three days after Shupai had been in the hospital, Dr Mutero came into the ward. He went straight to Shupai and handed her an enveloped letter. He said, "Greetings from Tafi. He's doing very well in his new job." Shupai noticed that Dr Mutero looked fatigued, as if he had had a bad night. She received the letter and he went on to see his other patients.

In the letter, he had briefly informed Shupai: "Last night four more patients from your 'work place' were sent to the 'sick bay' (his private surgery)." The message went on, "One of them is critical. News from the 'city' (the front), as you know...." The sentence broke off and then continued, "Is not always good news. They lost three workers." She could not believe her eyes. She read the short message over and over again. She was trying to imagine who the dead were and who the wounded were. She knew the number of the comrades she had left the night she had got herself a dislocated ankle. Now who could these be! She went on visualising in her mind all her comrades in Munongwa's unit plus those in Tafirenyika's unit she had worked with that evening, or even those in Tichaona's unit. She could not ask Dr Mutero during his rounds, or couldn't she? She asked herself.

When Dr Mutero came to her bed, she wanted to say something. Dr Mutero signalled to her to keep quiet by touching his lips with his right forefinger. He did that while extending his left hand for the note. She handed the letter back to him. She was sad, Dr Mutero noticed, but very brave, he thought. "How do you feel today, Sarah?" he asked.

He touched her ankle to examine it. She winced with pain. He removed some of the weights from the traction and asked, "How does that feel?" "U-u!" she exclaimed, "Doctor, that's painful," the words were squeezed out of the throat through clenched teeth. "I'm sorry," Dr Mutero said softly replacing the weights he had removed. He waited a bit. Then he added a few more. "Now how is that?" he asked, Shupai just nodded, her eyes closed. "Alright sister," he said this to the ward sister without looking at her. The ward sister did not acknowledge. She appeared completely disinterested. She had never liked this patient, thought Dr Mutero. Actually, she had never liked any single girl patients; he knew this because he had observed her for a long time. She seemed to be worse with this particular patient, however. "Sister Higgins," Dr Mutero said, rather politely. "We've increased the weights here. Let's leave the ankle like this for a couple of days and continue with the same anti-inflammatory medication." Sister Higgins continued to be indifferent. She particularly hated this girl she said it to herself, looking at Shupai. Stupid girls who went about hurting their legs then they come in here pretending, she thought, just to attract this stupid doctor Mutero here. He really becomes nuts. He's particularly too nutty about this one, I can see. Exchange of letters, indeed in my ward! He's not even ashamed of himself! She hated him, and the patient as well, Sister Higgins thought she could not wait for the day this stupid bitch would be discharged. Dr Mutero observed Sister Higgins looking down at Shupai. She looked as if she was about to belch. The hate that this woman had! Dr Mutero thought. "Sister Higgins, did you here what I said?" "Yes, very loud and clear. Why do you ask?" "You're not writing anything down."

"I'll remember, alright." She kept standing. Dr Mutero took the papers from Sister Higgins and wrote his instructions down. He called to a senior nurse, who was in the same ward. "Mrs Mhaka, I want you to make sure all the instructions written are followed." He turned to Shupai and said, "I'll phone your work place and find out more about the disaster." He continued with his round and then left the ward.

Shupai was in terrible pain after the examination by Dr Mutero. But the pain on the ankle was nothing compared to the pain she had to bear about her comrades. She kept on asking herself. Who could these be? Munongwa? Not him, please. She mentioned to herself the names of those she knew. When she came to Shonhiwa she felt like crying. Shonhiwa? Oh No! Not him. Not Shonhiwa Gidi. Zimbabwe is not yet free. No, he could not be one of them. Shonhiwa is my future....She covered her face with the bed sheet and actually cried. The senior nurse Mrs Mhaka noticed her. She came and uncovered her face softly, "Sarah, are you in terrible pain, can we call back Dr

Mutero? He is still around, you know." Shupai just waved her hand to say not. "But you are crying.

What is this disaster at your work that Dr Mutero mentioned? Is anyone dead at your work place?" Mrs Mhaka was actually patting her at the shoulders, concerned. Shupai just nodded her head. "What happened?"

"I really don't know. Doctor Mutero will phone for more details." "Try to calm down," consoled Mrs Mhaka, "I'll give you your medicines the doctor has just ordered." "Thank you so much Mrs Mhaka; you are so kind." Shupai continued to sob quietly. Then suddenly, a small voice inside her nudged: 'Look at you. You are actually crying! What kind of tears are these? You are not the crying type. After all the hardships you went through in your childhood? You never cried no matter what, now what?' The small voice went on, 'You want to mislead everyone in this ward to think you are in terrible pain? Is this self pity or something? Pain is there yes, but tears? No!' The voice was very decisive and clear. Okay, she agreed. But....she thought. 'But what?' the voice came back, 'There is a war out there, remember?' I haven't forgotten at all. Shupai said to herself as if answering the voice. These tears of mine are not going down for nothing! She now remembered the short report in Dr Mutero's note.

Munongwa's unit had been called to reinforce Tichaona's group. They had worked successfully on an operation, for almost the whole night. They had marched away from the point of engagement with the enemy, for a long distance. Most of the combatants were feeling the fatigue as the sun rose to reveal to the eye, Zimbabwe's natural beauty. Everyone felt like camping and resting. The guerrillas had not noticed that they had been spotted by an enemy surveillance team. This was a mercenary team which belonged to the crack Selous Scouts of the Rhodesian army. This mercenary unit was commanded by the blue eyed Lieutenant Wilson. Wilson was a seasoned mercenary. He was hefty and broad at the shoulders. He never smoked, but always chewing a gum. He fought in the Congo, in Mozambique, in Angola and Namibia. He even talked of the Mau Mau in Kenya, and some life in Latin America. He had excellent mercenary references. The Rhodesian army did not hesitate to take him in. Wilson managed, within a short time, to train some of the local men, black and white and came up with the best, most vicious and most dreaded 'soldiers of fortune' in the mercenary history of Zimbabwe. Anti guerrilla warfare became their piece of cake.

Wilson called his men together and quickly explained to them a detailed ambush plan againts the "terrorist unit" seen in the area of their base. The freedom fighters were going to be ambushed. That was part of the game in guerrilla and anti-guerrilla warfare. The training on both sides of the hostile forces involved lessons and exercises in setting up ambushes against the enemy, as well as in breaking out of an ambush. The ambush was to take place at a convenient time and place. Wilson knew that the "terrorist" group would camp.

He banked on the fact that the guerrilla unit they were following would be busy by night and usually lies low by day. "We'll stay clear of any engagement with the terrs. They'll settle down to rest eventually. Then…." He hit his clenched right fist into his cupped left palm. "The surveillance team will stick onto the bastards' tail."

Almost everything that Munongwa's unit did was closely observed by Wilson's surveillance team. Inforamtion was regularly relayed back to the main mercenary unit. There was nothing that would have raised Munongwa's or any of his men's suspicions about being tailed in the manner they were. Everything appeared normal. After some time of walking, Munongwa ordered his unit to halt and prepare to rest for the day. As a regular precautionary measure, Munongwa posted sentries around the resting area. Guard duty was only to last one hour because Munongwa wanted each man to have the much needed rest.

Wilson was sure that the guerrilla unit was finally settling down to relax for the day. He and his men now had to move in cautiously and wipe out the 'terrorists'. Wilson's ambush unit took its time. It was within the rules to make certain that the surprise element in the ambush was perfect so as to be effective. So, Wilson wanted to make sure that every member of the 'terrorist' gang was either dozing and dreaming or completely relaxed.

Two and half hours passed, and Wilson's unit began to prepare to take their positions. In about thirty minutes, there would be action. It was exactly eleven o'clock in the morning. Wilson, with a radio-man next to him kept his visual contact with the resting guerrillas. His right eye muscles began to twitch violently. This was a sign that Wilson's adrenaline level had become high. He had become extremely excited. His blue eyes had changed into a cold grey. He was ready for action. His men knew these signs. They readied themselves accordingly. He ordered his men to inch in towards the unsuspecting guerrilla unit and tried to encircle it. Forward they moved cautiously. The mercenaries stopped moving as Wilson had given the signal. He thought continuous movement might jeopardise the operation. They might be noticed and….

Members of Munongwa's unit had been schooled and drilled also in this type of warfare. They had not omitted any essential precautions in setting their camp. Camouflage was essential in these jungles. It could very easily save one's life. Munongwa had made certain that camouflage was effectively used by each and every member before he could lie down, doze and/or dream.

From Wilson's vantage point, only a few 'terrorists' could clearly be seen. That was not good enough, thought Wilson. The ambush unit had to move still nearer if they were to overcome the effect of the camouflage, which was making it difficult for them to see the 'terrorists' clearly for the assault. An effective ambush attack required a good visual contact with the enemy. Ambushes were aimed at a complete wipe out of the enemy, Wilson maintained. You could not afford to fire anyhow, uncertain of the target.

Wilson's men were forced to crawl forward nearer the enemy. But, as soon as the men moved forward on their tummies, their movements were quickly detected by the vigilant sentries, of Munongwa's forces. A signal was immediately whistled to the commander. Munongwa immediately gave the sound signal to his men. Every member of the unit grabbed and clutched close to his body his life-line, his AK-47 assault rifle and other weapons. They waited to receive further orders. Munongwa, received signals from the sentries who were pitched up in trees. Apparently Wilson's men had not seen that a few of the 'terrorists' had climbed up trees. Some had gone even farther away from the main unit. The sentries had discerned that they had been so surrounded by the enemy.

Wilson's men, unaware that they had been spotted, kept on crawling forward towards Munongwa's unit. Their FN Automatic rifles ready. Munongwa knew very well as did Wilson, that surprise was the best answer in the circumstances. He quickly gave his men an order to open fire against the advancing and unsuspecting enemy, and make a break-through.

Since Wilson's men were in motion, crawling, they were easy to spot. They became easy targets for Munongwa's and Tichaona's sharp shooters. The guerrillas opened fire first with deadly accuracy. They used hand grenades and their AK-47's. General and vicious shooting began. Wilson's ambush plan had been messed up. Wilson's men took the first volley of fire, directly from the freedom fighters. That volley, crippled Wilson's unit. Many of his men did not move from their crawling positions. They were dead or seriously injured. Munongwa's men broke their cover as they dashed from one end to another, concentrating their fire in the ordered direction in order to open a way out of the encirclement. After a few minutes of fierce firing, Munongwa's men had successfully broken out of the encirclement, but the firing continued from the mercenary group. Wilson was determined to wipe out the 'terrorist' unit. The freedom fighters, on their part, were determined to survive as a fighting unit.

As Munongwa's unit retreated, he ordered a few anti-personnel mines to be laid behind their escape route. As Wilson's men ran and fired after the escaping guerrillas, one or two mines went off. This caused Wilson to order his men to slow down. Two more of Wilson's men stumbled on the mines, and they had it. Wilson ordered the remainder of his men to halt. The pursuit was called off. Some of Wilson's men had been torn to pieces by the mines. Munongwa and his unit escaped.

It was a three hour journey westward before Munongwa ordered his unit to stop and take stock of its men and equipment, as well as rest. At this point they were sure that they were no longer being followed. Three combatants were missing. One of them was Shonhiwa. They had probably fallen in the fight to break out of the encirclement by Wilson's ambush unit. Four of the combatants had been wounded. One of them was Tichaona. His condition was serious.

Wilson's exact casualties were never known by the combatants. One thing clear was that many of his men fell or got disabled, Munongwa thought. The period between the warning from the sentries and the surprise first-firing by the liberation forces, had enabled the freedom fighters to grab their weapons and rations, ready for the break.

Shupai had read of the news of the battle with the enemy mercenary force from Doctor Mutero's second letter that day. Dr Mutero had to give her the messages, if necessary, about news from the front in writing. And the letter had to be destroyed immediately. The report in the second letter had said, the mercenaries, the Selous Scouts had tried to wipe out the unit to which she belonged including that one of Tichaona. She was aggrieved and was sad. But she was glad that the enemy's objective was not completely achieved. But the loss of three comrades! Shonhiwa was one of the missing comrades. No! He could not be dead, she refused to believe it. No! He must be alive. She told herself. She had a feeling Shonhiwa was alive there somewhere. He was a brave man. She thought, even if he died, he must have done so together with many of the enemy mercenaries. But she refused to mourn for him. Shonhiwa is alive, she asserted this to herself. What had happened was that, Shonhiwa had noticed where the heaviest of the fire was coming from. The guerrillas had been completely surrounded by the Selous Scouts. Something had to be done, Shonhiwa thought, or else not one of them would escape from the mercenary encirclement. He started on a diversionary stunt to pave way for the main body of the guerrillas to break through. He broke off from the others. He ran towards a group of the scouts firing his automatic gun. He managed to silence some heavy fire from there. Then he turned to the other direction, threw a hand grenade onto a group who were firing heavily.

Before his grenade had stopped them, he saw two of his comrades throw their weapons in the air and fell. They probably had also decided to divert the enemy, from the main body of the guerrillas, Shonhiwa thought. The sight of his comrades falling to their death made him to run amok. He was shooting and throwing hand grenades with tremendous accuracy. He had just thrown another grenade onto some enemy scouts and thought he had achieved his goal, and was about to turn for the run. He heard screams with the explosion then silence....He lay slumped over....His head gashed and bleeding from impact....His right arm shattered. He opened his eyes and closed them again quickly. The intensity of the white-hot sun was too great to bear. He ached terribly, pain overlapping consciousness. Something, somebody seemed to be pressing down on his head. He tried again to open his eyes, the sun, very small, and then a dark shadow and silence....A long time of darkness....

He heard a voice, his own voice. Then another voice, "What's your name?" the voice, female. "Your name please," the same voice again. He wanted to tell her to shut up. Too much effort. They may be dead back there anyway, he thought. His arm hurt again, a burning pain. He heard a door close. "He came round again matron," the same female voice. "Did he speak? What did he say?" another female voice, European, sharp and commanding.

"Something about hand grenade, matron." Where else can one find matrons except in girls' hostels and in hospitals, Shonhiwa thought. "Did he tell you his name?" asked the matron. "No, Madame," answered the girl, standing before the matron, fidgeting like some nervous child. "Stand peoperly, you," the matron commanded sharply, and went on, "I'll tell you for the last time, nurse Ruth. You are to address me as matron. You are not my domestic." The matron sighed, a blend of impatience and resignation. She promised herself to apply for transfer back to Salisbury. "Now remember nurse Ruth, you are on duty to your country," shouted the matron. "You should have asked for his name and where he comes from, do you hear?" The matron went on furiously, "I wish I wasn't working here in the Out-Places with such idiots like you nurse Ruth." Shonhiwa mumbled something. Matron turned to him and asked, "What's your name? Tell me your name!" no response. She turned to nurse Ruth, who stood near the medicine tray shaking a vial of Omnopon. "Just two cc's and tetracycline now, every twelve hours. Dr Patrick should prescribe oral medication for the pain in the morning that is if the patient will be able to swallow." It was past two in the morning. "You must never, never leave this patient nurse Ruth, understand?" That was sharp. "Let the blood drip in more slowly now. And before you go off duty nurse Ruth, you should make a clear report about this patient and see to it that the night porter wakes up Dr Patrick promptly at six."

"Yes matron." The matron looked down at the patient, felt his pulse and went out. The fat white bitch, Nurse Ruth whispered, and grimaced. She was anxious for the night to be through. After all there was a military police guard at the door outside, Nurse Ruth thought why should she bother about the patient's name. Matron, Nurse, Doctor, Blood Drip? Shonhiwa thought he must be in a hospital. But, "on duty to your country?" He felt some nausea, pain all over, a prick on his upper left arm. He heard some noise of instruments thrown into the receiver, some more darkness, black darkness.... Shonhiwa heard voices, as if from a far away distance. He slightly, opened his eyes. He saw some light. He closed them for another moment and opened them again. It was very bright in this white washed room, with a solitary bed. A man was standing besides the bed talking. Shonhiwa lay back against the pillows, not caring who or what this man was. Pain still pulsed through his body even though the drugs muted it. Twenty two stitches, he had heard the nurse say, from the bridge of his nose to his right ear. The scar would be brutal, he thought. His head was pounding and he felt nauseated. His right forearm was burning and oozing blood beneath the bandages. The man was saying to him in a deep baritone voice: "You know you have to talk. I must talk with you now. It is in your best interest, of course." The man, white, had a hawk-like nose. The cigarette between his lips gave the illusion of a bird eating a worm. He was stout and short. "What for?" asked Shonhiwa, weakly. "Can't we do this later?"

"I'm sorry, you've to talk to me before the police does...." Shonhiwa started, his eyes wide open. He attempted to sit up and nearly passed out because of the screaming pain. It shot along his nerves and rand in his head like a burglar alarm. He had to brace himself against the pillows. He had to close his eyes, fighting to maintain consciousness. He heard the man call for the orderly. He was wearied now, his adrenaline level falling. Shonhiwa, as if dreaming, mentally retraced his behaviour since contact with enemy mercenery scouts. He was a bit contented that he could have handled the situation in no better manner. It was only months of operational training that enabled him to do what he did. He thought, it was against all reason, all the instinctive desire to mind and body. It meant action. It was just hard luck that the enemy grenade explosion happened just at the last moment. He had made it, he thought, well, almost made it. He hoped most of his comrades had made it.

When he opened his eyes again his vision had cleared slightly. There he saw a big, powerful looking man, black, standing beside the short, stout white man with a hawk-like nose. Shonhiwa tried to place the black men and failed. He had never seen him before in his life. Who could he be? He almost drifted back to sleep...

"Who are you? What is your name? Tell us. What do you do? Where do you come from?"

Questions, questions, questions. Why the devil can't they leave me alone? He thought. He kept quiet, his eyes closed again. He was fighting hard to remain conscious. "Listen, you have to answer the questions," said the tall black man, harshly. "We know you don't know us. We've never met before." Shonhiwa sighed. His eyes partially opened. He was tired beyond anything he could recall, just wishing to be left alone. "I'm listening," he said weakly.

"Tell us your name, your work and where your home is," the short white man said tapping his cigarette at the window sill, spilling ashes onto the floor and across his shirt. "Why?" Shonhiwa looked at the big black man and he felt some horrors creep along his spine. He flinched with pain in his head. "Perhaps we should bring him up-to-date, all right?" The big black man had a deep barking voice, which was meant to create fear in the person concerned. The patient tried to nod. His chest was hurting now. The effects of the drugs probably were subsiding.

"You are a fighter," the short man started and paused for any reaction from the patient. Nothing. "You were captured at –ee- five days ago. You are the only survivor," the short man continued, "All your friends are dead." This did it. The patient attempted again to sit up, saying:

"Empty propaganda!" He struggled out of bed not caring anymore about the pain. The two men restrained him, "No, no, no. Please, relax," said the big man. "As he said, all your friend fighters are dead. You are the only survivor. You'll probably live....if you cooperate," the big man spoke, not caring anymore to be as persuasive as the short man.

"You don't believe what I told you," Shonhiwa's voice was shrill. "You don't believe me, do you? All right then." He pushed them with the power of the devil, staggering blindly as he stumbled onto the floor. "You!" he pointed to the big black man as the two men plus the medical orderly who had just entered, lifted him back onto the bed. His arm was bleeding profusely, his chest hurt badly. The room was reeling. He felt like vomiting and he belched convulsively on to the bed clothes. Rotten, sour stuff. It smelt, he thought, like rotten mangoes.

Gentlemen, please," the orderly said. "Can you leave him alone for a while again, please?"

"Okay. But don't give him any sleeping drug yet," commanded the big man. "He has to talk, or else...."

Shonhiwa closed his eyes and was quiet for a few minutes. Then he opened his eyes again. He was perspiring heavily. He passed his hand wearily across his eyes to wipe the sweat. Waves of nausea swept over him again. His mind seemed a blank, unable to concentrate. His throat was dry. His tongue was like a piece of course cloth and his mouth tasted sour. He wished he could vomit again. He belched again, this time only wind came out, teeth gritting. The faces of the men were blurred and he pushed his hand across his eyes again trying to focus properly. Everything in the room seemed to be moving, going round as if coming closer to him. He had to keep his eyes closed. The bed seemed to be lifted up and down. He still could not concentrate. The circling of his head stopped. He opened the eyes. Figures appeared again, distorted figures, their faces blurred still. He pushed his wounded hand across his face, wincing terribly, almost crying.

"What's this about talking?" he asked, the words hissing out between clenched teeth.

"Wake up, you," said the big man. His face was just in front of the patient, so close that the patient could smell the staleness of his breath. The face was still distorted, as if it was turned up-side down. "You have to tell us your name and the name of your leader."

"What leader?" asked the patient. "Stop pretending!" the man shook the patient's head roughly from side to side. The pain was unbearable and he screamed. He sat up, tried to stagger to his feet, reeled again. He suddenly faltered, feeling terribly sick, tears flooding his eyes. There were muttered voices in the background and he felt the needle pricking into his upper arm. His last image of the big man was a wide distorted face grimacing angrily beyond his contracting vision. Shonhiwa came awake slowly, annoyed by the persistent pressure on his arm. His senses, he felt, were dead and he wanted to return to the depths where he had been, no dreaming, nothing. He heard a far away voice. "He has slept for too long. Almost seven hours? What did you give him?" The voice was not familiar, he thought. Almost seven hours of sleep! He wished he could go back to sleep for seven more hours. He tried to pretend sleeping on. "He's awake, now, I know, he's just putting it on." Another voice, female, European. He seemed to remember that voice from somewhere. The matron he remembered. A light snapped on. He opened his eyes. The bulb was dim, but it felt as if a strobe had been fired. He blinked and tried to focus. He tried to shield his eyes with his left hand. The pain in the arm was sickening. He shut his eyes. He heard someone say:

"Details of the transfer of the prisoner to Salisbury are complete. Two plain clothed men will be here shortly to retrieve him." It was the short stout white man. "Get up?" shouted the voice of the big black man with the stale breathe. "You should have transported him to Salisbury's Harare Hospital while he was still asleep," said the matron.

"So he can't travel like this," said the big man, and went on, "Karoi is a long way to Salisbury. He's going to give us trouble." So I am in Karoi hospital. I wish Munongwa had known, Shonhiwa thought. "Then you have to put him under heavy guard," insisted the matron, "We can't have him here for any longer." "Then you give him another shot to put him back to sleep," suggested the short, stout white man. That could be better, thought Shonhiwa. "No," refused the matron. "It's due in another five hours' time. I'll write it in the report for Harare Hospital. Good-bye gentlemen."

Chapter 9

Shupai, lying in that hospital bed, grieved intensely over Shonhiwa's disappearance. But she, however, could not help thinking he was alive somewhere. She wondered who the other two cadres were. Their names were not released in Dr Mutero's letter. She read the letter once more before destroying it thoroughly. She thought of Tichaona. The letter mentioned Tichaona as one of the seriously wounded combatants. His condition was described by Dr Mutero as critical. Hope he would live. Shupai thought, that man, Tichaona, seemed to have been one of the unlucky ones in the liberation history. She began to recall the first day she had met Tichaona. Everything that happened that day and the following days and weeks started to flow into her mind as if it was just a few days ago.

It was one day, during school vacation when Shupai, then Lucia was travelling by bus to Salisbury, from Muzhanje Primary School, in Chiweshe Reserve. At one of the bus stops a man of about twenty four boarded the bus. The man was tall and well built with the appearance of an athlete. His hair had been cut very short and was pleasantly untidy. He had an agreeable face – a breezy, rather charming face. He was a handsome and attractive guy, she thought. As the man and Shupai, then Lucia smiled at each other, he came straight and sat beside her.

"My name is Tichaona," he introduced himself, "Tichaona Munyoro," he emphasised adding his surname.

"Mine is Lucia Kashangu," she responded, "I'm glad to know you," she added. After a close examination of Tichaona's face she asked: "Are you related to the old man Munyoro of Chakanyuka village?"

"Yes. He is my father," Tichaona replied.

The old man Munyoro was one of the peasants in Chiweshe Reserve whom Lucia had been politicising. Once, he had to pay a very heavy fine for refusing to pay poll-tax, for burning his chitupa and taking part in filling a dip-tank with sand and stones. Tichaona had informed Lucia that he had just come out of detention, he said, "I found my father away in jail. He had been arrested, and sentenced to some years in prison with hard labour or pay a heavy fine. He could not pay the fine. How could such an old man serve a six-year prison sentence?" he asked. "I only just managed to pay the fine for him and a very heavey fine too. Now he is at home." He added, "He is so disgruntled and so frustrated that I have to keep coming to see him as frequently as possible." Lucia whispered that she knew something about the arrest of the peasants, and was wondering what had happened to them. Then she asked to read that day's Herald, which Tichaona had.

As she went through the paper, her attention was caught by a statement made by the British Government. The statement praised the settler colonial regime for its efficiency in running its affairs despite a few disturbances here and there by the 'lawless, ungrateful blacks'. Lucia was infuriated and she commented: "These British! Aren't they the S.O.B's? She whispered to herself. Tichaona over-heard her. In response, he said, in such a low voice that he thought only Lucia, who was sitting next to him could hear: "That is the so-called Her Majesty's speech from the throne on the opening of the British Parliament. It lowers my respect – if I ever had any – for the British."

"It is obvious she had nothing to say to her people. How can she praise the white minority government here," whispered Lucia, "for oppressing and exploiting us?" They both spoke in such low voices that they thought no one could over-hear their brief impromptu political conversation, but....

"You two are under arrest!" a man sitting behind them said and moved from his seat to stand in front where they were in the next row. "Under what?" asked Tichaona, "And who are you? What have we done?" Tichaona asked angrily. The man pulled out his police identification card and showed it to them. The man arresting Lucia and Tichaona was in fact a member of the regime's brutal and notorious Special Branch, a secret political police force. The man had a puss pimpled face. He kept on blinking nervously as if he was in perpetual fear of being laughed at. There was commotion inside the bus as Tichaona and Lucia argued with the man about their arrest. The other passengers travelling with them started to shout at the man and threatened to beat him. The police officer ordered the bus driver not to stop the bus until they reached the town. The Special Branch man ordered Lucia and Tichaona off the bus, when the bus stopped at the bus terminus in Salisbury just near the Central Police Station in Railway Avenue (Now Kenneth Kaunda).

When Tichaona and Lucia kept resisting, the Special Branch Officer blew his whistle to summon help. Extra police officers in riot gear, arrived immediately, and a real battle ensued between the people at the bus terminus and the police. Lucia and Tichaona tried to escape but: "Arrest those two!" shouted the Special branch man pointing to them and blinking nervously. They were taken. More riot police arrived in trucks and started pushing men, women and children into police vans. Most of the people had nothing to do with what had just been going on. Some had just arrived on the scene from various directions, curious to see what was going on.

At the charge office, Lucia and Tichaona were separated despite Tichaona's protestations. He was forced away. Lucia saw him being led into a room at the end of the dark corridor. She wondered what would happen to him.

He was a very unlucky man, she thought, because ha had just come out of detention and had found his father....Now he was in again. Lucia was still looking towards where Tichaona had gone when she was pulled roughly by a white police officer. "This way and forget about him you bloody bitch!"

The African Special Branch man who had been responsible for their arrest had vanished into thin air. He had behaved like a cad, of course, thought Lucia angrily. Banishing his fellow Africans somewhere, among the rats, like that? Rat! Under the Law and Order (Maintenance) Act, Lucia was charged with insulting the imperial government, threatening to destroy the British flag, the Union Jack and for disorderly behaviour in public, likely to cause disturbance.

She was remanded in "Her Majesty's" custody for a few weeks without trial. She was then sentenced to three months in prison with hard labour, or a fine of two hundred pounds. Her uncle, Gumbo paid the fine. But she was served with a restriction/detention order.

"But why?" Lucia's uncle Gumbo asked about the restriction/detention order after he had paid such a heavy fine. He was told that, that was recommendation from the Director of Native Education. The Native Education Authorities now regarded Lucia as a dangerous political element. They had not forgotten that quarrel between her and inspector Bloomfield, at Muzhanje Primary School. Mr Bloomfield the Inspector had written a very negative report about her on that he had visited the Muzhanje Primary School very early that Monday morning.

Gumbo protested, demanding his money back, "You thieves, you knew you were going to detain her, why did you fine her in the first place?" Gumbo was quickly reminded that the state of emergency was still on and if he did not want to join her he had better shut up.

She, herself did not care about the order, although she had joined and supported her uncle in protesting against the fine and restriction order. She was not afraid of restrictions. Why should she be any exception? She asked herself. Thousands of Zimbabweans had been languishing in the settler jails, restriction as well as detention camps for years. If being in jail or detention was part of the struggle for the liberation of Zimbabwe, she thought, she had given her body, mind and soul to that task.

Lucia was sent to Marandellas (now Marondera) Detention and Restriction Camp, and no news of Tichaona. She wondered whether the same had happened to Tichaona who had been arrested together with her.

She wondered whether Tichaona had been sentenced to a prison term without a fine or whether he was as lucky as she was to come out with a fine and only, to be served with a detention order. These thoughts pained Lucia. She kept thinking and wondering what had happened to Tichaona. Fate seemed to be against him always, that man, she thought.

At Marandellas (Marondera) camp there was a group of well known political leaders like, Marufu, Mrs Chake, Makuva, Tichafa and others she did not know. There were some of the N. D. P. leaders whom Lucia had known in Highfield Township before the Party was banned, and many others except Murambiwa and Tapera and Miss Regayi. There were also among them, a few men and women from Chiweshe Reserve where she had been teaching. Some of them had been arrested on the same day as she. The restrictees were watched very carefully by guards, police and secret informers had been planted among them. They, Mrs Chake, Lucia and others like Marwei etc, nevertheless managed to meet clandestinely and discussed vital political issues. A group of two was adequate for quiet discussions and decisions would simply pass on between groups of two or three and so on. The police informers had been identified very easily.

Months had passed and some people from this camp were being screened and being released bit by bit in groups of four or more. New restricted people were coming in while others were being released after a few weeks of detention or restriction. However, among those to be released were never included those of Mrs Chake's group which included Lucia, the teacher who had been black listed by the Native Education Inspector, Mr Bloomfield.

During the state of Emergency and when Lucia was at Marondera, some Zimbabwean nationalists had managed to escape the settler police dragnet, and were exiled in neighbouring African countries. These were the ones who decided that political power in Zimbabwe must be won, but only through armed confrontation. They trained some of them in guerrilla warfare. Then highly armed combatants were sent back into the country. They were hitting the white settlers in by well organised acts of sabotage, ambushes and other hit and run guerrilla tactics. Local cadres were also being trained inside the country.

News of guerrilla activities filtered into the detention and restriction camps. The new development news was exciting but it also made detention very hard to endure. Lucia wanted more than ever to be free. She wanted to join the guerrillas whose actions of courage and bravery were bringing hope to the whole country's black majority.

Mrs Chake's "group" started to think of ways and means to obtain releases so that they could join the underground movement to aid the guerrilla effort. Each one in the group was given the task of thinking or planning any means by which the group or some of the members of the group could find their way out of the detention. If one of them thought of something, he or she would pass the plan to one of them and the information would be relayed around in that manner. This was done quickly and a consensus would be reached on the proposed plan. Many plans were thought of and proposed to the group but many were either physically impossible to execute or unacceptable on other grounds.

Day and night, Lucia thought of different plans which would enable her to be released. She thought of acting as a mentally sick person so that she could be taken to the hospital from where she could escape. She was convinced that the plan would work if executed properly. When this plan was passed round, other members of the group thought the plan was a good one. But at the same time, they thought Lucia might not be able to act effectively enough as a mentally sick person. Makuva volunteered to try the plan. Makuva was twenty two years old, strongly built, five feet eleven inches tall and a possessor of a very deep, loud voice. He was very pleased to be given this part to act.

Tichafa and Lucia suggested yet another plan. "What about some of us pretending to be in the settler police informer network?" suggested Tichafa. "This may enable some of us in this group to be released and then join the underground movement." Lucia and Marwei volunteered to act that part. This involved acting as if some detainees suspected them and a few others of being informers planted among the detainees in order to spy against them. Then Lucia had a bitter "quarrel" with Tichafa one afternoon, as planned. Tichafa started shouting at Lucia:

"You sell-out, running dog of the settler regime!" Tichafa, shouted at Lucia, loud enough for the guards to hear him.

"What have I done?" Lucia shouted back almost with a crying voice. "You politicians," she went on, "You make me sick. I have nothing to do with you. Leave me alone."

"We don't want to see you near us," said Mrs Chake. "The same applies to these ones here," she said pointing to Marufu and Marwei. "You are all here to spy on us, we know why you were sent here. You are not even ashamed of yourselves. Selling your own, for what," Mrs Chake emphasised, and the two guards and a policeman who were nearby moved closer to the scene. Lucia was in "tears". She was saying that she was in trouble with these silly politicians. She appeared to be talking to herself loudly, but she wanted the advancing guards and the policeman to hear the cause of the quarrel.

"I don't know why I am being kept here," Lucia said, "I don't even know why I cannot be released? I am not a politician but a simple school teacher."

She went on, "I have nothing to do with politics. I am a Civil Servant."

"Yes, we have discovered you. You have been hiding for too long," shouted Tichafa, who went on, "Informers are never capable of doing that. Sooner or later, we catch them. Now we have unmasked you. You are an informer." Tichafa added, "You are not ashamed to sell your own mother and father to the regime of those white people. Do you think the day we take over Zimbabwe and drive them out, you will go with them?" Tichafa was shouting like a gospel preacher. Lucia had her head buried deep in her hands "crying", and moving away from the rest of the people. "Leave me alone!"

"Leave me alone!" She shouted back. "I wish I could go back to my school, instead of waisting my time with these...." The African policeman said to Tichafa, "You will be dealt with accordingly if you don't stop your threats, you dirty bastard," the policeman went on, "This girl was not responsible for your being here." Then he said to Lucia: "You come here." They went to a guard-room and the constable asked Lucia how the squabble had started. Lucia told him that it was a long standing misunderstanding between her and some of the detainees. They had for a long time suspected her and a few others to be working for the police ever since she was detained.

"But I am not an informer. They have even been threatening to kill me. I, I can't have it any more. I have had enough!" Lucia said. The police constable told Lucia to go back and that he would see what to do about it. Lucia went back but she continued to pretend to the guards and the police that the trouble was getting worse. But every step that followed was carefully planned by the group to ensure its faultless execution.

One Friday afternoon Lucia was taken to the office of the Police officer-in-charge. In that office there was a white settler policeman. This officer was a different one from the one Lucia had seen several times before at this camp.

"Sit down!" the white officer commanded Lucia without looking at her. She sat on a creaking crooked chair. The settler officer was tall and heavily built. He had a large face, with jutting out ears, a big nose, furrowed cheeks, and sharp-blue eyes, deep under thick black brows. The mouth was just a slit under a hawk's beak-like nose.

He is as ugly and as ferocious as the bloody police hounds they set on us, Lucia thought. He was frightening. He gives me the shivers, Lucia told herself. I wonder....

The officer stopped fumbling with the desk drawers and sat down on a chair. He looked at Lucia with his gum-drop eyes for what seemed to Lucia as an intolerably long weekend. She noticed that those eyes did not blink. They did not blink even when he picked up the telephone receiver and dialled a number. The eyes frightened her so much that even the well rehearsed plan seemed now unconvincing to her. She had not thought it possible that so many different shapes of terror could come to her in such a short time. This man....

That was, however, a crucial moment which Lucia had worked and waited for. She had to be very careful and not to show any signs of fear, she told herself. After receiving no answer, the police officer banged down the receiver so hard that the noise went on ringing in Lucia's ears for a few more minutes. She thought that must have been heard a mile away. He still had those fierce eyes fixed at her when he said:

"How did you happen to be in this place? This place is for trouble makers, and what are you?" Lucia was sure that the white officer obviously knew why she was at Marandellas. She, all the same, explained:

"I am no a trouble maker sir. I am only a primary school teacher who happened to have been travelling on a bus in which some of the passengers started trouble with the police." He again looked at her for a whole minute without saying anything, without blinking. She felt very uneasy. She almost jumped up and ran out of the room. At last those words came: "I want you to stay here and work for me."

"Please sir, my wish is to be away from these people." Lucia pleaded. "I cannot stay here any longer because I will always be in trouble." She added, "These people are fanatics when it comes to what they think they believe in. Sir, please," she pleaded.

Then after a little more time of persuasion the white police officer gave in. He offered to release Lucia only on conditions that she would work for the police as an informer to "track down the terrorists".

My goodness! The plan had turned sour, Lucia thought. She had not expected the plan to round about turn that way. Should she accept the offer in order to secure release and then leave the job later? Should she refuse and remain in detention, vegetating and feeling useless and feeling sorry for herself? She could be outside doing the work she longed to do. And what would her colleagues say if she accepted this without consulting them? Gosh! She sighed visibly. Then she had another thought. She must accept. She would pretend to work for the settler police while doing more for the struggle. She thought she could work as a counter-informer for the underground movement.

But first she must consult the others, if possible. They might misunderstand her, she thought. This possibility had not been foreseen when they were planning the strategy for escape.

"You are wasting my time!" The officer barked at Lucia. She started, looking at him surprised, a bit frightened.

"I am thinking about your suggestion sir. I am not a politician," she said. "I don't want anything to do with politics please, sir I beg you."

"I want the answer now!" he demanded, banging on the table explosively. Suddenly to Lucia's relief, there was an animal-like sharp cry from one of the detainees. The detainees had been called out to assemble for the roll call. The sharp cry had come from one of the male detainees, called Makuva. According to the 'plan' he was pretending to be mentally disturbed, actually, really mad.

He had, all along, been behaving so "abnormally" that the guards had accordingly reported him to the officer-in-charge. And they were ordered to watch him closely. Makuva shrieked and screamed louder, and louder, as if in terrible pain. He screamed as if terrified by an ogre. The huge police officer rushed out of the small office leaving Lucia sitting on the creaking crooked chair. Now! Lucia thought, she would use this chance, thank Goodness. She picked up a piece of paper and pen from the officer's desk and very quickly wrote down her conversation with the officer. She added her own plan for accepting the offer. She rushed out and headed straight to where Marufu, Marwei Chakatama were standing, watching with wide open eyes at Makuva. They could not believe that Makuva could put such an effective 'act'. Using the confusion created by Makuva, Lucia handed the piece of paper to Marufu, who immediately disappeared to read the note and pass it on. Lucia explained, very quickly to Marwei, about what had transpired between her and the police officer. She explained the conditions for her release and her own opinion about it. Marweyi supported her straight away. Marufu, after reading handed the paper to Mrs Chake who slipped away to read the note and came back immediately to Lucia and whispered quietly: "Accept the offer, and I support your suggestion." Mrs Chake added, "The liberation movement will also need informers just as the oppressor does." Tichafa also concurred and simply whispered, when he passed by near Lucia: "We trust you Lucia," then moved away from her very quickly.

Makuva kept on screaming and shouting. The ugly police officer tried to create dialogue with him. Makuva only kept on pointing to the barracks and shaking his head violently. He acted as if terrified by something he alone could see. The ugly white policeman smacked Makuva very hard across the right cheek: "Shut up you baboon!" he shouted at Makuva, shaking him violently at the shoulders. 'The colonial bull is up to his inhuman work. Look at his jutting ears,' Lucia said to herself and almost rushed to the white police officer to protest against his hitting a 'sick' person. Makuva did not stop screaming even after the smack and the shaking from the heavy hand of the white policeman. He went on screaming. He screamed even more. His voice getting higher, getting lost at the highest pitch! He even rushed to hide himself behind the white policeman after the smack. He seemed to be hiding himself from someone chasing him. The settler officer shook him violently again. Nothing doing. Then he ordered that Makuva be taken to his truck under two guards. When the police officer drove off, Makuva was still shouting and screaming inaudible words. He was hitting very hard at his seat with his left fist, pointing to the barracks with his right hand. Then he covered his face and kept shrilling with a real mad man's voice. Amazing act, Lucia thought, hoping those roughnecks would not keep hitting him. They must take him to a mental hospital, she thought. That was the plan in the first place.

Lucia was momentarily forgotten. She had joined the others but she held herself aloof from them except Marwei. She had to keep pretending to be in trouble. She hoped that Makuva would be sent to a mental hospital straight away instead of the police custody. He would probably be put under heavy sedation with Morphine or Phenobartitone (drugs Lucia had read from a novel about a mental hospital) or whatever sedation they would see, to calm him down. But they would not continue sedating him, Lucia convinced herself. Makuva would then work his way out and escape from the Africa Mental Hospital and proceed to join the budding guerrilla movement.

Contact with the outside was not difficult to organise. This was not difficult because detainees were often visited by their relatives and friends. Word of the possible release of Lucia and others and about Makuva was sent to the underground headquarter.

The following morning during breakfast, after observing that the camp guards were nearby and watching, Lucia rushed out of the mess, sobbing. She had a mug of hot tea in her hand. As she rushed out, a piece of bread followed her, hitting her on the back. She picked it up and threw it back, where it had come from, shouting: "I am sick and tired of this! Can't anyone help me, please?" she called, obviously to the guards, who were nearby and had seen everything that had happened. After a moment Marwei also rushed out, followed by two pieces of bread. She was shouting at the people in the mess:

"I have never been an informer. You keep on accusing me without any proof at all! What is an informer anyway?" One of the camp guards rushed into the mess and without considering, began to hit everybody, at the same time demanding to know who had thrown the pieces of bread:

"Today you will have to talk. You are going to reveal the ring-leader of this mad business!" The guard threatened as he was swinging the heavy stick in his hands, forwards, backwards, and sideways like a rabid dog. Two black constables who had just arrived, called Lucia and Marwei to the guard's room and asked:

"Who is accusing you of being informers?"

"It is impossible to pinpoint anyone because when they start, they all talk and shout and threaten." Lucia replied.

"You will have to try to help us detect the real trouble makers," suggested one of the constables.

Lucia threw a glance at Marwei. Now they were being put to the test. They were being requested to nail down a particular comrade. The whole plan was turning even more sour, thought Lucia. If they were to name a colleague, who would that be? "This means staying here longer," commented Marwei as if to herself, showing great disappointment. "I don't think I can take it any more, I…." "Yes," said the policeman, and asked, "How else do you think we can stop this harassment once and for all? We have to get hold of the people making trouble against you."

"All we are asking for is to taken out of here, and we think the trouble will end," interjected Lucia.

"You are not going anywhere," said the policeman, "I suggest that you two go back to the others and pretend to be good to them as if nothing had happened. Then try to detect the ring leaders and report them to us."

"You people talk so gently and mildly about these political maniacs," argued Lucia. "You don't seem to know them that well. These people mean what they say when they say they'll fix us, and that we shall pay for our activities." Lucia continued, trying to be convincing, "There can be nothing like pretending to them to be any good as if nothing had happened. When they have suspected you they act accordingly." Lucia emphasised her point.

"That is all you have to do. Now go! Nothing will happen to you!"

Lucia and Marwei 'reluctantly' returned to the others. The situation was becoming more and more difficult. They had been asked to name the ring leader. That was hard. On the other hand they could not keep up the story that there was no leader or leaders. In the end, after a lot of soul searching and painful considerations, Tichafa volunteered to be named as the ring leader if the police should insist.

For more than three days, the two girls pretended to be shunned by their own colleagues. More disturbing incidents were staged. They waited to be called for questioning, but nothing happened.

Then one of the detainees, a man of about thirty or thirty-five, called Mandebvu, approached Lucia and asked: "Have you managed to detect the person or persons who are responsible for the trouble to you and Marwei?" Lucia looked at him calculatingly. It did not take long for Lucia to realise that Mandebvu was the real informer plant among the detainees. Lucia told him that she had not yet detected the leader but added that she was still trying to find out. She emphasised however that the isolation and harassment was increasing and that life with the others was becoming really intolerable.

The discovery of Mandebvu as a real informer made Mrs Chake's group to be more cautious. They watched him closely. Mandebvu often asked Lucia what the detainees talked about. Lucia pretended to be having a good friend in Mandebvu, when she answered his question about what the people talk about: "I hear every one talk about the liberation army," Lucia told Mandebvu. "But I'm not interested." "Do they talk seriously about this liberation army?" Mandebvu asked.

"Everyone talks seriously about that subject. Seems everyone wants to join that army," Lucia replied and added, "But all I want is to get out of here. I am a teacher. I am not interested in politics or in any liberation army."

"But remember you were given work to do here," warned Mandebvu and went on, "If you don't understand the work...." He paused, looked about then said, "You are supposed to detect the die-hards, the hard-core politicians among these people; the real trouble makers. You then must report accordingly. You can also report to me. But make sure that nobody here knows that I am your contact."

"You are a very clever fellow, aren't you mister Mandebvu?" said Lucia cynically. "You want me to bear the brunt of the blame from these crazy people while you hide yourself behind your skin? Very clever indeed!" She looked at him for a minute, then, "Let me tell you something. If I have anything or something to report, I will go straight to those people there and report to them," she said pointing to the guards. "I can get beaten by these people and may even be killed for this, and for all I know you will not come to my aid."

"Well, I have told you about your job, and those people will be expecting a report from you," said Mandebvu pointing to the guards. "I will send them reports, if any, but not through you," Lucia said. Mandebvu, disappointed, left Lucia alone.

After two days, Lucia and Marweyi were ordered by the camp commander, a white officer by the name of Mr Miller to collect their belongings. A truck driven by an African constable with three others sitting at the back was waiting for them. As they were preparing to leave, the other detainees, Mrs Chake's group pretended to be rejoicing at their departure: "Go away, you running dogs of the oppressor," shouted one of the detainees.

"Yes," said Mrs Chake with a hoarse voice, "And sell us and the whole country down the drain," she added.

"Say what you like," replied Lucia 'proudly'. "I will be free while you people languish right here."

Marufu had given the two girls pieces of cloth on which he had written names and addresses of their contacts in the underground movement. Lucia was given the name and address of a Mr Sanganai as her contact. She wondered whether this Sangani was the same man who was her former head-teacher at Muzhanje primary School in Chiweshe Reserve. Sanganayi had been demoted and was transferred to a remote school because of the incident with Mr Bloomfield, the Native Education Inspector. So Mr Sanganayi was a revolutionary after all? Lucia thought with great surprise and joy.

The two girls were driven away amid a lot of surprises among those detainees who were not involved in the 'plot'. "These girls are not even ashamed of being so open about being police informers. The judgement of the people will meet with them one of these fine days," said one of the detainees angrily.

"These will not only be informers, they will most likely be joining the notorious Special Branch," remarked another detainee. But those who were aware of the plan hoped that the girls would not change their minds and would serve the liberation movement of Zimbabwe.

The two girls were driven to a police station in Marandellas Town. They were ushered into an office. Lucia was astonished to see the ugly white police officer with jutting out ears, who had interviewed her the other day. He was sitting behind a desk as if waiting for their arrival so that he could strike. His jutting out ears seemed to be moving nervously. Am I seeing things? She asked herself, confused. She immediately felt the same different kinds of terror that she had experienced at that first encounter with this man. His gum-drop eyes seemed to penetrate through her anatomy. She felt some moisture under her armpits. But to their complete surprise, the two girls were quickly fixed with identity cards. They were instructed to keep in touch with the police and report anything that the settler police would normally be interested in.

Written lists of "do's" and "don'ts" were pushed into the hands of each one of the girls. Among other things, and more important, they were to continue their close contact with the African politicians. They must try by all means to infiltrate the "terrorists" themselves. They were to report continuously to the police all the activities of the "terrorists" and the whole African underground movement.

"Are we going to report to you directly, sir?" Lucia asked, adding the "sir" emphatically, to show great politeness to the "boss". What Lucia wanted was to be sure whether the white bull was going to be in close contact with them, but to Lucia's delight, he replied that they would report to the police in the area they would be appointed. How could she stand this terror for any longer? She asked herself. "Are there many girls like us doing the same work?" Marwei asked, politely. "Why do you ask?" asked the white man, curiously, looking straight at her.

"Because I think the work must be very hard. I am afraid that I may not be able to do it to your satisfaction, sir," replied Marwei showing all signs of politeness, doubt and lack of confidence in herself.

"If there are many of us doing the same job," Lucia took over, "It would relieve our fears and doubts," she added, "It would be encouraging to know we are not the only ones." "Of course, you are not the only ones," the police officer banged on the desk. "Many black men and women are ready to work for our civilised government. Dismissed!" he commanded.

"Can we meet some of them so that we can enquire how they go about it?" asked Marwei insistently. They were then told that wherever they would be, they would always be in contact with other members of the same trade. The girls asked all this information deliberately so that they would always be in a position to know and detect the real police informers. This would help the struggle more by identifying right way, the true enemies of the people. The ugly white police officer, they thought, didn't suspect any foul play. Could an African woman be intelligent? Could she question the validity of the white settlers' belief that Africans, especially the women, were too inferior and too unintelligent? No, and it was good that he remained unsuspicious, thought the girls.

The girls were each given a name and an address of a contact. It was in each case a senior woman informer. The girls were very happy about their conversation with the white police officer. They had already begun their work and the first source of the most vital information; that of the contacts in the settler informer network was this chief himself, she wondered what they called him. 'This is great' thought Lucia, 'Perhaps the job will not be too difficult after all. Knowing some of the senior informers already will serve the struggle a lot.' She was now anxious to get away from this white man to meet one of the senior woman police informers.

Lucia and Marwei were driven away to the main bus station in Salisbury in an unmarked police car. Marwei boarded a bus to her parents at Mufakose African Township. Marwei Chakatama had been one of a group of youths who were taken in by the police during the early days of the state of emergency. The youths had stoned the car of a passing white woman who had been lucky to get rescued by the police. Her car, however, was completely destroyed. But the youths were arrested and detained without trial.

Lucia did not go home to her father. Instead, she went to her uncle's house. Mr and Mrs Gumbo welcomed her with tears of joy. After a few minutes of settling down, they started talking about the situation in the country. They were surprised to see that she was somehow well informed about what was going on about the struggle. She, on her part, was very happy to know that they were still active and were also helping the underground movement. She did not, however, inform them about her own present 'role'. She merely promised to carry on with the struggle relentlessly and she meant it.

That same evening Lucia was accompanied by her uncle to the address she was given by Mrs Chake's group at Marandellas. Lucia was surprised to know that her former headmaster, Sanganayi stayed at this place though he was not there on that day. But Lucia's name had already been familiar to some persons at this address. It had been suggested by the local committee that Lucia must try to get a teaching post at one of the schools in a certain area. This was an area of active guerrilla operations. As she had been recommended very highly by the well known group at Marandellas detention camp, she was given the task of transportation. The strategy would be for her to try and obtain a car from her police informer "superiors" for easier and quicker communication with the authorities from the remote school.

But in reality the car would be to transport guerrillas to and from their respective activities. She would also easily look after them since she won't be suspected of harbouring any "terrorists". She would also help to mobilise the villagers around that area to support and help the freedom fighters. The villagers in that area, it was found out, would not be very hard to mobilise. They were the ones who had been evicted from their fertile and traditional areas in the same district where the settler Wiltshire Estates, were. Part of their land was declared "Crown Land" by the settler regime. These villagers were so embittered that they were ready to help anyone who would like to fight the settlers.

Marwei, on the other hand, soon got a job in the sorting department of the main Post Office in Salisbury. Many Africans men and women worked in this post Office. The settler informer, whose name was given to Marweyi, got her this job so that she could listen to African conversations and discussion at this Post Office. She was not the only one doing the 'job', she found out, as other individuals in the settler informer network were pointed out to her. This helped Marweyi to be aware of them, at the same time, pretending to be working with them for the settler police. The underground movement gained tremendously by having Marwei work at the Post Office. By virtue of her job, she was able to know some of the informers very well. These informers fed Marweyi with vital information on what was going on in the settler police circles.

Lucia obtained a teaching post at Chakara Primary School in Charter District. This was miles south of Salisbury. She had told her 'partners' in the enemy's intelligence network that she wanted to work near her mother's home. So she was given some names of some chief police contacts in Charter District. The nearest town to Chakara School was Enkeldorn (now Chivu) in the same district. Mrs Chake also came from this district. What a coincidence, Lucia thought.

Lucia had only worked at Chakara for about three months when she filed a request for a car from her police informer "superiors" in Enkeldorn. The reason she gave was well understood. She would necessarily need to travel to and from the town every now and then if need arose. So she needed fast and reliable transport to enable her to effectively execute her duties since she said she had discovered much of enemy activity in that area. In the end she convinced her superiors, and she was given a beat-up, dark green, second hand mini station wagon. It sure looked beat-up, but was in excellent mechanical condition. Bravo for the liberation movement, she thought proudly. After all, owning a car, no matter how old in those remote areas of the country, was a thing to be admired.

Charter district had some of the most fertile and rich areas of Rhodesia. Most of the African inhabitants of those rich areas were moved away from their ancestral places as the number of setters increased in Rhodesia. The victimisation of the indigenous peasants had increased. They were removed, by force, to very dry infertile areas. Their original areas were converted, by decree, into "white areas". The clear demarcation between the rich settler farms and the poor arid areas of the indigenous Zimbabweans, Lucia noticed, could be seen clearly.

The crops in the 'native' fields were sickly looking while the acres and acres of mealies (Maize), cotton and tobacco crops in the settler farms were richly green and healthy.

Something must be done, and it must be done very soon to give back the land to the poor African farmers, Lucia thought, after talking to some peasants who had a few acres each near her school.

"Teacher Kashangu, you would be surprised if I told you the amount of fertilizer I put in my field. But I still get these sickly looking crops," one of the peasant farmers said and added, "and yet these agricultural demonstrators advise us to continue using a lot of fertilizer. If I had as many acres of land as the white farmers, I would have left this part of my land to rest for some years."

Lucia said, "I wish the African politicians could do something about this," she said this as she intended to test the peasant farmer's reaction at the mention of politics.

"What can they do?" the peasant asked and added, "They have tried their best. But they are all now locked up and their mouths have been shut up for a long time. Besides, those Boers are powerful. They have the Army, the Air force and many guns. They have a police force, the B.S.A.P. and the numerous informers who live among us. The Africans have nothing." "Do you think those people who are left out like you can't do anything about it?" asked Lucia.

"What can a person like me do?" asked the peasant and added in a whisper, "I wish I could lay my hands on a gun I would shoot the nearest white settler I meet." "Could you help someone who would volunteer to fight the Boers?" asked Lucia also in a whisper. "I wish there were people who were brave enough to fight them," the farmer replied. Then he kept quiet all of a sudden. Lucia looked around to see if he had seen someone who was not to hear what they were saying. The peasant noted Lucia's surprise and said, "I am afraid I have crucified myself!" The peasant was really scared, Lucia noticed. "Why do you say so?" she asked.

"This talk is suicidal!" the peasant said and went on, "I may end up leaving my family and my sick looking maize crops for one of the many jails. I have committed treason by talking to you against the whites, against the government. People don't normally venture that far these days. It is dangerous to do so, especially with you female teachers....Oh my! What have I done?"

Lucia assured him of his safety. He was not to be afraid to talk to her about liberation. She, on the other hand wished to know of other peasants who were ready to help anyone who would volunteer to fight the settlers out of the blackman's land. The peasant said, "We, we'll see."

Chapter 10

Wiltshire Estates in Charter District covered miles and miles of rich fertile land. Thousands of black indigenous inhabitants of that whole area covered by the Estates and other settler farms had been evicted. Lucia was told this by one of the elderly teachers at Chakara Primary School. He was one of the people whose family was also evicted. He said, "We were banished to these concentrated areas of poor arid land, as you can see, the so-called reserves." He went on, "even those reserves we can see, are meant not for Africans to live on permanently. They are still reserved for the white settlers. We can see we are not to own land in our own country. We are to be labourers on their farms." The man sounded embittered alright, thought Lucia.

Concentrated and crowded areas of poor arid land were known as the "Reserves". Even those so-called "reserves" were meant not for Africans to live on permanently. The white government had other plans for these "reserves", because more and more white farmers, coming into the country needed land. Africans were settled on these only temporarily. Africans were not to own land. They were to be labourers on the settler farms; Lucia repeated this to herself, quoting the elderly teacher.

"Half of Wiltshire Estates lay idle, and the other half is used for extensive animal husbandry. The number of cattle, pigs, etc, in there is unknown" the elderly teacher went on, "Africans are employed on that ranch as herdsmen and so on and they work hard for a wage below subsistence level," the teacher complained to Lucia and added, "Rich farm lands occupied by other settlers adjoin the Wiltshire Estates, and these farmers are rich! I'm telling you."

One September night after Lucia had been at Chakara for about one year, one of the first major guerrilla operations in that area was to take place. The weather man, who had never been her admirer, had predicted a very clear dry day. She had told herself that morning that, weather men were eternal optimists. He was, however, right for the first time that day, Lucia thought. It was nice and dry. And Lucia could not wait for the moment!

At about eleven o'clock, that night, the Wiltshire Estates were set on fire. The fire was huge and it lit up the skies. It was spreading fast. The villagers had begun to be afraid that it was going to reach their settlements even though between their settlements and the fire, there were other settlers' farms and ranches.

From where she was, Lucia watched the fire with great delight. It seems to consume anything and everything that stood in its way. She knew by the size of the flames that the mission had been a success. It was a great inferno. The sky was bright with the "fire of freedom", she thought.

Lucia's work was to meet the combatants who had successfully carried out that big operation. She was waiting to take them to a hiding place. She waited impatiently. They seemed to be taking too long to arrive at the rendezvous. Then, two men approached. They reached the car which was parked under a huge Muhacha tree. But just as quickly, after seeing Lucia, they retreated. They took cover in the bushes some yards away, their pistols ready to shoot. They demanded for an explanation from her. They wanted to know why she was at that spot. The password was "WEVU" (of the soil), she loudly whispered the password. It meant one who belonged to the soil, also meaning an indigenous person, the owner of the land. The password assured the combatants that she belonged to the underground movement. The pistols slowly found their way back into their holsters. They greeted her. But why a woman? The two men were puzzled. They knew that, generally, girls were used by the settler police to infiltrate the underground revolutionary organisation.

"How can we know that this girl is not an informer in possession of the organisation's identity card, or password?" they asked each other. However they both got into the car and waited alertly, for the third comrade to show up. The comrade was the leader of the unit. After waiting for some time, Lucia asked, "What do you think has happened?" They just shrugged their shoulders but one of them suggested that he returned to investigate. She decided, rather desperately, that she would go out there herself and look out for him. "No, let one of us go," It was too late. She was already on her way.

The commander of the unit had been late coming because he was a completionist, or rather a perfectionist, thought his colleagues. He wanted to make sure that even those who would come to the rescue of the ranch would meet some real trouble. So he took some time planting land-mines on some paths and approach roads to the area. But he had also lost his way. At one point as he was running towards what he thought was the direction of the meeting place he had run into two wardens whom he gunned down and went on running. But suddenly he was shaking all over.

He sat down under a tree jittering and unable to believe what was happening to him, he heard explosions. They were the land-mines he had planted a few minutes before. But he did not know where he was and he was worried that his colleagues might be caught while waiting for him. He jumped up and started to run in a direction which he thought would lead him to the appointed place.

In the mean time, Lucia kept walking cautiously towards the scene of the explosions and the fire. She must have walked on for about a quarter of an hour when all of a sudden she saw the figure of a man running towards her. She decided to hide so that by mistake he does not take her for an enemy. He was passing just a few yards from where she was. She whispered loud enough for him to hear, "This way!" He stopped, reached for his pistol and even as he swung round with it in his hand, he was aware of how foolish he looked. He knew that the person behind him could easily have shot him down. He noticed a girl standing there carrying a small first aid pack on her back.

"It's alright! Let's go this way," Lucia told him, moving forward. "Don't move!" he said, "Who are you and what are you doing here?" still aiming his gun at the girl. "Talk or I will shoot!" he demanded, no more shaking.

She lifted her hands high, gave the password "WEVU" and quickly stopped moving towards him but went on whispering or rather hissing at him, "We are wasting valuable time comrade, don't be unreasonable." She was losing her patience. "Let's go or we will be caught in a network of confusion." He did not move. Even after she had identified herself to him as WEVU, the man was not satisfied. He did not trust women that is all. Women were a security risk, he thought. After all they can easily serve the interest of the settler regime as informers. Why did those people at Headquarters decide to send a woman to meet them? He wondered whether they were running short of able men now they were resorting to using women. This is putting us into unforeseen problems indeed!

If this woman turns out to be an agent of the enemy, I'll kill her, he decided, and continued to be very cautious and careful. But this couldn't go on indefinitely. Either way he would end up in the enemy's hands if he remained there or went with this woman. "Ok, you lead the way, with your hands up still, I'm watching you!" he commanded, using his pistol as a pointer.

She started moving gracefully and quickly among the trees and shrubs in front of him. Every now and then she would turn and look at him and smile. She seemed to have recognised this man. Finally they spotted the car parked under the huge Muhacha tree and suddenly he regained his bearings. The area became familiar. He used to lead his small commando unit to that place during their reconnaissance trips.

As leader of the group and commander in charge of that operation, he had visited the place several times. He was the one who, in fact, had recommended the very spot for the rendezvous after the operation, but the woman? He thought, they were not told that the driver of the mini station waggon car which would pick them up would be a woman. Just how far could these people trust her? Perhaps the enemy had already infiltrated the movement, he suspected. When they approached the car, his colleagues came out of the car. He recognised them straight away. He took them aside and secretly warned them to watch the girl very closely. "Any monkey tricks, knife!" he told them.

"Comrades," Lucia called, "You are being very difficult for no good reason at all. Let's move out of here quickly before we are caught in the maze." Two of the combatants sat at the back and the commander took the front seat still watching her suspiciously. Lucia got in quickly, glanced at the man besides her for a second then started the car. She drove fast and the silence in the car, she knew, was just as much not fear of the speed as of the suspicion that they still harboured against her. She again looked at the man besides her and smiled as if to say, 'I got you, if you decide to shoot me, we all die and for what?' She definitely recognised the guy. Tichaona Munyoro from Chiweshe, and she sighed, and then broke the silence:

"I know your pistols are trained and ready to shoot me in the back if I give you any reason to, comrades," she suddenly said to them, "but surely, comrade Tichaona, you of all people, have no reason to be as suspicious as the others," she added.

"What; why not?" Tichaona asked, tried to stand up from his seat; bumped his head onto the roof of the car, "What did you say? And how do you know who I am? What is this?" He fumbled, almost opened the car, and then decided against that.

"As a revolutionary fighter you must also train your memory comrade. Do they call you Tichaona, by the way or Mr Munyoro?" She asked, enjoying the advantage she now had over him. "Anyway, I thank God and I am glad you didn't knock me down at first sight a while ago. I am also thankful that the two shots I heard just before that were not aimed at you," she added and went on, "I'm just trying to get over the shock and the idea that you or anyone of you could have shot me down like a rabbit." She sighed loudly and thought to herself: this was close. We need to improve our set ups, then she asked, "What had happened back there; why the gun fire?"

"No," Tichaona replied hesitantly, then, "Two wardens came my way and...." He stopped talking and, as if a cloud had been lifted from his memory, looked at Lucia curiously, for a while. Then he exclaimed: "Say! My goodness! I know who you are! Wow!" He could not believe his eyes. "Who am I?" Lucia asked with a pleasant smile, facing him, momentarily.

"Yes man, I remember you, Lucia. Teacher Lucia Kashangu! How could I have ever forgotten you like this?" He went on, "This is terrible! Ever since that day, I have been wondering about you, what had happened to you and so on... I have been yearning for you. I've never managed to hear a bit about you." He sighed. "Now, there you are, and I almost finished you altogether today. My Goodness! Who, who is behind all this?" he asked and went on, "This is the worst arrangement ever planned so far. These guys should have warned us. Well...." He kept quiet for some time. Tichaona then introduced Lucia to the other combatants. He told them he had been thinking of this Lucia for a long time, wondering what had happened to her since that day but had never thought of meeting her under guerrilla circumstances. 'No!' he thought, 'Lucia is too precious to be involved in this kind of business. I wonder who talked her into joining this work.' Tichaona was thinking that she should be discouraged from this work right away. It's the work for men, he thought. 'She could help in another capacity but not this' he resolved to dissuade her from this business.

"I say, Lucia," Tichaona said after a short silence, "Tell me, what happened to you since we got arrested and separated that day at the Central Police Station?" "First of all before we go any further, what about you calling me comrade Lucia?" she asked cheerfully but meaning it. He stopped smiling, thought for a moment:

"Alright, comrade Lucia," he said reluctantly. "Tell us your story," Tichaona replied, not as cheerfully anymore, Lucia detected.

Lucia related to them the story of her past. She started it from the day she last saw Tichaona being pushed into a dark room at the end of the corridor, by a policeman at the Central Police Station, in Salisbury's Railway Avenue, up to this meeting. They were all surprised. One of the comrades sitting at the back of the car said, he now recalled the person called Lucia, being talked about at the underground headquarters. He had heard a lot about a lady school teacher by the name of Lucia being one of the intelligence people for the underground and also for transportation. But he had never expected that lady teacher to be involved this far. It's too dangerous for the woman, he thought to himself.

She is in danger of being harmed by any one of the combatants by mistake. It was about two o'clock in the morning when they arrived at the school. Everything was quiet.

Lucia had two bedrooms, a dining room and a kitchen. She had converted the other bedroom into a 'store room', big enough to accommodate more than seven people. One entrance to the 'store room' was in the kitchen. And it was not difficult to give the combatants what they wanted when need arose. No one could ever suspect that 'store room' to be a hide out for human beings....

The next morning, the police arrived at the school with the usual interrogations and searching. Lucia was called for private consultation by a member of the Special Branch (SB) whom she 'worked' with and was given some instructions to carry out in order to help the police to catch the saboteurs who may wander into the school grounds. She listened carefully to the instructions and at the same time asked questions which she thought could help her know the movements of the police so far and the extent of the damage caused by the terrorists. She was told that some suspects were held. Most of the African workers were arrested. But nothing was said about the spotting of any car or about her trip that previous night. 'We are safe so far,' she thought, saying goodbye to the SB men.

"The voice of Zimbabwe," a clandestine radio station operated by the guerrilla movement from a neighbouring country announced, "The revolutionary forces have destroyed one of the pillars of the economy of the enemy." On the other hand, the settler radio claimed that their forces had destroyed an incredibly high number of "terrorists" in an engagement of which the radio did not give details. The settler radio said nothing about the casualties and the damage they had suffered. Understandably, that was the psychological war-game being played. One side highlighted its own 'successes' and deflated its real setbacks. Nothing of substance actually remained in the Wiltshire Estates after the fire. Lucia had heard this from her informers in the Special Branch. Livestock and crops on the vast tracts of land which made up what was the Wiltshire Estates, the information said, were reduced to charcoal. It was impossible to save anything from that inferno, because anyone, the fire fighters, who tried to advance towards the fire, first met the land-mines, and were quickly blown to pieces. These Estates were the biggest suppliers of milk and meat, mostly pork. Now where the pigs were, one could just see the fat surrounding the burnt carcasses. It was terrible the Special Branch man had concluded his report to Lucia, shaking his head sadly. Lucia on her part had pretended to be very sorry and she promised to work hard to flash out the culprits, if she could. In her heart she was actually rejoicing for the success of that one.

The fire had spread to as far as the main road, past where Lucia had parked her car waiting for the combatants. The huge Muhacha tree was burnt down completely. Some neighbouring white farms were not spared either. That was one of the first victories for the suffering black masses of Zimbabwe, she thought. The three guerrillas spent three days in Lucia's house waiting for instructions from headquarters. By the end of the second day they had relaxed and Lucia was very happy, because she learnt how to use their fire-arms. No firing was done though, but she had all the theory grounded into her head. She had the fighters discuss with her the theoretical tactics of guerrilla warfare. Tichaona was a good instructor but was still reluctant; however, he tried to discourage her from getting too interested in becoming a combatant. He did not succeed. She told him she intended to fight with the others until Zimbabwe was free. In the circumstances, Tichaona, now that he had found her again, pledged secretly to work hard to try and dissuade her. He believed he would succeed, one day. He had fallen in love with her the very first moment he had met her in the bus the day they were arrested together. He had been crying for her all that time, hoping to see her again and....

Finally, instructions came from headquarters. Lucia was to drive the three commandos, including the one who had brought the instructions, to their next assignment. She was to wait for them at a rendezvous and then drive them away to another hide-out. She wanted to take part in that operation, but the comrade who had come from headquarters and joined the three combatants refused. Tichaona had thanked his lucky starts for that one. They reminded her that the instructions were that she was in-charge of transportation and nothing else. Tichaona was relieved. He did not want her in any actual combat at all. She was dangerously deep in it already he thought he didn't like it.

From the time he was arrested together with Lucia, Tichaona had been through very difficult circumstances. But he had never stopped thinking of her. He had sat down to tell his colleagues and Lucia the whole story from the day he was separated from Lucia, at the Central Police Station in Salisbury, up to now.

Tichaona was put in one of the interrogation cells of the settler police, he started his story, under a very harsh plain clothed white barbarian, he remembered, whom he said, behaved like an animal. The white man, he explained worked with two African CID's. And he commanded the CID's to beat Tichaona until he was unconscious if he refused to confess the truth. They waited for him to come round only to start on him again. The Whiteman himself took over with questions and heavy slaps on Tichaona's face. Everything which this brutal fascist policeman would think capable of forcing a confession from his victim was done.

The two black men did whatever he commanded them to do to the letter. "Just beat his lights out. He has to know something," the white officer had commanded the two black men who obeyed like two kids. In fact many such confessions were forced out of suspects. Many a times, the suspects made the "confessions" in order to save themselves from the brutalities that the white ape was capable of unleashing. Tichaona went on. His co-workers, the African CIS's, were afraid of him. They obeyed his orders instantly, without questioning.

"Now you bloody dog," the white detective shouted at Tichaona. "Tell me what's happening in your area? Why were you arrested? What did you do?" he demmanded.

"What do you mean?" asked Tichaona. The white man's forehead twitched. This was a very important sign to his African detectives. It showed them that he was getting angry, and he expected them to act on the suspect. The first detective, called Amosi, pounced on Tichaona like an excited cat, slapping him on the cheek. He shouted, partly to intimidate Tichaona into making a confession quickly, and partly to impress his white superior with his high sense of duty, devotion and loyalty to the white man personally and to the colonial regime generally, thought Tichaona, feeling sick.

"Those disturbances in your area," the black detective Amosi, shouted, slapping him again and again, "We know what you people in Chiweshe Reserve are planning," the black detective said. "Do you think we do not know?" and added, "We know more than you realise," he said furiously glancing at the white boss who was seated on a chair watching, his face still twitching.

"Well, if you know everything," said Tichaona, "Then what has that got to do with me?"

"Come on you bloody fool!" shouted the white man to the second black detective, called Herija, who was just standing there. He was expected to do the beating of Tichaona as his colleague was doing. African detective Herija started:

"You think you are clever, hm?" he asked and added, "We will serve you right, just wait and see."

"Do as you please. But you two can see that I am your brother and am innocent." This infuriated the black detectives.

"I have no brother like you, you fool," retorted detective Amosi. They began hitting on Tichaona with their fists, heads, kicks, and Amosi even threw his whole self upon Tichaona. They pounded his bleeding face with their uncontrollable fists and shoed feet.

"Carry on until the devil comes to his senses! I know he knows something," the white man commanded, and he went out leaving the African detectives, who went on beating the guts out of their fellow Zimbabwean. He was beaten so that he could tell the truth! The interrogators believed that since the peasants in Tichaona's area had created some disturbances some time ago, and since they were now quiet, they had to be planning something more dreadful against the settler authority. The detectives thought Tichaona must have known their plans because he came from that area. That was the logic of the ugly oppressor and his African detective constables. But was that the truth? Tichaona asked himself.

The truth of the matter was that Tichaona was absolutely innocent. He was only an ordinary Zimbabwean youth, who, like many other youths was becoming more and more politically conscious, he thought.

Tichaona's father, Mr Tendekayi Munyoro had been among some peasants in Chiweshe Reserve, who went to the "Native Commissioner" and in front of his office, burnt their "Zvitupa". They had refused to pay poll-tax and refrained from taking their cattle and other livestock to the dipping tanks. Many of them were arrested, including old man Munyoro. Many peasants, frightened to death by the appearance of some of these ugly and rough white police officers, confessed falsely in the hope that doing so would spare them from the beatings. They still received the beatings anyway and the heavy prison sentences or heavy fines even after the confessions. They could be punished for having done what they had confessed, even if falsely.

The Africans in Chiweshe Reserve, like others throughout the country had become quiet, helplessly quiet. The worst repressive measures had been unleashed against them by the settler regime's judges. What else did the settler colonial police expect from those helpless oppressed black people? When Tichaona came out of detention he had found his old man, Mr Munyoro implicated and facing a heavy prison sentence with hard labour or pay a heavy fine. Tichaona managed, with the help of friends, to save his father by paying the heavy fine. What truth now did those settler police want from him? He wondered.

"Brothers," Tichaona called after the white terror had gone out of the room. "What is it that I have done that you are so prepared to kill me for?"

"Save your breath, you bloody fool. You think the white man is here to fool around with idiots like you?" shouted detective Amosi. At that accusation, Tichaona spat a large amount of bloody spit right into detective Amosi's face and said:

"You running dogs of the white devils! Your days are numbered." He stammered on, "The day of judgement is coming; it's quite near for you now. You kill me today you won't stop the wind of revolution. It will start with all of you running dogs. Your settler pig bosses won't be able to save you. They will not be here to, save you. I.... I....will see ....to....to...that," he struggled to utter the last words, because the infuriated detectives had increased their ferocity, pounding, stumping, slapping, kicking and punching him. They wished their white boss was there to see just how well they could do their job. Tichaona stopped talking and started to cough and groan very deeply. All fell silent, and black all around him. A trickle of blood oozed from his nose and mouth. He was unconscious. The two fellow Zimbabweans had gone on without realising that they were pounding an almost dead body. African detective Herija stopped beating and shouted: "He is dead!" He rushed out of the room, wet, with sweat, to call the white detective who replied coolly: "You have killed him, not me. I wasn't there." He talked so lightly that detective Herija was rooted to the ground. For the first time something in Herija's heart was disturbed. He was stunned by the white man's remarks and obvious lack of appreciation for the work done so conscientiously well. Herija kept standing there sweating, waiting for further instructions.

"You bloody fool! Look at yourself. Do something about it then," the white man shouted, spitting terror through his teeth and viewing the trembling African detective all over as if he was something nauseating. Detective Herija could not stand it. He quickly ran out of the room to fetch a bucket of cold water. He ran to where Tichaona's body was lying slumped up and splashed the whole bucket of cold water on his head and body. Herija murmured to himself:

"I am not going to beat him again, not me. They can sack me if they want to. This man is innocent, after all, and I know it."

"Well," answered detective Constable Amosi, "I am not going to stop beating him because he spat into my face. He shouldn't have done that to me. No one has ever spat on me, let alone with his bloody spit. I'll beat him on," Amosi went on like a caged leopard. "He can't do a thing like that to me and expect me to be silent and only feel sorry for him. No; not me. May be before he had spat on me, but certainly not now! He shouldn't have done that!"

"Carry on my friend, please yourself," said Herija. "I am through with this job." At that same time the white detective entered the room.

"What did you say?" the white man asked his eyes straight at Herija. "You bloody devils; you don't know how stupid you are. Throw him into his bloody cell. He will be alright. If not, then you two have done it, not me." He said this marching out of the room. Herija was baffled. The white detective was actually accusing them of killing their fellow blackman. Did the white man care? Herija asked himself. No! He did not care. As long as he could use one black man against another for his express benefit, all was in order. In this case it did not matter at all if the black man died, Herija thought. What mattered was a white man to die at the hands of a black man! Herija, this time was thinking like a converted black man.

Tichaona did not know for how long he had lain where he was when he recovered his consciousness. Though it was dark Tichaona realised that he was back in his original cell. 'When did I come back here?' He started thinking. 'I know I left this room at dawn with two African men and was in a room where there was the most vicious white man I have ever encountered in my life.' His head was as if a heavy stone was pressing it down. His clothes were wet. He tried to get up. He fell back. Never before had his body ached so much with pain. They had reduced him to a cabbage! He thought. He was helpless. Never before had he hated another human being as he did at that time. He hated the oppressive system that was responsible for bringing him into that solitary cell. That was Tichaona's third day in police custody. He lay there in terrible pain, started thinking of the beautiful girl Lucia. Her face appeared in his mind. 'Are they treating her as they are treating me?' he thought and prayed, 'Please God, let this be for me alone. How can that girl stand all this?' he wondered whether he would ever see Lucia again; or whether they would both die in those torture chambers. His mind wandered here and there. He thought of things he had never thought would come into his mid at one time. But one thing puzzled him: how could those brothers of his, the black detectives, beat him more than the white man had actually ordered them to do? How can a Zimbabwean want to beat another Zimbabwean to death only to please the white foreigner? He wondered whether it was the fear of the white man, fear for the white man, or love for money that drove those black detectives to give him such a beating. He fell asleep again.

Tichaona was awakened by a loud order: "You, get up, you!"

There was light outside. He could see the light coming in through the small barred window high up near the ceiling. 'Another day? For how long I have I been lying in this place?' He could not remember.

"I said get up, can't you hear?" It was detective Herija, who pulled him up rather roughly. Tichaona could not stand. Every part of his body was in pain. He was very weak and hungry too. Amosi just peeped through the door and shrugged his shoulders.

Tichaona's mouth tasted like rotten eggs. When he staggered up, he felt dizzy, and he fell back and banged his head very hard on the wall and slumped down on the floor in terrible pain. His vision was blurred. He saw double images of detective Herija. Herija remained alone with Tichaona. Detective Amosi had hurriedly left the cell. Herija said to Tichaona: "I did not mean to do that", he whispered hurriedly. "Now listen very carefully. Carry on, pretending as if you are still unconscious. Even if they pour cold water on you or slap you do not stir or flinch. I am sure they will leave you alone, at least for a while." Tichaona was surprised by those words and advice from one of the men who had tortured him to near death.

He almost asked, "Why are you wasting your breath, you running dog?" But he had no strength to talk and so he obeyed. After a few minutes the white detective came in followed by detective Amosi. Tichaona was slapped twice across the face by the white detective. That was really painful but he kept still, praying that the slapping was not repeated, he would not take any more without moving, or fainting, maybe forever.

"Bring some icy cold water," commanded the white man. Tichaona heard heavy hurrying footsteps. They faded away and soon were heard again, each time becoming louder and obviously drawing nearer. Splash! The water was thrown on his face. 'Goodness, this is cold!' he thought, but he never stirred. The act was repeated and he was soaked all over in icy cold water. The white man felt for his pulse and said: "His bloody heart is alive alright. Leave him lying in the cold water for a while, he will come round," the white man ordered and walked out of the room hurriedly.

"He has been unconscious for too long." Tichaona heard. It was the voice of detective Herija who went on: "They must call a doctor or take him out of here." 'I have now got a friend here.' Tichaona thought.

"What?" asked detective Amosi. "He will have to be alright, otherwise, even if he dies I will beat his dead body to nothing. He should not have spit on my face yesterday." He then promised more beatings for Tichaona and went out.

'So I have been lying here in this state since yesterday,' wondered Tichaona. 'It's not too bad,' he consoled himself, 'I thought it has been more than a week,' Tichaona thought. Detective Herija, Tichaona's new friend had remained behind while Amosi had left the room. He was the one who had the keys to the cell. He said to Tichaona, holding him under the shoulders and helping him up: "Come on, get up and lie in that corner there where it is dry."

"Why are you trying to help me after all?" Tichaona asked weakly, while he was being helped to move from the wet spot to a dry corner of the cell. He wanted to say something else. "Sh, sh, sh, sh! Don't talk. Just obey. Don't ask questions," Herija warned. "Should I go on pretending to be a near corpse?" Tichaona asked. Herija nodded approvingly and said: "I will try to come and see you again myself." "I appreciate your help, son of the soil," said Tichaona, but he thought, 'I still don't see why you should do all this after beating all my guts out.'

"Shh....! Quiet," detective Herija ordered as he went out, locking the door behind him.

'Well, at least, there is a brother for me in this place. What next? I know I have to lie in the cold water for a while.' Tichaona went on thinking. He remembered Lucia again. Her image kept on lingering in his mind. The image of a suffering Lucia, after being badly beaten by a black policeman at the command of a fierce white police pig, kept on looming in his imagination. 'Lord! Why should she face such untold suffering? She is innocent. She is only too innocent, and….and….'

He was awakened from his imagination by footsteps, then the jingling of keys in his door. He tensed, and then thank goodness it was Herija. Herija had brought Tichaona a dry blanket. "I could not bring you dry clothes," he told Tichaona. Tichaona felt good, although he was still shivering uncontrollably, and the pain!

"What's the next thing brother?" Tichaona asked, his whispering coming through clenched teeth due to the cold and shivering.

"I don't know, but you are still half dead, okay? At least for another short while," replied Herija.

This time Tichaona felt confident to ask Herija about Lucia: "Tell me brother, how is the lady?"

"I don't know. I have not seen her. I only heard that you were arrested together with a girl," Herija replied.

"I hope she is not receiving the same type of treatment I am receiving," Tichaona whispered. His friend seems to have ignored this last remark, but he said:

"Listen, when you hear people coming to your door, keep the blanket to that corner behind the door. Move quickly to your original place in the cold water and lie as still as you were when we first left you," advised detective Herija. Tichaona nodded. He dreaded that moment, and shivered even more violently. Herija left and locked the room. Tichaona felt thirsty. There was the patch of water on the floor where he had been lying. He knelt, bent down and licked the floor for the water, like a dog. This made him feel better, although the shivering increased. For a long time, Tichaona, gritting his teeth, wondered how he would be able to keep still, pretending to be half dead if he went on shivering with the same intensity. He tried to take his mind off the fact that he was sick and was feeling cold. He thought of his father. His father had informed him that when he was under police custody, he was mercilessly beaten. He never elaborated. Actually, the old man did not want to remember that dreadful past. He never wanted to talk about it, not even to his son. Tichaona recalled how he had tried to coax his father into telling him what had happened, but failed.

Was my father beaten like this? Tichaona asked himself and went on. If he was, that old man must be very strong and courageous. But how can these devils treat such an old man like this? It's incredible! The devils….Several footsteps were approaching, and soon were right at his door. He moved fast back to the puddle of water and lay on his tummy with his face down. He had relaxed a bit, and only that way, lying on his tummy, could he keep still and not shiver violently.

People entered Tichaona's cell. Someone touched his temple and said: "He is alive." Tichanoa instantly recognised the voice of the fierce white detective, who went on, "Should I give him a slap on the cheek? He may wake up, you know." "Yes, some of these guys are very good at pretending, I know," said the shameless voice of African detective Amosi.

"And so?" asked the new European voice rather cynically. "You must really be good at beating political criminals," the new voice said, and went on, "Were you the ones who did this to this fellow?" and added sarcastically, "And you still want to go on doing it to him even if he is half dead?" There was silence for a few seconds. Even the fierce white detective said nothing. Then Tichaona felt hands touching his wet clothes: "And he is soaking wet! Where did the water come from?" asked the newcomer.

"We were trying to revive him, sir, by pouring icy cold water over him," replied African detective constable Herija.

"Did it work?" "No," Herija replied. "Then why did you leave him lying in the pool of water?" the man, who, by now sounded to Tichaona, to be a superior person to all those he had so far met, went on asking, sarcastically: "Did you want to drown him?" "These were orders from sergeant Fielding," detective Herija replied firmly. The big white detective looked sharply at Herija, and a very strong: "You bloody liar," accused sergeant Fielding, his forehead twitching, "Watch what you say, you bloody idiot!" he warned strongly, the twitching becoming more violent and spreading to the whole face and the upper limbs. Herija has put himself into trouble with his boss, thought Tichaona, listening very attentively.

And it was only at this time that Tichaona realised that the big white detective was called Fielding and he was a sergeant. 'I hope I shall meet this Fielding in the field of battle, one day' Tichaona thought, 'I'll beat his lights out in a minute, no matter how big he is'.

"Never mind Mr Fielding," said the superior man. "Get him out of here and give him dry clothes and something to eat and drink." Tichaona was surprised that even the ugly and fierce white man, who had ordered him to be beaten to death, the one who had sounded as if he owned that whole part of the world, could also be given orders and obey them without question. He is a paper tiger after all, even if he is the terror itself, thought Tichaona.

The two African detectives removed Tichaona by carrying him out of the wet cell, to another solitary confinement, not far from the cell he was being removed from. Amosi spat at Tichaona's face, "You thank your lucky starts. You bloody bastard...." Tichaona was confined to a lonely cell again, which was his bedroom, dining room and toilet – the unimaginable and unbearable rotten stench!

There had been a reign of terror in Rhodesia since the state of emergency. Many Zimbabweans, especially males, were beaten to death in those notorious cells which were known as "the grilling chambers for political prisoners." Those who came out alive could in most cases be mentally deranged. Tichaona did not die, nor did he become mentally deranged. After one month of solitary confinement, Tichaona was charged with insulting the Prime minister of the regime, and for threatening to overthrow the minority clique by violent means. He was sentenced to seven months in prison with hard labour. He was given no option of a fine.

Talking of hard labour, it was hard labour in the truest sense, Tichaona remembered. Tichaona's group, most of them political prisoners, plus some hardcore criminals were building a military road through the jungles of Zimbabwe to the North West of the country, right up to the Zambezi River that borders with a neighbouring country Zambia.

The beating and the hard labour that Tichaona encountered extreamly hardened him against the settlers. While serving his sentence he was quiet, followed all orders and worked as hard as was expected. The African prison wardens soon became friendly to him as they had no cause to hate or roughen him. He was quiet and followed their orders. He even helped them keep discipline among other prisoners. He used to tell his inmates: "Friends let us not behave like criminals, even though these people have tried to paint crime on us. Our day will come when they will all be criminals after our judgement." This way, Tichaona gained friends and respect among the prison inmates, as well as the prison wardens.

During the hard work, he never forgot the sneering face and the barking voice of sergeant Fielding. Another thing he thought of was the people's army. He kept thinking about it. He knew that one day he may need the knowledge of those surroundings. He would visually survey the area very carefully. Tichaona saw a big advantage in the building of that road. It would serve both the liberation and the colonial armies, he thought.

He completed his prison sentence. On his release, sme of his prison warden friends, secretly promised him that they would help the Zimbabwean nationalist movement in anyway possible. So he should keep them informed.

Tichaona went to his place of work but he found he had been dismissed. They don't employ terrorists, he was told. He therefore left for Chiweshe

Reserve where he started helping his father on the small field allotted to their family. He was restless. 'That sergeant Fielding!' he thought, 'A name I will never forget....A face I will never forget.' His restlessness increased. More thought about this sergeant Fielding always made his heart burn with rage. 'How can I fight back that white terror? I have to find a way.' He consulted his father: "Can't these white settlers be fought out of our country? If I think of that sergeant Fielding, I strongly feel a way has to be there someway to bring justice back to this country."

"Ah! Tichaona, I forgot to tell you that a liberation army has been formed while you were in jail and it is already very active against the Boers." His father told him about the existence of the underground movement. Tichaona stopped what he was doing and paid all his attention to the old man. He was surprised that the old man had all this information about the struggle! He felt so small and ignorant.

He asked his father to give him more information about the underground movement. His father gave him some details. In their area, one of the underground organisers was Mr Sanganayi, who used to be a headmaster at Muzhanje Primary School, where Lucia had been teaching. He was then a driver for the A.A Removals. He drove huge removals across Rhodesia to and from the neighbouring countries, transporting agricultural implements and other heavy goods. While thus engaged, it was easy for Sanganayi to give a 'lift' to freedom fighters, or lift their essential equipment within Rhodesia from one point to another, to and from some neighbouring countries.

In a few days Tichaona had made contact with Sanganayi, and informed him of his intentions. Tichaona had maintained his contact with his prison warden friends. When they learnt that he was going to join the revolutionary army, they also expressed their desire to join. He begged the wardens to remain at their work so that they would help the movement with vital information from within the enemy's camp. Tichaona's friend Herija, the detective, also pledged to help with information. Herija also in the end, turned out to be more useful to the underground movement, than the prison wardens, because of his place as a member of the Special Branch, in the enemy's establishment. He was very tactful and was never suspected.

There was this place where Tichaona and his fellow prisoners had worked, constructing a road between Salisbury and a border town of Chirundu through the deep forests to the north west of Zimbabwe. Tichaona had recommended this area as suitable for guerrilla training and other guerrilla activities. Sanganayi consulted the headquarters and within a few days some surveyors from the underground movement were sent to the area together with

Tichaona. This place was found to be suitable for the training of guerrillas.

Tichaona, some of his prison-mates and other men were given two trained comrades and one of them was Munongwa, to train them in guerrilla tactics and warfare. One of Tichaona's former prison wardens called Museve insisted on leaving his job to be fully involved in the training. He was accepted and they worked very hard together in their training. Tichaona, a very determined, strong and brave young man, who would have died in prison through heavy beatings, soon became commander of this newly-trained commando group. Tichaona's unit armed itself initially through what they called "requisition missions" against the enemy. These were special missions aimed at acquiring equipment and other supplies from the enemy depots, and carving out sabotage operations against the enemy. Naturally, these missions involved long distance walking, and running.

"It is my prison warden friend Museve here, and fellow prisoner Rukwa here," Tichaona told Lucia as he touched his two comrades' shoulders intimately, "with whom I was trained. We have carried out a number of missions together," he added, "more or less successfully," Tichaona concluded the account of his experiences so far. Lucia was really spell-bound by Tichaona's sad experiences. She felt sorry for him but was happy for his successes in the liberation army.

Now Shupai (Lucia), as Sarah in her hospital bed, in Sinoia General Hospital, realised that she had been thinking of Tichaona, ever since she had read Dr Mutero's report. Dr Mutero had described Tichaona's condition as critical. Poor Tichaona, she had thought, and prayed that he would pull through the serious condition and fight on. Shupai's mind had lingered back to the time of the Wiltshire Estates operation. Tichaona had sounded very aggressive and had promised to carry on with the struggle, no matter what, until he got hold of sergeant Fielding and punished him. Shupai also recalled the other work she had performed with Tichaona and others, such as the Rhodes and Founders' Operatoin. That was one of the first guerrilla activities she had been fully involved in, she thought. She remembered how Tichaona and herself kept quarrelling. He had not wanted her to be included. And had tried to discourage her not to be so involved, because he loved her and was afraid of losing her, he had pleaded with her. He could not succeed, however. Finally, he gave in.... Her mind flashed back to that Rhodes and Founders' holiday when she worked with Tichaona.

The underground movement had planned that throughout Rhodesia, certain strategic shops in towns and cities must be sabotaged. These were the ones owned by the minority regime's business supporters who practised strict colour discrimination. The attacks were to be carried out simultaneously against those targets, and a suitable occasion was considered. One of the holidays maybe, Christmas or Easter holidays? It was found out that the settlers respected their Rhodes and Founders' holidays in July more than other holidays of the year. These were celebrated for four full days, in honour of those first British pioneer colonialists, like Cecil John Rhodes and others, who supposedly founded or discovered the rich colony of "Southern Rhodesia" to add to the British Empire. The Rhodes and Founders' were the most important and most respected political holidays in this British colony. Most of the settler farmers and their families used to make sure that they spent these holidays drinking and merry making and relaxing in towns. Endless parties would be organised for the celebration of this occasion. During those holidays there would be more whites in the towns, especially the large towns like Salisbury, Bulawayo, Umtali, Gwelo, etc., than during the normal days.

Most of the African workers and their families, on the other hand, this was a good chance for them to spend the holidays at their rural homes with relatives and friends. They had no cause to celebrate, they thought.

The operation was organised for the day before the Rhodes and Founders holidays when the whites frantically did their shopping in the major towns' shops throughout the country. These shops, the underground movement decided, were an institution in themselves which maintained the policy of segregation in support of the minority regime. White settler farmers would be busy going from one department store to another doing thfeir last minute shopping and dining and wining in these department shops' cosy restaurants. Most of the blacks would be busy at the Musika (Market) bus terminus for long distance busses to the 'Reserves'.

These department stores in would usually be packed with goods in the periods preceding major holidays like the Rhodes and Founders'. Lucia, Tichaona and Museve were assigned to Salisbury. They were to join Marwei's group of two girls. Certain shops in Salisbury were well known for their colour discrimination. Among those identified were the L and M Silliards, Drumonds and Bollars, Serworks and Jacquelines and a few others. These were stores virtually for whites only. They also provided exquisite restaurants for the shoppers who could go on until late. The colour line was solid. Exceptions were, however, made for selected well dressed Africans who wanted to do their shopping in these elegant department stores. In these stores, prices tended to be higher than in others such as the OK Bazaars, Woolworths and so on. These department stores were in fact meant to serve the upper class of the white society. Most Africans avoided patronising these shops anyway. They hated, above all, the sneers they got from the scornful white and coloured girls who served at the counters, and the black watchmen, who were stricter and even more discriminative than the whites themselves.

The organisers of the sabotage operation had to do all they could to warn the Zimbabweans against being near the huge department stores on the day stipulated for the action. It wasn't difficult. They simply went round telling the people and reminding them of the high prices and the colour line: "Leave the whites to do the shopping in their own stores," the organisers persuaded the people. "Why be bothered by segregation? Why should you go there only to be humiliated, when your objective is only to buy, and to buy using your own money?" They went on, "Rhodes and Founders' holidays have nothing to do with us, any way." They asked, "Why should we pretend that we are happy with those days when we are not? We can do our shopping on other days which have nothing to do with the oppressor's days of happiness over our oppression." The campaign to warn the people went smoothly.

On the day before the Rhodes and Founders' holidays, Marwei and Lucia's group, of two smartly dressed young men and three girls, moved lackadaisically among the shoppers. They carried all sorts of "shopping bags" and "parcels", doing the shopping, in their own style. Their targets were the identified huge department stores. They went on, 'forgetting' some of their 'parcels' and 'bags' very conveniently and discretely among the packed goods and crowded shops. Shupai recalled how she had to buy a very expensive dress in Jacquelines in order to have a parcel to carry because she had just disposed of her last 'parcel'. They all had to buy something in return, she remembered.

The operation was successful. Lucia, Tichaona and Museve heard the news on her car radio on their way back to Chakara School. Marwei and her friends were back in Mufakose Township where they lived. The bombs went off at the time set. In Salisbury, the explosions could be heard a long distance away, in the segregated townships. Yes, that was destruction and a half! Lucia thought. The operation shook the wits out of the settlers throughout the country. The roots of white settler power were shaken. Many whites died in Salisbury and Bulawayo, Umtali, Gwelo and others. During the Rhodes and Founders' holidays, the rich white farmers and their families usually migrated into the cities. Even those in small towns had the habit of going to the large cities to spend their time and money merry-making. But this time....The few Africans who did not heed the advice of their fellow Africans not to be shopping in those stores or to be in the city centres around that time, were caught in the maze. The Rhodes and Founders' holidays of that year were turned into days of mourning instead of days of dining and wining, merry-making and laughter.

Rescue workers worked day and night digging out bodies buried in heaps of rubble; the radio reported the following day that L and M Silliards both in Salisbury and Bulawayo and Gwelo were the tallest buildings. They had the largest number of departments and cosy restaurants than other huge stores. L and M Silliards, naturally, produced larger and deeper heaps of rubble than the other stores attacked, the underground organisers noticed.

As usual the settler police had some suspects arrested. But that did not remedy the damage caused to property owned by settlers, nor did it help the lives that perished in the operation. Two settler farmers who had lost their families in the attack were talking. One said, "I have nothing to live for anymore," and went on, "I am packing my bags and am quitting this God forsaken place and country."

"Where will you go?" asked his friend and neighbour.

"I will go down south. It is safer there, than this goddamned kaffir country," replied the first settler, and went on, "Some crazy friends advise that I should stay and try to revenge the death of my wife and two sons. But that won't satisfy me. That won't bring my family back. These kaffirs are up to no good any more, man. They are up in arms against me, against us. They mean to kill us all." He continued, "This time they really mean business. They might catch me before I catch them, to carry out the suggested revenge." He continued bitterly, "I fought the Nazis in the Second World War. That was enough. I have neither the stomach nor the time to fight against these brutal and hungry Natives. After all, just as Hitler could not defeat us in our own land, we can't defeat these Natives in their own land."

"That's what you think. Well, me, I will stay right here. Any kaffir who provokes me will be in trouble." Declared the second settler farmer, "I'll make sure I kill six of them, each one for my mother, my wife, my daughter and for my three sons."

Many of these settlers left the country. Most of those who had farms bordering the "Reserves" left their farms altogether for the towns and cities, because they had become easy targets for the hungry and oppressed natives.

Immediately after depositing the several "shopping bags and parcels" where they were supposed to have been deposited, the sabotage teams had left the towns for the Reserves to spend the Rhodes and Founders' holidays with relatives and friends. Marwei and her two friends were the only members of the group who lived in Salisbury, at Mufakose Township. She and many residents of Mufakose heard, with pleasure the deafening explosions in town. That's it, she thought.

Chapter 11

The afternoon visiting time at Sinoia African General Hospital was from three to four. Mrs Mutero came into the women's ward to visit Shupai for the first time since Shupai was admitted. "Hi, Sarah!" she greeted quietly but cheerfully, hugging Shupai intimately and asked "How do you feel now?"

"Ah! greetings to you Mai Mutero. I'm quite alright except for the hanging leg." They laughed together while Mrs Mutero was unwrapping some parcels for Shupai.

Sister Higgins had for the past few days wondered why Dr Mutero's wife did not visit Sarah. This had confirmed her suspicions that Sarah was Mutero's girl. Just like some of the girls he brings in the ward, he seems a womaniser. When she saw Mutero's wife come into the ward she was curious to see what would happen, or how Mutero's wife would behave towards Sarah. She watched anxiously, standing at the door of the nurses' duty room. She was disappointed but somehow unhappy at the sight of Mrs Mutero; a very attractive woman, Sister Higgins noted and felt jealousy. The way they greeted each other....These two seemed to be long-standing friends. She observed the two, smiling widely at each other, hugging generously, talking quietly, intimately. Sister Higgins had been a secret admirer of Dr Mutero, a carefree and handsome black guy who could be a really capable lover, but he is always so busy, he doesn't even realised she loved him, sister Higgins thought to herself sadly and quietly. Mrs Mutero excused herself for not visiting Shupai often. "I've been extremely busy at the 'sick-bay', you know," Said Mrs Mutero in a low voice.

"I know. Dr Mutero told me. How are your patients?" Shupai asked.

"Tafi is doing very well," she whispered. "The other two are now okay and would be ready to go back to the 'city' in a few days' time." Mrs Mutero went on, "Tichaona's condition has improved tremendously. He's out of danger now. Last –e-e...." She fumbled in her hand bag and brought out a folded note and handed it to Shupai, saying: "Read this while I go to the men's ward to visit another patient of ours. I'll come back shortly" she said.

Shupai opened the letter: "Another colleague was brought to the 'sick-bay' two nights ago," the letter began. It was quite long, several pages, she observed and read on. "He is in a critical condition. His name is Guva-Makuva. The three 'work-men' who brought him are Chakanyuka, Makano and Keni the driver. I'm sure you know all of them. They are in the same team at one of your work places. They were all very happy to hear that you are recovering quickly. A dramatic story is behind all this." Shupai tensed and read on....

"In a heavy and bitter encounter with the enemy in the Bindura area," the note went on, "Chakanyuka, Makuva, Keni, Makano and others had decided to break engagement and run. They had suffered heavy causalities on their part. Makuva was seriously wounded and was captured. He was sent to Harare General Hospital. The police or army or the doctors at Harare Hospital could have left him to die. But one of the policemen insisted that the doctors perform extensive surgery on him to remove two bullets and some shrapnel from his body. He survived, however, and has been under heavy sedation and guarded heavily too. They aimed at extracting info from him, for sure. He managed to get away before they reached to that stage." Shupai put the letter down and closed her eyes. She tried to imagine Makuva. She knew him from Marondera Detention Camp. Makuva was the one who had play acted the 'mad-man' as part of the plan to get released from detention so that he could join the underground movement. Makuva had gone so far and now a strong combatant, Shupai thought, now seriously wounded in battle, and captured by the enemy and in hospital. My Goodness! Shupai was imagining how a person who had had such heavy surgery done on him could "get away." She picked up the letter and continued to read.

"You would, however, be pleased, to know that many people, of different walks of life, are now either overtly or covertly involved in the struggle. They are doing this in different and most subtle ways. This man, Makuva was heavily guarded at Harare General Hospital. He was never left alone. A policeman was at his side-ward door day and night. While Makuva struggled for his life in the operating theatre and in the ward, two of our people there, a male nurse and a female nurse were also busy. They were watching him as closely as the police were doing. Two nights ago, thanks to the two nurses, two of our "work-men" managed to enter Harare Hospital, removed the patient and drove him here." Dramatic and amazing indeed, Shupai thought, still tensed. How did they do it? She asked herself. She remembered Chakanyuka, tall strong and heavily built with a big head. His stature was almost that of Tichaona, athletic and quick. He was a daring young man who always aimed for success. Failure, to him was taboo. The other two, Makano and Keni were friends from the same school. Their driving force was Chakanyuka, she had observed. But the two were also strong and brave, she thought of Keni, the driver with his imaginary chewing gum. When he is excited he would chew away even vigorously. She remembered and read on:

"After eleven o'clock at night, the Senior House Officer on call had completed his night rounds with the sister-in-charge of the night shift. It was quiet again in the men's surgical ward and quite dim too in the corridor. Dressed like doctors, with stethoscopes hanging round the neck or peeping from the white coat pockets, Chakanyuka and Makano moved fast along the corridor towards the men's surgical ward. A black policeman on guard was sitting unsuspiciously on a chair near the door of one of the side-wards. He was dozingly watching the corridor with his back to the main ward. He saw two doctors moving very fast, past him and the side-wards and entered the main ward. They must have been called for an emergency, the policeman guessed. He stood up lazily and paced back and forth past the side-ward. He was young and seemed to be filled with self-importance. Promotion to corporal was his motto in this job, he thought of all the old African police corporals, who were about to retire. He stopped pacing and peeped into the side-ward and watched the prisoner patient closely. The prisoner was bandaged heavily about the forehead, his eyes partly covered by the bandages. His right arm was supported by a splint where the drip was flowing steadily. His other side, the left side and neck, and perhaps the whole body were bandaged, the policeman thought. Cabbage, the policeman said to himself. No, it is doubtful that this man would attempt escape, the policeman assured himself. He came back to his chair sat down and relaxed confidently, facing the corridor.

"The male nurse emerged from the main ward, and passed the policeman with confidence. He had a small metal receiver covered by a white cloth. He entered the side ward. The policeman strained to catch any conversation between the patient and the nurse. It was useless. There was no conversation at all except for the noise of a hypodermic syringe and needle thrown back into the receiver. The policeman looked at his wrist watch. The time was past midnight. The time for the patient's night medication, he guessed. The night was quiet. It was, however overlain with the cries of children and babies somewhere in the children's ward, he thought. While his attention was drawn to the side ward, the two "doctors" came out quietly from the main ward. Chakanyuka slugged the policeman hard at the nape of his neck. The man sagged and fainted quietly. They dragged him into the side-ward before he fell from his chair onto the floor. They tied his hands and legs to the bed and covered his mouth with adhesive tape. At once another nurse, female, appeared with a stretcher. Within seconds the stretcher had found its way into the elevator, going down with the two "doctors". The female nurse had remained up and returned quickly to the main ward. The male nurse had also been tied onto the bed and pretended to have been hurt in the side ward. When the two "doctors" reached the ground floor they wheeled the stretcher quickly to the side hospital entrance.

One of them, Makano, lifted the patient up from the stretcher and they rushed outside. A night watchman saw them, became suspicious, and came running to investigate. He received, from Chakanyuka, two heavy blows on the head, a kick, a push, and he fell down head first.

"Last night the BBC radio reported," the letter went on: 'The terrorists in Rhodesia are becoming more and more sophisticated. At Harare African General Hospital, in Salisbury, a policeman on guard duty and a male nurse were found by another nurse lying unconscious in a private ward where a prisoner patient had been under going treatment. This prisoner is believed to be one of the guerrillas who had been seriously injured in combat and was captured by the Rhodesian security forces. He was in a critical condition. It is suspected he was aided by some of his colleagues, who had come in dressed as doctors and managed to gain entrance into the men's surgical private ward by slugging the policeman who was guarding the prisoner patient. The male nurse who was attending to the patient at that time was found unconscious and tied onto the hospital bed. He is suspected to have received, instead, the injection he was to give the patient at that time because an empty hypodermic syringe was found in a receiver on the locker. Harare General Hospital is believed to be one of the largest referral African Hospitals in the country.' The report went on. 'One of the night watchmen was found lying dead behind one of the bushy trees at the side entrance of the hospital with deadly injuries on his head.' The BBC report ended. They are becoming sophisticated indeed, don't you think?" the letter ended.

Mrs Mutero came back as Shupai finished reading the letter. She handed it back to Mrs Mutero, and whispered, "Dramatic indeed! Really amazing!" and added, "This is the best news I've ever heard. Now I can appreciate how busy you've been." She said this holding Mrs Mutero's hand. "How is he now?"

"He's going to live. Actually, he's alright now." She looked at Shupai, detected some doubt in those eyes, she added, "Really, his condition has improved greatly, you know he's going to be active again in no time, thanks to the extensive surgery he underwent at Harare Hospital."

"Oh, I hope so." Shupai kept quiet for a whole minute. Mrs Mutero could see that she was in deep thoughts. Then she exclaimed, "Isn't this something? Oh how I wish I...." She tried to sit up but the traction....Mrs Mutero gently pushed her back on her pillows and fixed the pillows properly saying gently and quietly:

"Don't you worry, now. We'll keep you posted. The patient will be alright, I assure you. The two great "doctors" and their driver are back at their posts by now." She added, "They've sent their best wishes to you. But the big one," she lowered her voice even more, "Chaknyuka, appeared not to be amused when we told then about you. He sounded somewhat disappointed when he asked, 'You mean that teacher is actually fighting?' Mutero and Tafi nodded several times. 'And she got injured in battle? My foot! That woman is really something, something, isn't she? He kept quiet and sulked until they left. The other two, however, seemed pleasantly surprised."

"I don't even wonder at all," Shupai said and commented, "Him and I parted being at logger-heads. He believes very deeply that wars are the prerogative of men, and women must just stay appealing to men, remain in the kitchen and prepare delicious dishes for their husbands. He is not different from Tichaona."

"Male chauvinist, isn't he?" commented Mrs Mutero. Shupai just nodded several times. "Well, if he can't move with the times, let him be." Mrs Mutero stood up to leave. "Take care now, Sarah. I'll visit you some more." She was already moving towards the door.

After Mrs Mutero had left, Shupai got to thinking about Makuva, Chakanyuka and his group. She retraced the contents of the letter she had just read. The gallant act those boys put up, she thought proudly. Those boys had been great, ever since she had worked with them at Chakarara. She began to remember the first time she met Chakanyuka and his group. That was an encounter and half! She thought, she would never forget that group, and the opposition some of the men levelled against her, they could have killed her, she thought, and remembered....

It was a few days after the Rhodes and Founders' holiday operation. At Chakarara Primary School Lucia (Shupai) had received a message from the headquarters of the underground movement that she would receive a group of nine guerrillas. She would be required, the message went on, to distribute them to their respective assignments and hideouts. The message continued, "Nine combatants will be dropped by cars two miles away from the school. They will walk and arrive at the school in groups of three at three different times from seven in the evening." It would relatively be dark then, she thought, and read on. "You will meet each group behind the main school building, the one near the bush they would be coming from."

At seven in the evening Lucia waited eagerly, hiding behind the main school building near the bush. She saw three men approaching cautiously as if in doubt. She moved towards them to reveal herself. When the men saw her, they tensed, but kept on walking. They thought the woman was just a passer by.

But, to their extreme surprise, she extended her hand to greet the one in front, whispering "Well...." They started to back away, all eyes trained at her.

All had their hands in their pockets on their pistols or knives. One of the men at the back whispered: "Here we are, in real trouble." They stopped moving back, stood still, all closely watching her. Lucia realised the problem. She had to identify herself by mentioning the password, "WEVU" and she asked them to follow her to the house. They did not follow. They stood there debating among themselves: "That woman," the man who had whispered before spoke. "We did not expect a woman, did we, Keni?" "No," answered Keni, who seemed to be leading the small group. He was of medium height, strong, like a weight lifter and seemed determined. Before he joined the struggle he, Keni had worked as a driver with the Swift Transport Company. "Then what's going on?" asked the first speaker. "I don't know," answered Keni, "But let's find out. Be careful. No shooting if she turns otherwise." Lucia had moved forward expecting them to follow her. She looked back and saw them standing even further away from her. She returned. "Be reasonable comrades. It's getting late. We have to move fast." Command or persuasion? Keni asked himself. They followed her warily, to the house. She observed Keni. This one is foxy. A person who doesn't seem to be interested in saying much, she thought. What is he chewing? She asked herself and wondered if these boys were supplied with chewing gum. This one is chewing on so frantically, the gum of it could be shredded to bits and pieces in no time, she thought to herself. He kept on chewing as if absent minded; as if chewing a really big chewing gum. He was watching her every movement, Lucia noticed. He even followed her, to her horror into her bedroom after she had given them a bench to sit on in the room which she hides the combatants.

"Why, comrade?" she asked urgently. This is a queer one. What is he up to now? She asked herself. I have to be on guard against this one!

"I don't know who you are, that's why!" he demanded, chewing on at his imaginary chewing gum, she had noticed that he had no chewing gum in his mouth at all. This one is queer indeed, she deduced quietly.

"Who do you think I am; King Kong's wife?" Lucia asked with relative force in her voice to suit the mood of the man. She went on, "Why don't you and your comrades get out of my house and...."

"Okay. Okay," he said moving back to where his colleagues were and sat down. His colleagues were looking at him enquiringly. He just shrugged his shoulders and said, "I don't know," and chewed on.

Lucia told them, "I have to go and meet the others. You comrades, feel at home." And she went back outside.

The second group presented real difficulties for Lucia. Although she had given them the password, "WEVU", they did not believe her. A woman could not be their contact, they thought. They became rough and aggressive. The previous group, she thought, was better. Even Tichaona's group was much more gentle than these men, she compared. One of them, a tall man of about Tichaona's height and stature, an athlete with a big head sitting on top of a thick neck, got hold of her hand and dragged her roughly closer to himself and hissed: "Who are you? What did you say?" he demanded. "I said WEVU, comrade," she replied calmly. But she was shocked. She had to be cautious with these ones, she decided, or else she may be hurt badly. These men! "What do you mean by WEVU?" Before she could say anything he shook her violently, "Answer now, or...." One of them, a bit short, on the stout side with a neck as thick and as strong as a lions, interrupted: "Comrade Chakanyuka, let me go round the buildings and see if she is alone."

"Good idea, comrade Makano. Examine those empty class rooms also," advised Chakanyuka.

Lucia did not struggle. She was saying to herself, these guys are not even careful. They have already axposed themselves by revealing their names to me. But the stiff grip on her hands was hurting her. "Please, leave my hands, comrade Chakanyuka."

"What did you say? Who told you my name, you....?"

"I heard it from comrade-e- Makano there," she gestured with her head towards the school buildings. He did not leave her hands, even increased the grip. Then Makano came back and reported, he did not see any one else. Chakanyuka loosened his grip and let the hands drop.

She moved away from them and headed for her house. She silently thanked her lucky stars. Such situations were getting to be recurring, she said to herself. Her life was in real danger, if she is not careful, she thought, from her own comrades who did not believe that women could serve the revolution in such important capacities. They were so suspicious that they could even kill her. She recalled how Tichaona had almost shot her the night of the Wiltshire Estates fire: and how the men kept their pistols pointed at her in the car until Tichaona had finally recognised her. She turned round and saw they were just standing there, waiting. She said, "You wait for that man you had been expecting," and she disappeared behind the building. She entered her house and threw herself on a chair, agitated, disgusted. The first three men in the house suspected that something wrong had happened because she looked untidy and her hair was dishivelled.

One of them, Keni, carefully slipped outside. He soon saw three men wandering, walking very slowly, in great doubt and confusion. Keni went to them. That gave them confidence enough to come and enter the house. As soon as she saw them, Lucia stood up suddenly, closed the door and said:

"Put your guns away comrades, in that corner there," she pointed behind a curtain, looking directly at Chakanyuka, she burst out: "Why didn't the people who sent you here warn you that you were going to work with me?" She went on, "a freedom fighter, but a woman nevertheless? Isn't it enough that my life is in danger already from the settler enemy? Why, now, should I fear my own comrades as well?" She stepped forward in front of Chakanyuka and went on decisively, "I will not move from here now until I get strong assurances from headquarters that I won't be victimised anymore, by my fellow freedom fighters. I'm getting sick and tired of this!" She emphasised this in his face. Chakanyuka kept on standing there, defiantly glaring back at her. Makano and the other one just sat down shrugging their shoulders hesitantly. It was not anyone's fault, of course, they thought. They had to be cautious. Some girls like Lucia here could be dangerous, they thought. Girls could infiltrate the movement of the people rather easier than the men could. She could be an informer who has gone too far, they thought.

"We were never informed of you as our contact," Chakanyuka said, still sounding aggressive, Lucia noted.

"So what?" she asked and added, "We have work to do comrade. You sit down and forget about your chauvinistic ideas."

"You...." Lucia did not give him a chance. She went on breathlessly.

"Zimbabwe has to be free, with or without your archaic ideas, comrades." Chakanyuka kept standing there pointing at her. He felt some moisture under his armpits. Lucia observed some beads of sweat on his forehead. Anger or frustration? Lucia asked herself. "Well, I still have to go out there and meet the last group," she informed them. But the thought that she might be manhandled again, or even be killed urged her to say, "You, comrade Chakanyuka, you'll have to accompany me, please," the 'please' seemed an after thought. She thought she hated this big man who had treated her so violently, yet he still appeared as defiant as ever in her house. What does he want from me? Anyway, who doe he think he is? She looked at him and urged, "Alright, comrade? But you will have to remain in the background. Please, don't let them manhandle me as you...." She trailed off the sentence and cast a warning glance at the others. She observed that Keni had calmed down and was not chewing as frantically as he had been doing before.

"Comrade Jojo, you accompany her." Chakanyuka commanded one of the three men in his group.

"Why not you, comrade Chakanyuka? I don't bite, you know. Women don't bite, come on, but you stay in the background." she urged and he followed her outside still as suspicious as a cobra. The third group, thogh at the sight of her, had started to run, gave no problem at all. The men had quickly retreated a few yards away when they saw her. But one of them, curiosity having an upper hand, had come back to investigate. She lifted up both her hands and quickly mentioned the password "WEVU".

"I will knife you if you move an inch!" he commanded. He moved slowly, closer to her. With a blast of alarm she, recognised the men. Guva Makuva, one of the men who had been with her at Marondera Detention Camp; the one who had pretended to be really mentally sick to fulfil the plan for escape from the camp so as to join the armed struggle. She remembered the way he had screamed and shrieked that day, like a real mad man. Makuva, himself, after some minutes of looking really very close at her, recognised her. He became really confused and started thought cracking. He was surprised to see Lucia there. He looked around. He was still expecting someone else who was to meet them, a man, of course. He looked back at the girl, more closely; he could not believe his eyes:

"Lu-Ah-Lucia!" he exclaimed and asked, "What are you doing here? I thought...."

"Thank Goodness!" Lucia gave a deep sigh. "At least someone has been good enough to recognise and remember me." The other two moved closer too. She extended her hand to Makuva and remarked, "I say, mad man, when did you recover from your mental illness?" and added, "U-u, I'm so very glad to see you, comrade Makuva. So our plan did succeed after all, didn't it? I was worried about you, you know, in the hands of that white terror with jutting out ears, do you still remember? What was his name by the way?" She sounded excited, indeed, Chakanyuka over head her.

"Umm...." Makuva sighed, "I managed to bluff my way out of that mental hospital in a few days' time." She beckoned them to follow her. Makuva kept rooted to where he was standing. "Lucia!" He still could not believe his eyes. "Have you gone this far?" He asked after realising that Lucia was actually their contact. "I can't believe it," he said still hesitating, holding back the other two who had almost started to follow her.

"What do you mean I have gone this far?" Lucia demanded. She was getting annoyed by Makuva. He cannot start to give her any problems, especially after she reminded him about the plans they had together at Marondera, plans to join the armed struggle.

"I mean....gone this far with revolution," replied Makuva with a tinge of mockery in his voice, she detected.

"I know you don't want to admit that a woman could also go this far in the revolution, do you?" Lucia retorted. "Your idea of a woman is someone who gets onto a chair and shrieks loudly if she sees a mouse. That is all prehistoric now, comrade. That idea only remains in the minds of the backward people, backward men." She said with a mocking laugh.

"I see," said Makuva still doubting, but followed her slowly. Lucia led them to the house and ushered them in. Makuva saw the other comrades and was relieved. But he observed that they were all looking very sad, actually, worried, their faces cast down. Then Chakanyuka entered and seemed to light up their spirits a bit. Lucia said after minutes of dead silence:

"We are all looking and feeling so unhappy and confused because of one little thing," she looked around at the men who had now all lifted up their heads to listen to the speaker, their eyes fixed on her curiously. "It seems as if the people at the headquarters are the only ones who have become enlightened in this business. I mean, they are the only ones who believe that the liberation of Zimbabwe needs the efforts of every Zimbabwean – men, women, young and old. I am only one of the many women in Zimbabwe who are trying their best to be involved fully in the struggle for our motherland. Women are also oppressed you know. In fact, they are the most oppressed," she went on, "You are here. You have a serious job to do, yet you are so perplexed just because of the presence of a woman. You make me sick!" She sat on a small stool. She looked around at them defiantly as if challenging them one by one. They all seemed to be looking at her as if she was a sly little woman who was up-to-no-good. She became even angrier. She stood up and said directly to Chakanyuka, who never wanted to sit down. He kept standing at a corner, watching her every move.

"You all look so confused, I'm beginning to doubt whether you will be able to carry on with the job at hand without confusion and messing up," she went on, "I'm telling you, I'll hold you people responsible for any mistakes or for any failure at all.

Remember, the struggle for a free Zimbabwe cannot be the monopoly of men as most of you seem to think." They were quiet. She went out of the room into the kitchen, and left them alone. They thought this woman is a real wild cat. Some of them appreciated her quietly, however.

Lucia was unhappy about the attitude of most of the men towards women and the struggle. Yet she fully understood why her presence and role in the underground movement could not be made public knowledge. Revelation of her presence and role in the struggle would have interfered with her double duties. She would be found out by the settler police and informers and would be arrested. The struggle would suffer, she thought, she would be locked in again, and would never get another chance of helping to liberate Zimbabwe. Lucia thought she had to rely on her lucky stars that she could not be killed by a fellow comrade during these encounters or confusions. It would be terrible to be wiped out by a colleague by mistake rather than by the enemy in combat. She recalled again as she went on thinking. Tichaona almost shot her after the Wiltshire Estates Operation. There was dead silence in the house. They could almost hear each other's peristalsis. Everyone seemed to be having a debate within him, as she returned from the kitchen. It was Makuva who recovered first from his introspection, to break the ice.

"Lucia," Makuva called quietly. She seemed to be going on with her internal debate. She did not seem to have heard him. "I say, sister Lucia," Makuva repeated the call, forcing some cheer into his voice. She looked at Makuva for what seemed to him as a long weekend. He felt uneasy. His shoulders hesitated on a shrug. Then she looked round at each one of them slowly. Her eyes rested at the defiant Chakanyuka, still standing there unflinchingly.

"I–beg–your–pardon–comrades," she spoke slowly with a lot of emphasis and added, "I would rather you all address me as comrade, Lucia. You are going to work hand-in-glove with me, whether you like it or not. I would not like to be disregarded. Not at all." She shifted her gaze from Chakanyuka back to Makuva, then to Keni, the one who carried on with his imaginary chewing gum, "We are colleagues, please, remember that, okay comrades?"

"Well....I...." Makuva stammered for an answer, "I wanted you to tell me what happened after I was taken away from Marondera Detention Camp as a mad-man." She looked at Makuva, and around to the others. She brightened up a little as she recalled that day. The big white man, she had never bothered to know his name, she thought. She only remembered him as the white terror with big jutting out ears, ears larger than those of Mr Spock of the T.V. series "Star Trek"; the man whose eyes never blinked. She thought of all the different kinds of terror she felt the first day she came face to face with that man.

"U-u-! That white terror!" she exclaimed. "Do you remember the hard slap he gave you across the face? I almost forgot my part in the act, and almost rushed to him to protest against his hitting a 'sick' person." The others now seemed to be listening with interest. She went on. "You acted really sick, you know, really mad. Everyone including the white terror himself, was utterly convinced you were mad in the true sense of the word. That screaming!" she laughed. He joined in. Everyone started to relax. They apparently had heard about how Makuva had escaped from the detention. But the story, told by an eyewitness.... She went on, "You know, I kept on worrying and thinking about how you fared since that day you were taken in that truck. The way you kept on shouting and pointing to the barracks as if you were seeing an apparition. This one!" She exclaimed, pointing at Makuva. He is such an actor and a good one after all."

After some quiet and relaxed laughter all round except for Chakanyuka, who sat there glancing at Lucia like a bulldog about to....there was a short silence. "He didn't hit me anymore," Makuva replied and added, "I was taken directly to the Harare Hospital Psychiatric unit. I had kept my eyes shut. My voice had become hoarse but the scream had not subsided. I heard a voice say urgently 'Psychosis! Largactil or Lagactal, I can't remember, 25 milligrams I.M. stat!' The injection knocked me out flat at once. When I woke up, I didn't move, but started to think of my next move. Getting out of there soonest, before they started their investigations was the best, I thought, or else I'd be forced to play act again. Perhaps fail this time or get another needle. I got out that same night. Now here we are."

"Absolutely incredible indeed. This one!" commented Lucia, pointing at Makuva, laughing and went on, "Now, about myself...." She told them everything about her, up to that moment.

"You were involved in the Wiltshire Estates Mission and the bombing of the racist shops in Salisbury?" asked Makano in astonishment. "Isn't this something?" he asked, looking at Chakanyuka who just sneered at him, openly. The snob, Lucia thought.

The narrations by Makuva and Lucia served to brighten most of the combatants. It introduced a new mood and a fresh atmosphere among them. Some also had interesting stories to tell about how they joined the armed struggle. Most seemed satisfied and happy about how they joined the armed struggle. Most seemed satisfied and happy except Chakanyuka and Keni, Lucia thought. Chakanyuka just sat there sneering at her. He never took his eyes away from her as if she was something that could turn out to be nasty and he had to be on his guard all the time.

Keni was frantically chewing away, as if indifferent to what was going on. Wonder who the ones I'm going to work closely with are? she asked herself silently returning a care-free-look at Chakanyuka. An ice-berg indeed, more than the cold itself, she thought. Then she called one of them called Jojo to accompany her into the kitchen. They brought two large dishes full of curried rice and another one full of stewed beef with a lot of gravy. Each had to dish for himself the amount he wanted and they started to enjoy the well cooked and delicious meal, talking quietly to each other until all the dishes were empty. Then: "I think it's time to discuss the serious operations at hand, comrades, don't you think?" Lucia reminded them, after the meal. There was silence again. She regarded them questioningly then rested her gaze at Makuva.

"What do you know?" Makuva asked, and added, "Perhaps you should brief us before we have any discussions."

"What discussion?" Chakanyuka demanded harshly, and added, "We do know what we have to do, don't we?"

"For sure you do," replied Lucia calmly, looking at him directly. In return he glared back at her contemptuously. Still very aggressive, Mr Chakanyuka, she noted. She glanced around quickly and thought she observed that not all of his comrades supported his attitude. She looked back at Chakanyuka who seemed to be thinking of his next move against this woman. She awarded him a cool smile and said, "I'm to drive five of you tonight to a place in Enkeldorn where you have a mission. Does that agree with what you have?" she asked Chakanyuka. It was Makuva again, who answered:

"I'm one of that group of five." He pointed to the other four, "two, three, four and five."

"Good," she commented, and, "By the way, comrade Makuva, you and your group," she informed, "are going to Mrs Chake's place tonight. Do you still remember Mrs Chake at Marondera Detention Camp?"

"I remember her alright."

"She's going to look after you."

"It's a small world, isn't it?" Makuva commented pleasantly. Lucia turned to Chakanyuka, and the other three, Makano, Jojo and Keni. So these are the ones....she thought, and she awarded each one of them another very cool smile. The leopards or foxes and one sheep, she thought with a bit of resentment and said:

"The other four have to remain here with me and wait for further instructions. Is that correct, comrade Chakanyuka?" she asked. He did not say a word nor did he remove his eyes away from her. He hated the whole idea of having to sort of rely on this woman, he thought.

Women are never to be trusted, let alone relied upon, he continued silently to himself. What can a woman do anyway? He asked himself. Women are never as strong as men physically and otherwise, anyway. What can she do, especially in real combat danger? Those people at headquarters don't seem to realise what fire they are playing with leaving all these important details to her....

Chakanyuka had never forgotten how his own sister, Roda, had reported his presence, at his home village in Mr Darwin, to the police. That was the time he had come back from Mozambique with three of his colleagues. His sister, Roda, was a girlfriend of one of the police constables at Mr Darwin.

She had wittingly or unwittingly, he'll never know, he thought, remarked to the constable, "I'm so happy today, you know. My brother Roy has come back at last." She had said this happily.

"Come back at last? Come back from where?" asked the constable.

"I don't know. From –er....He went away two years ago," she explained. "No one knew where he was. Oh! I'm so happy. Everyone is very relieved. He is like the prodigal son in the Bible. Every body in the village is rejoicing."

That was it. Fortunately she had not mentioned that he was with the other three guys. These managed to escape. He was found without any arms, fortunately. He was arrested nevertheless and was beaten! That was some beating, he remembered. They decided to release him after they had confirmed that he was not a "terrorist". He had shown them a certificate of typist-stenographer he had obtained from the Blantyre Technical College in Malawi. He got the terrible beating altogether anyway, he thought, hating this woman in front of him. Women are not careful. They may unwittingly sell you down the drain, remember? Chakanyuka reminded himself. He had never stopped wondering whether his sister Roda did that purposefully or not. But women, however, are never to be trusted and he told himself to be ever on guard against this woman....she knows too much or pretends to know too much.

The following day the instructions to go ahead with the next operation came. Lucia reported to the combatants, "The operation will be tonight." Chakanyuka hated the idea that this woman was actually kind of giving them orders. She actually is the one receiving the instructions? He hated it a lot.

"Tonight? At what time?" asked Keni chewing away frantically. "I can't wait!"

"We...." Lucia was cut off suddenly by Chakanyuka.

"We?" he asked and demanded, "What do you mean, we? You have a mouse in your pocket?" Her teeth were on edge as she met his inscrutable look. This guy Chakanyuka! He is a....

"No comnrade. I don't have a mouse in my pocket," Lucia answered calmly and firmly. She added slowly but forcefully, "I am to drive you to this mission and back here. Were you told otherwise?" Her voice was deliberately sarcastic, but he was unscathed by her sharpness, and sarcasm.

"No! If I had known it would be a person like you, it would have been otherwise." His dark brow arched with taunting scepticism that was both condemning and disdainful.

"Now what are you going to do? Call it off?" Her eyes smouldered with resentment, but she had managed to keep the anger out of her voice.

"Comrade Keni here will drive us," he said decisively pointing at Keni, but keeping his ice-berg eyes on her.

"No ways!" she replied forcefully. "I'll handle the transport side. I've done so several times and you are not going to be any exception. So, we'll leave at eleven thirty tonight." She walked out of the room into her bedroom. Her teeth were gritting with temper. These people, she thought angrily. As if it's not enough to manhandle me, they are actually refusing to work with me. Cowards, she scolded. They are afraid of their weakness, I'm sure.

Jeaney Junction was one of the largest settler military training centres for whites and colours. It was an elaborate complex, surrounded by elaborate security measures. It was situated in the jungles between Gwelo (Gweru) and Bulawayo. A road branched from the main Salisbury to Bulawayo highway leading to the Jeaney Junction.

The commando guerrilla unit led by Chakanyuka with Jojo's help had observed that the trainee soldiers and their instructors left the camp by road, in open lorries and trucks. They left every morning at five o'clock for their respective training areas. They almost always made their return trips back to the camp, to their barracks around six in the evening.

Jojo (Alexander) was a coloured soldier, who had been trained at the Jeaney Junction. He had deserted the colonial army and ran out of the country to join the liberation forces. He travelled to Zambia en-route to Tanzania and Mozambique where he joined Chakanyuka and others. Then, he came back and integrated into the guerrilla warfare. He was one of the several guys who could perform several "duties" in the struggle. He could pose as an enemy agent when necessary....very effectively. He had worked very closely with the commando unit commanded by Chakanyuka, collecting vital information for them and fighting side by side with them.

Chakanyuka's men had carried out close reconnaissance of the activities of the enemy soldiers at Jeaney. Their commander, Chakanyuka used to spend hours up in a tall Musasa tree observing the activities of Jeaney Junction. He was observing, precisely, what time the trainees and their instructors left the camp for their training areas, and what time they returned. This information was vital for the success of the group's planned operation. Through other intelligence sources of the underground movement and Jojo, it had been learnt that the settler soldiers of Jeaney Junction made regular outings four days a week to train away from the Junction area. Lucia and two men from the local headquarters of the underground had driven previously to Jeaney Junction as far as where the road branched off the main road. They wanted Lucia to familiarise herself with the road when she would drive the combatants there for their operation. They also reconnoitred for a suitable place to hide the car and for a tree which she could climb and stand watch, in waiting for the combatants to return. Jojo had also learnt that on that particular week's Thursday, there would be special events out of the training camp and most of the big guys of Jaeney Junction would be out with the trainees.

So, Lucia and Chakanyuka's unit drove to Jeaney Junction that Wednesday night. It was very quiet at the junction where the road to Jeaney Junction branched off from the main highway. The men got off the car. Lucia drove the mini-station wagon to where it would be hidden waiting for the combatants to come back. Lucia had expressed her wishes to participate in the mission. She was quickly and firmly reminded, by Chankanyuka, she was not a combatant but only in-charge of transportation. Chakanyuka's men started planting land mines and time bombs. They started some few yards away from where the road branched off from the main road to about a mile or so away from the training centre. The bombs were placed conveniently along the sides of the road.

They did not want to waste time digging the tarmac for the land-mines but they managed to conceal them effectively besides the road. They worked very fast and walked away quickly. They made sure that they had got rid of all their loads because they did not want to travel back with any of the deadly arms, in case they were met with suspicion on the way back. After four hours of quite heavy work they returned to where Lucia was watching and waiting for them. She was up in a tall tree away from the car. She was to sound a bird-like whistle to warn them if she observed anything unusual, and or any suspicious movement. Fortunately nothing unusual or suspicious happened. No car, and nothing travelled to or from Jeaney Junction.

"Thank Goodness!" Lucia exclaimed. When every one had settled in the car she said, "I think the waiting is more strenuous. It's a worse cause of anxiety than the action itself. I wish I could be personally involved in these operations in future." Lucia started the car. The men just looked at each other and shrugged. Makano and Jojo did not seem to object, she thought.

"I don't see why not," Makano commented, looking at Chakanyuka. But Chakanyuka could not agree with him. Chakanyuka, like Tichaona, had his own beliefs about women, Lucia observed. He thought that the war was for men. Lucia had even gone too far, already, he thought regretfully. She should be somewhere in the kitchen preparing some nice dishes for her family. He remembered the nice food they ate at her house; that's the job she should be doing. He believed she should not be out here driving guerrillas to and from dangerous missions, against such a ruthless enemy like these settlers. At this particular time, he thought, such an attractive woman should be in bed with a man, and be at a dinner table in the evening after he came home from work. What a waste, he thought.

Lucia some how, intuitively, sensed Chakanyuka's thoughts, and she looked at him and laughed quietly. She did not say anything. She only knew that, actually there was nothing so difficult and as ugly as male chauvinism, and Chakanyuka was drunk with it and tried hard to maintain it. But the other three comrades, including Keni, actually admired Lucia. She noticed this through their comments. They admired the way she handled difficult situations. The way she kept cheerful even when faced with an anxious situation like the one they had just handled. It was amazing, they thought. She never showed any sign of fear or tension. The way she handled her transport task was admirable, Keni the driver thought. She drove fast but carefully, they observed, and thought, with more women of her calibre, Zimbabwe would just be around the corner.

They reached the school at about four thirty in the morning. Everyone at the school was still quiet, in bed. Lucia got out of the car after parking it very close to the door. She opened the door of the house and each guerrilla jumped out of the car and entered the house quickly and quietly.

The combatants heard about the Jeaney Junction disaster from a foreign news bulletin. Most of the settler military men, the news had said, from the new recruits to the higher ranking officers who happened to be on those military lorries died, and some, were seriously injured.

Help for them could not reach the disaster area quickly or early enough because, the rescuers who tried to go to the centre from the main road were hampered by mines as soon as they branched off from the main road. The report went on. Rescue had to be flown to the disaster area later by helicopters. Even those rescue workers flown in, met considerable trouble from time bombs which continued to go off every now and then. Many time bombs had been left lying behind bushes and trees along the sides of the road. All had been going off at different times. In the lunch time bulletin, the announcer said that even at the time of reporting the bombs were still exploding, at random. The rescuers' work became so dangerous that the settler anti-bomb squad had to spread out all over the area searching for bombs. Although using mine detectors and other sophisticated equipment, the settler squads could not discover all the bombs which the freedom fighters had planted in and around the area. The reporter also said:

'Elsewhere in the country, that same night, the settlers were battling against fires and other disasters. Two of their ammunition dumps and a police outpost in Enkeldorn were burning,' the report continued. 'A bridge and a rail-road were blown up, about sixty miles to the north of Salisbury. Some Crown Lands in Bindura and Mt Darwin were on fire, and the white farmers there were frantically working hard to save their crops and livestock.'

"Your scheme, comrade Chakanyuka, has worked," Keni said jubilantly, slapping Chakanyuka, lightly on the back. Chakanyuka became cheerful right away and began to speak. He had been sulking ever since the operation last night.

"The attacks on the ammunition dumps, the police outpost in Enkeldorn, and all those around the country mentioned in the news, including many others not mentioned," Chakanyuka explained to Lucia happily, "were synchronized with this one of ours as a necessary diversionary act in the scheme. This keeps the enemy busy indeed." Was that Chakanyuka talking to her in such a nice and cheerful way? Lucia wondered why. He went on, "You see, the enemy had to be split in order for him to deal with the widely separated incidents." Chakanyuka, Lucia quietly observed, relished success. He was happy now though still wary towards her. Chauvinists and pessimists like Chakanyuka needed to perform and succeed then they become happy. They became edgy and rough before an operation because of fear of failure. She thought she did not like to work with such people. They are cowards sometimes. You never know with cowards and people who become cheerful only after an achievement....

At three thirty that afternoon, the police, one white and two blacks with two black police reservists came to Chakarara School, in search of "terrorists". Lucia went to them as soon as she had seen them. She knew the white sergeant from Enkeldorn and the two reservists. She asked the white sergeant, "What is going on, sir?"

"I'd like to ask you the same," he answered.

"These saboteurs, now are really becoming a great nuisance, don't you think?" Lucia commented and asked innocently.

"Wait until I lay my hands on one of them," he replied as if jokingly, and asked, "How are things around here?"

"Nothing unusual," she replied, looking towards the other policemen. She spoke for a short time with the white sergeant then she went on to where the two police reservists were. They didn't stop talking to each other when they saw her coming. She was their contact there. She greeted them and then excused herself for interrupting them and repeated the same comment she had uttered to the white sergeant, and asked, "What's going on?"

"Any terrs around here?" one of the reservists asked. Lucia shrugged her shoulders saying:

"I also heard the news about the fires and the bombs. How far true is that? Where are we going?" She sounded quite concerned.

"It's true," answered one of the reservists. "In Bindura and Mt. Darwin, those Crown Lands, even the European farms adjacent to the Crown Lands, the fire could not discriminate."

"Ya," agreed the other, "I hear one of the farmers was seen frantically loading into his Land Rover, a few of his belongings, a frightened wife and three kids. They had just moved when the homestead was engulfed in the inferno." He went on, "The farms that side, at this time of the year, you know, are full of dry maize, and the cotton and tobacco are all nice and ready. What a pity!"

"Destruction of the highest order!" exclaimed the other police reservist. They laughed looking at each other. They seemed to enjoy the idea, Lucia thought.

"Do you think these terrs will succeed?" asked Lucia. "They are just destroying things," she remarked, seemingly concerned.

"Ya, because those things, being destroyed, do not belong to any black person."

"Oh!" Lucia exclaimed. But she was secretly delighted to note that even among the police reserves, the "boys" have some support.

"Morale among the whites has begun to sag, you know," commented the police reservist, and added, "They now realise that their regime is unable to prevent loss of their property, death to their children and wives, or even to themselves." He went on, "What do you think about the disasters during the Rhodes and Founders' and the Wltshire Estates?"

"That was terrible indeed!" replied Lucia innocently.

"Yes. It has become really hot for them now," said the other police reservist, and added, "Some are abandoning their farms and their big businesses. They are already collecting their belongings to leave the country altogether."

"Where do they go now?" asked Lucia showing a lot of surprise and concern.

"To South Africa, back to Europe, Australia, New Zealand, Latin America, back to Britain and so on."

"How do they go with all their property?" she asked again. "They fly," replied the police reservist.

"But all their movable property is taken by road and rail down to South Africa or Mozambiqu for shipping," said the other police reservist. He went on, "The removal transport companies are having a booming time now transporting these things out of the country, mostly down South.

"Ho-o?" remarked Lucia and commented, "They are being clever, I guess." She slowly, started to move away from them saying, "Well, some of us are just small fries who just watch where the wind blows, see you again."

She went back to her house. She was happy about the information she had just got from the conversation with the police reservists. Excitedly, she reported it to Chakanyuka and the others. Quiet jubilation reigned. Then Lucia became quiet, into deep thoughts, Chakanyuka asked:

"You don't seem to be happy about our accomplishments, do you?" Lucia thought he sounded suspicious. She ignored that and answered:

"I was just thinking about all that property being taken out of our country," she went on, "You see, it's taken to South Africa and Mozambique by those removals...." She trailed off, looking at Keni the driver. "That property belongs to this country, why should we let it slip through our fingers like that?"

"Ya, man!" exclaimed Keni, "Swift transport business must be having a booming period these days. I must get in touch with Sanganayi and the boys, soonest," suggested Keni sounding urgent. Silence followed. Everyone seemed to be thinking of some ideas to....

"Right!" exclaimed Lucia, "We must get Sanganayi immediately," she said, urgency in her voice, and continued, "These people can't be left to leave the country as smoothly as they came in. Something has to be done." She suggested, "Let them fly away without our property. After all, it's our sweat and blood."

"That head is full of ideas, isn't it?" Chakanyuka said, and remarked, "Revolutionary ideas!" Lucia looked at Chakanyuka and asked herself, Praise? Admiration? Sarcasm? Envy? She could not make out Chakanyuka's notion at that moment. At least that's a sign of admitting this woman into his ranks, Lucia thought. She did not care whatever notion he had, this Chakanyuka. She ignored his remarks but said:

"After I drop you at your destination this evening, I'll proceed to Salisbury to see Mr Sanganayi," suggested Lucia.

"I think, Keni, you should go with her," said Chakanyuka. Keni nodded in agreement.

"You still think I need a driver chaperone, don't you, comrade Chakanyuka?" she asked sarcastically.

"No! I didn't think that at all," replied Chakanyuka, a note of apology in his voice, Lucia noted. He stood up from the stool, walked slowly to her and stood, towering above her, very close for her liking: "You see, Keni and Makano were working with Swift Transport Company," he explained, "Keni will contact some of the boys at Swift....including Sanganayi, at the A.A." The ice in those cold eyes had melted a little, she thought. Such men are not to be trusted with women! She warned herself.

"Oh!" Lucia looked at Keni. Him and his imaginary chewing-gum, I don't think I cherish his company at all, she thought regretfully. She said, "I'll drive though." They all nodded. The whole mood, after the news of the success of their mission, she thought, had changed surprisingly to a happy and friendly one, anyway, especially with Makano, Jojo and Keni, and as for Chakanyuka....? Lucia chose to let him be....

In the evening, at about ten thirty, they left Chakarara School. After some distance, Makano, Chakanyuka and Jojo dropped off near somewhere, where they were going to rendezvous with Makuva and his group who had operated around Enkeldorn. Lucia and Keni proceeded to Salisbury. The journey became quite interesting, she thought. Keni, who had seemed, to her, as a man of few words, turned out to be a talker. Very funny and interesting stories he told her about himself and his friends. She noted, he had actually stopped chewing the imaginary gum for the whole journey to Salisbury. A nervous wreck, she thought. How he came to be chewing like that, she wondered. He could chew and chew, increasing the velocity as he gets more excited and anxious, she had noted.

Two weeks later, Lucia went to Enkeldorn to visit one of the police reservists, she had talked to the other day at her school. In the course of their conversation, she commented, "Things seem to be quiet these days, don't you think?"

"What?" asked the man in surprise. "Things are even getting hotter these days," he argued and commented, "You are too far away from civilization and the happenings, you know. You should come and teach here in Enkeldorn town," he advised. "That's a good suggestion, worth digesting," she agreed with him, and she asked, "What is happening then?"

"Those removal transport companies, we talked about that day?" She nodded. "The booming period ended in terrible disasters." "Why? How?"

"The boys, I mean the terrs have been on them, I'm sure," he said confidently.

"Why do you say so?" She asked.

"The accidents reported from there are queer. Quite queer, you know, between Fort Victoria and Biet Bridge, and along the Umtali road near the Mozambique border," he emphasised, and continued, "I think they are staged. Others are outright ambushes by the bo....com....by the terrs."

"Reports? We don't hear anything about accidents on the radio."

"These things are never reported in the news media. But the transport companies are losing their removals by the dozen."

"How do you know? They must, at the same time be losing many drivers then?"

"I'm not sure about that. But the military has now taken over. Cars moving down south are now escorted. They move in convoys to try and stop the 'accidents.'"

"Is that effective?"

"What? You don't know those military boys. The private drivers are made to drive at very high speeds. Anyone who slows down the traffic, is forced to speed up and this is dangerous plus, plus."

"Oh, well, I guess a solution will be found one of these fine days."

"A solution in favour of the boys, I'm sure," the police reservist hoped and forecasted, "They won't stop harassing until they get what they want. I don't blame them you know...."

"What do you mean?" asked Lucia, pretending to be puzzled.

"Well, look at what's happening. Africans have to buy land, the land that is rightfully theirs." He went on. "The Wiltshire Estates, you know, which were burnt down some time ago, are now being sub-divided into small farmsteads or plots, to be sold to the Africans as the Native Purchase Areas. The whole deal is a farce, don't you think?"

"As I said before my brothers, some of us are just small fries," she replied and bade him farewell to which he answered: "Hope you heed what I said, for you to come and teach near here where there is civilization and light."

"I'll think about it, for sure," she was already on her way.

She was in a very joyful mood and heading for Mrs Chake's place. She relayed the news about the 'accidents' and about the Wiltshire Estates being divided into plots for African's to buy. And she said to Mrs Chake, "I wish I could participate fully in the armed struggle."

"What do you mean?" Mrs Chake asked and commented, "What you are doing is already full participation."

"No," she argued, "I mean the actual combat, with guns," she talked emotionally, shaking her clenched fists towards Mrs Chake. "Why can't I? It's about time some of us carry the guns."

"Well, I'll send your wish to the headquarters. We are going to have a meeting shortly. By the way, Miss Regai is working for the Uniform and Clothing Factory in Salisbury. We are, somehow, able to get some 'clothes' for our boys, you know and she is doing a great there. She has also managed to recruit other girls like Marwei to work in that factory."

"Oh, that's great," she remarked and said, "I hope you'll support my request, Mrs Chake. I really want to do the real fighting. I know Miss Regai and many other girls are doing their best to help the revolution, but me, I .... Well, goodbye then." She extended her hand. ""Don't forget my request, I mean it." she reminded Mrs Chake.

The organisers of the underground movement, in their meeting, after Mrs Chake had told them about Lucia's request, thought and agreed that Lucia was serving an important task as a teacher and one of their close contacts in the civil service. So, as a matter of compromise with her requests to hold the gun, they urged her to ask for transfer to Masowe Primary School in Sinoia/Karoi/Chikuti /Chirundu areas. Masowe Primary School was only three years old and the parents were quite agreeable and eager to be friends with their children's teachers. The Police Post was not very far away from the school, either. She could 'work' close with the police without much problem, and also flush out their real informers.

The area had become too important for the guerrillas. It was one of the training bases for the guerrillas as well as one of the best links between those guerrillas trained in other friendly countries and those trained locally. Lucia was needed to help Sanganyi and other transporters and in the transportation of the trained combatants to different parts of the country. Lucia's work was confined to Sinoia, Chikuti, Karoi, Hurungwe and Chirundu areas only. She mostly would take guerrillas to and from their respective assignments; help in covering and protecting them just as she did at Chakarara School. The peasants collaborated well with her in supplying food and other necessities to the guerrillas.

In order for her to secure transfer from Chakarara to Masowe, she had gone to her police informer superiors in Enkeldorn and, "I gather that the Karoi, Hurungwe, Chirundu areas have become very important terrorists' hideout," she informed and suggested, "I believe very strongly that I'd serve a lot by trying to infiltrate them." Then eagerly, she asked, "What do you say?" The superior had showed interest straight away and had not doubted her at all. She had done well so far.

"Do you know of anyone there? It's too remote for a girl like you and it could be quite dangerous, you know." She answered that she had an uncle in Sinioa Town, and would not have any problems.

Chapter 12

To the settler police, Lucia usually had to struggle to get anything at all to report. She, usually, had nothing to report. One police sergeant, Marova, asked her when she first came to the area. "What is a pretty girl like you doing in these back woods, away from civilization?"

"My uncle, the one who brought me up, works in Sinoia Town, and," she went on, "I'm as you know, always on police duty and there is a very important reason why I was transferred here."

"Of course, of course, we were informed, I know," said the sergeant. "I was just....Well, you know...." He looked at her as if to size her up or to ascertain her integrity, then: "Be careful, these jungles have ears and eyes."

As a 'police informer', she was never, just like at Chakarara School, suspected of harbouring any 'terrorists'. There were times she had to tactfully divert the police and soldiers to false directions. She would give them false reports about the whereabouts of what she suspected to be the "terrorists" in order to pave way for the guerrillas. She was working closely with Sanganayi, her former headmaster at Muzhanje School in Chiweshe, who drove one of the A.A heavy removal Lorries to and from Zambia.

Sanganayi would go via Masowe School to pick up some 'passengers' from Lucia. These were guerrillas who had either completed their training and were to be taken to their respective assignments, or guerrillas who had been assigned to 'special duty' in the Sinioa/Karoi/Chirundu area. Sanganayi had managed to recruit several other drivers in the company he was working as well as in several other heavy transport companies. So the movement of guerrillas to and from different parts of the country was easily afforded.

One week after a series of operations by freedom fighters, around the country, more and more settler strategic projects and infrastructure had almost become paralised. More soldiers were sent into the country from South Africa. Lucia's area became infested with the settler security forces. They pitched camp near Masowe School. Lucia, as usual, had three guerrillas hidden in her house. The guerrillas had been waiting to be taken away to their other hideouts after the previous night's assignments. That was a very dangerous situation she was in, Lucia thought, because those soldiers did not know that she was 'working' for the police. They could at any time, decide to rampage the place and start searching even the teachers' quarters for 'terrorists'. What could she do? She thought that, this time the chips were down for her.

If she could manage to get out of this one, she decided, she would quit pretending to be working for those settler fools, and go into actual combat against them. 'Gosh! What can I do?' Lucia cracked her head, searching for what she could do to save the combatants and herself. The boys in her pantry, although as guerrillas, they were prepared for any consequences if the worst came to the worst, were beginning to despair. They were going to be taken like sitting ducks, they thought. And Lucia on her part, though trying hard to find a solution to the problem; she never showed any sign of panic. The combatants were surprised by her calmness. Come what may, she had thought. This time she was prepared for any eventuality.

Lucia, due to the desperate situation she was in, had now started to think of what she had actually done for the struggle. She was not satisfied. She felt, she had not done enough, for her people. To her it was the duty of every Zimbabwean to do anything possible and tangible. But she thought she had done very little. The situation had turned out to be hopeless for her. She could not find a solution to it. It seemed obvious that she was going to be found out harbouring the 'terrorists'. This held a death sentence. Just imagine, she said to herself, dying by the settler hangman's rope rather than his bullet in combat! Lucia thought, she was a freedom fighter and not a common criminal. She would rather die in combat than to be hanged by the neck as a murderer. Suddenly, Lucia had an idea. Could she not try and divert the soldiers? There was a slight chance there. She would try it, she decided. It was on a Saturday. That afternoon, she locked the combatants in the pantry, took a basket, went out and locked her house. She entered her car and drove towards Chirundu. The soldiers saw her leave. They seemed not to worry about her. She drove away as if everything was normal. She hoped nothing 'drastic' would take place at the school while she was gone. Nothing like a search and breaking into the teachers' houses....She was taking chances.

After some time before sunset, Lucia came back, arriving at the school in such speed as if the devil was after her. She drove so fast that some people had to jump out of her way. She drove straight to where the soldiers were gathered, lazily talking to each other. She was shouting! She squeaked the brakes, jumped out of the car demanding to see the sergeant major personally. Her car, it appeared, had really met with serious trouble. It was strewn all over with mud and pieces of grass. Her own dress had a long rip from the right shoulder to the hips and right sleeve was hanging by a few threads. Her hair was terribly dishevelled. Lucia really did look terribly shaken, the soldiers observed, all rushing towards her. The sergeant major, a hefty brown eyed white Rhodesian, rushed to her: "What's the matter?" shouted the hefty tall sergeant major.

"They've attacked me! Some men! The terrorists I think." Lucia replied breathlessly, pointing to where she had just come from. "Where?" asked the sergeant major urgently.

"There, on my way back from Chirundu. Not, not far from Chirundu itself." She explained stammering breathlessly. All the soldiers surrounded her anxiously, their guns ready. She was crying now, real tears streaming down her cheeks. "My God that was close!" she exclaimed and asked, "What did they want to do with me?" She was shaking with 'fright'.

"Calm down!" the sergeant major commanded, shaking her shoulders a little. "Which direction did they come from?" And without waiting for an answer from her, he went on with more questions. The questions came out quickly, one after another, "Where did they go?" he went on, "How did they do it? How many were they, do you remember?" She stammered on for sometime, as if unable to explain anything because of the shock.

"One-sickly-looking man was lying on the side of the road, almost in the road," Lucia explained in gasps. "I slowed to a halt to look at the sick man, to give any help possible, you know. Then suddenly, someone grabbed me from the back, attempting to drag me out of the car. I think they were three of four of them, including the sick one, who jumped up quickly and came towards me. They could be more there." She went on, "I struggled and managed to step on the accelerator and drove off. I think I hit one of them who had stood in front of the car throwing things onto the windscreen. I could not see properly. I was terribly frightened! I...." She stopped talking breathlessly. She was breathing heavily, heaving her chest up and down as if she was really out of breath. She threw herself onto the flat stone and sat down to 'calm' herself down. In a few minutes, all the soldiers were on their way to the mentioned area. Not a single soldier remained behind. The sergeant major's jeep was right in front and all the others jumped into their jeeps and Lorries and drove off towards Chirundu.

Once certain that the soldiers had left, she slowly stood up and drove to her house. She unlocked the front door, and went straight to her comrades, "You should be ready for a journey now comrades," she warned them and went out to clean the car. She changed her torn dress. The boys did not know what had transpired outside; they only saw Lucia bursting into the house with a torn dress and telling them to get ready for a journey now comrades. How were they to get out of the house and into the car with all those soldiers scattered all over the school area? The comrades asked each other. Lucia had to tell them what she had done.

They were utterly astonished. Lucia was playing a dangerous game now, they whispered to each other, agitatedly. "That was very clever and very brave comrade," one of them commended, "but don't you think that was too melodramatic to believe?" She just shrugged.

It had become dark when Lucia and the four comrades drove away. The men lay flat on their seats, so that only Lucia could be visible in the car. They were taking chances, they thought. They could meet a bunch of soldiers on the way and could be stopped and Lucia could be recognised, and....

Lucia took the combatants to a farm of an African family in Chitombo Native Purchase Area. When she came back, the whole school area was extraordinarily quiet. Lucia thought she did not like the rather too quiet atmosphere around the place. Had anything happened? Were they laying low waiting for her to come back? Did they suspect her? These thoughts raged in her mind like a whirl wind. She went on asking herself more questions. She was afraid of coming out of the car. She sat in the car for some seconds:

Had anyone seen her when she departed with her three passengers? She remembered that she had not checked the whereabouts of other teachers when she left, and that was a serious security slip, she blamed herself. Well! She exclaimed uncertainly, and came out of the car. She opened the door and went into the house. She closed the door behind her and peeped out through the window. Lucia stood there stupefied! Walking slowly round her car was a man. He was peeping inside and bending over to examine the wheels. Lucia noticed it was Mr Mwenje, the headmaster of Masowe Primary School. What was he doing? What was he looking for? What did Mr Mwenje know? Lucia wondered. She put on the candle light. When the man saw the light, he knocked at Lucia's door. She confidently opened the door. She anxiously waited to see and discover what Mr Mwenje was up to or what he knew about what was happening.

"Miss Kashangu," called Mr Mwenje quietly. "You are a queer person. Very queer, in fact," he accused. "You presented us with very queer movements of yourself this evening and...."

"Just what do you mean?" Lucia interrupted him.

"You came rushing around claiming that you had been attacked by thugs," he said sarcastically, "then you immediately drove off again in such darkness, alone." Mr Mwenje asked, "Isn't that queer?"

"I agree," said Lucia. "It appears queer indeed, but I had no choice," she went on. "You see, I had promised my uncle that I would spend the weekend with his family. I was going straight there from Chirundu if I had not been attacked. But I had to go and notify them about my encounter with the terrorists," she explained, trying to be convincing.

"I am still surprised at you Miss Kashangu," Mwenje insisted, "How can you drive alone, at night, in such darkness? What are you up to Miss Kashangu? Is there something you are not telling us? Tell me...." Mr Mwenje looked at her suspiciously for a whole minute, and then looked around the room as if expecting to see or detect something unusual.

"Well," Lucia replied, "I thought it was safe since the area was so full of security forces." Lucia then asked, "Why do you sound as if you are very much concerned about me, Mr Mwenje?" She asked trying to sound surprised.

"Of course, I am concerned," he answered sharply, and went on, "If you are here alone, as you are, by yourself, you are under my protection. I am, you know, responsible for your security here." Lucia asked a few more questions, to deduce whether Mr Mwenje had seen her passengers or not. It appeared to her, she thought, Mwenje had not seen her passengers nor was he suspecting anything on those lines.

"Thank you so much Mr. Mwenje, for your concern. I am really grateful."

The following day she waited anxiously to see whether she would be asked by anyone else about the events of the previous day. The police and the soldiers were all over the place but nobody asked. Lucia wanted to know how the soldiers went about last night's task. She approached one of the police officers who informed her that, a group of men were arrested in and around Chirundu, last night.

Lies, she thought, deep-blue lies. Lucia knew that those men arrested were just innocent peasants. It was not uncommon, she knew, for those settler forces to just frantically collect any peasant they came across during their search and destroy operations against the freedom fighters. It was a painful thing, though, she thought, but that was part of the struggle. But she was also thinking about another thing she did not like. She did not want to testify in the settler court. She might be called to identify those who had been arrested. Luckily she was never called upon to do so. She, however, wondered for a long time what had happened to those poor peasants who had been arrested that Saturday night. Probably, they were still languishing in detentions without trial, she regretted this thoughtfully.

When something happened in a certain area, the settler police and army rampaged the area frantically. They would then make announcements to the effect that their security forces had arrested or killed so many 'terrorists'.

This was always said even if no Zimbabwean guerrillas had been arrested, or killed, or even when those arrested indiscriminately were innocent people. It was intended to boost the morale of the white settlers and to demoralise the freedom fighters and the masses in general, thought Lucia.

At the end of that year, Lucia managed to persuade the underground movement to allow her to leave teaching altogether and join the armed combat. She resigned. But she did not stop pretending to be working for the settler police where and when such pretence served the revolution. This was the time Lucia was taken to the guerrilla training camp commanded by Munongwa. She was given the guerrilla names Shupai Zvenyu. She had to keep struggling hard, she recollected, to be accepted as an equal in combat against the settler enemy. Munongwa, like Tichaona, Chakanyuka and Tafirenyika was hard to convince. He took time to accept her not as a woman but as a combatant, and a brave one, as he later realised.

Someone bumped against the traction on Shupai's leg. The pain forced her to jerk suddenly. She looked around, as if confused. Some of the patients were looking at her curiously. The patient next to her was saying: "I am sorry, I did not mean to disturb you." Did this patient sound sarcastic? Shupai thought she did not like the tone, and the looks from the other patients.

She had spent some time recalling and recollecting all that had happened before now. In her flashback, she remembered certain vivid incidents which appeared very funny now, buts interesting. The incident at Masowe Primary School with the Rhodesian security forces, especially, she thought, was the funniest. She had pictured herself ripping her dress from the right shoulder to the waist-line, splashing mud and pieces of grass in and onto her car. The ripped off sleeve hanging unceremoniously by the thread, and her hair... The way she demanded to see the sergeant major, personally; the way she told them she had been attacked by the 'terrorists'. Dramatic indeed and quite theatrical! She had actually laughed or giggled unconsciously.

The other patients had observed this and had assumed she was being delirious, a bad sign of severe illness and near death. This patient next to her, whether out of curiosity or out of pity for Shupai, had sneaked over to the ward sister Higgins, and told her: "That patient called Sarah is acting funny."

"So what?" sister Higgins had asked.

"She must be very sick, sister," the patient had informed and went on, "Come and see her."

"Go to your bed, just now you!" Sister Higgins had commanded and had not even bothered to go and see the patient called Sarah. She never cared about that Dr "Matero's" patient. Sister Higgins had never managed to pronounce the Shona syllable 'mu' but pronounced it 'ma' as in 'mud'. So the other patient had returned to her bed and had decided to deliberately bump against Shupai's traction by way of waking her from the delirium.

After three days the traction was removed and Shupai was allowed to walk on crutches. She could now drag herself to the toilet. That was great, she thought, rather than having it in her bed. Toilet in bed, blanket bath, the smell of antiseptic, the sneaky women patients, she thought, these were the worst parts of her life in that hospital. After a few days with the crutches she was able to limp around without any support. Shupai requested Dr Mutero to release her from the hospital. The doctor had certain orders to follow. Orders connected with the underground movement. Usually when Dr Mutero had a guerrilla patient in this hospital, he was requested to try and keep the patient in hospital if possible, until the patient was fit enough to join the combat right away. Dr Mutero had the duty, a national duty, he knew he had to comply with these orders. A slight disregard for such orders or any mistake on the part of Dr Mutero could mean a surprise capture of a combatant by the enemy forces. At the same time, he knew he had to be careful. He had to have a good reason for keeping the patient in the hospital.

That day, when Dr Mutero had had his round, the ward sister, Sister Higgins, asked without any respect at all, Dr Mutero thought. "Why is that girl," pointing to Shupai, "Not being discharged today?" A bitter argument ensued between the sister and Dr Mutero in the nurses' duty room. By right a nurse was not to question a doctor's order, Dr Mutero thought. But Sister Higgins was white and he was black, so the rule did not apply. "Listen," Sister Higgins shouted, "If a patient is well enough to be discharged from the hospital I don't see any earthly reason for such a patient to remain in the hospital."

"Who told you this patient is well enough to leave the hospital?" Dr Mutero asked. "Any way, who decides whether a patient should stay or leave the hospital?" Dr Mutero demanded.

"Of course, I can see that, can't I?" argued Sister Higgins and went on, "That Sarah is just pretending to you. She's not sick at all. She was never sick in the first place."

Dr Mutero looked at the Sister and thought, 'This woman is up to her racist dirty tricks again. This time I will show her the game is up', he promised himself. Sister Higgins and Dr. Mutero had always been at logger heads.

Sister Higgins resented getting orders from a black man, never mind how much education he had. After all, this man had never paid any attention to her even if she had tried to attract him by some love moves. Before he could utter another word, Sister Higgins quickly answered Dr Mutero's second question:

"Of course, I know that you make decisions as to when a patient should be discharged," she said with great contempt. "I thought it was better to remind you, Dr Matero," the sister said, the 'doctor Matero' was emphasised sarcastically. Then Dr Mutero said slowly but firmly:

"Alright Sister Higgins, you follow the doctor's orders and keep this patient here until the doctor decides otherwise. Agreed, sister?" He asked with a contemptuous voice and bustled out of the nurses' duty room. The sister headed for Shupai's bed with the speed of a tornado. Shupai was unaware of what had just transpired between Dr Mutero and Sister Higgins. She was sitting on her bed peacefully and thoughtfully after her request to leave the hospital was turned down by the doctor. He had recommended that she remain in the hospital for a few more days. Shupai had thought she could get out of that place, away from that Sister Higgins, but....

"Sarah!" A sharp voice shot out from the nurses' duty room door. Shupai paid attention as she was meant to! All the patients stared! Shupai looked up towards where the voice had come from. Sister Higgins was rushing towards her. "What do you think you are doing here?" the sister screamed at Shupai who was spell-bound. She gazed at the sister with wide eyes and open mouth. "Can't you hear me?" the sister screamed again. At this point, Shupai wondered whether Sister Higgins had made the fatal discovery as to who she really was. This thought drove cold chills down her spine. Goose pimples sprung all over her skin. She had never felt so frightened before; not even during battle, faced by enemy guns. She had never experienced that type of fear before. The terror she felt in the hands of the white man with the jutting out ears at Marondera detention campwas incomparable with this one, she thought. For a few seconds she was almost convinced that somebody had discovered her and Dr Mutero. If that was the case, then trouble is not the word!

"I can hear you all right sister. I heard you the first time who wouldn't?" replied Shupai with all the fake politeness and at the same time forcing a smile she could manage to master. "But what do you mean when you ask, what I am doing here?" she said looking straight into the eyes of the advancing woman.

"You pretend so much to that Dr Matero of yours," the sister accused Shupai, "so that you can continue to stay here."

"Sister, I still don't understand what you mean by everything you have said to me so far," said Shupai, at the same time trying very hard to look and appear normal to the woman she had grown to dislike so much.

"I know you are not sick anymore. You can walk very well. You are ready for home and work. What do you want to stick around here for?" Sister Higgins shouted. "This is not a pleasure house or a holiday resort, you know," she went on. "We want this bed for genuinely sick patients," she went on shouting at the top of her voice, moving round Shupai's bed like an accursed spirit. "You will sleep on the floor if you want to stay here for no good reason," she threatened. Shupai had not moved since the sister had had started shouting. At this point Shupai could tell from the way this sister was talking that the sister was nowhere near suspecting Shupai as being a guerrilla in hospital. As soon as she realised this her temper changed. It changed to a point that she felt she could not stand listening anymore to Sister Higgins' vituperations. These revealed Sister Higgins' devilish, racist nature and her oppressive character, Shupai thought. She stood up cautiously, and firmly held the sister's right hand at the wrist and demanded:

"Sister Higgins, what do you mean by 'sticking around here?" she asked and went on quietly. This time she squeezed the wrist hard. "You better explain yourself Mrs or Miss Higgins. I don't understand what you mean. And shouting at me like that makes me sick right up, in my head." Her words hissed out through her teeth. She was trembling. The fear she had experienced a few minutes ago turned to rage and anger. The shouting from the ward sister had reminded her of some of the white nuns at St Paul's, she thought, that establishment that had made an indelible mark in her life. She remembered sister Aquilina and Mother Superior at St Paul's Mission and saw their representative in Sister Higgins.

The hefty Sister Higgins tried hard to free herself from Shupai's grip. She started appealing to the nurses to come and help her. The three nurses, including Mrs Mhaka the staff nurse, did not move from where they were. Higgins, her face sweating, turning all shades of purple and pink, was not aware she was in the hands of a tough, trained guerrilla; a battle seasoned soldier; a fighter in her own right who had a burning desire to destroy everything that symbolised oppression. The nurses were having a ball watching the notorious Sister Higgins being humbled by a patient. This was something they had never dreamt of. It was great and funny, the nurses thought. Only Dr Mutero had stood up against Sister Higgins before. For the first time, the nurses noted and thought that Higgins was a paper-tiger after all. They thought she could fight back the patient's grip, but she couldn't. Instead she was appealing for help.

"You are not my doctor," Shupai told Sister Higgins, harshly applying more pressure on the grip. "You have no right to talk to me like that. What kind of a nurse are you anyway?"

"Leave my hand!" the sister demanded, "I am not just a mere nurse," she was very annoyed by being referred to as a 'nurse'. She went on, "I am the nursing Sister-in-charge of this ward," she shouted, still struggling to release her hand from Shupai's iron grip, but getting nowhere. Shupai's eyes were glitering with fury. She accused:

"You are not fit to be near a sick-room, then. Your bed-side manners are appalling and terrible," she accused and roughly let go of Sister Higgins' hand. She limped slowly over to the nurses' duty room.

"Please, call Dr Mutero and ask him to come immediately and solve this problem," she asked the staff nurse, Mrs Mhaka.

"No nurse!" Sister Higgins shouted, almost hitting the staff nurse. "I will call Dr Clark, the superintendent of this hospital. I can't have this in my ward, not anymore."

Sister Higgins grabbed the receiver and dialled a number. She was shaking all over, the receiver almost slipped from her hand. Shupai waited quietly behind her. The phone was answered. The nurses who stood behind Sister Higgins were smiling and giving a-thumbs-up sign to Shupai indicating that Shupai was fighting their immediate and direct oppressor – Sister Higgins, and was succeeding.

"Dr Clark?" Sister Higgins shouted into the receiver. "Come quickly to the women's surgical ward. I...." The sister terminated her speech because Shupai had snatched the receiver from her and was already giving her own version of the situation.

"Come quickly doctor, please, we need your immediate help. Sister Higgins is getting out of her mind trying to fight a helpless patient." She sounded like one of the nurses.

"Whose patient is it?" asked Doctor Clark.

"Doctor Mutero's patient," answered Shupai, and said, "Please...."

Shupai did not finish the report. Sister Higgins had snatched the receiver away from her and started blurting onto it. Shupai and the nurses exchanged glances of amusement and stood there listening and watching.

The ward sister sounded really out of her mind, thought Dr Clark on the other end of the line, as he listened to the shrieking voice of the enraged Sister Higgins. Doctor Clark decided he was not going to be involved in the fracas, especially as it involved Dr Mutero. I will be in serious trouble with that son of terrorism, thought Dr Clark.

I wonder why the police can't just arrest him under the Law and Order (Maintenance) Act, or even under any emergency regulations! I am sure there must be a regulation under which they can pick him up so that we can enjoy some peace in this hospital. But that Sister Higgins also....Dr Clark thought, he did not want a confrontation with Mutero anymore because of Sister Higgins. He put down the receiver and ordered his secretary to phone Dr Mutero and tell him to go to the women's surgical ward right away.

Sister Higgins, back in the duty room was still trying to phone Dr Clark who had hanged the phone on her. She was very surprised to see Dr Mutero himself rush in.

"What's going on here?" he asked coolly. Sister Higgins grabbed the phone again, dialled a number and started screaming into the receiver at Dr Clark:

"Dr Clark! You dirty son of a....!" Doctor Mutero took the receiver from her and very gently told her to sit down and explain the trouble to him. He was trying to give her a chair to sit on.

"You!" Sister Higgins burst out pointing at Dr Mutero, "You! I don't want to see you here! You take this woman," pointing at Shupai, "out of here or else I...."

"Or else what? Now listen to me Miss Higgins," Dr Mutero said firmly and decisively, "You are going to get out of here if you don't want to listen to me, is that well understood?"

Sister Higgins started screaming. This time, tears actually streamed down her oversized cheeks from the small eyes which had turned from grey to green. That slit of a mouth situated between fat cheeks, could not open wide enough to let out the scream. She looks terrible, thought Shupai.

"You! Why?" she said between sobs. "Why do you talk to me like that? You have no right to talk to me like that! You bloody Kaffir!"

"Because you are not doing your job professionally; I am the doctor around here. You better learn to obey the doctors' orders, too," Dr Mutero said and then went into the ward where almost every patient was up watching the drama in the nurses' duty room. He politely ordered the patients to go back to their beds. Shupai did not go to her bed immediately. She pleaded with Dr Mutero to discharge her from the hospital right away. The incident with the sister was something she would not like to be repeated. But what is it with this Sister Higgins? Shupai wondered. She just hates me, or there is something else?

Dr Mutero rejected Shupai's pleas for discharge from the hospital. His part in the struggle was to look after the health of those freedom fighters that were under his care. He had to look after them well until in his own opinion they were physically ready to rejoin the rigours of the war. So far he had had no problems with these 'special patients'. He had always kept many of them under hospital cover for as long as was necessary. This particular one happened to be a woman but he was not going to handle her differently from the other fighters. There was no separate set of laws in the struggle for Zimbabwe. Dr Muetro was determined to ensure that Shupai remained under the hospital cover until he was satisfied about her safety on release and about her physical condition.

Dr Mutero ordered Shupai back to her bed. Shupai silently obeyed and limbed back to her bed. She sat on her bed with a bowed head and went into deep thinking, regretting her own actions against Sister Higgins. She thought she really had forgotten herself and had run out of self control. This hospital is run by white authorities. If they find out about her and Dr Mutero, there would be trouble, Shupai thought. She was afraid for Dr Mutero, more than for herself. Dr Mutero's cover must never be broken, Shupai went on regretting. His services to the liberation movement are very valuable. As for her, she would....

She was not aware, however, of how strong Dr Mutero's position had become at this hospital. She was also not aware of how notorious Sister Higgins was, even among her own kith and kin. Dr Clark, the Superintendent, had not even listened to Sister Higgins' story. Instead, he had listened to Dr Mutero and had ordered Sister Higgins to rest for two weeks. After the two weeks she would be transferred to another department of the same hospital or be transferred to another hospital. In discussing the incident with his all-white colleagues in the all-white administration block, Dr Clark had warned, "The political situation in the country is changing very rapidly, ladies and gentlemen. As I see it, it is becoming worse and difficult for the government to contain."

"So what?" demanded the matron.

"Everyone of us, I am sure, is thinking about his or her life," said Dr Clark, and continued, "his work, his position here, whether one should leave this country, or not when the black people take over," Dr Clark went on, "I don't know what you say, ladies and gentlemen, but I, personally, think that Dr Mutero is very powerful among the black political agitators. If we treat him recklessly, especially in this case, things may turn sour or even worse against us."

"What do you mean?" one of the white medical officers asked, and added, "Our security forces are containing the terrorists effectively. The terrorists will never win a war against us! Where did these black people ever fight a war?" He asked, and went on, "I mean a real war with guns, bazookas, machine guns, mortars and tanks, and planes and bombers?" He emotionally looked round at his colleagues and his eyes rested on Dr Clark.

"Most of us are out of touch with the actual situation, I think. I can't forget what happened in Kenya," commented one of the doctors who had been sitting, quietly, listening.

The emotional medical officer argued, "Kenya is different from Rhodesia, you should know by now. Did we not defeat these people in the eighteen hundreds?" he asked and went on, "After all we have help from South Africa and from the Selous Scouts and other mercenaries. He informed and asked "How can they dream of defeating us now?"

"Yes. How?" the matron joined in hesitatingly, "Dr Mutero is black. We are white and powerful. We can very easily get rid of him," she suggested, "The police will listen to us and not to him if we tell them that we suspect him to be dangerous agitator and most likely a terrorist collaborator. They'll take him away. It is quite simple. A black man's word against a white man's, that's all," she continued, "If we do that he will leave this place faster than he came. But, I think, at the same time I must be frank as a Christian. Can we really say Dr Mutero is a terrorist collaborator when he is not? We know that he is not, and we know te is a good doctor who knows his work well. My conscience bothers me," she said, her voice getting a bit faint. She planted her eyes to the floor, as she concluded, and watched a column of ants fighting over a crumb of bread.

"I don't support the suggestion at all," Dr Clark said decisively. "Some of us have been in this country for quite a long time. We do not dream of leaving it. We are prepared to stay and work for and under any government that is running it." He went on, "After all, who is ruling us right now? Is it not but a few, a handful of men? The rest of us are down here, toiling as workers in the capacities of doctors and nurses, boiler men or what have you. If an African government came to power we would remain doctors, nurses and boiler men that we are today, wouldn't we? I, personally, don't believe that these people will drive us out. After all, some Africans, a lot of them, are among my best friends. What I have heard them say is that they want to participate in the running of the affairs of this state. Those who rule now are preventing them from doing this. Anyway, I am not a politician but a physician. It looks to me it's going to be, 'each man for himself and God for us all'. I have seen it in other African countries. The whites, who wanted to remain after the white regime left, remained and some of them are still there. They are working and they are happy," he concluded. The majority of the whites present in that meeting agreed with this view. They greed that as professionals whatever regime came to power, the country would still need them. So they had nothing to fear. Their services as medical people should be to people, irrespective of colour, religion or sex, they concluded the meeting.

The following morning after a sleepless night, Shupai did not see Sister Higgins. A different ward sister came into the ward. She was short and plump. Not bad looking though, Shupai thought, but too white and pale for her liking. She came in the ward accompanied by a tall white man in a white coat. They were greeting and talking to every patient and when they came to Shupai's bed, the man introduced himself as Dr Clark. Shupai did not know what to expect after the introduction. She, however, remained cool, and said to herself, 'Now what?'

"I apologise for what happened yesterday," Dr Clark said, adding, "Everything will be all right now. Sister Alice here," he said, lightly patting Sister Alice on her shoulder, "will look after you." Shupai could not even smile back in reply to a wide smile from Sister Alice. She could only manage a simple nod of her head. Dr Clark then asked her: "How do you feel?"

"I'm still limbing badly but am ready to go home, I think," Shupai answered, struggling hard to award Dr. Clark with a smile.

"You think, and you're not sure?" asked Dr. Clark smiling pleasantly. Dr. Clark was very handsome during his young days, thought Shupai. His white coat sat perfectly on his shoulders. His black tie was geometrically precise. His white shirt-front gleamed like porcelain. His white teeth shone. His hair, greying at the temples, was well brushed back. Just how long this man takes to prepare for each day, Shupai wondered, must be a life time. He was spotlessly smart and he knew it too. He is very likable, Shupai told herself.

After the squabble between Shupai and Sister Higgins, the other patients and especially the nurses in that ward started to regard Shupai as a heroine. They started to be curious about this daring and tough girl who could stand against Sister Higgins. To the patients and African nurses, Sister Higgins was the symbol of white tyranny in that ward. She represented the might of white powers in Rhodesia. Yet she was a mere state enrolled nurse, thought Mrs Mhaka, the staff nurse in that ward. Higgins was an S.E.N., which is a State Enrolled Nurse from England. But here she had the title of Sister-in-charge because she was white.

She was receiving three times the salary of the Zimbabwean registered nurses, who taught her the work when she first arrived from Britain, Mrs Mhaka had told Shupai. "You know what, these white so-called sisters are recruited from Britain or elsewhere to come and work here. They are promoted to state registered status straight away and we have to struggle to train them. We do the work for them in fact."

Each nurse and patient in that ward wanted to have a chance to talk to Shupai but she tried hard to keep her distance, introducing herself as a school teacher from the neighbourhood a cousin to Dr Mutero's wife who got injured during sports with her students.

"We all thank you for helping us to get rid of that terror of a white girl from this ward." Mrs Mhaka was fourty eight years old with tremendous experience as a State Registered Nurse (SRN). She had worked at Sinoia Hospital for a long time. Her husband, Reverend Mhaka was in charge of the Sinoia Diocese of the Church of England (the British State Church). Mrs Mhaka told Shupai that she received many of those white girls from Britain and taught them the nursing and the treatment of tropical diseases. Most of those young white girls were State Enrolled Nurses (SEN's), and some were not even trained, Mrs Mhaka asserted. They were ward assistants who had just been recruited from the various hospitals in Britain to come and reinforce the number of settlers in this country. Mrs Mhaka went on to tell Shupai, that while she was training those girls, the girls were already designated as 'Sisters' the title given to senior SRN's. They were in fact already rated double above an African SRN, and earning thrice as much as Mrs Mhaka, besides the numerous fringe benefits and pensions they received. Miss Higgins, Mrs Mhaka told Shupai, was among some of these so-called nurses whom she had trained, and some had been transferred to other hospitals. "Some of those girls are not such bad people at all when they first come," Mrs Mhaka commented. "Miss Higgins wasn't. She stayed on here at Sinoia Government Hospital. She was nice, young and not so fat when she first came to Rhodesia," Mrs Mhaka told Shupai and commented, "I wonder what came over her."

"It is the laws created by these settlers which change into brutes even the best white people who happen to settle in this country," Shupai said quietly to Mrs Mhaka and the other two nurses. "Not all settlers are bad, you know. They only have to obey the laws of their settler society which demands that every white person must rate an African as a third class citizen, a servant all the time. Miss Higgins is one of those many whites who became really bad, as you say in order to serve the selfish interests of their community."

"Now about my husband," said Mrs Mhaka insistently. "He took over the diocese from Reverend Williams, a white man. Rev. Williams was living in a very big beautiful house. When we came we were not allowed to stay in that house. We were told that it would be turned into Bible class study rooms and so we were forced to stay at Chinyemba Primary School together with the teachers. The huge comfortable car that Rev. Williams had been using was shipped back to Britain for Rev. Williams' use there. My husband is now using a bicycle. Rev. Williams was receiving a large salary, but my husband is told to get his money from contributions donated by the church members. Just imagine! How much do you think that can be?" Mrs Mhaka asked Shupai, shaking her head.

"It is clearly discrimination, even in the service of God, isn't it?" Shupai said encouraging Mrs Mhaka to go on.

"This makes me feel very bad about my husband's work. Does the church have to practice such discrimination against those who would like to serve God so faithfully, but happened to be black?" Mrs Mhaka asked emotionally.

"Mrs Mhaka, you have the same ideas that many of us used to have. Of course, it was the white people who brought the church into this country. Perhaps, some of them had good intentions, but the individuals who ran the colonial government took advantage of the church and used it as a means of exploitation and oppressing the black people." Shupai was trying very hard to be mild. "The church has had its positive side, though. It was the church which started to teach the black people to read and write. In fact, as time went by, it was the Mission Schools which offered better education for the black people than the settler regime run schools. It is also important to know that it was not the church that enacted the law which says white churchmen must not live with black churchmen. It was the settler regime, serving colonialism and imperialism. In fact, many people, including myself, came to realise later that the church as such was not responsible for the oppression and exploitation of the black people in this country," Shupai asserted, "These white people, no matter how humanitarian they are, who run the churches are given ground rules by those few who run the government in Salisbury. And if they want peace from harassment, the church authorities have to abide by those ground rules. For instance," she went on, "There were people such as Bishop Ralph Dodge of the United Methodist Church; Bishop Lamont of the Anglican Church in Manicaland, and many other church people both men and women who were victimised for supporting Africans. Ordinary white citizens or non-citizens were also victimised by the few white rulers in Salisbury. Remember Dr Terence Ranger, John Reid, Peter Mackay and many others, who suffered detentions, restrictions and even served terms of imprisonment. It is true that some white church leaders do behave in a racist manner.

We, too, tend to look at them, because they are white, as being part and parcel of the oppression system. It is the system of government which refused your husband, a black pastor, to live in a big house where a white pastor lived. This system did not want to see a black family in a nice house – it was a white house by law, not a black house."

Mrs Mhaka thoughtfully said, "I think what you are saying is quite correct. Rev and Mrs Williams are not bad people at all. We knew them in Britain when my husband was doing his Theology and I was doing my SRN's training. Some of these Britons are not such bad people in their country you know. But when they come here…." Mrs Mhaka went on, "They begin to speak a different language and begin to behave like brutes. They despise us as servants, as if they have servants in their own country. You would be surprised to see the white men collecting gabbage cans and emptying them in gabbage trucks, and their women sweeping the streets. Yet they call these jobs 'kaffir' jobs, when they come to Rhodesia, isn't that sickening?" Mrs Mhaka addressed the question to the other nurses she had with her.

"Do you know what is going on in Seke Reserve where I come from?" the patient next to Shupai who had been listening quietly, asked, "People have been told to give all their cattle, goats, sheep and donkeys to the 'Native Commissioner' so that a six foot high barbed wire fence can be constructed around the villages making them one huge protected village with a curfew imposed?" The woman looked around her and lowered her voice, "They have been told that there are killers and thieves roaming the forests who want to kill the villagers, if the villagers do not give these killers food and places to hide."

"Well, perhaps those so-called killers may be our liberators," Shupai said with a staged up note of doubt in her voice. "They are not supposed to kill their fellow Africans. Perhaps the villagers should try to help them in any way possible." Shupai said this as if she did not know anything about those forest fighters.

Three days after the Furore had occurred Shupai was lying quietly in her bed. She was just wondering where Dr Mutero had been for the last two days. Perhaps he had also been transferred like Sister Higgins, Shupai was thinking, when Dr Mutero walked into the ward. He handed her that day's Rhodesia Herald saying:

"I had been to Salisbury for the last two days." Shupai received the paper. A photograph on the front page hit her in the face. With a blast of alarm, she blinked. She could not believe her eyes. She looked again and held her breath. Shonhiwa Gidi? She sighed painfully as she recognised him and went on to read the accompanying head line:

"CAPTURED TERRORIST LECTURES COURT IN THE DOCK". The Rhodesia Herald reported the highlights of the trial in the magistrate's court in Salisbury the day before. Shupai looked at Dr Mutero sadly, questioningly.

"That's where I was," he told her quietly, and went on, "He totally refused the services of a lawyer. There's nothing we could do." Shupai just could not say a word at that moment. They avoided any discussion associated with terrorists with Dr. Mutero.

Chapter 13

After Shonhiwa was transferred from Karoi Hospital to Salisbury's Harare African General Hospital, he had been heavily guarded. Several plain-clothed men, both black and white had visited him with questions and more questions. There was this white man who was sort of in-charge, Shonhiwa noticed. He was present almost at all times Shonhiwa was being interrogated. He had introduced himself to Shonhiwa: "I'm detective Inspector Gaylord," he went on, "I'm with the division of the legal department of political habits within the country." He continued breathlessly, "Political activities sometimes parallel criminal activities, you know." He spoke, the last sentence, voice so close that Shonhiwa could smell the staleness of his breath. He had a face of a drinker, with burst capillaries beneath his skin, Shonhiwa observed. He wore a pair of fearsome sun-glasses. When he removed them, his eyes were pouchy. His eyelids flickered. "We have vetted your background and I believe you are what they say you are," Inspector Gaylord informed. "They? Who are they?" Shonhiwa asked.

"The people who brought you here."

"What do they say I am?"

"A freedom fighter of the highest rank." The inspector sounded sarcastic, Shonhiwa thought.

"So what?"

"What's your position in this er-er?" Shonhiwa did not answer. Another man came into the security side ward. He was a tall black man with large pimples under his chin probably from constant shaving with a blunt razor blade. He stood there snarling at Shonhiwa and picking onto his pimples violently. Inspector Gaylord, asked, "What's your name?" "Shonhiwa Gidi".

"Liar!" shouted the pimpled black man angrily, and he turned to inspector Gaylord, "These people use phoney names, you know." "Your friends have told us who you are," Inspector Gaylord lied confidently.

"Then what do you want from me?"

"The bloody fool!" the black man said sternly. He wagged his finger strongly in Shonhiwa's face. "He still thinks we are joking," remarked the black man.

"We must remove you from here as soon as possible," suggested Inspector Gaylord smiling at Shonhiwa amiably. 'Save your mocking, mocking smile Boer,' thought Shonhiwa to himself. Gaylord reached out a hand and patted Shonhiwa gingerly on the head as if he (Shonhiwa) were a large strange dog.

"We do not want to fall into the same situation as before," Gaylord said this to the black man.

"Don't worry. He won't manage to escape," said the black man glaring at Shonhiwa hatefully. "Not this time. I'll see to it myself." Shonhiwa wondered whether anyone had ever managed to escape such conditions. He was never left alone. Two policemen, one just outside the door, and the second one was stationed right inside the small room at a corner. Shonhiwa's food, his nursing treatment, even his medication was administered by the police. No chance, Shonhiwa thought resignedly.

What Shonhiwa did not know was that one of his colleagues, Makuva, had managed to escape from that same side-ward a few days ago. The tight security manned around this ward, this time made it impossible for anyone, not even the two nurses who had helped in Makuva's case to think on those lines.

The two officers stood there both looking at Shonhiwa. Inspector Gaylord smiled at him again, and he awarded Shonhiwa another amiable tap on the head. Shonhiwa flinched. This time the tap was harder on the wounded head. The white pig! What is he trying to prove? Shonhiwa almost uttered these words. He just looked at them sourly as they left the room.

He leaned back and watched the armed policeman, who had been standing outside come in and locked the door. I feel as if I am in the slammer already, he thought. He lay there, on the bed, feeling tired, and broken and trapped. The door was unlocked again. Another set of interrogators came in and he said to them weakly, "I'm for the hangman. This, I know." He dismissed them with his heavily bandaged right hand. The pain on the hand throbbed violently, sending a flood of nauseating fluid in his mouth. "I wish you could leave me alone, at least for now. I'm not going to be hanged tomorrow morning, am I?" He said this knowing it was on deaf ears. But he was surprised, he was left alone, not interrogated, for the rest of that day.

As soon as he looked a bit better, he was quickly removed from the general hospital. He was taken to the remand prison pending trial.

Shonhiwa was tried by a white magistrate, who wore glasses which seemed useless because he kept removing them to clean them. "May the accused, please, stand up," said the bespectacled magistrate. "Does the accused understand the charges as read to him? If he does, does he plead guilty or not guilty?"

The court was crowded. The crowd turned its eyes on to the accused. Dr Mutero and other members of the underground movement were among the crowd. Shonhiwa, the accused himself, appeared calm and relaxed, thought Dr Mutero. His hands and face, Dr Mutero observed, bore obvious marks and scars of torture. His right arm was scarred from elbow to wrist with burn tissue and the skin looked puckered. There was a nasty and brutal scar on his forehead, another from the bridge of his nose to his right ear. He walked with a pronounced limp, Dr Mutero had observed, when Shonhiwa had walked into the courtroom. People gasped when he stood up. Some even avoided looking at him. Those scars!

The scars must have been either from the battle field, guessed Dr Mutero, or probably from the interrogation tactics employed by the settler minority secret servicemen. Many die in those torture chambers of the settler regime. Shonhiwa obviously survived, Dr Mutero thought. He is a toughened guerrilla fighter, with an unbending spirit. Pity, Dr Mutero regretted that his colleagues at Harare Hospital had not been helpful this time. They only notified him about this patient the day before the patient was removed from the hospital and was sent to the remand prison. He had no time to organise the 'boys' for the rescue. Shonhiwa had been thought dead by his comrades. They did not know he had survived that ambush bid by the mercenary Selous Scouts led by the blue eyed Wilson.

Tall and dignified, Shonhiwa in the witness stand, stood beside his guard. All ears in that court waited to hear from his own lips what he thought about his actions against the government. Was he going to denounce his role in the liberation movement? Was he going to tell the usual story? Dr Mutero wondered, the story that he was lured by promises of scholarship overseas before being forced into the 'terrorist' army? Was he going to plead guilty, hoping then, to plead and beg for mercy? Was he going to compromise and offer to work for the regime as an informer? Dr Mutero thought Shonhiwa would be a very effective informer and very damaging to the liberation movement. Dr Mutero tensed. But Shonhiwa, once on his feet, said nothing. He kept looking down at his feet. Shonhiwa had refused the assistance of a lawyer, the underground movement had organised. He had refused even to see and talk to the lawyer. He was going to defend himself, he had told them.

"Does the defendant plead guilty or not guilty?" repeated the weary, thin magistrate rather impatiently. Shonhiwa looked at the magistrate. The magistrate was a small bespectacled man, balding, with thin hair combed straight across his sunburned scalp. His glasses were forever sliding down the bridge of his hooked nose. Shonhiwa thought, these British Jews, who are still hunting down the Nazis, even up to now.

Shonhiwa cleared his throat calmly. "Guilty or not guilty to what?" he asked. His voice was deep and surprisingly composed, thought Dr Mutero.

"To the charges brought against you by the state prosecutor," the weary magistrate said firmly.

"I have not been told the charges, and up to this moment I have not been shown the charge sheet. How then am I expected to plead guilty or not guilty?" The magistrate was so surprised that he unconsciously let his glasses slide down the bridge of his nose until they fell onto his desk. The court laughed. The prosecutor was furious. The accused was calm and composed. The magistrate put his glasses back on.

"I will ask the prosecutor to read the charges again. Please listen attentively. It is for your benefit," said the magistrate, showing signs of uneasiness and annoyance. The burly prosecutor, a white man with a Jewish or German name, did his duty. He was tall and heavy. His eyes were a cold blue ice. They sent a tingling of cold fear up Shonhiwa's spine. But Shonhiwa knew he was a condemned man already anyway. The cold fear, he reminded himself, was quite unnecessary under the circumstances. No mercy, he knew.

The prosecutor read the charges. There were seven: "waging war against the lawfully constituted government of the land; leaving the country unlawfully; undergoing military training outside this country together with others now not before the court; bringing into this country instruments of war without the express authority or knowledge of the government; re-entering the country clandestinely and failing to report his re-entry to the rightful authorities; inciting tribesmen against the legal government of this country; and in conjunction with others unknown and now not before the court; recruited tribesmen into the terrorist army for the express purpose of overthrowing this government." The prosecutor sat down. His mouth was foaming and the nauseating white stuff was all over his lips.

"Has the defendant now heard the charges against him?" asked the magistrate. He was perspiring. "The court will now proceed," announced the magistrate looking straight into Shonhiwa's eyes. He, obviously, expected him to plead guilty. Shonhiwa kept quiet for a whole minute, looking at the prosecutor whose eyelids and lips twitched nervously. Shonhiwa expected an epidemic of complaints from the prosecutor, but the court was quiet, with the quietness of the grave. Then he said, still looking at the prosecutor:

"My plea is that I am both guilty and not guilty." The court exclaimed:

"Ah!" and there were whisperings and murmers all round. "Silence in the court!" the magistrate shouted.

"If it will please your court, I will explain my plea," said Shonhiwa, looking at the magistrate. The prosecutor was on his feet:

"Objection your honour! The accused cannot explain a plea," the prosecutor went on, "He must only plead guilty or not guilty if he feels so. Thereafter the court will proceed on its usual course."

The magistrate was curious to hear what Shonhiwa had to say. "Objection overruled!" The magistrate quickly overruled the prosecutor, saying that the case was not an ordinary case, hence the strange plea. "The outside world must not be given the impression that the accused was bamboozled through some complicated court procedures. Let him go ahead and explain his strange plea."

"I am guilty, if by guilty you mean that I am a freedom fighter," Shonhiwa started. He spoke calmly. "I am a soldier, prepared to fight to the end against any form of oppression against my people. I am a soldier because I am militarily trained. If that is an offence, then I am guilty. You, the people of Britain," he pointed to the magistrate, "together with almost the entire world, united to fight against the monster that was Hitler. Why did people of the world fight against the monster that was Hitler. They did so because Hitler was a Nazi fascist; a murderer of millions of innocent human beings. He had mighty forces, but the world fought those forces until it brought them down to their knees. The world defeated them. The people of Asia challenged imperialism, feudalism and colonialism which the monster Japanese regime of that time imposed on them. You, sitting there, and the prosecutor here," he pointed to the burly prosecutor, "hated Hitler's oppression and all those who supported him. You hated his fascist government because of its wrong and evil policies towards its fellow human beings. Were you guilty for taking up arms against fascism, dictatorship and Hitler's aggression?" he asked and continued, still very calm. "Were those nations which stood agaist Hitler guilty or not guilty? And what is the difference between your regime and that of Hitler?"

The presecutor jumped to his feet "Objection your honour!" The magistrate beckoned him to sit down. He sat down glaring at the magistrate openly.

"Were those killed by Hitler," Shonhiwa continued, "more human than our people who ever since the arrival of the settlers have been deprived of all their rights, robbed of their wealth and denied their humanity? Are murder, rape and robbery more heinous when committed against Europeans than against our people here? If not, how then can it be right to call those who fought against Nazi fascism heroes and those like myself," he pointed at his chest, "who fight no less crimes be called criminals and terrorists? The white minority has taken the lion's share of my country. My people suffer untold poverty and disease." He stopped talking and was quiet. Everyone thought he had finished. The prosecutor sat on his chair, tensely, with one buttock.

"Our people are killed in detention camps just as Hitler killed people in the concentration camps and the gas chambers," Shonhiwa went on, "Our entire nation has been sentenced to death by starvation. Our country has been turned into one massive prison for us, with the so-called protected villages, forming the internal concentration camps." There was silence of the dead in the courtroom. The prosecutor could not believe his ears. He kept on trying to object. The magistrate kept on beckoning him to sit down. Shonhiwa went on:

"Can I be guilty when our cause is just? Those who fought against Hitler and defeated him were not guilty. Their cause was just. And how can the robbers and murderers be judges?" He paused for a moment, and continued. "Only my people have the right to judge my actions. But they do not have the seat you are sitting on now. If they did, they would not find me guilty. Our entire nation is at war against your racist regime. Victory belongs to the Zimbabwean people. Now...."

"Your honour, please!" the prosecutor, this time, thought he could not be stopped. The accused had gone too far. The prosecutor snarled at the accused; glared at the magistrate who did not seem to have heard the prosecutor's objection plea.

"You racists," Shonhiwa pointed to the prosecutor, "and your litany of murder, brutality and racial discrimination you imposed on our people is comparable to some of the work of the Nazis. You should face the Nuremburg type trials. You must be hanged." Shonhiwa went on as if possessed by the devil himself. He thought he had to say his piece despite the prosecutor's protestations. He thought he had nothing to lose after all. "Or you should face the gilotine like during the French revolution."

"Objection! Objection! Your honour, I object, please!" shouted the prosecutor. The court room was talking. It was in disarray. The accused had to shout his last piece: "No amnesty!" He pointed to all the whites on the prosecuting bench. "No amnesty to all of you."

"Your honour objection, please!" The burly prosecutor jumped up. He stood there in the centre of the courtroom like a bull that has disposed of one matador and is glaring round in search of another. His lips twitched dangerously. His cold blue eyes became cold grey ice. The court became quiet.

"You!" the accused started again, pointing to the glaring prosecutor. "No ma...."

"Enough!" the irritated magistrate cut in sharply with a loud bang with the gavel on his desk. His spectacles slipped and dropped onto the desk emphasising the noise. He did not bother to put them back on. He went on, "I am registering a plea of not guilty against the name of the accused. I summarily find the accused guilty on all counts as charged." He pushed his spectacles on to the right place. "This court will accordingly pronounce its verdict and pass it on to a higher court for appropriate sentence," announced the magistrate, banging his shaking right hand on the desk, at the same time, declaring, "The court is adjourned!" He left the court without much ceremony.

Shupai, in her hospital bed, read the article with a mixture of pride and pain. She was proud of Shonhiwa Gidi's courage, bravery and dedication. He had struggled against the oppressor even right in his own so-called court of law. She was sure that members of her unit, as well as the whole liberation movement, felt the same as they read or heard about Shonhiwa's speech and adventure in the dock.

She was sad, on the other hand, because it was as sure as sunrise, that the enemy high court would sentence Shonhiwa to the gallows. Shupai was sad not only because she was losing a courageous comrade-in-arms. He was, she recalled, the only man who readily accepted and understood her. He had, at one time, almost succeeded in moving her feelings from the battlefield to serious thought of marriage. They had finally promised each other marriage in a free Zimbabwe. Shonhiwa was, therefore, special. His death....She sobbed quietly....He would die an honourable death, as a brave son of Zimbabwe; a hero. The Zimbabwe of tomorrow, she was sure, would read his name and would remember what him and many others like him did for its people.

Dr Mutero had watched Shupai read the paper, and he noticed her crying. She was so sad that he decided to discharge her that morning. Mrs Mutero came to pick her up from the hospital.

That evening they listened to the BBC. The most exciting news item announced was: "The white minority leader in Rhodesia has agreed, in principle, to majority rule." The report went on, "He is willing to have a round-table conference to discuss the peaceful transfer of power from the minority to the majority," the report said.

"This is fantastic!" remarked Mrs Mutero. But somehow Shupai was sceptical about the whole affair.

"It can't be true," Shupai argued. "The minority fascists must be up to some monkey tricks, I'm sure."

"Surely, if he is genuine in his intentions, the move is definitely significant," Mrs Mutero retorted, and asked, "But who knows?"

"Who knows, really?" Dr Mutero supported his wife and went on, "The minority regime may have had enough of our blows by now, you know," this was addressed to Shupai. He went on, "He may now be ready to engage in serious negotiations with the nationalist leaders of Zimbabwe."

"This man also, we must not forget, is a liar of the first order," Shupai reminded. "All he may be doing is to pour icy cold water over our whole liberation struggle and to sugar coat our bullets. He may be trying to woo us away from the battlefield." She went on, "If this is his aim, then he is fooling himself. Nothing short of complete and absolute transfer of effective political power can woo us." She went on debating, "Our objective is not to put our guns down once the enemy says he is prepared to talk."

"I think the leaders should agree," suggested Dr Mutero, and recommended, "The talking can on while the fighting continues. I, however, sincerely hope," Dr Mutero said doubting, "that our nationalist leaders would not be duped or be fooled by this latest gimmick by the white minority leader."

"I wonder what made him change his mind rather so abruptly." Mrs Mutero mused. "Not so long ago he was so arrogantly shouting that no black majority rule would come in his life time. He even went on to say; 'I have the happiest Africans in Africa' now why does he want to talk? We know he is too conceited and much too arrogant to talk to black people."

"I think people must be very careful," warned Shupai thoughtfully, "I suspect the liberation war has become so bitter for him that he plans to create a buffer so he can reinforce his demoralised forces. He wants to get time to plan for more drastic strategies to combat us."

"You are quite right," conceded Dr Mutero, "We need to be quite on our guard against these fanatic fascists. But as I said earlier, our blows may have forced them to concede to our demands. While at the conference table, however, we must remain very wary and vigilant against any of their foxy tricks."

The next day, in the evening, the BBC announced that a venue for the Constitutional Conference on Rhodesia had been agreed upon. Geneva, Switzerland, had agreed to hold the talks under chairmanship of the British government.

"The very best thing for us to do is to engage the enemy fiercely with our guns while the conference is in progress," recommended Shupai. "Yes," Mrs Mutero agreed. "We must never give him time to breath. He must be choked until he is asphyxiated. Then he will agree to our terms."

Shupai stayed with the Mutero's for another few days more. She was much, much better, but was waiting for the instructions for her to be taken back to the front to join her unit. For the days she was at Dr and Mrs Mutero, the issue of the Geneva talks was hot both locally and internationally. The Rhodesia Herald reported that the African chiefs had been organised to, launched their own political party, for Geneva, as the 'true representatives of the African people in Rhodesia.'

"This must have been instigated by the settler regime. It hopes to hoodwink the international world into believing that the chiefs were still important in these issues," remarked Dr Mutero.

"They hope to form a puppet government led by the stoog chiefs and some moderate Zimbabweans," commented Mrs Mutero. "And this will still serve the interests of the white minority settlers."

"Who in the present political circumstances of this country would remain moderate?" asked Shupai. "Shame on these chiefs!" she exclaimed. "They'll never learn. Can't they see the haven they are living in is nearing the end?"

"Don't worry," consoled Dr Mutero, and assured, "The chiefs' party is an abortion, a non-starter in fact. It will die a natural death," Dr Mutero prophesised.

For sure, the chiefs' party was already becoming a still-born in the fact that it was not taken seriously by the Zimbabwe masses. Shupai noted this after reading a short, hidden article in the Rhodesia Herald. "Zimbabweans were never interested in the chiefs, let alone their party," the article said. "The chiefs' party is a white man's party in black man's skin for white man's interests."

The voice of Zimbabwe, the external wing of the liberation movement information service broadcast, from Tanzania, in its comment about the chiefs' party said, "When the white man set his foot in our country, he turned our chiefs from being the traditional leaders and the custodians of the customs and traditions of their people into paid up traditional henchmen, collaborators and tax collectors. They are happy to continue serving in that capacity till death do them part," the broadcast went on, "The Zimbabweans, the chiefs have to be reminded, have long realised that they do not have anymore of the traditional leaders. So the chiefs must be well assured, will die, together with the main body of the white men, being appendages...." This was very encouraging, Shupai thought, and wished she were out with her unit. She wanted to hear what her comrades were saying about the current developments on the political front.

Dr Mutero then received instruction through his usual channels to drive Shupai to Masowe Primary School. Mjiba Doro, the teacher, would lead her to where her unit was operating. Once he received his orders, the patriotic Dr Mutero carried out the task with great pride and precision. Just before Dr Mutero whisked the gallant fighter away, Mrs Mutero hugged her fondly, "It's a pity you have to leave," she said emotionally and continued "Your presence here always enriches my political knowledge, you know."

"Thank you so very much for everything my sistser," Shupai said. "I know I have very, very good friends here. You've been like a loving sister to me, really." She smiled generously and hugged Mrs Mutero back then she left.

Shupai arrived at her destination and joined her comrades. They were happy to see her. She had managed to carry the newspaper that carried Shonhiwa's trial and told them what had happened to him. The jubilation for Shupai's return turned to sadness about Shonhiwa's predicament. They all concluded, sadly, he was going to be hanged by the settler regime. Shonhiwa was a gallant fighter. He would die a gallant death....

They also discussed the negotiations that the British Government was suggesting between the Rhodesian Government and the Nationalists. They all agreed that they will not put down their arms until they have total independence for Zimbabwe.

A few weeks later, in Geneva, Switzerland, a constitutional conference on Rhodesia began. It was chaired by a representative of the British government. The Rhodesian government delegation was flanked by what the minority leader termed, "the very true leaders of the happy African people of Rhodesia," the chiefs' delegation.

Just after the first session the Zimbabwe nationalist representatives went into caucus. The leader had felt there was an urgent need for consultation among themselves. "I don't know what you say, comrades," started the leader "but I, personally, think the minority leader has cheated us to the conference table." He went on, "There are clear signs that what we mean by majority rule is not what he means at all."

"It's quite true comrade," supported the other member, and added, "It's very open that the minority regime does not mean the same ONE MAN ONE VOTE as we know it." He explained, "His majority means," he made the open and close quotation signs in the air, "only those few Africans he has managed to accept in his 'general voters' roll. And of course, adult suffrage means to him one white man one vote."

"That is correct," agreed the leader and said, "So, comrades, what do you say?" Without waiting for their opinions, he suggested, "We must stick to our guns! We have been struggling for ONE PERSON ONE VOTE and nothing," giving a strong negative gesture with both his arms, and repeated, "Nothing, nothing falling short of this demand, comrades, is acceptable to us." He looked round at his colleagues. They were all nodding frantically in agreement. He relaxed a bit. "Alright then," he sounded relieved, "Let's go back there and tell them," and he warned, "We may have to walk out of that conference room. So, be ready to pack your bags for back to the front line."

They all laughed. But they were very serious when they seated themselves again around the conference table.

The Rhodesian delegation had also consulted. Nothing falling short of their wishes was to be accepted. They wanted to keep ruling according to their own terms. Democracy to them was the choosing of a few African leaders, only "acceptable" to them. They felt if they accepted the nationalists' demands, then civilisation and Christianity which they believed to represent in this part of Africa would be thrown down the drain. "What have we and our fathers worked for then?" the leader had asked, and strongly suggested, "We must stick to our beliefs and demands, or else the whole civilized world will laugh at us." They all agreed, nodding their heads and clapping their hands.

The Geneva conference quickly flopped. It was the Rhodesian government delegation which staged a walk-out in protest against what they called the violation of the civilized and the enlightened reason". The combatants who had radios heard this news from the six o'clock a.m. BBC news. Munongwa's unit, for example, actually felt relieved.

"Now, this is the greatest news since the history of our struggle," commented Shupai, "Our leaders are great!"

"Well," Munongwa said, "We know that the enemy had hoped to pour cold water on our liberation fire," he talked happily, "by pretending to be for majority rule and agreeing to a so-called round-table conference with our leaders." He continued, "Hats off to our militant and gallant leaders," he took off his cap and held it high, and others did the same, "who could not be hoodwinked by the enemy chicanery!"

"Down with the minority oppressor!" the other combatants replied throwing their caps onto the ground in agreement with their commander. "Forward with our leaders!" they shouted. While Munongwa wanted to continue addressing his comrades, a bird like whistle was sounded to announce someone's arrival. It was 'Mjiba' Doro. He could be seen waving a black and red squared cloth anxiously, running towards the comrades (every 'mjiba' had to carry this kind of cloth and should show it whenever coming to the combatants with a message. This was for his own safety otherwise he could be mistaken for an enemy).

"Pamberi, makomuredi (Forward Comrades!)," Doro greeted the fighters breathlessly. They returned the greetings. Doro seemed he had a very important and urgent message. He did not waste any time, for there was no time to waste in the struggle, he thought.

"Comrade Munongwa is wanted at the headquarters immediately," he said, and added, "Your unit is to join comrade Tafirenyika's unit under you comrade Marufu," he said pointing at one of the combatants and went on, "Comrade Tafirenyika's unit is now at the Cave, waiting for all of you, minus comrade Munongwa and Tafirenyika of course."

Munongwa was taken to the District underground Headquarters where several unit commanders were gathered including Tichaona, Chakanyuka, Makuva, Tafirenyika and other commandos, from different parts of the country.

The purpose for this high level meeting was for the chief political commissar, Tangai, and other high command representatives, to brief the field commanders. They were briefed about the implications of the failure of the Geneva constitutional conference:

"Comrades, greetings!" started Tangai, tall and slim, but very strong and quite ambitious looking. He went on solemnly, "Let us stand up first of all comrades, and observe a moment's silence in remembrance and honour of our heroic and beloved comrades, Shonhiwa Gidi and the others we have lost in battle. They all stood up in silence with their right fists raised high in salute. After the minute, "Thank you comrades," Tangai said wiping his forehead with a cloth. Then he went on after they had seated themselves on the floor, their faces up, anxious.

"I'm sure you are aware of the success our leaders achieved in Geneva." The combatants nodded. "The implications are that we will have to intensify our war efforts against the enemy. And this is the only weapon that can bring us a valid and solid solution, total liberation." He paused for a short while. Then he went on calmly, "This means that more Zimbabweans have to be prepared to suffer, serve and sacrifice for this total liberation. We must resolve to push the enemy harder in the battlefield. This will force him back to the conference table. He must come ready to face and to accept reason." He pointed out, "The enemy remains arrogant. He has not yet felt our power. That is why he still dilly dallies in the hope of watering down our efforts. Comrade Hondo Iropa (war is blood) here," Tangai pointed to one of the high command representatives, "has a few announcements to make. I'm sure you'll be delighted about what he is going to tell you."

Hondo Iropa stood up and said, "I have some good news for you, comrades." Hondo was short, stocky and wide at the shoulders with a neck as thick as his thigh. He had hard muscles around his arms and was a bit loud in speech. "We have received new weapons from the Organisation of African Unity's Liberation Committee in Dar-es-Salaam," he announced and went on, "The new weapons would enable us to raise the level of our effectiveness in the battlefield for the final onslaught against the enemy forces." There was applause with clapping of hands followed by murmurs, then:

"Comrade Commissar," called Tichaona. "We hope the new weapons include more hand grenades and different types of zvimbambaira (sweet potatoes). This is the name the combatants gave to the landmines. Tichaona went on, "These are very effective in stopping or slowing down the enemy forces from pursuing us each time we break-off engagement with them. The enemy also uses a lot of hand grenades on us."

"Very effective," Chakanyuka supported Tichaona.

"We wish we could have those surface-to-air missiles too" said Tafirenyika and recommended, "We could combat that enemy better if we reduced his freedom in the air." He pointed out, "As we are now, even with hand-grenades and landmines, those enemy gun ships and choppers," he made a flying gesture, "still harass us so effectively that we find ourselves, most of the time, on the run and taking cover."

"Yaa! That's true, comrade," agreed Munongwa and went on, "I think that's how we lost comrade Shonhiwa and the others. They got cut off from the rest of the unit by one of those choppers," Munongwa added a bit doubtfully.

"Your concern is known and well understood, comrades," said one of the commissars and went on. "As we are talking right now, those things you have mentioned are being landed into the country," he went on to reveal, "You will have them within a few days, together with some conventional anti-aircraft batteries from a friendly progressive country."

"That would be great, comrade commissar!" interjected Chakanyuka. "This will definitely enable us to consolidate our grip on the already liberated areas."

"Yes," Makuva agreed and went on confidently, "I think we are doing fine in most of the rural areas, so far, aren't we, comrade Chakanyuka?" Makuva and Chakanyuka were in the same commando unit, specialised in sabotage work. Including Tichaona's unit, they always moved from one part of the country to another, paralysing enemy efforts. That is why they could tell the progress of the liberation war in some rural areas.

"That's a fact, comrades," answered Chaknyuka.

"Then, I suggest that now we should try and move into the urban areas, do you remember the Rhodes and Founders' mission?" Makuva went on excitedly, "Let us concentrate some of our efforts in the urban centres now." Makuva was applauded by his comrades and the commissars.

"Good idea, comrade," commented Munongwa in approval of the suggestion and recommended, "There are courageous commandos among us who are well trained in sabotage techniques and tactics and urban guerrilla warfare." Munongwa went on, "They could go in and attack important projects of the enemy's economy. You know what? We have already identified these as forming the power base of the minority regime and we need to paralise them immediately."

"Comrades," said Tangai, "We are very relieved and encouraged by your work and your enthusiasm," and he said, "Now, do you want to choose the commandos who have to organise the activities right here?"

"That is not a problem, comrade commissar," replied Tafirenyika, and reminded, "Do you comrades remember the Jeaney Junction operation, and that of the Wiltshire Estates and many, many others?" He went on without waiting for their reply, "Have you heard of how comrade Chakanyuka here," pointing at Chakanyuka, "and his commandos entered Harare Hospital and rescued comrade Makuva here," he asked pointing at Makuva, "Amazing! Wasn't it?" They laughed jovially.

"Yaa! Amazing indeed! We have brave soldiers there!" emphasised Hondo Iropa, and added, "We should now direct such big operation efforts against the enemy's urban enterprises." There followed a long pause. Everyone seemed to be brain-cracking for suggestions or something to say. Then: "We will need some women to work with," suggested Chakanyuka and added, "There is one already I'm thinking of. That one is good. She could organise the other women very effectively, I'm sure."

"Who is this?" asked Tichaona. "I feel I know the one you mean. When did you last see her?"

"She is the one who helped in the Wiltshire Estates and the Jeaney Junction affairs. I remember she managed the transportation very well." Chakanyuka went on, "After the Harare Hospital affair, I heard she was in Sinioa Hospital with some injuries she had sustained in the battle, isn't she something?" Munongwa and a few others laughed heartily, showing that they knew the person.

"Do you mean comrade Shupai?" asked Munongwa.

"She must be the one, a different name though. She was a teacher at Chakarara Primary School at the time of the Jeaney Junction," informed Chakanyuka. "Though I don't trust women, that one bit me....Lucia, yes, that's her name. I remember her suggesting that the removals transporting the settler goods out of the country must be sabotaged, and that was done and was very effective, remember?"

"Of course, that's the one. Comrade Shupai's most effective work is intelligence," said Munongwa proudly. "Remember, she is the one who discovered about the poisoning of the water. She's one of the best people to involve in some of the important operations," Munongwa recommended, and went on to say that she should be sent for right away. "The planning must be done while she's there."

Chapter 14

Some special task force units of two, three, four or five especially trained sappers were formed. These were from among the unit commanders and other combatants including Chakanyuka's and Tichaona's commando units to operate as urban guerrillas. They were to penetrate difficult but important enemy targets. Special women's units were assigned some jobs. Women could carry 'handbags' and other unsuspicious 'parcels' around towns, into shops, hotels and other important offices even some settler country clubs without attracting any attention.

From that time onwards, for a long time many targets were sporadically attacked. These included mostly shops, high class restaurants, exclusive whites'only clubs, hotels and other vulnerable buildings like government offices and police posts. However, after a series of these attacks, especially, the bombing of government offices around the country's towns and cities, the women's units, were withdrawn. The units could not operate effectively anymore. The minority government had begun to frisk and search every handbag or parcel of any person entering some buildings including some shops. This exercise was carried out throughout the country in the towns and cities and the in some clubs. The searching was performed by what the urban guerrillas called "vanahudhu", a country-wide home and guard system. But major operations were in the pipeline.

"Do these people think this frisking business will stop anything?" Tichaona asked. He was talking to Makuva, Chakanyuka, Makano and Keni, the driver.

"Let them wait until this assignment is through," Keni said. Keni who was always chewing at an imaginary chewing gum went on "They'll realise that small bombings and explosions they are trying to stop now are peanuts, just monkey-nuts," he emphasised.

"I can't wait for that moment," said Chakanyuka, "when the nerve centre of the white minority's economy would be on fire." He continued, "That whole oil and petrol storage complex, I can imagine, would make the biggest bonfire ever...."

"It's going to be the biggest and the greatest day in the history of guerrilla warfare," Makuva commented with his face turned up to the ceiling. The guerrillas were in a spare room of a house in New Highfield's Lusaka section. They had to whisper to each other to avoid being heard.

There was a light tap-tap on their door. They knew there was someone they were waiting for. Makano opened the door and Marwei entered all smiles. She was carrying a bag which she threw on the floor. Marwei was one of the girls who worked at the Uniform and Clothing factory with Miss Regai in the heavy industrial area in Salisbury.

"Everything is okay, I'm sure," said Tichaona greeting her. "It's all written all over face."

"You bet it is," replied Marwei and she informed, "It's all set, ready for the go," she whispered excitedly, slapping Tichaona on the shoulder. "The uniforms have been made to fit." Marwei went on, "You can try them on later. Have you eaten, yet?" They nodded. "We better set the day and the time now," she suggested, "Shupai, you know, doesn't want any mix up. Everything has to be planned thoroughly, and has to go according to the plan."

"Tell her not to worry," Chakanyuka said, reassuringly. "Everything will have to be carried out as planned. Day after tomorrow, Friday evening. Nine thirty sharp, alright?"

"Good. See you after the thing then," she looked at them for a few seconds, then, "Good luck to all of us." She shook their hands amiably and said to Keni, "Driver, I wish you all the best of luck with the wheel." When Keni is excited, he chews more frantically on his absent chewing gum, Marwei thought, as she observed Keni. He just stood up, shook her hand with both hands and sat down, throwing nervous glances at his comrades. Marwei waved goodbye, left the room and went out cautiously.

At the oil storage complex in the heavy industrial area of Salisbury, one Friday evening, Munjera, one of the night watch men had come on duty. He had done his first round, had consulted his three colleagues inside the complex and was preparing to settle on his stool for the night at the main gate post. A man approached him. "Good evening Mr Munjera," the man greeted him and added, "It's a quiet evening here, isn't it? I'm sorry, I'm late."

Munjera answered quietly. The man did not introduce himself. This was Makuva, one of the urban guerrillas on a mission. Munjera noticed that the man had a navy blue overall and a cap. The uniform was exactly the same as that of Munjera's and other watchmen. There was no question about it. Makuva went on naturally, "It hasn't been very quiet here for me this afternoon. You see these people," pointing to the administration office building some yards away from the gate, "wanted me to go on night duty next week," Makuva explained, "yet I had plans of my own and I had requested them, for next weekend. How could they do that to me?" he asked. "They finally agreed that I take up the night duty, on condition that I commence today so that I could be free for next weekend."

"What do you mean?" Munjera asked, puzzled.

"I mean I have come to relieve you, Mr Munjera, I should have been here earlier." Makuva said and went on to explain, "You are starting day duty on Monday and you have been given the weekend off as from today."

"I don't understand." He was really surprised. "I didn't know I am to start day duty?" Munjeral asked. He sounded doubtful indeed, Makuva realised and hoped Munjera won't be difficult, he wouldn't want to harm him.

"I know you didn't, Mr Munjera. You should have been informed, but you have no phone at your house. As I have just told you...." Munjera interrupted:

"Well, whatever is going on here who can refuse a whole weekend off?" Munjera asked and hesitated a bit. Looking closer at Makuva, he asked, "Are you new here?" He picked up his overcoat and stared at Makuva again, "Who are you? I have never seen you before." Munjera talked quietly as if to himself. He thought there was something not quite straight somewhere. But what can it be? He asked himself. There is nothing wrong with this man. He has the latest company uniform on. He could be unfamiliar to him but, this was a big establishment. This man could be one of the several watchmen employed here. But he kept looking doubtfully at Makuva without leaving.

"Ah! Mr Munjera," Makuva exclaimed, interrupting Munjera's thoughts, "you surprise me. You really do surprise me." Makuva came closer to Munjera and said, "Look at me again Mr Munjera. Don't you know me?" he asked and went on confidently, "Don't tell me you would be so sleepy every morning that you can't notice people, your colleagues?"

"Well. Never mind," said Munjera. "I'm off then?" He hesitated still. Glancing at the office block inside the yard, he said, "I think I better check."

"Mr Munjera, what's wrong with you?" Makuva asked quietly and added, "When are we ever going to trust each other, we Africans? You go and find out on the duty roster if you insist. Or why don't you ask Thadius? He is on duty with you, isn't he?" Thadius was one of the night watchmen who was working with the guerrillas on this project as the inside person. Munjera went to him and consulted. They came to the gate together.

"What's going on Sam?" Thadius asked Makuva.

"Ah! Munjera here doesn't want to go off duty. He says he doesn't know me so he came to check with you." Makuva replied.

"He must have forgotten who you are," Thadius said jokingly and turned to Munjera, "It's these people's fault," he said pointing to the offices. "They should have informed you this morning anyway, before you went off duty."

"Alright...." Munjera said quietly. "I'll see you on Monday morning then." He took his things and left.

After a few minutes of Munjera's departure, three more men arrived. They wore the same navy blue overalls and caps. They looked just like any other watchmen employed by that establishment. The three men, Chakanyuka, Tichaona and Makano, consulted with Makuva and Thadius and disappeared inside the complex led by Thadius. Makuva remained at the gate.

Munjera had reached the main road and was walking towards the Highfield bus stop, a car passed him and then stopped a few yards away. "Are you going to New Highfields?" a voice shouted.

Munjera, already running to where the car was, answered, "Yes!"

In the car, a Peugeot 404, sedan, were two women one of them driving, and two men occupying the back seat. Shupai was the one driving. Marwei was sitting in front beside Shupai. The men were Munongwa and Tafirenyika. The four, especially the girls knew Munjera and his movements in and out. Munongwa had opened the door, stepped out to let Munjera in. So he sat between the two men.

"Are you not working today?" Marwei asked, avoiding to mention his name.

"No, I'm just going off duty," Munjera answered, then frowned, looking at the girl who had just spoken. I don't know this girl. But she asks as if she knows I should be at work? "Do I know you my sister?" Munjera finally asked.

"No, I don't think so, Marwei replied and added, "But you are familiar. I see you every morning when I pass your gate on my way to work." Marwei went on, "I work at the Uniform and Clothing Factory. We are the ones who make your uniforms including those of the army, the police, the air force, the prisons, the United Bus Company to mention those few."

"Ho-o?" answered Munjera, seemingly interested in the girl and the conversation. "How can I know you? There are so many women who pass by our gate to go to that factory." He commented, "In fact I think there are more women than men in that factory, isn't that so?"

"The men are many, many more than women. You see and notice more women as they pass by your gate but you can't notice the other men," Marweyi talked jokingly and they all laughed happily. The car headed towards Beatrice Road, Munjera noticed. He informed the driver that he lived in the Egypt section of New Highfield:

"How much do you charge for the ride up to that section?" Munjera asked.

"Only twenty cents," answered Munongwa. As they neared the turn off for New Highfield from the Beatrice Road, the car slowed down but did not turn.

"Which road do you take to go to Highfield?" Munjera asked. "Don't worry Mr Munjera, we'll get you there," said Shupai, who had been quiet all this time. Munjera started, sat forward and asked:

"You do know my name? I didn't tell you my name, did I?"

"You didn't," answered Shupai and added, "But we know you. We are your friends. We know you are supposed to be on duty guarding one of the most vital installations in the country, the oil storage tanks establishment." She glanced back at Munjera then in front again she smiled at Marwei. "You have left your guard post. Someone has informed you that you have been given a weekend off and you believed them." Shupai stopped talking and continued driving slowly. There was deep silence. They could hear Munjera's deep breathing. His adrenaline level had forced his heart into his throat and almost choked him. He was quiet, mouth agape, throwing eyes from one to the other. Then:

"Stop, stop the car! Who are you people?"

"We are your friends, as she told you," Marwei said, "Now listen...." The sentence tailed away. Munjera was fumbling in his overcoat pocket for something.

"What are you looking for?" asked Munongwa holding Munjera's right hand firmly.

"I must pay your twenty cents. Please stop the car and drop me right here." They had gone past Waterfalls towards Hunyani River.

"Don't you know, Munjera," said Marwei warningly, "that you have put yourself into a lot of trouble?"

"What kind of trouble?" Munjeral asked anxiously.

"If anything happens, fire, for example, to the oil tanks you have to answer for that. Don't you think?" Marwei went on, "Petrol and oil are very important, you know that. Your job is very important also. You are trusted very much. But you have left it. What are you going to tell the police?"

"I....I will tell them that I...."

"You'll tell them what, Mr Munjera?" asked Shupai. "If I were you I'd just do as I'm told," she looked at her watch and pulled the car slowly to the side away from the road. It was exactly nine thirty.

"What do you want to do with me? Why have you stopped? Please let me go!" Munjera almost opened the door to dash out when Marwei said: "Wait Mr Munjera. Do you know where your work place is from here?"

"Of course I know," he answered, looking back towards the industrial sites. "What's that? My Goodness! What has happened? What have I done?" he groaned, almost collapsed. Munongwa supported him.

"Your work place is on fire, Munjera," informed Munongwa slowly. "Now you are in real trouble. The police will be looking for you in a moment. They would want to know, naturally, why you are not at work when you are supposed to be," he went on, "you have put the oil tanks on fire Mr. Munjera...."

"But....But....that man....the other watchman told me.... And Thadius...." Munjera stammered and could not continue.

"As we have told you," said Marwei, "We are friends, we can save you if you do what you are told."

"What? Who....? What are you talking about? Who are you people?" Munjera shouted all these questions showing all signs of realisation, shock, disbelief and perplexity. "But that man...." He finally let out some words, "The other guards told me I have been given an off duty?" Munjera gaped at the fire that had begun to illuminate the sky, shooting fire missiles high upwards and sideways. He looked at the girls and the men beside him and exclaimed in horror, "My God! What have I done? Who was that man? But Thadius, what's happening....?" He was talking to himself. Then he made a quick move, opened the car door, dashed out and started to run back towards the town. Munongwa ran after him and apprehended him.

"Don't be a fool Munjera," Munongwa spoke harshly, and went on threateningly. "We can take you to the police, now and hear what you are going to tell them."

"I'll tell them the truth," said Munjera struggling to be released. "You'll tell who the truth? That you left your guard post for home and let their valuable petrol and oil be destroyed by fire? Your story is not convincing, my friend. Get into the car and be sensible, come with us," Munongwa pushed him back into the car and warned, "Don't make us start to manhandle you, okay, you are a very valuable son of the motherland. Now, behave like a mature man."

"The alternative is for you to be found at your house," said Shupai, "get arrested, and after a hell of a torture, be hanged like a cat. What would you choose?" Shupai asked urgently.

"My God!" Munjera sighed trying to remember the last time he ever prayed. In fact, he could not remember. "What's going to happen to me?" he whispered.

"Nothing will happen to you if you come with us," Marwei reassured him, "We will look after you for sure, that is, if you co-operate."

"Let me go and tell my wife...." He stopped talking and started as if he had just realised something. "My wife....My children....I have a wife and four children...." He gasped the last sentence out. "Please!" he pleaded.

"Leave that to us, Mr Munjera, please," Marwei said persuasively and added, "Your family will be very okay, we assure you." Marwei touched Munjera's arm. He was shaking and shivering like a leaf. A fire engine siren sounded. It sounded as if it was very near. Munjera started and then slumped back as if he had fainted. He started mumbling inaudible words. Munongwa shook him violently.

"Now, would you like to get out and go home?" asked Shupai, "We want to leave this place. You're wasting our time."

"Kusiri Kufa ndekupi nhai amai (either way is death mother)," he whispered. Shupai started the car and Munjera was driven out of Salisbury to a hide-out in Mhondoro Reserve, west of Salisbury.

At the oil storage depot, the fire was not just a large fire like the ones the fire brigade had been battling against lately, in the different urban centres of the country. This one was an inferno, thought the residents of Salisbury. The oil was burning furiously sending missiles of flames up in the sky.

The navy-blue overall dressed guerrilla sappers who had with great precision staged the operation could see the illumination miles away on their way towards their base in Musana Reserve, North East of Salisbury. "That is a fire of fires, don't you think," remarked Makano happily slapping the others on the shoulders. Keni was at the wheel calmly.

"I can imagine the shock, the disbelief and the realisation among the Boers now," Thadius the watchman spoke, "that such a well guarded complex could be hit."

"It has been hit, thanks to you and your calculations, comrade Thadius," commended Chakanyuka patting Thadius on the shoulders. They all laughed shaking Thadius' hands. "Welcome to the bush comrade Tee." Said Chakanyuka and went on, "This will be your guerrilla name from now on, Tee."

"Thanks, comrade Chakanyuka. I was getting tired of operating in towns anyway," said Thadius. "I wish to stay out for a while."

"Well, that depends," remarked Tichaona and continued, "on the assignments. We wish to intensify our struggle in the urban areas from now on. So you'll still be needed comrade Tee." Tichaona glanced back toward Salisbury, "Uwi!" he exclaimed. "Look at that!" They had gone very far and were almost arriving at their destination in Musana.

They all turned to look. Keni, who was driving, stopped the car to see what the others were admiring. They came out of the car. The flames of the fire illuminated the sky above Salisbury. It looked as if the whole Salisbury area was on fire. The flames appeared to be majestically swimming towards the heavens. He started to sing "Lord Salisbury is burning; Salisbury is burning, draw nearer; draw nearer. Fire, fire; fire, fire; pour some water. Pour some wate."

"I'm sure most people in places such as Seke, Domboshava, Chihota,

Marondera, Goromonzi, Murewa, Mazoe, Beatrice, Mhondoro etc. can see that Salisbury is on fire," remarked Makano.

"But must be wondering what could be burning so furiously in the capital city," said Thadius.

"Ya! The enemy will be very busy tonight, including all his teeth." Keni said, happily chewing away, adding, "And he is split into bits and pieces too."

"What do you mean he is split into bits and pieces?" asked Makano, puzzled a bit.

"His fire brigade is split into bits and pieces, don't you remember the strategy?" answered Keni proudly.

"Oh ya!" Makano remembered the strategy. There was going to be all sorts of fires around Salisbury and in other small and big towns simultaneously, including some false alarms. The enemy fire fighters were to be split and be spreared around in small units, therefore making them less effective. "I hope that fire there, continues until all the oil is burnt out."

"Once the oil has caught fire," Thadius said, "it has to burn until it's finished and dried up. It will be very difficult to put the fire out. Wow, the nerve centre of the British colony has been hit! That's marvellous news indeed!"

"Well, we've done our bit," commented Chakanyuka. "Let's now get rid of these overalls, they've done their bit."

"How? Make a bon-fire?" asked Keni, jokingly chewing on.

"Perhaps we could bury them" suggested Tichaona, "Who knows? They may be of some service later."

"By the way, comrade Tee, how did you manage to get hold of these brand new overalls?" Makano asked.

"Through the task force of the Women's Brigade," replied Thadius, "Some of the women, including sister Marwei, who work at the Uniform and Clothing Factory belong to the Women's Brigade," he explained. "They are led by Miss Regayi, who is in the finishing and packing department of the factory. So...."

"So, Miss Regayi worked in conjunction with comrades Marwei and Shupai," Keni completed the sentence.

"I'm sure those two comrades including Munongwa and Tafirenyika have succeeded with Munjera," said Makuva and continued, "The man almost posed a big problem if it wasn't for comrade Tee here," Makuva touched Thadius on the thigh, "whom he trusted so much."

"Comrades Shupai, Marwei, Tafirenyika and Munongwa will handle him alright, don't worry," assured Chakanyuka

The following morning at ten o'clock, three policemen, one black and two whites, came to Munjera's house in Egypt's New Highfield Township. Mrs

Munjera had been wondering why her husband had not yet showed up from work. She had not listened to the early morning news and had no idea about what had happened at her husband's work place. At the sight of the police, Mrs Munjera showed grave signs of apprehension but did not say anything. She only wondered to herself....

'My husband, where is my husband?' she asked herself watching the three policemen, especially the whites.

"Is this Munjera's house?" shouted the black policeman. "Where is he? Talk woman! Where is Munjera?" the policeman asked intimidating her already trying to enter the house.

"Where is my husband?" she asked in reply and added, "My husband is supposed to have been here by now. He works night duty. Since he left for work yesterday evening, he has not yet come back," she explained, "He has never come home later than eight o'clock. Has something happened to him?" She enquired frantically, "Tell me please. Is my husband alright? Where is he then?"

One white policeman had entered the house and searched, came out, "Come, Kaffir woman! Into the car!" commanded the other white policeman, pushing Mrs Munjera into the truck.

"So my husband is not alright!" she shouted, "Something has happened to my husband! What happened? Please, tell me!"

"Shut up!" shouted the black policeman. "You are making too much noise!"

"Now....Where are you taking me?" she asked, "My children....!" Mrs Munjera was taken to the central police station. For three days she was interrogated about the whereabouts of her husband. In colonial Zimbabwe (Rhodesia), interrogation was fully accompanied by beating and torture of the highest order....Mrs Munjera, sulking, told her friends about this after she was released. She found her children being well looked after by a child minder, a middle aged woman who did not say much. The children who were going to school had new uniforms bought for them, and there was so much food in the kitchen to show that her children were in good hands of the Women's Brigade of the underground movement. They also told her about the welfare and safety of her husband.

Meanwhile in the industrial area, each time an oil tank exploded, it sent fragments of fire missiles flying to all directions. These missiles were lighting the adjacent buildings, most of them settler factories.

"This bloody fire brigade of ours is becoming fuckin' inefficient," angrily remarked one of the settler factory owners, who had a big part of his factory lighted by fire from the burning oil tanks. He went on talking to the manager of his half burnt factory, "I hear that the bloody fire started, and they took so long to arrive at the fuckin' scene! Now, look at that. They could have prevented all that," he spoke pointing to the dark smoke and the flames which seemed to be connecting heaven and earth. "The bloody fools!" He went on, "Where were the security guards at the oil tanks complex in the first place? These bloody kaffir boys are never to be trusted anymore."

"The fire brigade was overworked last night, you know," said the white manager of the factory, "I hear there were several bad fires last night. In Borrowdale, in Waterfalls, in Greendale, in Cranborne, almost everywhere," he went on, "Some petrol stations were also burning. And to top it all, the police kept on receiving hoax calls about fires or accidents here and there. This served to divert them away from the real danger."

"The bloody fuckin' bastards!" scolded the factory owner and added "They must all be killed now, every black person. We must kill all of them. We can do without them." He was pointing at his African workers who were busy removing some charred bits from the burnt part of his factory.

"True, the government has got to do something about this," agreed the factory manager. "But what can it do?" he asked and went on, "The activities of these terrorists have become so widespread and so sophisticated that, I think our army is finding difficulties to contain them."

"What? I think the army can do better than what it's doing now. Just eliminate all the bloody fuckin' kaffirs, that's all there is to it," suggested the factory owner. "In Australia it was done, you know."

"I know it's easy for us to talk like this. Australia almost did it, but there are terrorists for us everywhere in this country and across the borders, you know."

"The air force should cross the borders and bomb those Kaffir countries which are aiding the fuckin' terrorists."

"They are preparing to do so, I hear," the factory manager informed, whispering. "But on watching the unquenchable fire going on, one would think that's the end of the British Empire."

"What? You talk like a coward. You are helpless. Be careful the way you talk," the factory owner warned, and left the manager gaping after him....

In a newsletter to the underground movement's external offices, for instance in Zambia, Mozambique and in Dar-es-Salaam, Tanzania, the internal wings' publicity office reported:

"Congratulations to our urban guerrillas who, with great precision are carrying out difficult operations. The successes are tremendous!" the letter report went on, "If the settler government does not go down on its knees this time and beg the owners of this land for mercy, he is just out of his mind. This time he was hit right in his middle. The fire at the oil storage depot in Salisbury kept the army, the police and the fire brigade busy for more than two and a half weeks. It was difficult to extinguish that fire even from the air. In fact, that fire was never put out. It stopped on its own after it had completely burnt out all the oil. The settler back bone was being violently destroyed. He could not help it. He just stood there watching and cursing. The masses of Zimbabwe are rejoicing," the report continued. "Though in other urban centres, Bulawayo, Gwelo, Umtali, Fort Victoria, to mention a few, similar engagements were also taking place, the biggest event was in Salisbury! The British colony is undeniably coming apart at the seams. It is as if the settler colony has begun to suffer from a sort of senile hypertrophy.

"We are also pleased to inform you that as the liberation war continues successfully," the news letter continued, "There are now certain areas where the settler forces, not even their planes could venture unless they are flying very high. These are the now liberated areas of the country. Many enemy aircrafts including their helicopter gun ships which used to harass the fighters are now meeting with hot opposition from our anti aircraft fire and ground-to-air missiles. Thanks to the O.A.U. and the friendly progressive countries of the world. The peasants can now see that the boys have become really hot on the settlers. They can now see that the settlers are going to be defeated.

The peasants, even those who have been placed in the so-called protected villages are doing their best to help the boys. More news in the next mail," the letter ended.

Elsewhere in the country, the war was raging fiercely between the settler security forces and the liberation army. In the Wedza District, just behind Wedza Mountain itself, two old men reported what they described as the horror of their life. These two old men, Mhunga and Gwara came from Gandamasungo village near Sabi River. It was very early one morning when old man Gwara came to wake up Mhunga and told him, "I did not sleep well last night. Can you hear that noise from down there?" Gwara asked, pointing towards Sabi River, and urged, "Listen." Mhunga wiped his eyes and listened. There were cries and mourns as if of pain and torture. Shouts of angry voices were heard coming from that direction.

"I wonder what is happening," whispered old man Mhunga.

"This has been going on since the first crowing of the cock this morning," Gwara said and he added, "I could not go back to sleep then."

"Let's go and find out what's going on," suggested Mhunga, who was younger and stronger than old man Gwara. They agreed to inch their way towards where the noise was coming from. As they neared the place, they crouched behind a thick bush. They saw four men standing in a line with their hands at the back.

"The boys have been caught," Mhunga whispered.

"We can't see properly," said Gwara and urged, "Let's move a bit closer so we can see well," They crawled to another bush nearer. They could count something like twelve soldiers, seven Africans and five whites. The old men could see quite clearly, that the four men standing in the line had their hands tied at their backs. As they looked more closely, to their horror, they saw two bodies stretched full length on the wet ground.

Two soldiers were shouting at the same time. One soldier was waving a long sword-like knife that looked like a machete. "Talk!" the soldier with the knife shouted. "Say you surrender now!" The men standing in the line with hands tied at the back kept quiet. The soldier pointed at one of them with the knife. "You, say you surrender now!" He waited. "Say you surrender now!" He shouted again lifting up his knife slightly, intimidating.

"Go home!" shouted the four men together. The soldier lifted his hands higher quickly and slashed the head of the nearest man off as if cutting a young sapling of a tree off the main branch. The head was severed and it went bouncing on the ground. The body fell and joined the other two on the wet ground.

"O-o-o....!" the two old men exclaimed in unison. This happened so quickly that they could not imagine. On closer visual examination the old men could see that the other two bodies lying on the ground had their heads also decapitated. They could see the heads scattered around like round black stones.

The soldier, waving his bloody machete, moved nearer one of the three remaining men. "You, do you still resist?" The man did not reply. The soldier went on shouting, "If you don't want to join your friend over there," pointing to a tree, a few yards away, "you better surrender now." The two old men glanced towards where the soldier was pointing at....

"A-maiwe-e-e! (Mother)" the old men remarked together, twisting their faces with horror and disbelief. Dangling from a tree branch was another man. His tongue was hanging out of his mouth and his eyes protruding out of their sockets as if someone had actually squeezed them out. "Amai nababa murikudenga, batsirai vana (mother and father in heaven, help the children)," old man Gwara prayed. Old man Mhunga who had appeared stronger had fallen down and had started to vomit, lamenting inaudible words to himself. Suddenly they heard a burst of machine gun fire. They saw some of the soldiers fall; some threw themselves to the ground and returned the fire. Silence followed. The three men in the line with their tied hands had also thrown themselves onto the ground.

After some time, only four of the soldiers stood up, staggered, and then started to run firing aimlessly. Another burst of machine gun fire and they dropped. Another short period of silence, then two men appeared at the scene moving cautiously. They started to untie the hands and feet of the other three men alive who had kept on lying down helplessly.

"Let's go and help the children," suggested Gwara to Mhunga who had then stopped vomiting but had kept on praying.

"Ah! Iwe! (You!)" exclaimed Mhunga. "Be very careful," he warned and added "What are you going to say to them? They may suspect us to be working with the soldiers, you know. You never know with these boys. Have you forgotten what they did to Chimombe's father at Badza?"

"Aiwa (No), don't you know that Chimombe's father was a real informer. He had gone to report about the presence of the boys at Badza School. Then he was foolish enough to come back pretending as if he was for the boys. I didn't blame them. But we are not informers. The ancestors know it. They'll lead and protect us. You'll see."

They stood up and started to descend slowly towards the scene. One of the other two new men had climbed the tree where their comrade had been hanged. He had finished untying him when he saw the two old men coming. He held up his rifle, trained it towards the old me, "Hold up there!" he shouted. The other men down there threw themselves onto the ground for cover, and readied their weapons.

"Please don't shoot us," shouted old man Gwara, his voice coming out in a shrill because he was very frightened. He went on to explain, "We are your grandfathers. We heard the noise. We have witnessed everything. Now we have come to help." He went on, "We know we are helpless. We did not know what to do. We just watched in horror. Please, believe us," he pleaded.

"Alright, come, with your hands on your heads and don't try any monkey tricks!" the man on the tree commanded. "Shasha!" he called to his friend who was busy bandaging one of the three men who had had his shoulder slashed by the soldiers. "Let them help us. I'll watch them from here."

The two old men arrived with their hands up. They were searched by Shasha and then they started to work. Old man Mhunga bent down to touch one of the white soldiers who, was lying in a pool of blood. The soldier opened his eyes all of a sudden, and looked straight into Mhunga's face. Mhunga jumped. The soldier did not move. He only closed his eyes again and whispered:

"Please, help me!"

"This one is alive!" old man Mhunga exclaimed. One of the men who, was called Shasha, came and lifted the white soldier from the pool of blood and examined him. He gave him a gulp of water. The soldier opened his eyes again, looked at Shasha. When he saw the AK47 rifle, he crinjed and tensed, could not get up, slumped back and closed his eyes.

"Please, don't kill me. I....I'm so....I surrender," he stammered.

"The pig!" Shasha cursed and added, "As if he is in a position to do anything now." Shasha turned to Mhunga and said, "He's been shot through the right shoulder and he has lost a lot of blood. We'll take him with us and if he tries to be funny...." The white soldier was the lucky one, thought old man Mhunga, who noticed he had been missed by several bullets which just scratched him leaving him with several lacerations but horribly looking. He must be in terrible pain, Mhunga realised.

"I won't. I promise, honestly," the soldier uttered these words in whispers.

Shasha tied the soldier's hands and legs and called out, "Karl! Come down, let's go. Vanasekuru (grandfathers)" Shasha addressed the two old men, Mhunga and Gwara, "Can you please, bury our comrades here," he pointed to the decapitated bodies plus the one who had been hanged. Shasha, helped by the other combatants, had collected the scattered severed heads and placed each on to the neck of the owner. "You can also bury those settler soldiers if you want. We are taking this one with us." Shasha, Karl and the other three blindfolded the white soldier and left. They had to carry him because he was so weak that he could not walk.

At the base, the soldier with his legs kept tied together and blind folded, was treated and nursed until he was strong enough to eat by himself. Each time the blindfold was removed he pleaded not to be killed, "You are such good people. What are you going to do with me? Please, you are not planning to kill me, are you?" But they could have killed him already instead of nursing him to life, he reminded himself. What is their reason for treating him so kindky? He asked himself, but shuddered at the thought of hanging or his head decapitated after all.

"You said that you are a Zimbabwean," Shasha said, "Karl here, suggests that you join the liberation struggle or else...." Karl was the commander of that unit, which was operating in the area behind Wedza/Gandamasungo Mountain near Sabi River. He was a young man of few words. Shasha, the medic and his second in command was the talker. Karl had sulked so much over the loss of four of his men in what he termed a 'clean capture by mercenary soldiers.' He and Shasha had gone to look for some supplies of food. Well, he thought, he had at least saved some, but....

"I'll do what ever you say, whatever you want me to do," the soldier spoke urgently. "What do you want me to do?"

"We want you," answered Karl, "to write a letter to the British and the American newspapers."

"Give me paper and pen," the soldier said anxiously, "What do you want me to say?" he asked, breathing so fast that his words came out in gasps with excitement.

"Here," Shasha gave him sheets of plain paper and a pen, "Write what you think, what you think the international world must know about...." The soldier had already started to write:

"I am Colonel James Peterson of the Rhodesian army writing from Wedza at one of the guerrilla bases. I have been captured in combat. I'm writing voluntarily. This intensification of the war has completely drained our resources. We are incurring heavier and heavier casualties by the day. This has demoralised many young soldiers like myself. I'm the only survivor out of a company of twelve soldiers.

Tens of African soldiers are deserting to join the guerrilla forces. I'm joining them too. More and more young whites are emmigrating to other countries in large numbers. I'm sure countries like Canada, Australia, New Zealand, Sweden, Britain, USA, South Africa and even Latin America don't know what to do with more and more of these Rhodesian soldier deserters. Our morale is definitely sagging, mine has already. I thank God for being alive. We now have no way out but to begin to talk seriously about a genuine settlement with the guerrillas. The so-called internal settlement which brought about the Zimbabwe-Rhodesia is an abortion. The black Prime Minister has no power at all. The Zimbabwean freedom fighters are winning the war. I had thought," he went on writing, "that the effects of the oil disaster in Salisbury would send us reeling to the conference table. This time, I think, the pinch of the armed struggle by the Zimbabwean guerrillas has gone deeper down our flesh, up to the bone-marrow. There are so many distressing reports from the war front. Whole companies of soldiers are perishing in combat against a highly illusive enemy." He ended the letter by saying "I do hope this message reaches the powers that be in Britain and the United States and in other countries. Something must be done as soon as possible!"

Then he handed the letter to Karl, the commander, saying, "I don't know whether that'll do." Karl read the letter and smiled cynically and looked at the white soldier. 'Are you genuine?' He asked in his thoughts, and commented, "Yes, this'll do. It'll do very well," said Karl and added, "Sign it."

"What else do you want me to do?" James Peterson asked, after signing the letter quickly, anxiously.

"Stay here," Karl answered bluntly while tying the man's legs and his hands. "Remember, you are a prisoner."

Chapter 15

The settler air-force decided to cross the borders and bombed some Zimbabwean refugee camps in Mozambique and Zambia. But this only served to intensify the war inside the country, foreign newspapers reported. Some reports even went on to suggest that the British government should intervene militarily. Yet some of the reports alleged that the British government's warships had already docked at the Beira harbour in Mozambique and were getting ready to attack Rhodesia. The Rhodesian leader ordered a thorough investigation. None of the reports were confirmed. He became so unsettled that he angrily picked up the receiver of his private phone, and dialled. A pause, then: "What is this that is being reported by your papers?" shouted the minority leader through a long-distance call to the foreign office in London.

"Um, we're pleased you've phoned, Mr. Prime Minister," answered a voice in the British foreign office. "When you come to think of it, no-one here likes the war business exercise you are clinging on to." The voice went on, "These so-called terrorists seem to be winning the war against you, what do you say?"

"What?" the Rhodesian leader asked. He was very surprised. "This is ridiculous!" he exclaimed, angrily, "I did not expect such from a conservative government officer." There was silence. Each party did not seem to have anything more to say. Then: "It's a pity that you can decide to dump us like this," the minority leader said. He had let out his steam, and was now speaking a bit calmly. "Now that we are all alone in this world, without anyone on our side, I am telephoning to say we can attend another conference to settle this problem once and for all." The minority leader added, "I'm afraid civilisation in Africa is coming to its end."

"This is the most sensible news item I've just heard from you since UDI, Mr. Prime Minister." The Prime Minister snarled in the receiver, but did not say anything. The British Officer went on, "We'll be glad and are ready to host a constitutional conference between you and the so-called terrorists."

"They are terrorists of course! What do you think?" the Rhodesian Prime Minister snapped and went on agitatedly. "You must instruct them to cease-fire first before we come to the conference table, these barbarians."

"You know they won't agree to that. Have you forgotten the Geneva experience?" the foreign office man in London reminded.

"But, they'll come to the conference table anyway, if you summon them." the minority leader stated.

"Of course, they will," replied the British man and added, "But this time,

Mr Prime Minister, you'll have to agree to their terms."

"Their terms? Ma-a-y foot!" he shouted into the receiver, "That'll be sacrificing Christianity and western civilisation to the dogs!"

"That's your own opinion, down there. We in...."

"Alright, then," the minority leader cut the British man short and added, "We'll see when we meet at the conference table," and he banged the receiver down cursing, "The bloody fools, real idiots, the British! They want to sell us down the drain. We are not going to allow this to happen to us. We represent the civilised world here, don't we?"

This man was Prime Minister of Southern Rhodesia since 1964. He was an ardent advocate of white rule, who had argued that the west no longer had the will to stand up to Communism that he said was represented by black rule in Africa. His party was named the Rhodesian Front (RF). He said that Rhodesia was the front-line and the whites were not engaged merely in a battle for their existence but a battle to preserve civilisation and civilised values and white supremacy. He had managed to convince white Rhodesians that they could continue to defy world opinion: "I don't believe in black majority rule over Rhodesia, not in a thousand years," he had proclaimed. And thousands of whites mainly from Britain and South Africa had come into the country during this time to enjoy the advantages of white supremacy.

He had divided the land into two, with the 278,000 whites getting the most fertile half, and the 6.1 million blacks the other half. The indigenous people who had lived on fertile land for generations, such as the Tangwena people, to mention only but a few, for example, were unceremoniously evicted in 1969 to make way for whites and their families, who were flocking into the country at the invitation of the minority regime.

This man was the first native-born Rhodesian to lead the country. Some thought he was a simple man, blunt, unemotional and lacking a sense of humour. They thought he was socially awkward and he disliked publicity. His taste in clothes, was drab but his craggy, rough-hewn image, other people, noticed, concealed an astute tactical mind and a talent for political infighting. Some of his political opponents, however, once remarked that "dealing with this man is like trying to nail jelly on a wall," and added, "Make no mistake; this is a ruddy, ruthless man."

It is said, he was one of the many Rhodesian whites who interrupted their studies to join the British Royal Air Force (RAF) Squadron in 1939, and was deployed during the North Africa campaign. His Hurricane crashed on take off, smashing his head against the instrument panel. It is said that, his face had to be surgically reconstructed, and the operation left him with a somewhat menacing stare. He was still very eager to carry on fighting for Great Britain. His spitfire was shot down over the Ligurian Alps, and he had to spend a few months fighting with the Italian partisans. He eventually managed to escape over the Alps into France, where the allied forces had landed. He is said to have finished the war in Germany.

His war experiences left an indelible impression on him, and the fact that Rhodesia had done more than any other colony to help the mother country, Britain, would become central to his sense of betrayal by post-war British governments, who did not seem to recognise these efforts. This is his story: The former spitfire pilot who was shot down over Italy in 1944 and spent some three to five months fighting with the Partisans was Prime Minister of Southern Rhodesia. 'Surely with all his war efforts, Britain has to support his policies,' he was quite encouraged. His white extremists supported him fully. He caused one of the greatest political crises of the post-war era by unilaterally declaring independence (UDI) from Britain in 1965.

Southern Rhodesia had been part of the Federation of Rhodesia and Nyasaland which was formed in 1953 under a white Prime Minister. In 1961 the federalists had supported a new constitution that would allow limited representation for black Africans in parliament. The spitfire fighter man as chief whip opposed this move vigorously and was instrumental in founding the Rhodesian Front Party (RF) that would be committed to negotiating independence from Britain with a government based upon the white minority.

Due to the successful struggle for independence by the two partner states, Northern Rhodesia and Nyasaland, the Federation was dissolved and Southern Rhodesia reverted to its former status as colony of Great Britain with the name Rhodesia. The Africans in Southern Rhodesia had not been quiet. The agitation by the African Nationalists was also becoming hot. So, as Prime Minister and leader of the Rhodesian Front, he moved very quickly to show he meant business. His first official act was to authorise the arrest and banishment of four Black Nationalist leaders and others. Serious unrest and disorder in the country followed but it was suppressed vigorously by the police under sweeping emergency laws. He kept white moderates' opinion carefully emphasising that he wanted a proper settlement with the British government.

To his supporters on the Right, however, he asserted he would never compromise on the fundamental issue of white supremacy and civilisation. He even made a trip to London for talks with the conservative Prime Minister of Britain. During the talks, it is said, the British Prime Minister outlined the British terms or principles for the independence of that colony. These included immediate improvement in the political status of the black population, unimpeded progress to majority rule and progress towards ending discrimination.

The man responded by demanding independence under the 1961 constitution which he had opposed at the time of the Federalists. He told himself, 'If I can prove to the British government I have the support of the majority, they will grant me independence on this constitution and on this franchise.' So he summoned some 600 chiefs and vllage headmen to give their views. These so-called chiefs and headmen had no say at all in the politics of the country. They had no idea at all of what was going on. They only boasted later, after the meeting about the recognition accorded to them by the white government and of eating on the same table with the whites on that day. Their authority over the people, they boasted, had been strengthened. They dutifully voted in favour of the independence based on this constitution which allowed limited representation for black Africans in Parliament. Of course, some of the chiefs would be part of those black representatives.

This view was endorsed by the country's whites in a referendum where the black people were not involved. But the British government refused to accept the results as valid. The spitfire fighter man was severely accused by the British of reneging on their undertakings. Most whites in Rhodesia believed him and blamed Britain, the mother country, for a shameful act of treachery and great betrayal of its own.

There came a new Prime Minister in Britain under the Labour Party. This Prime Minister underestimated the gathering momentum towards UDI. He was against the use of any force should Rhodesia decide to go it alone. There were several fruitless talks between the two Prime Ministers but in November 1965 UDI was declared and a state of emergency gave the white minority government sweeping powers including censorship.

Expecting a quick victory, the British government imposed some economic sanctions on Rhodesia, which were failing dismally even though they were also supported and applied by the U.N. Security Council. These slow measures were almost counter productive because, not only did they enable Rhodesians to solve their own difficulties at an easier pace, they also served to unite white Rhodesians around their Prime Minister. The only problem was with recognition of the Rhodesian minority regime.

Not one foreign government was prepared to recognise this government except South Africa. Therefore, access to the world's money markets became more and more difficult. The regime could not get the capital funds to sustain development. On the British side, the failure of these sanctions obliged the Prime Minister of Britain to return to negotiations.

In 1966 the two Prime Ministers met on board the British Cruiser Tiger, off Gibraltar. They worked out a set of constitutional principles in line with the original terms for a settlement. The Rhodesian Prime minister made several concessions. In exchange, the British Prime Minister agreed and that majority rule should be postponed beyond the end of the century. But the talks broke down over the issue of how Rhodesia could return to legality. The British prime Minister demanded that interim powers be handed over to the loyalist Governor of Rhodesia (Sir Humphrey Gibbs). This proved unacceptable to the Rhodesian Prime Minister and the Tiger proposals were rejected.

The British Prime Minister tried again, and met the Rhodesian Prime Minister, this time, aboard the assault ship Fearless. Again the negotiations ended in failure. The Rhodesian Prime Minister and his team came back to their people and told them; "It was clear to us throughout the talks that the British were obsessed with the question of African majority rule." The Prime Minister asserted again, "I am telling you, there will be no African majority rule in my life time, or my children's time, never!"

So now, he felt the way was open to install a new constitution that would "entrench the government in the hands of civilised Rhodesians for all time". The draft constitution enshrined the concept of "parity" under which the black population would achieve equal representation with the whites in the distant future. Blacks were allocated 16 seats, to the whites' 50 seats. That was a proportion which would remain fixed until the black population paid at least 24 percent incometax. In 1969, this constitution was endorsed in a referendum by 78 percent of the (white) electorate; no blacks involved, and in March 1970, Rhodesia became a Republic under the Rhodesian Front.

The same year, the British Foreign Secretary (Sir Alec Douglas Home) returned to the quest for a settlement. He was more sympathetic to the white Rhodesians and was prepared to go much further in appeasing white opinion than in the past. He proposed a formula that endorsed the principle of one-man-one-vote, but on a majority of Rhodesians with certain property and educational qualifications. While this did not exclude the possibility of African rule, it postponed it for long enough for the idea to be acceptable to the Rhodesian Prime Minister.

In 1977, they, the British Foreign Secretary and the Prime Minister of Rhodesia announced their agreement on the above proposed settlement. What remained was to test its acceptability.

The African Nationalist leaders decided to fight that agreement vigorously. Then in early 1978, seven teams of Commissioners under Lord Pearce were sent by the British government to find the "true voice of Rhodesia". The response came as a rude shock to them. Despite the emergency powers, riots broke out in most of the big cities – Bulawayo, Gwelo, Fort Victoria, Salisbury, Umtali and every where the commissioners went, they were greeted by rowdy and angry crowds of Africans with a big 'NO'. On his return to Britain, Lord Pearce's verdict was unequivocal: "In our opinion the people of Rhodesia as a whole do not regard the proposals as the basis for independence."

By mid 1978, the security situation in Rhodesia had become increasingly desperate as the guerrilla war had spread deep into the country and into the urban centres. The American secretary of state, Henry Kissinger presented the Rhodesian Prime Minister with a draft settlement providing for "black majority rule within two years". The Rhodesian minority leader decided to play with time by agreeing to the deal, although he insisted that the work "black" should be deleted from the "majority rule", thus leaving the meaning ambiguous, and ensuring that whites should be able to retain control of the crucial portfolios of defence, law and order and finance. Mr. Kissinger, meanwhile, found that the deal was totally unacceptable to the Black Nationalist leaders and the Front-line African presidents, but he decided to suppress this information.

So, the Rhodesian Prime Minister duly went on Rhodesia television to announce the agreement. The white population in Rhodesia reacted with stunned disbelief. Although many assumed it must be yet another of his ruses, the fact that he had been prepared to contemplate "majority rule" within two years had an enormous psychological impact. In that year, Rhodesia saw a net loss of more than 7,000 whites, the largest exodus in more than 13 years.

Agreement with the nationalists, however, could not be reached. By now the Rhodesian minority leader believed that his only hope to holding on to power lay in coming to an internal settlement with some of the more moderate black leaders including chiefs and the head men. So, he announced that he was prepared to accept the principle of one-man-one-vote as a basis for discussions and he invited three black leaders (one of them a president of the council of Chiefs) to meet him for talks. A series of meetings culminated, in an agreement which provided for a legislature of 100 members, of which 28 would be white and 72 black.

Crucially though, the whites could veto any legislation affecting their privileges and would retain control of the administration, the security forces, the economy and for the interim period, parliament. So, in a referendum among the whites held in January 1979, 85 percent were in favour of this new constitution; and in the general election in April, one of the more moderate black leaders emerged with 51 of the 72 black seats in the new Parliament.

The Rhodesian Front took all the 28 white seats. But this did not include any black nationalist leaders.

Although the white leader resigned as Prime Minister, staying as Minister without portfolio under this black moderate leader, there was little doubt where power really lay. It so happened that four days after this black leader took office, Rhodesian forces raided Mozambique to the East of Rhodesia. It is said the raid began at three in the morning and this black prime Minister was not informed about it until three or four hours later. This, however, did not help to bring an end to the guerrilla campaign which caused the Rhodesian armed forcers to be seriously short of manpower. Then there was a new Conservative prime Minister in Britain, Mrs Margaret Thatcher. It is said that her natural inclination was to recognise this new Rhodesian government and lift sanctions. The black African states warned her of a serious trade boycott. The Rhodesian minority leader was forced to accept Mrs Thatcher's invitation to a peace conference at Lancaster house in London.

This man, the spitfire fighter for Britain, was nursing a deep sense of "betrayal" by Britain, which he felt should have supported him totally. He put Rhodesia's collapse on almost everybody except himself. He even ruminated: "During UDI we had the greatest national spirit in the world, a fantastic country, great race relations and the happiest black faces in the world...If our friends hadn't betrayed us, we would have won. After all, white rule was better for all races in Rhodesia." He loved Rhodesia passionately. He was a crude racist and that his resistance to African advancement caused an unnecessary war. But he denied he was racist because he thought he had good relations with many black people who would have consented to continuing white leadership as representing the best deal available for all Rhodesians, black and white.

It is said, when his delegation met Mr Harold Wilson in their long and fruitless talks, observers were struck by the fact that the white Rhodesians were all older men who had fought for Britain in the war. They were tough guys who thought their opposite numbers naïve. Mr. Wilson himself was taken aback and railed at the Rhodesian leader as a "tin pot dictator". The Rhodesian had turned his back on him in a long silence before replying:

"Look here, Harold, if you and I are to get on, you can't talk to me like that." It was Wilson who had to retreat. The key to understanding this minority leader, one observer noted, was that, like other white Rhodesians, he clung to an almost Victorian view of the world both in moral values and in the easy assumptions of British primacy that characterised the empire. Such emotions made it automatic that he would rally to the defence of the mother country,

Britain in 1939, his wartime service, undoubtedly, the central experience of his life. He remained passionately committed to the fellowship he found among the RAF friends, especially when he visited Britain. He remembered he had faced death many times for the mother country, Britain. His wounds had cost him great pain in his face, knees and back ever afterwards. This left him, he thought, a supremely self-confident man, unafraid of pretty much anything. He told his supporters, he had been bitterly disappointed by Britain he had encountered in the permissive 1960's. It was obvious he was in love with a Britain long past; he had been so all his life, a Britain of the King-Emperor, Kitchener and Kipling. He was in love with a Britain that remained far more alive in the minds of those whites in the colonies than it did back home in Britain.

The tragedy was not just that this brought him into bruising conflict with modern Britain, but that he had given his heart to a country that no longer existed, that he could only dream about as still going on by paying undue attention. A natural leader, some of his opponents observed, he had sought to preserve some of what he thought was best in that anachronism in an unlikely but beautiful country in central Africa. But now will end up like all those who followed him, lost souls who remain forever devoted to another country that now no longer existed.

To him, Harold Macmillan's 1960 "Winds of Change" speech meant the propagation of white minority rule in Southern Rhodesia. These "winds of change", he thought decisively, cannot affect the Rhodesians, not the white Rhodesians who supported and fought on the side of Britain during the war. The spitfire fighter had decided to fight to preserve the Rhodesia of empire as epitomised by a royal visit to Southern Rhodesia shortly after the Second World War. This man was in the motorcycle escort for the Queen's entourage during the royal visit in 1947. Youthful, he remembered of hurricanes, spitfires, Lancasters…No; he had vowed with all his might, he would not live to see this beautiful country slide under a communist, ignorant, uncultured and uncivilised black leader. No, he vowed, the black devils must never be allowed an inch of rule, not in this country; this is a white enclave, a haven we created for us and for our posterity, for the British Empire. These new British governments do not know how we suffered to preserve this British colony. This white man never dreamt of ever coming up out from that past dream indeed….

It took the British government hard work and a lot of diplomatic shuttle to try and persuade the Zimbabwe Nationalist guerrilla leaders to come to the conference table for a negotiated settlement with the white minority government.

"Have you forgotten about Geneva?" asked one of the guerrilla leaders when the British High Commissioner to Tanzania met the guerrilla leaders in Dar-es-Salaam. "We are not prepared to be ridiculed again. We know our enemy. You don't," the guerrilla leader declared standing up to leave the room. "After all they are your kith and kin. What do we have?"

"No, no, no, please, sit down. This time...."

"Don't waste your time," the British officer was quickly interrupted. "The barrel of the gun will bring our enemy on his knees. It's already doing so if you didn't know."

"That's why a genuine settlement is now necessary. Lord Soames himself will personally be in charge of the conference proceedings."

"What difference does that make?" asked the Zimbabwean guerrilla leader. "He is for whom anyway? And you?"

"The British government is for a genuine political settlement in your country, that's all." Dead silence followed, as if they could hear each other's heart beats. Then the guerrilla leader sat back onto the chair again and said:

"Listen, we will come to the conference table. But we shall not be dictated to," He cautioned, "We have our own terms and no negotiations, understand?" And he, followed by his colleagues, stood up and marched out of the room.

The Lancaster House Constitutional Conference on Rhodesia was quickly organised by the colonial power, Britain. After a few days of wrangling and bickering, the Zimbabwean guerrilla leaders came out of the Lancaster House victorious. A cease-fire would be organised under Lord Soames and a Commonwealth military force. Soames would be the last British governor in Rhodesia to oversee the General elections, which would be conducted under one person, one vote regardless of colour.

So, some of the guerrilla leaders and the high command representatives organised a meeting with the guerrilla commanders scattered throughout the country's guerrilla bases. The Lancaster House terms for the cease-fire had to be explained carefully to these fighters for them to understand and accept. After the meeting, the commanders returned to their bases with good news!

Munongwa's unit was assembled at the Three Stones. He arrived there very early in the morning. His unit had been waiting anxiously to hear what the next step would be. Munongwa was all smiles as he greeted them and said: "Comrades," he called. "Victory for the Zimbabwean masses!" he shouted, lifting his right fist high, and announced, "We have received word from the high command. We should cease fire." Munongwa continued, "This is, as we all know, the result of our gallant fighting and our determination at the war front that led to the Lancaster House negotiations. And one-man-one-vote demand has succeeded, comrades."

"Ye-ye-ye!" the guerrillas shouted lifting their rifles up in the air and at once, one of them started to sing:
"Taigara mumakomo"
(We lived in mountains)
"Kutetereka nemasango senherera"
(Wandering in the forests as if we were orphans)"
"Taitambudzika"
(We had a lot of problems)
"Tichigara nenzara mumasango senherera"
(Staying hungry in the forests as if we were orphans)
"Taitizira mumapako"
(We had to rush into caves)
"Tichitiza muvengi akatora nyika yavabereki"
(Running away from an enemy who took our parents' land)

They sang and danced this song until they all started to sweat. After this song, Shupai started a more sober one:
Ngatitendei mhepo dze Zimbabwe
Nyika yedu ino yamadzibaba,
Zimbabwe-e Zimbabwe
Nyika yomute-e-ma.
Zimbabwe inyika ye-edu, nyika ye-e-du.
(Let us thank the winds of Zimbabwe
This country of our fathers
Zimbabwe the land of the black person
Zimbabwe is our, our country)
Madzimai ridzai mipururu
Kutambura kwose nhasi tapedza
Hatinga manikidzwe
Munyika yedu ino
Zimbabwe inyika ye-e-du, nyika ye-e-du.
(Women should ululate
All the problems have been finished
We cannot be oppressed
In this our country
Zimbabwe is our country, our country).

Munongwa continued addressing the combatants after the revolutionary songs: "Soon, we shall be required to move to established assembly points," he announced, "from where we shall triumphantly move to Salisbury." He went on, "On the 18th of April, after the elections a new country by the real name,

Zimbabwe will be born. Comrades, every one above 18 years of age will vote."

Shupai imagined the jubilation that was there throughout the four corners of Zimbabwe. She sat there quietly, attentively. She, as any other combatant realized that victory had finally come, with the cherished liberation of the motherland. Zimbabwe is now definitely free, she sighed, but, will this liberation of Zimbabwe come with the liberation of the women of this beautiful land? She asked herself. No, she concluded. The struggle to liberate Zimbabwe, even if the women participated fully in many ways, did not mean their automatic emancipation from the men's chauvinism and general backwardness. The Zimbabwean men, at least most of them, she knew, were still too backward in their relationship to women of this land. Shupai thought, with a tinge of sadness in her eyes. She remembered how she had to struggle, during the liberation struggle, to be accepted as a human being let alone as a freedom fighter and not just as a woman. Did I succeed? She asked herself. No. She realized she still met a lot of opposition from some of her male counterparts.

The struggle continues then, she declared to herself. The women have to continue the struggle for their own liberation and emancipation. She vowed silently to appeal to all the women of Zimbabwe to carry on with the struggle for their own emancipation. She went on debating silently.

She and many other women had fought side by side with the men. They had served, suffered and sacrificed for Zimbabwe like any other Zimbabwean man. She though it was gratifying to know that the struggle for a free Zimbabwe had ended positively. But the Zimbabwean males, most of them, she thought regrettably, are selfish, chauvinistic and jealous of their women folk. Most of them are real put downers, who look down on their women folk as always ignorant beings. They would rather have their women back to the kitchen after this bitter struggle together, Shupai thought with a bit of bitterness against the men. The Zimbabwean men do not want to see a woman succeeding over them, she thought, she....

When she looked at Munongwa, she realized she had been lost in her own thoughts while he was still addressing the combatants. Somehow, he was looking at her as if he had noticed that she was absent minded. She smiled at him generously. He continued with his speech. Well, Shupai said to herself, what remained for her now was to join the masses of Zimbabwe to experience life in a free Zimbabwe. She sat back and leaned against her AK47 and said to herself: 'I've done my bit.'